"Sci-fi fans can't afford to miss this series or its truly unforgettable heroine! *Guardian* is a poignant story about what it takes to be truly human—and, perhaps even more importantly, what it means to love. Author Cathy McCrumb has firmly secured her place on my auto-buy list."

— STEFANIE LOZINSKI, author of the Storm and Spire series

"With an immersive setting and intriguing characters, *Guardian* combines some of my favorite sci-fi elements—space travel, high-tech heroes, and monsters swarming the halls. Grab yourself a drone and plug in!"

— KERRY NIETZ, award-winning author of *Lost Bits*

"With a deft hand, Cathy McCrumb weaves the final threads of the Consortium series into a beautiful tapestry that will satisfy those who have been waiting for the final book. A rewarding conclusion to an excellent series."

— MORGAN L. BUSSE, award-winning author of the Skyworld series

"A powerful conclusion to a poignant series. With its courageous exploration of the gift and burden of our humanity, the power of a single choice, and the value of every 'bright life,' *Guardian* left me feeling genuinely proud to be human."

— K.T. IVANREST, author of *The Windward King*

"*Guardian* is chilling, philosophical, exciting, and achingly romantic. For those who have been on the fence, now is the time to pick up this splendid, heartfelt series."

— AMBER KIRKPATRICK, author of *Until the Rising* and *Unleashed*

"I wondered how this series would end. You see characters spiraling to a resolution. You watch as things go from bad to worse. You wonder how the author will pull off a satisfying but believable ending. McCrumb doesn't disappoint. In fact, now that I'm finished with *Guardian*, I'm going back to Recorder to enjoy the thrill ride again. Highly recommended!"

— LISA GODFREES, co-founder of Havok Publishing

GUARDIAN

GUARDIAN

CHILDREN OF THE CONSORTIUM | BOOK THREE

CATHY MCCRUMB

Guardian
Copyright © 2024 by Cathy McCrumb

Published by Enclave Publishing, an imprint of Oasis Family Media.

Carol Steam, Illinois, USA.
www.enclavepublishing.com

ISBN: 979-8-88605-094-3 (hardback)
ISBN: 979-8-88605-095-0 (printed softcover)
ISBN: 979-8-88605-097-4 (ebook)

Cover design by Emilie Haney, www.EAHCreative.com
Typesetting by Jamie Foley, www.JamieFoley.com

Printed in the United States of America.

For all the stars obscured by storms
Who yet hold fast to light.

Subzero surface air hissed through the closing hangar doors, its sulfur burning my nose and its cold creeping through my inadequate black jacket. Nate spun me around once again, and grit and dust swirled around our legs. I coughed into my elbow before resting my bare cheek against his armored chest while the debris settled.

On the far side of the shuttle, the hanger doors thundered shut, and their magnetic seals clanged into place. Circulation fans roared, replacing the moon's atmosphere with less noxious air and reducing the chill. Behind us, Jackson barked commands and a second warning for the marines to keep their helmets on, reminding me that Nate and I were not alone.

But I did not care who saw us. I had no desire to leave the hangar if it meant leaving his embrace. What was mere cold or potential illness? *Thalassa* remained in orbit about Pallas, and I had not lost my Nathaniel after all.

Even so, Nate stepped back and tipped my chin up. Behind his faceplate, those green eyes skimmed over me and lingered on the spreading, unhealed bruises on my neck and jaw. Perfect eyebrows drew together. "You're okay?"

"You are here, my heart." Each syllable emerged visibly into the chill in uneven puffs. My lungs tightened, whether from the frigid air or from my impulsive dash from the crematory to the hangar, I could not tell. But how could I have done anything except run to see him when we all had feared the shuttle had been lost? I caught his gloved fingers in my bare ones. "That is all I need."

Nate studied my face. "Seems like we've got some things to talk about after you get warmed up."

"Timmons." Jackson's gravelly voice rattled over his helmet's speakers. "Get her back to civilization."

"My thoughts exactly." Though not a member of the marines, Nate saluted before guiding me toward the door.

I frowned. Jackson must have meant our center of operations. We were yet inside Pallas, one of the larger moons orbiting Krios, nearly a light-hour away from New Triton and Ceres. The underground research station was infested with behemoth insects and enemies of the Consortium, who wanted all of us dead, from Recorders like me to the Eldest herself.

Civilization was a gross overstatement.

When Nate released my arm, dizziness washed over me, and I wavered on my feet. He caught me and called, "Alec?"

"Yeah, Tim?" Alec answered from a knot of marines near the shuttle's ramp.

"I'm taking her back to thaw out. Bring her suit as soon as you can."

Behind his faceplate, Alec grinned, but the expression faded as he studied me. "She's turning blue. Get her warm. I'll bring it once we've unloaded the shuttle." He took a datapad from a pocket and addressed the marine in charge. "Jackson, can you spare a few more hands to load the bot with food and medical supplies?"

Several of the marines cheered at the mention of food, but their noise was hidden by the growl of an industrial cleaning bot. The towering machine settled into a steady, low chug as it left its garage to remove debris blown in by the shuttle's return. People dodged out of its way.

Across the hangar, near the small office, Jackson clapped a woman in marine blue on the back. "Smythe, Parker." He nodded at the two men in the mottled grey-and-black of Consortium-sanctioned suits. "You."

The woman strode toward the shuttle, the men close behind her. Alec entered a code on his datapad, and the cargo hold near the shuttle's tail crept open. Dust swirled again as a squat transport bot lowered itself to the ground.

"I don't see their drones. Your jamming devices still working?" Nate murmured, and when I nodded, he said, "Good."

The woman averted her gaze as she passed, but both approaching Recorders—droneless, *former* Recorders—slowed as they approached. The talkative former Recorder who wanted to be named Daniel Parker welcomed Nate back before he joined Alec, but James, my first friend, paused. His silvery eyes flitted from Nate to me.

"You must exhibit more caution." The helmet's external speaker made James's deep voice slightly hollow. His gaze darted to the newly arrived marines then fastened on my right shoulder. "You have not recovered, and moreover, you cannot with certainty trust them all."

Without another word, he walked on.

Nate's gloved fingertips grazed my cheek. "Recovered?"

I did not want to lie to my Nathaniel, so I remained quiet.

After two seconds, he tipped his head toward the marines. "They're good people, but maybe James isn't wrong. Regardless, do me a favor and wear your suit, okay?"

Again, I did not answer him verbally, only nodded, even though the light armor had done little to protect the people who had been injured by roaches over the previous ten-day.

"There's still a lot of particulates in the air," Nate continued, "and you can't go running around without some sort of respirator. Jackson was hollering about contamination when we stepped off the shuttle. I'm not sure what he was yelling about."

Guilt propelled the admission: "I am."

His full attention snapped to my eyes and then my bruises. "What do you mean?"

My heart seemed to constrict, and when unexpected vertigo slammed into me, I widened my stance to stave it off. A lack of balance would exacerbate his concern. I wished there was no risk, no need for helmets, respirators, or armor, so I could touch his cheek and soothe his tension away.

"It is a story best left for after you have met with Jackson and the others," I said. "But keep your suit on while you are outside the clean rooms."

Nate's lips compressed into a thin line.

"Do not worry, my heart," I said with utmost sincerity, though the adjuration implied more truth than it held. "When I have a suit, I shall wear it."

As one, we traversed the open floor, our boots scuffing through occasional shallow drifts of fine silt. The industrial bot continued to prowl near the giant double doors, rumbling like external anxiety.

"Nate?"

"Sweetheart?"

The term of endearment brought a flood of contentment. People had called me *Recorder, Zeta, Izzy,* and several less-kind epithets, but when Nate called me *sweetheart,* the word felt more like my name than any other bestowed on me thus far.

I cleared my throat. "James said *Thalassa's* usual channels are down. No one on Pallas knows what happened."

"They're down, sure enough." Nate exhaled sharply. "Pirates, or whoever they were, hit *Thalassa* with an EM cannon strong enough to knock out the main computer, comms, and the engines. Followed it up with a missile to the main external comm array. Nothing else, though. No attempts at cutting through the hull, like pirates usually do. It's more like they wanted us out of the way, though that doesn't make much sense."

But it did. Those people who had kidnapped Kyleigh and effectively killed Freddie and Lorik were not here for anything on the ship. They were here, like we were, because of the virus now swimming in my veins. "*Thalassa* was merely an obstacle to their goal."

"If it was, they shut her down pretty well. She's still a bit of a mess. Backup systems are running at a third normal power. The captain has crews replacing the comm unit so we can contact New Triton."

"Contacting marines or marshals stationed at Krios Platform Forty-One would provide more immediate assistance."

"That too."

We walked another seven meters before I said, "Adams was in a medical tank. Others were injured. Are they well?"

"Miller and Adams are fine. The chem generators kept the infirmary and basic life support going. *Thalassa's* artificial gravity was uneven for a while, which caused its own problems, but the tanks sealed right away, like they're supposed to. Medical nanites in the tanks weren't affected."

"Because they are bioelectrically driven," I stated unnecessarily. "I had forgotten."

A single eyebrow rose at my admission. "Are you sure you're okay? You don't forget things."

"I . . ." I should have told him I was not well, but I could not. Not then, not yet. I refused to surrender the temporary peace I felt being at his side. Instead of explaining that the injury on my neck was from a jet injector loaded with the virus we had traveled to Pallas to defeat,

I selected my least alarming symptoms. "I have a headache and have not been sleeping well."

His long strides slowed. "Your eyes are a little bloodshot. They should've found a suit for you by now."

"Kyleigh needs one as well."

"She has one. Freddie painted flowers on it." Nate angled toward me. "Why does she need a new one?"

"It is a longer story than I have breath to tell."

"That doesn't sound promising."

I did not answer.

"Well, once you have yours, keep the helmet on and let its air filtration reduce the dust and clean out your lungs." The crack of a single shot echoed down the concrete and rock hall, and we increased our speed. "But you're right about nanotech working fine. Kinetic and bioelectric systems weren't affected."

Nagging concern pressed a question from me as we reached the door leading into the station's inner network. "Was no one harmed?"

"It would've been bad if anyone had been undergoing surgery, but everyone's fine." A dark shape on the ceiling snared our attention. He tensed, but the shadow was merely cast by ductwork. "Everyone except the ship's Recorder."

I had not enjoyed any interaction with the woman, but memories temporarily blinded me to my surroundings. *My drone's destruction. The Recorder who had taken the name Rose Parker curled in a knot of pain, then going limp.* "She lost her drone. Did she die?"

"Not yet, but it isn't pretty. Edwards isn't a surgeon. She needs Max."

My headache pounded, likely worsened by my impulsive dash and the hangar's cold. When I returned to the quarantine room, however, Williams or Max would have medication. The pain was a small price to pay for walking at Nate's side.

"Other than the Recorder and a ruined meal, the worst of it was the cats." Nate's dimple made a brief appearance when he grinned. "Cam Rodriguez and Eric Thompson had a time and a half cleaning up the cats' room, even with bots. Seems the cats didn't do well with sudden absence of gravity." He chuckled. "And I thought their waste box was bad. Cam and Eric scoured the walls and floor, then scrubbed the cats themselves—which they didn't appreciate in the slightest. No one wanted anything to do with either young man until they'd showered. Twice."

"And Tia Belisi?" I asked. "And Edwards?"

"Edwards is overworked. Tia . . ." His expression tautened. "She's doing well, but . . ."

"But?"

"She shouldn't have come. Don't know why they let her."

Anxiety threaded through me. Perhaps I should have inquired after the other people I knew, but instead I asked, "Bustopher is well?"

"Unhappy, but well. That cat keeps escaping their room and prowling the infirmary." Nate quirked a smile. "I think he's looking for you."

The warmth of being wanted almost drove away the lingering chill from the hangar. My nose tingled, and I dug through my pockets for the tissue I had brought to Freddie's undocumented memorial service. I ducked my head to wipe my face. Red seeped through the flimsy paper. My nose was bleeding? Like Freddie, like Lorik, like Rain? I hid the tissue in my pocket again. Nate watched me closely but said nothing.

We reached the junction leading deeper into the station and took the left passage which led away from the control room. Nate nodded at the marines at the corner. They deactivated the laser barricade, but their sharp attention never left the halls, flickering back to a crack in the ceiling eleven meters to our right.

I drew closer to Nate, trusting that the hallway's bright light would suffice to ward off the behemoth insects infesting the station. We should be safe.

Nate hefted his weapon as we passed the fissure. "You're not wearing your commlink."

My hand flew to my clavicle where the communications link he had given me last ten-day should have been. "I must have forgotten to put it on."

He frowned. "You're forgetting a lot of things."

"There was no need to wear it to the crematory," I protested. "Not with the marines in attendance."

"Crematory? Stars, sweetheart," he said sharply. "What happened down here? Who was cremated?"

Suddenly all too aware of how cold I was and how my head throbbed, I wrapped my arms around myself. "Jordan, Zhen, and Kyleigh are well."

The faintest lift to the corner of his mouth hinted at a dimpleless smile, and he tapped the side of his helmet that housed his communications link. "I know that much from Zhen's ongoing commentary. Alec's had an earful, as well." His expression shifted. "What? Freddie's dead? We brought his meds, and—"

When he halted, I did as well.

He stared at my neck.

My stomach clenched. Zhen DuBois must have told him the truth: Freddie had died after he, the Elder, and I had been dosed with the virus.

"What on all the worlds are you doing out here?" Another shot rang out. Nate's eyes darted toward the fissure behind us, then scanned the ductwork and piping overhead, checking for any sign of insectile movement. The hall was clear, and he focused again on me. "You've been injected with that virus?"

"This is why Jackson warned of contamination."

"Why aren't you in bed?" he demanded. "What happened?"

I wanted to shrink, though I had not done anything wrong. Well, nothing entirely wrong. Kyleigh assured us the virus was not airborne, and I did not regret running to greet him. "What else did Zhen tell you?"

"Freddie died after you both were dosed with that virus by"—Nate's jaw tensed, then his smooth tenor roughened—"*Ross*? Tell me she's joking. That voided waste of carbon is back?"

"Your statement is not entirely accurate," I began, ignoring his personal criticism of Julian Ross. "He protested when his colleague injected Freddie. He himself did not inject anyone. Other members of his group did."

"Other . . .?" Nate growled an imprecation. "Walk and talk." He motioned down the hall, but his tone gentled. "Unless you need me to carry you?"

"Nathaniel." I set a hand on his arm and peered up at him, studying the features I already knew by heart. "I have not yet succumbed, and for the most part I have regained my sense of balance. I can walk under my own power." A smile crept out of my heart and onto my face. "After all, I ran to see you."

"You did." He checked our surroundings again before continuing, "Come on. I've got a rogue Recorder to get back to quarantine."

While *rogue Recorder* was not as pleasant a label as *sweetheart*, somehow, when Nate said it, I did not mind.

The hall grew busier as we neared the quarantine room where Kyleigh and I were staying. The occasional percussion of weapons' fire echoed through the drab hallway. I hoped they were practicing, not clearing another incursion. Perhaps it was better not to know.

Then without warning, sounds, movement, and colors blurred. I blinked hard, but dizziness hovered at my side like a drone, encircling me with invisible tendrils. We had not gone far when my knees buckled. Nate dropped his weapon to dangle on its tether and caught me before I hit the floor. The grey hall and its blue safety lights swam. He scooped me up, and the pounding of his steps seemed like hammers on my temples.

"Stay with me, sweetheart." Nate's voice seemed to come from a distance, though I knew he held me close. The discrepancy disordered my thoughts.

He spoke again, but not to me. A few steps further, and the quarantine room's vestibule door swung open. While we waited, chemicals rushed around us to clean potential contamination. Warm liquid dripped down my upper lip; my nose was bleeding again. Blood trickled down the back of my throat, and I choked.

"Tip your head forward. Pinch your nose," Nate ordered, but his voice shook.

I tried, but red seeped through my fingers. Tissues. Why did I not carry tissues? No . . . I had. But they were in my pocket, and I could not reach them. The vestibule narrowed around us.

"Max, she collapsed, and her nose is bleeding . . . I don't know! How would I possibly know if she has—"

I gagged and coughed into my sleeve, grateful the black fabric hid any red.

The inner door flew open, and cool air whooshed from above.

"Over here. We'll get that stopped easily enough." The doctor's deep voice soothed my rising anxiety.

Nate lowered me onto a hoverbed, and Max gently pried my hand away. I clenched my eyes shut. A sharp puff up one nostril made me flinch, and a gloved hand caught the back of my head.

"You're doing fine."

Another puff, then a damp cloth wiped my mouth and chin.

"There. And Timmons? Clean off the blood before heading out." Max spoke calmly, as if my blood on Nate's grey-and-black suit was a simple, meaningless thing. As if the blood might not summon the roaches. As if it might not be a precursor to the virus devouring me from the inside out.

"Not heading out yet, Max."

"I know," the doctor answered quietly. "Kye, see if you can find a clean tunic for her in that stack over there."

Teal, white, and green flashed as Kyleigh, uncharacteristically silent, dashed to the tidy box of clean clothing. Her hazel eyes grew huge as she handed a marine-blue tunic to Max.

Freddie's incomplete murals, which covered most of the grey wall behind her, seemed to writhe, but I concentrated on them until their flickering stopped.

I should have reassured her, but not knowing what to say, I remained silent while my fingers fumbled with the closures on my blood-stained jacket. Nate eased it from my shoulders, then disappeared from my line of sight. Kyleigh helped me into an unsoiled tunic, but when a sharp light shone directly into my eyes, I jerked away. Max steadied me, then helped me settle back on my pillow. The monitor in the headboard chimed.

His suit clean, Nate stepped close and rested his gloved hand on my head. "Hold on," he whispered. "I've got you."

Selfishly glad for his presence, I closed my eyes while Max administered pain medication. My coughing fits became more frequent, and when they struck, all air seemed to vanish from the room.

I could do nothing but wait, wait, and wait again. Seconds, minutes, and hours lurched forward in heavy, uneven bursts before slowing to a lethargic crawl, dragging me behind them like a reluctant child.

Nate dozed at my bedside until Max ordered him to leave, eat, rest. The room spun when I tried to say goodbye. His fingers brushed my cheek, and he promised to return.

Kyleigh took Nate's place at my bedside, and Williams arrived before Max left. When pain intensified, Williams dosed me again, her safely gloved fingers precise and steady.

Sometime later, Kyleigh retreated to her bed, and I heard her crying. I had dim memories of Nate, though I could not be certain he was truly present.

No, time did not function as a constant while I waited to find out if I would die.

"So why isn't she dead?"

Static netted through the unfamiliar soprano that tugged me from what passed for rest. In the stillness after the stranger's question, air filtration units hissed steadily. I shifted under a blanket unlike the soft cotton bedding in *Thalassa*'s infirmary. Three seconds ticked past before I identified the material as a thermal blanket.

I blinked. My eyelids scraped over dry corneas. Overhead, lights buzzed faintly, and the word *EXIT* glowed over the door centered in a grey concrete wall of Pallas Station's quarantine room.

"What's different about this case?" the woman continued. "Nothing about her is special."

A masculine grunt disputed the woman's assertion, and I rolled to my side, toward whomever had disagreed. Nate sat in a chair next to my bed, glaring at—I glanced over—Williams? She had not spoken.

My attention flickered back to my Nathaniel. Fatigue bruised his eyes. He needed rest.

"Well, she's the sole member of the Consortium who hasn't succumbed as soon as she was infected. I'd say human connection might be a factor, but citizen deaths rule that out."

I searched the room for the woman, but only Nate, Max, Williams, and Kyleigh were present. Given my condition, Kyleigh Tristram should have been wearing a respirator, like the others.

"We're missing something." Williams's gentle voice held an edge. "Something obvious."

"Exactly," the unfamiliar woman responded. "The others died."

An ache swelled behind my sternum, not as sharp as the pain in my head, but as impossible to ignore. My fingers found the bed rail and curled around it as, wincing, I pulled myself upright. Nate braced my back.

The quarantine room was much as it had been, though the omnipresent hum of Pallas's circulation system was muted by the metal plates that had been bolted over the ventilation opening. Fresh sealant leaked unevenly down the wall, but I could not tell whether the sealant had cured and the sharp fumes had faded or Max's treatment had impaired my sense of smell. Or perhaps the two filters next to the door and the third one near my bed eliminated the odor as they attempted to purify the air of the virus I carried within me.

Freddie's empty hoverbed lurked in the far corner, neatly made, and a box emblazoned with the red cross denoting medical supplies rested on his bedside table. Disheveled blankets and pillows cluttered the bed next to Kyleigh's computer terminal and its old-fashioned keyboard. Kyleigh herself hunched on a wheeled stool, a marine-blue T-shirt hanging on her small frame. Williams, however, sat rigidly at a second desk cluttered with various datapads, and her small computer projected streams of data into the air.

Gloved fingers caught mine, and Nate's thumb traced circles on the back of my hand. "Easy," he murmured.

"You're awake," Kyleigh exclaimed. She seemed frailer, somehow, which might have been a faulty perception based on her pallor and the circles under her eyes.

Max crossed the room to study my headboard's readout. "It's about time you woke up. How are you feeling?"

"Thirsty."

Williams brought me a bottle of water, and my hands shook as I accepted it.

Max offered me a half smile. "How's the pain?"

After a brief internal inventory, I confessed my joints felt better but my head still hurt. He turned to retrieve medication.

I startled when the staticky female voice complained, "We need to find a cure. You need to quit dithering with Recorders so we can save people."

But no one else was present. I searched the room again. Surely, no one had invented invisibility while I had slept.

"Saving her *is* saving people," Williams snapped. She took the empty bottle and added under her breath, "It's a voice link. Zhen got comms working. She's in the labs on *Thalassa*."

Zhen was on *Thalassa*? Or was the woman? Williams was usually more precise.

"Fine, fine." A chuff grated through the speaker, and anger slivered through me at her dismissal of my friend. "So what sets this Recorder apart?"

"Could it be something about *Thalassa* itself?" Williams asked. "Although other than better food, the difference is the cats."

"Those animals try to get into everything," the woman complained over Max's uncomplimentary observation about felines. "Unsanitary. I can't see how the captain allows it."

"She helped me with them on the voyage back to New Triton, Dr. Clarkson," Kyleigh said. "But Freddie and I had spent time with them long before we went into stasis, and that didn't—" She broke off suddenly, and her eyes watered.

"Good stars! Is Freddie sick, too?" the woman, who must have been Dr. Clarkson, demanded. "At the rate this virus takes out citizens, I don't see how he stands a chance."

There was a pause, then Williams said, "Freddie isn't sick."

Confusion nearly prompted me to rebut Williams's implied untruth. Freddie was not sick. He was dead and cremated. Nate's fingers tightened around mine as Freddie's request came rushing back—that none of us would mourn, that I would transfer his identity to my first friend so James could escape the Consortium. Did this Dr. Clarkson not know? I gripped the stiff blanket with my free hand. If she could not be trusted . . . if she discovered Freddie was dead and James had taken his place, we would all be in danger. My empty stomach writhed.

Dr. Clarkson snorted. "You had me worried, Williams. You could knock that young man over with the proverbial feather, let alone a real one. Poor boy is nothing but a skeleton."

"Besides," Williams put in quickly, "with the cats roaming the ship, the Elder must have had contact with them, as well, and he was sick."

"But we don't know what happened to him for certain."

Her scratchy soprano was beginning to irritate me.

"I told you," Kyleigh said. "They stole the Elder's armor, stabbed him, and that horrible man shot a jet injector of the virus into—"

"You can't possibly know what was in the purported injector," Dr.

Clarkson interrupted. "Without proper testing, you can't verify that those criminals who kidnapped you were telling the truth."

"But the Elder was symptomatic," Kyleigh protested. "I read the reports from *Agamemnon* and those other ships, as well as from Lunar One. He had a fever, his nose was bleeding, and his eyes . . . He wept blood. It was horrible."

"You can't prove it. Where is this Elder now?"

Max's deep voice rumbled, silencing the disagreeable woman. "Enough, Clarkson. Freddie was there, too, and both he and the Recorder here described the events and the Elder's symptoms. Given the fact that the Recorder's virus is confirmed, it seems likely."

"Freddie told me the Elder did not make it over the rubble blocking the corridor and that the roaches were coming," Williams said. "No one is going to climb through rocks, concrete, and giant insects to get you samples."

She did not add that cockroaches scavenged. Even if someone volunteered to venture past the debris, it would be fruitless to search for Lorik's remains.

"The point, *Williams*," Dr. Clarkson said with peculiar emphasis, "is that if he did have the virus and *if* the difference for this Recorder was the cats, their obnoxious presence did nothing to keep him safe."

"No," Williams protested, "it is possible. She was sick on the trip to New Triton. Toxoplasmosis, because of the cats. Could it be the medication used to treat the parasites?"

Max hummed, then clarified, "Pyrimethamine."

"Founders' sakes. Fine. We'll go over it all again," Dr. Clarkson drawled. "She grew up Consortium. Was on *Thalassa* on the first trip to Pallas. Found the survivors." A few taps sounded over the speakers before she continued, "She took samples of the debris. Her drone was destroyed. Oh! Do you suppose it's the cockroaches? Her suit was compromised. She could've inhaled something."

Nate shifted his weight beside me. "It's not the bugs." He glared at the speaker beside Williams's computer. "You keep saying you want test results, but you aren't reading them. I have, and there's no trace of anything insectile in any testing."

"And what would *you* know, Timmons? You're just hired muscle."

Her disrespect burrowed into my skin like a metal sliver. "He is a pilot and a chemical engineer."

Nate winked and gave me a brief smile.

"But not a virologist. The problem is that nothing is conclusive. It could be a systemic response triggered by the insects." A long exhale rattled through the room. "Never mind. Back to the Recorder. She was transported to *Thalassa*, where Maxwell removed her chip, and she seemed fine. There was her incident with Elliott Ross—"

My face heated. Did the whole system need to know Elliott had kissed me without my consent? Nate squeezed my shoulder.

"And she got sick."

"She wasn't sick from the virus, though," Max interjected. "As Williams said, she contracted toxoplasmosis from the cats."

Dr. Clarkson grunted. "And we're back at the cats again."

Kyleigh tugged on her short curls. "But Freddie and I both had been exposed long before. Max, you said my infection was dormant?"

"True."

A sharp crack echoed from the speaker, as if Dr. Clarkson had slammed something down. "We aren't getting anywhere. Maxwell, you need to get your hands on Pallas Station's records. You're the only one who's qualified. Williams is just staff. The marines and security team don't have the training—or capacity, to be honest—to dig through medical information."

Incensed by Dr. Clarkson's belittling remarks, I began to refute her assertions. Nate nudged my shoulder, then rolled his eyes and quirked a dimpleless smile. I fell silent.

Her scratchy voice continued, "DuBois said the self-destruct damaged some of the core, but I've studied the plans. There was a deep storage backup, and the information has to be there. Maxwell, you'll have to leave patching up injured grunts to their field medic and track down evidence regarding the bioweapon's beginnings. And get some more blood samples from that Recorder—"

"She's not going to have any blood left, if you keep taking it," Kyleigh objected.

I could not help but smile at her concern. "An exaggeration. I will be fine."

Dr. Robert Maxwell's brows drew together, like they did when he worried. Surely, he could not be concerned they would drain my veins?

"You will be fine, if Williams, Edwards, and I have anything to say about it. But," he added as he returned to my side, bearing two jet injectors, "you did show signs of parasitic activity again. Your immune system has taken a beating the past few days, so I've asked Johansen to bring some pyrimethamine back today."

"I don't like your risking *Thalassa* by sending marines up here," Dr. Clarkson whined.

Max did not address her concerns but smiled briefly at me. "In the meantime, let's get you something for the headache and a few extra nanites to boost your ability to fight off viral attacks." The tip of a jet injector touched my inner arm.

"Wait!" Kyleigh cried out.

Max rotated toward her. "What is it?"

"We've been looking in the wrong place!" Her face was ashen. "It's the nanites! Stars above, think about it! Back on *Thalassa* before we reached Lunar One and Ross ran off, I came to tell you the Consortium nanotech in her blood had changed." She spun toward me. "You were all talking about names and—" She stopped and snuck a look at the speaker, then concluded, "It's the tech."

"Don't be ridiculous," Dr. Clarkson scoffed. "Maxwell removed the Consortium chip from her brain."

"But even though Max got the chip and the nanowiring, there's Consortium-specific nanotech in her blood—"

"Kyleigh," the virologist said, "in case you don't recall, citizens don't have chips."

"That's not what I'm talking about." Kyleigh placed her fists on her hips. "After she was sick last quarter, the nanites in her blood were different, both in shape and locomotion. We know Ross used nanotech encapsulation to carry the virus. What . . . what if that was merely the first stage?"

"You showed us a side-by-side comparison," Nate said slowly.

"Can you pull up your findings?" Max asked.

"The records on *Thalassa* were damaged when Ross deleted them, but I backed them up on—oh." She sank back onto her stool. "On my datapad."

"The ridiculous flowery one?" Dr. Clarkson asked. "You took it with you. You can transmit the information to *Thalassa,* and—"

"I-I lost it."

I caught my breath, for I knew she lied. Kyleigh had given me that datapad to create the jamming devices that would free Recorders from the Consortium's network and protect them from their drones. Whatever other information it had held was long gone. Williams slumped into her chair, and Nate squeezed my shoulder.

"Then *that* theory does us no good," Dr. Clarkson remarked. "But whatever ridiculous hypothesis you have doesn't matter, since citizens don't walk around with Consortium nanotech in their veins."

A chill swept over me.

The Hall of Reclamation where I would be assigned if I could not find a way to escape. Rows of tanks full of deceased donors and living Recorders who had disobeyed Consortium directives. Recorders and Elders sentenced to serve the citizenry with their very selves, part by part, until they could serve no longer.

"No," I said. "In fact, they do."

Max pivoted toward me, angled brows knotting over his tired eyes. "Via donations?"

Nate's grip on my fingers grew uncomfortably tight, but I did not pull free. The verbal affirmative tangled in my throat. I could but nod.

Dr. Clarkson snorted. "That's ridiculous."

"It's why—" Kyleigh's lips trembled, then she burst into tears. She tried to speak, but only *Freddie, eyes,* and *ever* were distinguishable.

Williams dropped her datapad onto her chair. Uttering soft shushing noises, she enfolded Kyleigh in her arms.

"Why what?" Dr. Clarkson's irritating, disembodied voice demanded. "What donations? Tristram, I can't understand you when you're blubbering like that. Maxwell, calm her down—dose her with something if you have to. The girl is too excitable." The woman's groan grated over the speaker. "I don't know what made the powers that be think sending veritable children on this assignment was a good idea."

"Enough, Clarkson." Max strode across the room to give Kyleigh a tissue. "She's the sole nanotech specialist who was willing to go, and she's the one who discovered the separate parts to the delivery system. The past few days have been hard on her."

"Right, right. I forgot. Being kidnapped and quarantined and all," Dr. Clarkson acknowledged. "Does she have symptoms yet?"

Yet? Anger beyond indignation arced through me like a drone's reprimand.

Nate's response was terse. "No."

"Well, take samples—"

"Already done," Williams said through clenched teeth. "But to answer your previous question, yes. Organ donations."

"Which are willed by citizens," Dr. Clarkson stated.

Williams glanced at the ceiling, where the inactive Consortium camera stared blankly into the room. "Not all."

"You can't mean there are Recorders? That's almost civic-minded and self-sacrificial of them."

Yanking my hand from Nate's, I pushed off my pillows and faced the speaker. "You think we do not care? Because we are not to display bias, that we have no emotions? That we would wish for others to die unnecessarily?"

"You're putting words in my mouth," she argued.

Heedless, I continued, "Is it not enough that we are stripped of connections and our sole name is our shared title? Or do you think merely capitalizing it expresses worth? From infancy and our very first step into a Caretaker's arms, we are raised to serve—to protect and preserve human life. Or perhaps you believe we are not human and cannot desire good for others?" A distant part of my brain registered Kyleigh's stifled sobs and Nate's low *sweetheart*. I did not care. "You know *nothing*. Nothing of our constraints, emotions, even dreams, all held back and suppressed to serve the people who—who—"

"Abandoned you," Max said quietly.

Regret cascaded and drowned my outburst. A kaleidoscope of emotions I could not parse flashed through me, narrowing into the single, aching need for absolution. I had not meant to implicate Max, of all people, in rejecting Recorders. Not when he had no contract over twenty-six years ago, no power to prevent his children's mother from gifting them.

"Max," I began, "I—"

"Whatever else is going on, it's quite clear why you were up for review by the Consortium," Dr. Clarkson said flatly. "Founders' oath, what a mess."

Williams released Kyleigh and glowered at the speaker, as if Dr. Clarkson could be aware of—or would even care about—the intensity of her reaction. "Some of those Recorders are in the Hall of Reclamation against their will."

"What would you know, Williams? You're only Consortium staff." A staticky chuff filled the room. "None of which matters, because putting someone in a tank against their will implies they're still alive. You can't possibly mean they are parceled out like goodies at a kid's birthday party, because *that* would be a death sentence, and execution is illegal. We're beyond such primitive behavior."

Williams lifted her chin. "As Consortium medical staff, I spent the final quarter of my internship in the retrieval rooms, assisting with donations. So, yes, I know."

"Your lack of knowledge does not negate the problem, Dr. Clarkson," I said before the woman blurted another ignorant response.

Max's jaw was tight. "No one will want to believe the truth about the Hall of Reclamation. I didn't. But facts are facts."

"It's unlike you, Maxwell, to blindly accept such a wild idea," Dr. Clarkson said. "But on the off chance you're right about donations from Recorders, and if Kyleigh is right about the bioweapon altering Consortium tech, we might have a bigger problem than we thought."

I held my breath for the count of three before asking, "Williams, can we verify the presence of nanotechnology in citizens' bloodstreams? In Freddie's?"

She tilted her head. "With the proper equipment, yes, providing we can compare older samples with—"

"Just get new ones," Dr. Clarkson ordered. "He can spare a vial."

"With any changes." Williams scowled but gave Kyleigh one last pat on the shoulder before picking up her datapad and scrolling through data. "No, no evaluation of nanotech in the previous reports."

"Clarkson," Max said, "start reviewing files for organ transplants or blood transfusions in *Thalassa*'s crew and the marines. Last we knew, the citizen death rate was around sixty percent. I find it hard to believe such a high percentage of the population has Consortium nanites in their blood, but the hypothesis is better than none at all."

For once, the woman did not argue back. "I can check. We haven't found much else, to be honest, and if—*if*—you're right, at least we can separate the ones at risk. I'll talk to Archimedes about restricting trips from Pallas to here until we figure this out."

"How will you get samples if you limit trips?" Williams asked.

Dr. Clarkson did not acknowledge the question. "Stopping the spread is a priority. Fortunately, as far as we know, the exposure was limited to four ships and Lunar One, though where those terrorists who started all this went before coming here is beyond me. People must be panicking by now, though with long-range comms down, we have no information from New Triton."

A sharp click was her farewell, and I slumped in relief when the link fell silent. Kyleigh blew her nose before resuming her work at the computer. Max stood, arms crossed, and stared at the wall behind me. Eyes on her datapad, Williams lowered herself onto her chair, and her fingers flew through its small cyan and amber datastreams. For twenty-three seconds, no one spoke.

"Kyleigh." Max waited until she swiveled around on the stool. "We'll need you to take another look at Freddie's final samples, the ones we were saving to send to the virologists. And yours and hers." He nodded in my direction. "Williams, message Edwards. You are both Consortium, and I have to assume you have their tech in your blood."

"Imogene Clarkson won't warn him," Nate said. "She'll wait until she can prove it and take credit."

"I'm warning him now." Williams finished her message and set the datapad back on the chair. "I have never had anything more than vaccines, but Edwards had an emergency appendectomy on *Manitoba*."

Max's nostrils flared. "They should've used a tank rather than resorting to surgery for something that simple."

Williams held up her hands. "It was not about Edwards being staff. We had injuries after a run-in with pirates, and the medtanks were full. The doctor was positively gleeful to be able to 'practice something so primitive.' He said it kept his skills up."

Max rubbed the back of his neck, though the action could not have been beneficial while he wore a suit and helmet. "That might not have required any transfusions."

"It is unlikely that such a high percentage of the citizenry has undergone surgery," I said. We were missing something.

"But the nanotechnology angle seems likely," Nate said.

"It's the best explanation." Kyleigh heaved a sigh. "But Williams, don't worry about Edwards. He always follows procedures."

"I know, but . . . I am concerned."

Tanks. Procedures.

"Moons and stars," I blurted. In an instant, all attention fixed on me. "Your search might not be broad enough. I was in the medical tank on *Thalassa* and in the emergency transportation tank on the shuttle.

It was before any contamination by the bioweapon, but Consortium devices could have mingled with the tank's medgel."

"But the tank filtration system should have cleaned it—" Williams interrupted herself with a groan. "But only of biological waste, bacteria, and viruses, not Consortium technology."

Kyleigh gasped.

"So we need to expand the search to anyone who has been in a tank." Williams glanced at me and Nate. "It might need to be even wider."

The small circles Nate rubbed on my back slowed, then stopped, and he lowered himself beside me. "How so?"

Her gaze bored into his, then shifted to mine. "Elliott."

Nate's expression darkened.

"But he apologized, for what it's worth," Kyleigh said, her voice small and thin. "And he helped us get away."

"Which is not the issue." Williams focused on Nate. "Transfer via saliva, Timmons. I know you've never been in a tank or had a transfusion, but . . ."

As surely as if someone had hit my solar plexus, I could not breathe. Elliott had contaminated me, and that meant when I had kissed Nate, I had placed him at risk.

I twisted toward him. He cupped my face in both gloved hands, and his speaker amplified the whisper: "I don't regret a single second. It'll be okay."

But if it hurt him, *I* would regret it for the remainder of my life, until I served to nothing in a Consortium tank.

"Oh, stars above." Kyleigh's voice cracked, and another frisson of fear ran through me. "That means me, too, doesn't it? I helped carry the Elder and Freddie through the tunnels after that hateful, evil man injected them. And I kissed Freddie goodbye." Dashing at her tears with her sleeve, she reached for a tissue, blew her nose loudly, and dropped the tissue into the biohazard waste bin. When she reached for the sanitizer, she paused. "If it's in the tech, I don't suppose killing germs will do any good."

"Use it anyway, Kye," Williams said gently.

"Well, I'm not sorry. Freddie was—" Kyleigh's right hand drifted up to the green-and-white mourning band around her left arm, then she raised her chin. "No. Freddie still *is* worth every single kiss and every single second I spent with him. I knew I was risking things when he was dying. So how is this any different?"

"Perhaps it isn't," Williams said, though when she turned away, I caught the pinched expression on her face. "Kyleigh, you isolated the original nanites, didn't you?"

"Yes, I did, though Julian Ross destroyed the files when he erased *Thalassa's* documentation and the security footage. I backed it up, though it was all on my flowered datapad, which was overwritten to make a jammer. So that information's gone."

Nate, who had been silent, spoke. "But we have two Recorders down here. Neither James nor Daniel has been exposed, that we know of. Check their nanites against hers."

Max nodded. He studied the readout behind my hoverbed, then turned wordlessly and searched through the container of medical supplies.

"Kye," Williams asked, "what will you need to check for nanites?"

Kyleigh waved a hand at the small centrifuge and microscope on the counter opposite her computer. "More powerful stuff than this. I need the portable equipment from Georgette SahnVeer's lab."

"You probably shouldn't go traipsing about the station, given roaches and insurgents, but there might be enough room in here if we can gather what you need." Nate squinted at Williams's desk. "Given the power fluctuations, a backup generator is a good idea, too." He stood abruptly. "Looks like we need an expedition."

I swung my legs over the side of my bed.

Nate caught my arm. "What do you think you're doing?"

"Is it not obvious? The materials Kyleigh requires will be located in secured sections of the station, and someone must gather them for her."

His face softened, and he tucked a curl behind my ear. "And that someone won't be you."

"I have a suit now, Nathaniel. My presence will not put others at risk."

"Not the point. You need to rest."

"Very well," I said stiffly. "I shall not traipse about. But you cannot expect me to lie here and do nothing."

"Oh, can't I?" But he said it softly, as if the words meant something else altogether.

I turned away to look for my datapads—my own navy-blue one and the green one that had belonged to the station Recorder. They were gone, though two datasticks rested in an otherwise empty glass beside a container of tissues. Freddie had given me one to create an identity for James, but . . . where had I found the other?

"If you're looking for your commlink and those two datapads, they're charging by Williams's station." Max brought me more water and two small, white pills in a disposable cup. "It seems I rely too heavily on nanotechnology. This is the sole oral analgesic we brought down. Take these. I'll send for more, next shuttle trip."

No sudden scent of lavender and pine calmed me when I swallowed them, though I knew the nanodevices' absence did not indicate inefficacy.

Williams, who had been gathering necessary supplies to draw more blood, added, "We do have stronger IV drugs, in case we must put you under. Maybe the doctor who so gleefully removed Edwards's appendix had a point about primitive medicine?"

"All right." Kyleigh placed her hands on her thighs and stood. "I'll go."

Max shook his head. "No. You don't have symptoms, but we need to keep an eye on you."

"But if they need access to the computers and the sealed rooms—"

"James and Daniel were Recorders. They will figure it out," Williams said. "And if James is anything like his father, that is good enough for me."

Max's response was buried in an avalanche of sound as the station's alarm blared. Immediately after the initial screech, both his and Nate's communications links chimed.

"Tim. Max." Jordan's alto spilled over their links, giving the impression she spoke from two places at once. "One of Jackson's teams had another run-in with the bugs near the hangar. Dropped out of a crack in the ceiling on top of them."

The doctor growled something under his breath, then turned to his assistant. "Williams."

"The blood samples can wait until we are back," she said. "And do not worry, Kyleigh. Someone will track down the equipment you need."

The two moved in unison to the vestibule, and the door closed behind them before Jordan spoke again.

"Tim, there's been a change in plans. Johansen will be back in about thirty minutes, but your run tomorrow is on hold."

"By whose orders?"

"I don't know."

Nate raised an eyebrow. "Can't see Archimedes falling for Clarkson's line, but staying here for a while is fine with me."

Jordan made an indeterminate noise that might have indicated agreement. "What equipment was Williams talking about? If we hold off on shuttle runs, we'll have to make do with whatever we have here."

"I need some gear from Dr. SahnVeer's laboratory. Sending you a list." Kyleigh's old-fashioned keyboard clicked. "You'll need an alternate route, though, because one of the marines said they ran into company when they were last in that section."

"We'll figure it out," Jordan said. "In the meantime, Tim, Jackson needs as many boots in the tunnels as he can get."

Nate exhaled. "Guess that means me."

"You guessed right." She paused, and her voice lowered. "How is she, Tim?"

"She's awake."

Jordan repeated his statement, and several cheers sounded over the communications link. "Stars, Tim, but that's the best news of the day."

A tiny flush of warmth lit in me at their concern. "Thank you, Jordan."

Nate's gaze held mine. "And she's staying here."

"I have a suit, Nathaniel, and my assistance—"

"Isn't necessary," Zhen DuBois's voice snapped over Nate's link. "Traipsing through roach-infested halls the day you emerge from a sickbed is a stupid idea."

"You cannot know the halls would be overrun with insects."

"Oh, can't I?"

"Simmer down, Zhen." I could easily envision Jordan holding up one hand. "Kyleigh, this is quite a list, but we'll track down your supplies."

"If we have a current map with the intrusions, fissures, and collapsed hallways marked," I offered, "I will find a safe route."

"Nope." Nate crossed his arms. "You'll rest. Let Zhen earn her keep and puzzle it out."

"But, Nate—"

"Let her find a way, and let us handle any locked doors. If you overdo it . . ." His eyes met mine. "Please, sweetheart. Don't do that to me again."

Although I had not intended to be ill and he could not expect me to remain behind and do nothing, my protest vanished when the light over the vestibule changed to green. Max and Williams were through, and the small area awaited its next occupant.

"Please," Nate repeated. When I nodded, a vestige of a smile touched his lips. "I'll see you later."

I clutched his hand so tightly my fingers ached. The possibilities that rose in my mind validated the Consortium's disapproval of imagination, for potential disasters—the bioweapon, the roaches, the people who hated Recorders and wanted all of us to die—outweighed any potential good. I did not want Nathaniel to leave me and venture into such chaos.

His gloved fingers slipped from mine.

The vestibule door closed behind him. For fifteen minutes, Kyleigh and I watched the red indicator light as his suit was scrubbed clean of contagion. The light shifted to green. Nate was gone.

Kyleigh rose and gathered both the blue and green datapads, which she set carefully beside the glass with the datasticks.

"Rest," was all she said before returning to her computer, effectively leaving me alone, a prisoner of my own blood and a bioweapon that had already claimed lives.

When I was a child at Consortium Training Center Alpha, the Elders and Recorders had frequently expounded upon the importance of patience. Waiting for others to speak allowed the free exchange of information, but the quarantine room's unnatural quiet settled more heavily than a weighted blanket. When minutes seemed to stretch past their allotted sixty seconds, I began to doubt the reliability of the Elders' assertions.

In all the time I had known her, Kyleigh's verbosity had been a constant, even when her unexpected transitions confused me. Yet now, though she cast furtive glances in my direction, she said nothing.

About an hour after Nate's departure, a chime from her computer preceded a staticky voice I recognized at once. Despite the situation, I smiled.

"Hey, Kye."

"Tia! How'd you sneak access to comms?"

"I didn't sneak," Tia Belisi protested. "Captain Genet gave me permission to chat for a few minutes. Maybe he feels bad I spend most of my time shadowing Officer Smith."

Kyleigh groaned. "Having been on a ship with Adrienne Smith, the captain has a point."

Tia chuckled, then sobered. "Are you two all right?"

"I am. Just a little cough once in a while, but Max says it's mostly debris from the tunnels and I'll be fine soon enough." Without turning to ascertain my status, Kyleigh lowered her voice. "She's resting."

"But . . ." The word wisped over the speakers. "We heard she's better?"

"Max thinks so. Her fever's dropped, and she seemed more like herself, except she blasted Dr. Clarkson. I've never heard her that angry before."

"She can put people in their places pretty well," Tia said. "She did on *Agamemnon*, at any rate. But, yes, Clarkson was complaining about 'that unRecorder's inappropriate opinions' and 'sass' pretty loudly at dinner. Eric and Cam were about to tear into her, but what's-his-name from engineering shut Clarkson down. Over half the people there cheered when he did."

Kyleigh hid her face in her hands. "Tia, it was awful. Like Freddie all over again, except her eyes weren't bleeding."

Unwilling to allow them to worry unnecessarily, I said, "I am well enough."

"Stars above!" Kyleigh spun on her stool to face me.

"Zeta!" Tia exclaimed.

"Indeed."

"It's good to hear your voice." Tia paused. "Cam, Eric, and I have been worried about you."

Nate's concern for Tia echoed in my mind, and I struggled to formulate an adequate response.

"I'd better go," Kyleigh said abruptly. "She needs to rest."

"Right. I'll check back tomorrow, if the captain lets me. Send me updates, Kye? For both of you."

"Sure."

Tia signed off, and Kyleigh swiveled back around. Her fingers resumed tapping at the old-fashioned keyboard.

The unfinished faces of Freddie's mural stared blankly at me, and after several minutes, I ventured to Williams's computer to work on . . . On what? Scrolling aimlessly through files would create new lives for neither James nor the talkative former Recorder. I tapped my thigh with my right fist and returned to my hoverbed. Dizziness snagged my vision, and the room seemed to tip. Kyleigh half rose as I caught my balance on the railing, straightened my covers, then crawled under them. When I met her eyes, she looked away. Still, she did not speak, though her typing slowed.

I stared at the ceiling, the murals, the vent's dried sealant, and Kyleigh's back. It seemed all I had done in the past quarter was wait between periods of frenetic activity and panic. Nate sent no news, and neither Max nor Williams informed us of the injured marines' fates. I was tired of waiting.

The chronometer on the wall clicked toward seven, yet sleep did not come. I rolled to my side and watched the green light over the door, sitting up when it turned red eleven minutes later, but Kyleigh must not have noticed. She did not look away from her data. I watched the indicator, hoping for my Nathaniel but expecting Williams to emerge with needles and Kyleigh's equipment. Instead, when the light flashed green and the door opened into the downdraft of cool air, James strode in, a large, sealed bag in each hand and a third over his shoulder.

Kyleigh jumped. "You startled me, James."

His growing brows—as straight and angled as his father's—lowered behind his faceplate. Moving slowly, as if precision would better accomplish the task, he set the larger bags on the floor beside her desk. "Such was not my intention, Kyleigh Tristram. I shall send notice next time."

"I didn't mean . . . I didn't know anyone was coming. Hold on." Her fingers clattered over the keys, and the streams of data pixelated and disappeared. "There. Just had to save my work."

"It is well."

"I didn't mean you had done anything wrong. And you can call me Kye," she said with an imitation of a smile. "I see you've come bearing gifts. You didn't bring dinner by chance, did you? I haven't eaten in forever."

"I did." James pulled the smaller bag from his shoulder and placed it precisely on the desk. "Prepackaged meals have adequate nutrition and calories, though the quality does not compare to meals onboard *Thalassa*."

James pushed the bag toward Kyleigh, who opened it, skimmed the package labels, and groaned.

"Fish and potato casserole," she said, then added hastily, "It's not that I don't appreciate it, just that fish is much better fresh than in a sealed container. Still, it's better than isopods."

He dipped his head once. "I shall remember."

Intent on their conversation, neither seemed to notice that the light over the door turned red again.

"I didn't mean you did anything wrong, James," she said.

His silvery eyes widened.

"It's just that everything keeps getting worse, and there's nothing I can do to fix it."

"I have confidence in your efforts," he said, "and do not believe the current disaster cannot be undone."

"Disaster's about right." Her gaze dropped to the packaged food in her hands. "Deep down, I know it isn't my fault, but if I hadn't run off to get the paints for Freddie . . . I should've stopped to think."

"It was not your doing, Kyleigh Rose Tristram. It was theirs." James took the brown-wrapped meals from her and placed them beside the keyboard.

"It doesn't feel like that." Her voice was very small. "It feels like I killed him."

"You did not. You are not to blame for others' evil actions."

A tear tracked down her cheek. "I'm responsible for my own choices, which put him at risk. I put them all at risk. Freddie and the Elder are gone, and my friend"—her voice dropped—"is dying."

She did not glance in my direction, as if I were not there, as if I could not hear her. Perhaps she assumed I was asleep. Perhaps my presence was a reminder of all she had lost, bringing her more pain. But whether or not I was dying, the fault was not hers. It was I who had charged thoughtlessly into danger.

He reached toward her, then withdrew his hand. "Despite my limited experience, I believe I understand."

Teary eyes rose to his. "You do?"

"Yes. Last quarter, I acted in violation of my training, and though my actions saved citizens, there was a cost." James's deep voice emerged in a monotone, and his gloved hands fisted. "My choices condemned me and cost a citizen her life."

"No, James. You saved them."

His breath caught, and the sound propelled me upright. Had Max not told him who he was? If he had not yet learned—

"You did the right thing." She wrapped her arms around her waist. "I'm sorry that your mother died, but she couldn't have saved them by herself."

"You . . . you cannot know." He moved away from her. "I did not reveal illegally obtained facts; I have told no one."

"Oh." Her eyes went wide, and she dropped onto the stool.

"How is it that you know my name?" James asked. "Since we arrived here on Pallas, people have addressed me by the name my mother said my father had chosen, but such knowledge cannot . . ." He paused, then began again, "I have done my best not to respond, not to convey awareness, as if it were mere coincidence, but how do you know how my mother died?"

My pulse pounded, and Kyleigh's cheeks flushed, then drained of color.

"How . . ." My first friend drew a deep breath. "How do you know who I am?"

"Stars above." Kyleigh's hands rose to her suddenly flushed cheeks. "I've done it again."

Whether or not it was my story to tell, I shoved the blankets to the foot of the bed and stood on unsteady legs. "I told her."

They both turned toward me. Behind his faceplate, James's silver-grey eyes met mine, then lifted to somewhere past my right shoulder. His posture grew unnaturally rigid, and his hands curled tight.

Kyleigh shot to her feet. "James?"

He did not respond.

"James?" Her eyes sought mine. "He's so still."

Holding onto my bed's railing for balance, I shuffled toward him, all attention on my first friend's vacant expression. "It is well. You are safe, and our knowledge will endanger neither you nor us. Indeed, it is one of the reasons Freddie bequeathed his identity to you."

James did not move.

"I viewed the record." I counted the seconds as they passed—sixty, ninety, one hundred twenty, one hundred thirty-seven—then spoke evenly. "I am sorry the Elders stole the incident from your mind. I am sorry for the reprimands and for the pain of a memory download, which I viewed in the records. After watching the woman assert you were her son, I verified her claim. It was not my place, but I had other reasons for my search."

"Other reasons," he repeated blandly.

Relief surged that he had finally spoken, but it was quickly supplanted by the conviction that I had no right to tell the rest of the story.

He drew a shuddering breath and refocused on me. "So you know also of my sister."

I nodded.

"Do you . . ."

When he did not finish, Kyleigh stepped to his side. In the oversized shirt, she seemed very small beside his broad, armored shoulder.

"Do we what?" she prompted as gently as a Caretaker would a frightened novice.

"She is missing," I said to forestall his answer, "but only presumed dead."

"I know. I viewed that information." He clenched his hand, then relaxed it. "And my father?"

Kyleigh touched his forearm. "You don't know?"

"No. The Elders stopped me before I learned who he was." His gaze locked on hers. "But you do?"

She nodded. "He's been searching for you since your mother gave you both away."

The memory of Max's ashen face when he realized he had met his son rose before me, but a whoosh of air interrupted us.

Zhen DuBois stormed in, glanced down at the bags by the desk, and pursed her lips. "Good. You brought the suits."

At her abrupt arrival, my thoughts scattered.

James said, "I did."

"Is that what's in those bags?" Kyleigh asked.

"Indeed. I have brought the Recorder's and a spare for you, Kyleigh Tristram. Pallas Station is not safe without some level of protection."

"So." Zhen faced me. "It turns out, you were right. I found a way there, but we need you after all."

Kyleigh folded her arms and leaned back against her desk. "Where?"

"To get the equipment. We've got a problem."

"Which is?" Kyleigh asked.

"Access. Unless you want to send your retinas separately, Kye, you need to suit up. Don't worry, though. I'm going with you, and Jackson is sending a couple of marines." Zhen's voice softened slightly. "Recorder-who-isn't, you need to suit up, too. I don't like it, and Tim will kill me for taking you out of here, but we need your help."

"I am unsteady, Zhen," I said.

She glanced at the sealed packages of food and huffed. "You haven't eaten yet? Moons and stars, but you two need as much supervision as children." She grabbed a package, ripped it open, and handed it to Kyleigh. The nauseating, briny smell of overprocessed fish seeped through the air. The filters' hiss grew louder, and the odor faded slightly. Zhen tore open the second package and crossed the room to hand it to me.

James watched her but said nothing.

"You'll be steadier with calories to burn." Zhen steered me back to the bed and placed her hands on my shoulders, gently forcing me to sit. "Eat."

The unpalatable tray of food glistened oddly in the overhead lighting. "I do not understand. As you and Nate discussed, you are more than capable of—"

"I can do a lot of things, but not this." Zhen folded her arms. "As much as I hate to say it, we need a drone."

Internal chaos barred my ability to speak. I sat, open-mouthed, my attention shifting rapidly between my three friends.

"What?" Kyleigh shoved away from her desk and waved her hand in my direction. "We have that, which is all we need, right?" My heart pinched until she continued, "We don't need a drone. All we needed last ten-day when she made those jamming devices was that datapad's codes."

Unjustified hurt lifted, but her statement was not entirely true. I had required parts from my old drone to establish the connection, but again, the explanation stuck in my throat.

"I'm not talking about a jammer," Zhen began. "We need—"

"Stars above!" Kyleigh put her fists on her hips. "What you *need* is to leave her out of it and leave the drones alone. Activating one right now is as good as shouting, 'Over here!' You'll alert all the wrong people."

"You are not entirely incorrect." James shifted his weight, but his expression remained neutral. "The Elder would have notified the Consortium Center on Krios Platform Forty-One, which is eight days and three hours away. Even if the Consortium did not react quickly when a Recorder's drone malfunctioned, they would for an Elder's."

Kyleigh spun to face him. "If they already know, that makes everything a thousand times worse! They'll be here soon. We simply can't risk alerting them by reactivating anything."

James stared past her at Freddie's mural. "If his call for assistance went out over the network approximately five days ago, a ship could arrive in three days."

Zhen drew a sharp breath. "We're walking a thin line."

My dull, constant headache swelled, and thought became difficult. "Again, reactivating their drones could betray our intent to hide both former Recorders from the Eldest. It would be better if—"

"Then we won't." Kyleigh raised her chin. "But shouldn't the jammers keep them safe?"

"The jammers merely shut down local communications." James waited for my nod, then continued, "They hide our neural implants but do not disconnect the network itself."

"Which makes using a drone dodgy, I know." Zhen's jaw muscle jumped. "I don't like it, either, but we need one."

Kyleigh pointed wildly at the door. "You can't haul her out of here as soon as she regains consciousness! Use that drone in the control room, that one she hooked into the computer the first trip down here."

"As I told Jackson, removing it from any established connections and utilizing it for other purposes will draw suspicions," I said. "Additionally, I do not know if the Consortium network was disrupted when *Thalassa* was hit."

"It sounds to me like avoiding suspicious behavior is already impossible."

"There is no need to risk our friend and to draw attention to our irregular activity. The jamming devices remain powered." James withdrew his focus from the mural and met my eyes. "That should suffice when I reactivate my drone."

"No. We aren't going to let the Eldest stick you in some organ donation tank," Kyleigh stated flatly.

For a fractured second, I envisioned James inside a medical tank, the green gel obscuring his silvery eyes. My stomach cramped.

Kyleigh crossed the room to place herself between me and Zhen DuBois. "And you can't put *her* in danger, either. I'm not debating saving the system from a bioweapon. I'm saying you can't haul her off a sick bed and into danger. Not only will Timmons kill you, *I* will."

"Kyleigh, listen—"

"She nearly died. *Died.*" She reached past the glass holding the datasticks and snatched a tissue from the box on my bedside table, violently blew her nose, and tucked the wad inside her sleeve. "Max said she has to rest. Wandering off to deal with drones isn't resting."

"Whether or not you like it, we're getting that drone." Zhen darted a glance at me and pointed at my tray of food. "Eat, and I'll explain."

My stomach betrayed me and growled, despite the colorless tubers on my tray. Resolute, I unwrapped my utensils and, eschewing the flakes of grey fish, took a bite of overprocessed vegetables.

"Please eat, Kyleigh Tristram." James slid the meal across her desk and waited.

She sighed, trudged across the room, dropped onto the stool, and stabbed a piece of fish with her fork.

Zhen watched us eat a few bites, then began, "After preliminary results on the marines who had roaches drop on them, Jackson put a rush on the medical files and your equipment, Kye. He sent two teams. Neither achieved their objective. Alec's team went after the equipment. The lock needs a retinal scan, and there's security even beyond that. Daniel says fail-safes went into effect after the station's self-destruct activated. If he's right, we need a drone to access Dr. SahnVeer's lab, even after Kyleigh's eyes get us in."

Kyleigh set down her fork. "'Neither team' and 'that team' means there's another one that wasn't successful. What happened?"

"Daniel was on the first team." James stared over her shoulder. "I volunteered for the second, but having no experience with weapons, Jackson insisted I stay behind."

"Jackson made a good call," Zhen said.

Worry twisted through me. "What has happened?"

"The second team headed down to the station's deep storage to retrieve information about the virus's construction. The trip didn't go well." Zhen crouched beside Kyleigh's desk, read the bags' labels, and carried the slightly smaller one to Kyleigh's bed. "Tim, J, and the rest interrupted a feeding frenzy."

Kyleigh gasped, and my utensil clattered onto the tray. I could not summon the words to ask if Nate was—if they were—uninjured.

"Evidently, Julian Voided Ross's cronies tried to break in, which activated some fail-safes." Zhen shrugged. "Whoever it was didn't pay attention to the warnings. One less genocidal murderer to worry about."

Horrified, I could not speak.

Kyleigh blanched. "It . . . it wasn't Elliott, was it?"

Bile rose in my throat. I had not considered that possibility.

"Hard to tell at this point." Zhen unzipped the bag. "Though probably not. The best guess is the fail-safe was what caused the power to flatline last ten-day, and you saw Elliott Ross after that. Anyway, they left whoever it was and ran."

An incoherent exclamation escaped Kyleigh, and she slumped backward.

"Zhen DuBois," I managed past the knot which filled my throat.

She pulled the armored suit from the bag without looking up. "What?"

"Has Nate—are they uninjured?"

Her dark eyes flickered to me. "No casualties reported, but they're not back yet."

Whatever else happened, I could not do nothing. I crossed the room with as much assurance as I could muster and hefted the remaining bag.

Kyleigh jumped to her feet. "She's sick, Zhen. You can't send her."

"I will go," James announced. "Kyleigh Tristram is again correct. Our friend is not well enough to leave isolation. You can open a direct communications link and tell me exactly what to do."

The still-new joy of being called *friend* flashed as brief and bright as burning magnesium, but I said, "No, James."

He raised one eyebrow—an act that again stirred petty jealousy since I had not mastered it—but calmly said, "Who else is there? I will not sit idly and allow others to risk themselves when I can be of use."

"We need her, James, not you," Zhen snapped. When he flinched, she softened her tone. After she finished laying out Kyleigh's suit and helmet, she helped me with mine then tilted her face toward the ceiling and closed her eyes. "Moons and stars. I don't like this. Neither did Alec, for that matter, and Quincy is livid. I don't want to be around when Tim finds out, but Jackson is adamant. You were training to be an Elder. Could you activate a drone and observe it from here? Maybe give it directions to follow citizen orders?"

"Perhaps," I said hesitantly, though I could not remember who Quincy was or why his opinions mattered. "Although I would rather maintain control—"

Zhen's sharp laugh shattered my train of thought. "Wouldn't we all? I don't know how to muddle through all this, but you're the only one who has the knowledge and doesn't have those blasted neural implants."

"Your reasoning is solid," I said.

"Of course it is. Finish eating. We need to go."

"I know this whole horrible situation is a 'last ten-day' kind of thing, and I'm not trying to say it isn't." Kyleigh skewered another bite of fish. "But even if we find a solution in the next twenty minutes, we're still stuck with *Thalassa* locked above us in synchronous orbit, and the ship still doesn't have the power to return to New Triton."

Zhen stood. "If the Consortium ship doesn't show up, we'll limp our way to one of Krios's platforms, and one of their ships can sprint back to the inner planets with what we've learned. But we need the information and the equipment for the injured marines Max and Williams have been working on for the past four hours."

"They were attacked by the cockroaches," I protested. "No one indicated they encountered the terrorists—Skip and his ilk. They could not have been injected with the virus."

"You're right and wrong. It seems—" She closed her eyes briefly, cocking her head to the side, as if listening. Her short lashes were dark against her cheeks. "Alec's team is back, and everyone's fine. Tim and J's team had another brief encounter with bugs, but they're due back in"—she rotated to check the chronometer on my bed—"an hour."

"But they are well?" I asked.

"No casualties so far," Zhen answered. "If we hustle, we can get that drone onto a temporary power supply, get you back here, and set up a computer so you can follow along without leaving home. As safe as we can make it."

I wiped my fingers clean with a paper napkin, then used it to hide the fish and potatoes. "Very well."

Zhen studied her gloved fingertips. "I heard about Clarkson being as stupid as an amoeba and refusing to acknowledge the Elder was sick."

"Clarkson is as sensitive as raw ore," Kyleigh huffed. "What does that have to do with anything?"

"We have proof now, in a roundabout way," Zhen said, but her hesitation told me what she did not.

Max had said that the marine named Michaelson was in danger not because of the amputation after a roach had mangled his arm, but because the roach carried *E. coli*, *Streptococcus*, and other bacterial strains it had acquired while scavenging for food.

But the Elder, Lorik—the people who had injected me with the nanodevice-born virus had also injected him. He had offered himself as a diversion to allow me to escape with Kyleigh and Freddie so we could live. Those roaches would now carry Lorik's nanodevices and his infection in their saliva. If my guess was correct, the insects themselves would be bioweapons. My Nathaniel, my friends, the people I loved, faced those insects every time they went out in the station's corridors.

"The roaches' saliva carries the virus," I said through suddenly parched lips. "How many were bitten?"

"Both of them."

"Stars above," Kyleigh whispered.

"And we have but one tank and no way of ascertaining if the nanotechnology in it is a blessing or a curse," I murmured.

The room swayed when I stood to pick up a piece of armor.

Zhen leaned forward and caught my upper arm. "I'm sorry. Truly. I know you're sick, but we need a drone if we're to save them."

I steadied myself and squared my shoulders. "In that case, Zhen DuBois, I will need your help."

Weapon ready, Zhen continually scanned the hall as she led the way to the control room. Kyleigh and James walked on my left and right, ready to take my arms, should I falter. Three marines in blue armor ranged around us, and the evenly spaced overhead lights made their bulky, unfamiliar weapons cast strange shapes underfoot.

Though short, the walk took longer than it should have. Halfway there, I had to rest, and while everyone waited, the marine who wore a red-and-white medic badge on her upper arm adjusted my suit's oxygen flow. She asked a series of pointless questions before motioning to Zhen. We continued at a slower pace. Somehow my boots carried me down the hall, but when the pale-blue safety lights along the base of the walls blurred, I closed my eyes. Kyleigh wrapped an arm around my waist, and James took hold of my right forearm to steady me.

Finally, I heard the tap of fingers on a panel and the sound of the control room's double doors sliding apart. I risked opening my eyes and winced at the subsequent brightness. Industrial floodlights illuminated the vast room's every corner, leaving no place for a behemoth insect, or even a smaller one, to enter by stealth. Spotlights hurled lumens at the dark volcanic rock ceiling's tooth-like structures, and their shadows huddled at their bases, not daring to creep down the walls. Flecks of mica, obsidian, and quartz caught the light and shimmered overhead like distant, bound stars.

The three marines accompanied us past a sentinel and a knot of men and women at a computer halfway through the room. We stopped less than four meters from the main console, where I had connected the drone to the computer. It hovered in the same position, like a spider awaiting prey on a web of tentacles, tendrils, and cables. A fine layer of dust had dulled its metallic body and the black of the cables anchoring it to the console, but its appendages shone.

"Recorder!"

Transfixed by a machine that had been both ally and enemy, I did not respond. James set a hand on my arm, and I glanced up at him. He inclined his head toward the man who had called me.

"There you are," one of the marines boomed over the communications link in my helmet. It took but two seconds to summon his name from my lagging memory. Lars. "Good to see you up and about, Recorder-who-isn't. We weren't sure you were going to—"

A chorus of voices interrupted him with varying impolite requests for his silence.

Lars grimaced. "Well, a couple of us thought you'd have to be recycled or something. You sure you should be out here? You look like you'd fall over if someone sneezed on you."

Someone groaned, and a woman I did not recognize suggested, "Then don't sneeze on her."

"Can't." Lars knocked one gloved hand against his helmet. "Not with this on."

Zhen flashed a glare at the man but tapped my arm. "Go ahead and get started. I'll be right back."

As she left, Lars waved at the drone attached to the console. "I remembered you telling Mike, back before the bugs got him, that you needed to leave that one alone, so New-Parker helped us wrangle the other ones for you. Over that way." He jabbed his thumb toward the corner, then walked beside me. "Good thing you're here, though. Lytwin and Patterson are in trouble. Everyone says you and Tristram"—he angled sideways and addressed Kyleigh—"good to see you—can figure out this mess once we get that equipment. None of us know the first thing about drones. Well, maybe New-Parker does. Didn't think of that before. Should've asked."

"It is well," I said, even though I concentrated more on my steps than his sentences. Kyleigh tightened her arm around my waist, but even with her help I was out of breath when we reached the table in the back of the room.

Lars bent over to peer through my faceplate. "Never seen anyone that color green, except once in hi-G training when that one guy washed out."

"If that is true," James said, edging between me and the tall marine, "you should bring her a chair."

"Right." Lars straightened, then walked backward toward a nearby computer station. "I really don't think Timmons will be too pleased you're up. Spanos wasn't. He and Quincy argued with Jackson something fierce. Be right back." He jogged past the vacant console's dusty chair toward the group of people on the far side of the room.

Kyleigh and James stared after him. She shook her head, and James brought me the chair. After brushing the seat with a gloved hand, he offered it to me. I sat gratefully and allowed my eyes to close. Fatigue reached deep into my bones, nearly erasing the reason I had abandoned my bed.

Unwilling to allow myself to forget, I clung to the fact that Max needed to know if Consortium nanodevices contaminated the medgel. If the virus was inextricably linked to the technology which ran in all Consortium blood, we needed to utilize that knowledge to save the marines who had been bitten. The key to that might be to track down why I yet lived.

With my eyes closed and my thoughts circling, I startled when someone touched my shoulder. Kyleigh knelt before me, and James stood like a guardian at her side.

"Are you all right?" she asked quietly.

"I will be." It might have been untrue. I could not tell.

Bracing myself with the chair's padded armrests, I studied the drones arranged on and beneath the thick concrete table. Like all Elders' primary drones, Lorik's was three-quarters of a meter across. The Elder's larger secondary slave drones rested on the polished floor. The two Recorders' drones were smaller, but mine, which Zhen, Jordan, and I had retrieved from the medical bay where a roach had mangled it, was absent.

They rested on neatly folded arms, giant silver ellipsoids on tidy silver cubes. With their writhing tendrils and tentacles spooled into the interior, they were peaceful, more like giant metallic water-smoothed stones and less like the mechanical jellyfish to which I had compared them all my life. They seemed harmless.

Lars appeared again, pushing a large, overstuffed rolling chair with a small, zippered duffel bag leaning against the lumbar support cushion. He gave it a final shove, and it eased to a stop beside me.

"Ah, good thinking with the other chair. Sorry I took so long. This one is better, though." Lars picked up the bag in one large hand, and its contents clattered. He rotated the chair toward me. "Give it a go."

I heaved myself from the dusty chair and into the softer cushions. Even in my suit, I could feel the difference, and a sigh escaped.

Lars grinned. "It's my favorite. Whoever's at comms usually takes it, but I figured you needed it more. Found it in a posh office just down the hall."

"It's Christine Johnson's."

We all turned to Kyleigh, who stared at the chair. James nudged the dusty chair in her direction, and she dropped into it.

Lars's smile evaporated, and he shifted his weight. "Oh. D'you mind?"

"No." Her voice thinned to a thread of its usual energy. "There's no one who will mind now."

When they fell silent, my heartbeat echoed in my ears. I slowly scooted the chair closer to the table, all my focus narrowing to the familiar Consortium shapes before me. Regardless of the absence of people mourning whoever Christine Johnson had been, we could not allow the two bitten marines to die like the citizens on *Agamemnon* had. Like Freddie had. Like I could. I had to choose a drone.

Which one . . .

The bag clattered again.

"Brought you wrenches and pliers and some of that cabling, like the stuff that hooks that other one to the computer system." Lars set the zippered duffel between Lorik's slave drones, but I eyed it with askance. The marine meant well, but I questioned his knowledge in packing appropriate supplies. He tapped one of the drones with the toe of his boot. "Tell you what. Pick one of these big ones. Never know when more power will come in handy."

"But have you worked with an Elder's drone before?" Kyleigh asked.

"No," I answered. "I have not."

Which one . . .

Was using the Elder's worth the risk? If a Recorder's drone went rogue, I could shut it down, but if the codes for an Elder's differed, would the threat to both citizens and escaping Recorders outweigh the benefits of activating it?

Images overlay the table before me. *Lorik's blood-reddened eyes and pain-etched features. The darkness in the tunnels as he repeated the codes, making me promise to use them for . . . something.*

Either fatigue or the virus scrambled the numbers and letters in my memory. I closed my eyes, searching for accuracy, pleading with myself to remember. It had not been long ago. I should not have forgotten.

Which one . . .

Familiarity warred with dangers and benefits.

I had to gain access to the storage areas, true, but Lorik's drone would also allow me to access Consortium records and create new lives for the talkative former Recorder and James. Their freedom was worth whatever I needed to do, as long as I kept the others safe as well. My eyes opened. Despite the risks, I knew what I needed.

I sat up straight and pointed to Lorik's personal drone. "This one."

"Not one of the really big ones?" Lars asked. "You're sure?"

"I am certain."

Light footsteps brought my attention around.

Zhen nodded at the tool bag. "I assembled that kit based on what you used when you set up the jammers. Will you need anything else?"

Relief trickled through me. "I have not checked, but if you assembled it, I am not concerned."

"I'm glad someone appreciates me." She came to a stop two and a half meters from the table. "What next?"

"I need a conference room with a lockable door."

Zhen's expression descended into a frown. "But if we aren't hiding it—"

"This is not about hiding but about containment. I do not know what this drone will do, and even though it may do nothing, putting others in danger is not an option." The room spun around me when I tried to stand, so I sank back in the chair before looking up at James. "You must stay far from the area while I attempt to activate it. I do not want it to record your presence or put you in danger."

My first friend stiffened. "You cannot do this alone."

"On the contrary, I do this alone, or it is not done."

"Right." Zhen clicked a button on her wrist. "I need those

microantigravity units we used to move these beasts in here. And check with Jackson about conference rooms."

Over the communications link, the talkative Recorder said, "You got it."

Grabbing the comfortable chair's armrests, I rotated toward the approaching man in the Consortium suit. The talkative former Recorder removed a microantigravity device from a box and tossed it to Zhen, who caught it one-handed.

She studied it for a moment, then frowned at me. "We aren't going to finish before Tim and J get back, so be prepared for the scolding of your life."

"You can't let her go off on her own when she's been so sick," Kyleigh protested, and her assertion did nothing to increase my self-confidence.

James's expression mirrored hers. "Indeed."

"I have to say"—Lars glanced at Kyleigh and James—"they're right."

"Exactly," the talkative Recorder said, all hint of his usual good humor gone.

"Oh, she'll go alone." An incongruous smile blossomed on Zhen's face. "But like I said last ten-day, I'll go with her."

Unlike when Jordan, Zhen, and I battled inertia and a malfunctioning microantigravity device to tug my defunct drone from the medical bay, transporting Lorik's drone took little effort. With the marines' more powerful units, the drone glided smoothly down the dimly lit hall, but the ease of moving it did little to alleviate my concern.

Despite my insistence that the drone could put her in danger, Zhen refused to let me reactivate it alone. Though she was armed, she focused primarily on the controls for the microantigravity units. The drone itself floated in front of us, right behind Lars. The possibility that it could injure someone looped through my mind, as omnipresent as the pain in my head and my shortness of breath.

James remained at my side, the bag of tools in his hand. Though I had argued against it, he and the talkative former Recorder—Daniel, I reminded myself—had convinced Jackson that they would be able to assist me, should I falter once the drone was active. Strangely, Kyleigh had not disagreed. She, of course, had no such reason for accompanying me, but after she promised to return when ordered, no one protested her presence. Daniel's quick steps followed behind us, and occasional glances over my shoulder proved he held his rifle ready.

Given the potential of roaches, gratitude for an armed presence remained foremost in my mind, followed closely by the assurance that Kyleigh and James would be escorted back to the control room once I had activated the drone in a secure location.

We had taken but two turnings when Lars stopped us before a hinged door with an old-fashioned knob.

"Unless the station map is incorrect, this is not a conference room," James said in an undertone.

I bit my lip. The probability of James failing to recall something was unlikely.

"It isn't," Lars said. "Figured close was better than a longer trip into bug zones."

When James answered that his supposition was correct, Lars beamed.

Zhen tapped the datapad in her hand, and the drone hovered at her side like a floating silver egg. "As long as it has power and we can secure the door, it should work."

"Power was on earlier." Lars glanced at Kyleigh and me. "We started sealing the vents today to keep the bugs out. It should be fine. I took care of this one before lunch, so the fumes shouldn't be as bad."

"Our suits have air filters, Lars," Zhen said.

He grunted. "Point. Tristram, you're heading back with me and New-Parker?"

"Daniel Parker," the talkative former Recorder reminded us.

"Right," Lars said. "Dan."

Kyleigh's short-lived smile did not reach her eyes. "Yes. I'll head back to the control room until we leave to get the equipment from Georgette's lab. I just came to make sure my friend was all right."

The lack of sparkle in her eyes prevented me from reminding her that an armed presence would do more to ensure my safety than Kyleigh's observations.

Lars gave her a quick nod. "Good. Wouldn't want you to be sad or anything, Tristram. Wait here."

He motioned us back and pushed the door open. The room's lights flickered on, lending a warm hue to the corridor's cool, dim grey. He entered alone.

While James watched the door, Zhen and the talkative Recorder—Daniel, I repeated internally—scanned the hall, up and down, as alert as any drone could have been. Mere seconds ticked by before Lars stuck his head back through the doorway.

"Clear."

Zhen ushered the drone into the room. I followed, but the contrast with the sterile, empty halls jarred me to a stop.

While investigating the incident leading to the deaths on Pallas Station, I had utilized *Thalassa*'s VVR to walk through recordings of several locations. Neither Charles Tristram's cluttered workspace nor John Westruther's austere one resembled this.

The office itself was as large as the conference room where we had first secured my drone after fleeing the insects in the medbay, but buttery-yellow matte paint transformed the grim concrete walls. Framed watercolors of flowers altered them further. Overhead, a delicate fitting of cut glass replaced the standard fixture and softened the glare, splitting full-spectrum light into tiny rainbows. Underfoot, orange flowers and olive-green vines twined around gold geometric designs in the thick carpet that muffled our footsteps.

Slippers, perhaps a size and a half larger than Kyleigh would wear, rested between a chaise lounge and wooden side table. Pale residue clung inside the abandoned glass resting on a crocheted coaster, and warm, incandescent light spilled from a delicate ceramic lamp with a creamy fabric shade. As if it waited for its owner to return, a lacy cardigan draped over the back of the overstuffed chair facing the wooden desk. On the back wall, lacquered black frames boasted of academic accomplishments and commendations, and gilded frames displayed pictures of children alike enough to be siblings.

Over two years' worth of dust overlaid everything in a thin film, belying the office's comfort. I suppressed a shudder. Whoever had chosen these amenities was long since dead, as surely as the skeletal fern that crouched in the corner, its splayed, twig-like stems reaching over the dry, brown mound of leaves littering the thick carpet.

Lars pointed between the fern and the desk. "Power strip's back there."

While Zhen settled Lorik's drone onto the carpet, Daniel let out a low whistle. "This is where you found that chair, isn't it? I thought you were exaggerating when you said it was posh."

Zhen retrieved the equipment from James, but she said, "Lars, keep an eye on the hall."

"Watch for bugs. Right." Lars gave Zhen a salute and strode to the door.

Daniel, the talkative Recorder, studied the room. "I haven't seen anything that flaunted credits like this since I was assigned to the Founders' Hall in Albany City."

Zhen dropped the duffel beside the drone and arched a brow at him. "You were assigned to the government center? How did that go?"

His chuckle seemed out of place in the office's soft desolation. "It did not work out well. I was there for less than three ten-days before I was sent to tribunal."

"That is not long." I frowned. "The Elders should have found you a position that better matched your temperament."

"Not if they wanted to be rid of me."

Before I could respond, Lars spoke from the hall. "Sounds shady."

"The official I was sent to assist did nothing illegal," Daniel said, "but standards of moral conduct should supersede mere contracts."

Kyleigh still faced the empty, dust-covered chaise lounge. "Tia and I talked about that on the trip out here."

When she did not elaborate further, Daniel continued, "I refused to ignore predatory behavior and filed an incident report. He countered that he had not violated any contract or law, and therefore, I displayed bias. The Elders agreed with him."

Zhen huffed. "That doesn't mean you're wrong." She narrowed her eyes, but I could not tell whether her apparent displeasure was aimed at Daniel's remarks or at the drone. Tools clattered as Zhen searched through the bag. She motioned to me. "Am I doing this right? I studied the one in the control room, but I've never handled a functioning drone before. I don't want to get zapped."

Of course. The drone.

I took two rapid steps, but dizziness loomed again. I dropped to the floor beside Zhen, thankful for the carpet's cushioning effects.

"Be careful. I need to get you back to the quarantine room in one piece," she said.

"Do not be alarmed. We cannot be 'zapped' until it has become active."

"Well, it's that Elder's machine, there's probably some sneaky Consortium wiring going on. Kyleigh, I need . . ."

Her words petered out as her gaze lingered on Kyleigh, who stared vacantly into the room, arms tightly crossed against her chest.

James touched Kyleigh's arm. "Are you well?"

"I'm fine," Lars said.

"Not you," Zhen snapped. "Kye?"

"Yes. It's . . ." Kyleigh blinked rapidly. "This room is the same, but different. Like when you find out that the meaning of a poem you've learned by heart is the opposite of what you thought."

For a moment, Daniel's posture softened. "You miss your friend."

"Christine Johnson wasn't my friend." Kyleigh crossed to the overstuffed chair facing the desk and ran gloved fingers over the upholstery. "I don't think she liked many people other than herself and Ross, though sometimes I felt like she was using him, too. She was rude to Elliott when Ross wasn't watching and tolerated me because she worked with Dad. She was decent enough to Freddie, though his dad was the station director. She wouldn't have wanted to get on John Westruther's bad side. Not that he had one."

James tilted his head, silver eyes intent on the young woman by the chair. "And yet, you mourn her?"

"I suppose I do. This room—it's so Christine." She picked up the lacy sweater and folded it carefully. Rather than returning it to the chair, she held it against her chest. "I wonder if it still smells like flowers. She used to wear expensive perfume, but I can't recall what kind."

"Probably smells like dust now," Lars commented from the hall.

Zhen rolled her eyes before pointing at the cabling. I double-checked. She had done well: only one attachment required adjustment.

I made the correction. "That will suffice."

"Sufficient, it is, then. Where's your datapad?"

My hand went to the pocket on my thigh, but it was empty. "I . . . I must have left it behind."

Zhen's attention locked onto me. "Right, but you needed it before to find the frequency for those jamming devices. We don't need that now."

Kyleigh resumed as if we had not spoken. "She paid extra to have her furniture brought here. Freddie, Elliott, and I placed bets about what ridiculous item would arrive next. I lost a week of dessert to Elliott over this chair, although Freddie gave me his when Elliott wasn't looking." She sighed. "She was kind of like me in that she didn't have any family."

"You still have your mother," Zhen said.

"I haven't seen Mom in years. She was supposed to join me and Dad here." Kyleigh placed the sweater on the desktop and smoothed the fabric. "Mom was waiting for me at Lunar One, but with the restrictions, I never saw her. Archimedes tried to convince someone to let us communicate, but the authorities thought it was a security risk."

Zhen snorted. "That's rubbish."

Kyleigh rounded the desk to straighten the infinitesimally crooked pictures. "This is Christine here, the blonde, with her older sister, Agatha. The toddler is their little brother, Xavier. She told me her sister died years ago."

"While I'm sorry about her sister, if she couldn't see you for who you are, I don't care how smart she thought she was. Christine Johnson sounds like a drossing idiot." Zhen uncoiled the thick black cable, stretching it toward the power strip at the base of the wall. "Here we go."

"We should wait until they leave," I said.

Eyes on the access panel, she made a noncommittal noise. "If it doesn't work, you and I will have to walk back alone. That didn't go well for Michaelson when that voided bug about chewed his arm off. First we find out if it works, then they go. With this drone, you and I will be a little safer from the roaches."

"Zhen DuBois," I said, and she shot me an incomprehensible look. "I do not agree."

"Too bad."

The cabling connected with a click, and the drone's power light flashed from red to orange. I settled on my knees. Slowly, as if surfacing through a viscous liquid, the drone lifted from the floor, the microantigravity units magnetically attached underneath like fist-sized parasites. The underbelly's panels slid open, and the tendrils began to unspool.

Zhen jumped to her feet. "I think that does it. Nothing to do now but wait."

"They should leave." My helmet's speaker scattered my words through the air. "*You* should leave, Zhen DuBois. I do not know what it will do."

"I don't think so." She turned to the door and said, "Lars."

He glanced back. "Yep?"

"You and Daniel escort Kye and James back to—"

Sharp, percussive shots echoed in the hall, and Lars doubled over.

08

"Down!"

Zhen darted around the drone to Lars's side. Kyleigh dropped behind the desk, but I froze, as if my knees had been welded to the floor. A high-pitched buzz in my ears rivaled still-deafening shots.

Lars shoved himself upright. Another series of bursts shattered the air. He staggered sideways, steadied himself, and raised his weapon. Brutal sound stabbed my ears as he edged into the office.

Despite the gentle flow of oxygen in my helmet, I could not breathe.

Daniel was at the door, sighting down his weapon, and sound punched my chest. Sparks flew from the metal doorframe. The ceramic lamp shattered. Words—short, terse, and incomprehensible—penetrated the chaos, and James's deep voice responded. Grabbing my upper arm, he pulled me behind the drone, which became our barrier from the door, though its dangling tendrils provided no true protection.

Numbers. Someone—Daniel?—listed unsequenced numbers.

Kyleigh left her hiding space to crowd with James and me between the drone and the wall. She removed my arm from James's grasp and turned it wrist up, flipping open the communications panel. Voices disappeared, and weapons' fire dulled to pops.

Ignoring the drone and its emerging tendrils, Kyleigh rotated me to face the wall, then caught my helmet with both hands. In the absence of sound, I watched her lips. After she repeated the same thing twice, I understood.

"Two. Three. Five. Seven."

She paused, waiting.

"Eleven, thirteen, seventeen, nineteen, twenty-three," I continued.

Kyleigh gave me a tight smile, then said—or mouthed—*"Breathe."*

James cast a quick glance at the door and stood. Panic bit at me. I reached to yank him down, but Kyleigh put a firm hand on my shoulder and climbed to her feet as well.

The drone jostled me as it ascended. I grabbed it, and it tugged me upright.

The door was shut. Daniel was closing the small access panel beside it, and Lars leaned against the wall. No blood leaked down his suit's marine blue, but two deep scratches ran across the left thigh, and the right shoulder was scuffed. He rubbed his hand over an uneven divot marring his chest plate.

Zhen turned to Daniel, who bent his head toward the chaise lounge. How long had it been? Minutes? Seconds? I had not counted.

The drone slid from my grasp as the ovoid machine drifted up. Thicker tentacles unspooled from their interior cavities, and its four jointed arms unfolded. Its tentacles dangled underneath and pooled on the flowered carpet, but its extended tendrils writhed wildly. It came to a stop, hovering at shoulder height, tethered to the wall by the black cable.

One hand splayed on its silver side, I whispered the code the Elder had told me before he died, flexed my fingers, and input the numbers and letters, hesitating but once. The small screen on the top flashed.

>>*Assigned Elder not detected. Network not detected. Enter CDN.*

Again, my breath caught.

Did I enter my own Consortium designation number, or did I enter Lorik's?

Whether due to my delay, the charging process, or a malfunction, the words pulsed across the screen: >>*Enter CDN.*

Three whip-like tendrils twined around my ankles.

Which identification number?

Indecision swelled. The Consortium must know Lorik died. Without the neural implant, without the network, with our physiological differences, the drone would immediately identify me as an imposter. I was no longer a Recorder training to become an Elder, and surely, the drone would recognize my number. To proclaim my identity when I was considered an aberration and a rogue would surely activate security protocols.

>>*Enter CDN.*

I clenched my jaw, then entered, >>*Zeta4542910-9545E.*

>>*Unauthorized. Access Denied.*

One long tendril slithered up my legs and around my torso. Another twisted its way to my neck.

James grabbed my shoulder, and a tendril reached for him. The drone issued a reprimand, and sudden pain made my eyes water. Kyleigh tried to pull me back, but when I pushed her hand away, one of the appendages encircling my legs released me and snaked toward her. The one around my neck tightened, but whatever happened to me, I would allow neither James nor Kyleigh to be harmed. The tendril around my waist wound higher, but before it could pin my hand to my side, I entered the universal stop code.

For the space of two breaths, nothing happened.

Then, the tendrils withdrew, disappearing again into their internal pockets. The tentacles wound back into the interior, and its arms folded into tidy cubes. As the drone floated down to rest again on the microantigravity units, its screen flickered off, though the orange charging light still glowed.

I sagged backward. James caught one arm and Kyleigh the other. My nose tingled, and I sniffed back a trickle before lifting my gaze from the drone's smooth surface.

Zhen met my eyes from across the room. Slowly, she lowered her weapon. Daniel seemed coiled like a spring, ready to rush to my side. Lars had maneuvered himself upright. All color had drained from his face, and his weapon shook in his gloved hands.

Whether or not my error lay in giving my identification number instead of Lorik's, without the drone, we could not access the equipment. Without the equipment, no one would be able to discern whether or not the medgel necessary to treat the injured marines would instead end their lives. The tingling in my throat grew stronger as the weight of unmet responsibilities pressed down, crushing me as surely as a singularity.

The marines and my friends had overestimated my abilities, and Lars had been shot. Now we were trapped in the elaborate yellow office with its cut-glass fitting while unknown assailants fired at us.

My limitations and lack of control over my physical responses had led us here, trapped, with a drone I could not control. I did not wish to return to being a functional Recorder. I wished to help the others.

But as light split over two years of dust in the abandoned office, I could do nothing at all.

09

Deep green ferns crouched in squat, red-glazed pots throughout the paneled room, like giant botanical spiders lurking in the corners. A three-meter, braided ficus leaned toward the window, and Tia knew enough about plants to know that someone should rotate it before it became permanently uneven. Odd, really. In such an opulent setting, someone should have remembered. While she watched, a single leaf dropped, pirouetting through the air to the floor's geometric tiles. A bot detached from under a side table to clean it up, then hummed its way back to the charging station.

Tia glanced at the receptionist, who seemed enthralled by the small projection over her desk. It was a nice desk. Real wood, if Tia wasn't wrong, as polished and smooth as the warm cherry-toned paneling on the walls. The whole room practically screamed credits. Even the high-end, uncomfortable wooden chairs put visitors in their place. Products imported from Ceres were rare enough, so the plethora of carved designs and wooden furniture made the subtle point: Citizens were welcome, if temporarily, in the shrine of bureaucracy.

I'm more than a mere citizen, though. Everything will be fine.

Being nervous was ridiculous, but this was so very different from everything in her mother's modest flat. Tia wrapped her fingers around the wooden armrests, the dark finish almost as smooth as synthetic material. Philippe wouldn't be annoyed that she showed up at his office, would he? Maybe she should have waited until their next date.

A bubble of nausea rose in her throat.

Well. Maybe not.

The receptionist powered off her display and patted her elaborate tower of braids. Inadequacy washed over Tia, but she didn't have time or credits for sophisticated styles. Besides, he loved her hair down. Tia stood and smoothed her best, most professional tunic, feeling like a schoolgirl when the elegant receptionist bestowed an empty smile.

"He'll see you now."

The panel behind the woman's desk slid into a pocket, and Tia steeled herself and passed from the waiting room into an even richer office.

His desk faced the doorway, and he threw her a languid smile. A portion of her worries evaporated. This was her Philippe with his agate eyes, his long hair tied into a loose yet artistic tail, his elegant masculinity. Everything would be fine. He loved her, and she loved him.

The whole situation was simply a bump in their relationship. They would be fine.

"It's good to see you, gorgeous." His voice, as polished as his cherry desk with its tapered legs, soothed her nerves. "Unexpected, but not unwelcome."

"I couldn't wait," she began.

His lids lowered, half shuttering his eyes. "And certainly understandable." Rising from his chair, he strode to her and combed his fingers through her loose hair. "I love these waves tumbling free."

See? Everything will be—

"Recorder," he said.

"What?" Startled, Tia jerked back. Her confusion morphed into a rush of adrenaline as the subsequent whine of a drone drew her attention to a gaunt Recorder stepping from an alcove, a drone tangled about her neck and torso.

"We won't need you," Philippe said. "You're dismissed."

The Recorder's drone released her, and she took two solitary steps toward the door.

"Take that drone with you."

"All business performed in service to the people of Albany City must be documented," the Recorder intoned.

"This is personal."

The Recorder's hollow focus zeroed in on him. "You have an appointment in thirty minutes."

Phillippe flicked a smile at Tia. "Which will more than suffice."

"Documentation of attempted blackmail or coercion—"

Tia's stomach flipped, but he chuckled. "I'm not worried, Recorder, so you shouldn't be either. Besides, it's your last ten-day here." He waved a hand at the door. "Take some time for yourself."

The Recorder ignored his taunt and fastened her eerie eyes on Tia. "Is this so, Portia Belisi? There is no need for concern?"

She knows my name? Tia suppressed a shudder. "Not at all."

"Very well." The Recorder hesitated a moment. "As you say."

The door slid shut behind her and that monstrosity of a drone, leaving them alone.

He frowned. "I'll be glad to get a new one. That old drone . . ." He shrugged, then turned to stroke Tia's cheek with his knuckles. "But I'm even gladder that you came."

Resisting the urge to melt into his arms, Tia caught his hand, and he stilled. She wetted her lips and said, "That's not . . . I need—we need—to talk."

His soft expression shifted into something more mechanical. "Do we?" He released her and went to the sideboard in the corner next to another hulking fern. "A drink, before we—"

"No," she said quickly. Too fast. She'd answered too fast.

He turned to face her.

She wrapped her arms over her stomach. "No," she repeated. "Thank you, but I don't . . . I don't want one."

"If you insist. Have a seat, my dear." He turned back to the sideboard, and ice clattered. Liquid poured twice.

"I told you I didn't need anything."

He held out a crystal glass with clear liquid, keeping the amber one for himself. "Water. You're always thirsty when you're ill at ease. Have a seat."

She accepted his offering and lowered herself into a sleek fabric chair.

He leaned back against the cherry desk and took a sip, his eyes never leaving her face. "So what is this topic you and I need to discuss?"

"We've been seeing each other since my second year. No one has ever made me feel as special, as beautiful, as you."

A half smile flickered.

"You and I . . ." Condensation dripped from the glass, leaving a dark splotch on her tunic. She scrubbed at the uneven shape, dulling its edges, then took a sip of water and forced herself to say, "I want a contract."

"No." The single word flew out, sharp, abrupt, even faster than her earlier refusal.

The glass's geometric design suddenly felt slick in her hand. "You didn't even—"

"Tia," he said. "I already have one."

The air must have all vanished, for Tia couldn't breathe. He had to be lying.

He swirled the ice in his glass, downed the amber liquid, and then said evenly, "I assumed you knew."

Her body went cold, and his statement momentarily trapped her response in her throat.

"No? I find that hard to believe," Philippe continued. "You know who I am. Most people do their research or keep up with gossip sites and current events."

"You know I don't read those."

"True. One of your positive attributes." He tipped the glass at her. "My partner and I have been together for, oh, ten, eleven years. She understands me, and I understand her."

Ice rattled in Tia's glass, and rather than allowing it to bear witness to how her hands shook, she set it by her feet. "Does your partner know? About me?"

"Not specifically. It isn't like I talk about"—he waved an elegant hand—"this. That would make poor conversation, don't you think? But she understands. We have an open but exclusive contract."

"Open but exclusive," she repeated like a file error.

He set his glass down on the beautiful wooden desk. "You weren't worried about being caught in legal suits, were you?"

"No." *But I am now.*

"So why does this matter?"

"How can you ask that?"

He pushed a grimace away with an artificial laugh. "You wouldn't try to contact her or blackmail me."

"Of course not."

"Good, good." He motioned to her glass. "Drink. You sure you don't need something stronger than water?"

"Given the circumstances," Tia managed, "that wouldn't be wise."

He froze, and his gaze ranged over her figure, lingering over her middle. She fought the urge to twist her fingers around the hem of her tunic.

After an everlasting minute of quiet, he said, "Ah."

"I'm so close to graduating." Her words almost ran over each other in their hurry to escape. "I only have three sessions after this one. And you know policies don't allow . . ." She steadied her breath. "Please, I just need a short-term contract, maybe a year. I promise not to burden you."

"Impossible. Tell me I don't have to explain how exclusivity precludes additional contracts, Portia."

"But you love me." The protest emerged in a whisper. "You said you loved me."

His demeanor shifted to gentleness, and he crossed to kneel in front of her and pick up her drink. "Of course I do, gorgeous."

Under his watch, she choked down another sip. The water sloshed, so she rested the crystal glass on her knee. "I don't know what to do."

His eyes ranged over her face. "Sometimes you are so very young."

She stiffened. Was that what had attracted him in the first place? Being young? Being naïve?

"A contract isn't your sole option," he murmured. "Public service is another. You're bright. I'm brilliant. The combination would be a valuable gift."

A gift. Her mouth fell open.

He chuckled. "Don't act offended, Portia, and don't be stupid. Gifting to the Consortium isn't a bad decision."

Why did it hurt to breathe? "Maybe not."

Plucking the glass from her hand, he stood and carried it to the sideboard, where the ice in his own was melting down to nothing.

Nothing. It all comes down to nothing.

"So. You face three choices." He returned to sit behind his desk, elbows on the surface, long fingers steepled. "Gifting, a contract, or losing your future."

"A contract?" A spark of hope lit. "But you . . . what do you mean? You refused."

"I already explained," he said as smoothly as pouring oil. "Open but exclusive, my dear. Nothing we did broke that, but a dual contract is out of the question."

Silence billowed around her. In vids, there was always a separate sound, like an archaic clock or the whoosh of the ventilation system, but not here, in this expensive office, sitting across from the man who'd said he loved her. Moons above, she'd been a fool.

"One of your young friends could be an option."

"How can you even suggest someone else, like—" She broke off before she could say, like *I don't matter*. He had a contract. Of course she didn't matter.

"Now, personally, I don't see why they would want to saddle themselves with your baggage for another twenty years, but they might not mind. There's that red-haired boy who didn't seem to like me." His derisive smile made her bristle. He leaned back into his chair. "He's a belter, I think. They have a different perception of reality in the inner belt. He might be willing to—"

"Leave Eric out of this," she ground between gritted teeth.

Philippe waved a long-fingered hand. "Then you have but two choices. You're young, and your life is before you. Without a contract, you will be ejected from university. I didn't make those rules," he added quickly, "but they make sense. You can't divide your attention between studies and other responsibilities and expect to be successful. I can't help you, so you either gift it, or you quit university. If you don't want to ruin your future, gifting is your best choice." He glanced at the alcove by the door. "The Consortium certainly needs quality Recorders."

For a fraction of a second, Tia saw a miniature version of herself as haggard as the Recorder who just left, standing in that empty alcove, a drone floating at her side, empty eyes staring back at her. Tia shoved the mental picture away. That old Recorder was the exception, not the norm.

Tia made one last attempt. "But if you love me—"

"Love." Unnaturally white teeth flashed. Why hadn't she seen how unnatural they were before? His mellifluous voice mocked her as he said, "Love is a complicated construct when we are but biological machines with chemical responses."

She didn't want to provoke him, so she suggested, "What if you could sponsor me? I could still—"

"I won't deal with your mistakes."

Her cheeks heated. "*My* mistakes?"

"You're the one in the predicament." He shrugged. "A gift is a simple thing. The world will benefit, and you'll be compensated."

"But you said—"

"Life as you know it is over if you don't." He smoothed the front of his gold-embellished jacket. "You'll have no recourse but to take a menial job and give up your goal of . . ."

She almost choked on her answer. "Being a forensic accountant."

He had the nerve to smile. "That's right."

Her gut roiled. He hadn't been listening when they sat, fingers laced, and she'd spilled out her dreams.

Philippe leaned back. "Of course, you could take a job in the inner belt."

She gaped at him.

"It's rough in places, but they are willing to take dropouts with baggage." He studied his fingernails. "I could put in a recommendation for you, get you to a safer location."

She could hardly breathe. "You're trying to get rid of me."

"Portia, there's no need for theatrics."

"Really?" She stood. "And yet you play the melodramatic villain so well."

He adjusted the datapad on his desk, not even having the decency to look her in the eye. "Don't be a child."

She swallowed her rising gorge and spat out, "Well, you won't get rid of me. I will always be here. No matter what it costs."

Very slowly, he raised his head. "Is that a threat?"

"It's a fact. You won't ship me off to some forsaken asteroid to appease your guilt—"

"I'm not at fault here."

"Or your precious partner."

Cold eyes bore into hers. "She is not your concern."

"Oh, so you care for someone after all?" It was either laugh or cry, so Tia forced a laugh. "Or were you lying about that, too? Is that why you don't want me to contact her? Don't want her to find out she's the older, cast-off model?"

His nostrils flared. "Get out."

"Don't think you'll get a credit of the compensation I'll receive for gifting."

"Credits?" His well-modulated tone descended into a sneer. "You think *I* need credits? That I want compensation? Everything I wanted from you"—he snapped his fingers—"I already had. I wouldn't accept payment for such small favors."

Tia's cheeks burned as she stormed from the room. She wouldn't take a contract with him now if the Founders returned from the dead and deeded her the whole system.

The elegant receptionist jumped to her feet when Tia barged through the embossed door and ran headlong into that Recorder, knocking her back against her drone.

"Excuse me, I . . ."

Her words ground to a halt when the Recorder laid a thin, vein-laced hand on Tia's arm. "Portia Belisi."

Tia's throat tightened. "Yes?"

Pale eyes searched her face. "Are you well? Do you"—she glanced at the receptionist, her drone, back at Tia—"have anything you need to document?"

What was there to tell anyone except that she had been . . . tricked? Deceived? Stupid? That she'd made a perfectly legal, humiliating mistake that would ruin her future? The receptionist took a half step in their direction.

"I serve elsewhere next ten-day," the Recorder said. "You will not be able to contact me."

She wasn't as old as Tia had first thought, not unless the Consortium had some strange antiaging tech. Not a single wrinkle marred her almost skeletal, sallow face.

"Are you all right? I don't mean to be rude, but do you need to sit down?"

The Recorder blinked mahogany lashes. Surprise laced her voice. "Irrelevant."

But it wasn't. And Tia couldn't find the words to ask what she wanted to—did the Recorder regret her own gifting? Was it the right thing to do?

"Do not worry for me." The Recorder wobbled, and her drone sent a thick arm around her waist. She leaned into it. "The Consortium takes care of its own."

"I'll still be here, though," the receptionist said. "If you . . ."

She never finished her sentence.

Tia took a hair tie from her pocket, twisted her loose waves into a bun, and secured it. She inhaled and lied, "I'll be fine."

Their concern gave her the presence of mind to keep from dashing from the building. Instead of taking public transport, she began the long walk back to the dorms. Her anger didn't fade, but disappointment deepened. Fear welled up to keep them both company.

Her last work-study tour was coming up in a few ten-days. And after that, she'd make her gift and finish up her degree. Ruining her future, the one she'd worked so hard for, was out of the question. She wouldn't allow Philippe—that voided piece of *rubbish*—to ruin her. He'd done enough damage.

A blister formed on her heel, so she stopped at a bench under a mimosa tree to take off her dress shoes. The tree's delicate pink blossoms dipped slightly as the mammoth overhead fans pulsed, and dappled light filtered through the leaves. Tia set her shoes beside her on the bench, put her face in her hands, and cried.

10

Something trickled down my upper lip, and I clamped my mouth shut while I unplugged Lorik's drone. Since I could not control it, allowing it to power up would endanger others. It was disconnected when James extended his hand. I surrendered the coils and shifted away without raising my head. The others should not be given additional cause to worry. If my nose bled, it bled. There would be nothing anyone could do unless I removed my helmet, and I had promised Zhen, Kyleigh, and James that I would not.

While James finished packing the bag, I pushed myself to my feet. I faltered, and Zhen appeared and caught my elbow. Without meaning to do so, I met her eyes.

Her gaze flickered to my upper lip, and she frowned, then tapped her helmet. Very slowly, almost so slowly that I did not understand, I saw her say, *"Turn it on."*

Shaking my head brought a surge of vertigo. She anchored me, then pointed to my wrist and held out her hand, but I folded my arms against my chest.

James lifted the overstuffed chair and settled it against the wall, where the desk blocked my view of Lorik's drone, and Zhen and Kyleigh guided me over to it. Dust ascended in faint puffs when I lowered myself onto voluminous cushions, even though I merely sat on the edge, waiting, clutching my wrist lest someone attempt to reactivate my communications link.

As clearly as VVR, my mind replayed the previous moments. *Lars doubling over, the lamp shattering, the drone's tendrils stretching past me.* Again and again.

My attention snagged on the shattered lamp. Vivid yellow glaze sandwiched shards of bone-white ceramic. Broken. Beyond repair. Discouragement grabbed at me, and I surreptitiously tapped my thigh.

Zhen pivoted from the door, a scowl on her face. I looked away.

Eventually, my respiration slowed, and I fell back against the cushions. Fatigue gathered me in invisible tendrils, and I slumped sideways, my eyes flickering open and drifting shut, making time uneven.

A sudden flurry of movement jarred me upright. Daniel entered something on the panel, and the door swung open. Marines poured into the room. A hover gurney eased toward the chaise lounge where Lars rested, and he scooted awkwardly onto the flat cushions. Once he was settled, the medic tightened the safety straps, and another marine tucked Lars's weapon into the bed's undercarriage. James left Kyleigh's side to meet another man in grey-and-black armor. Together, they wove through the sea of marine blue at the doorway. I dropped my gaze.

Familiar black boots entered my line of sight, halting on the carpet's twined flowers and geometric designs. When I did not stand, Nate knelt in front of me. I kept my eyes on my gloves' thin, black ribbing rather than admitting how I had erred.

He switched over to his external communication unit, and I did not resist when he turned my arm wrist up and enabled my own. Sound resumed—the faint hum of microantigravity devices, the clatter of weapons against armor, the muffled thuds of footfalls on the thick carpet—but since everyone used the communications links, the absence of conversation was loud.

"Hey." Nate's speaker combined with my helmet's reception to make his tenor slightly tinny, slightly distant, but it was still his own. "Look at me, sweetheart."

The gentleness in his voice brought my head up. His eyes roamed my face, lingering for a second at what must have been the dried traces from another nosebleed.

I whispered, "I am looking."

The corner of his mouth lifted slightly. "How're you holding up?"

"Nate—I cannot . . ." I glanced over at the gurney, where Lars held one arm tightly across his chest as the marine medic flashed a light in his eyes. My inclination to ask who had shot at us was ridiculous. The marines would not, and the roaches did not bear arms. That left Skip, the knife-man, and their accomplices—the ones who had injected Lorik, Freddie, and me with the virus. All I said was, "Lars is injured."

He grimaced. "Yeah, but the armor did its job. Max or Williams will check him out once we get back. Probably some nasty bruising, maybe a cracked rib. Not that being shot is particularly fun, but he'll be fine."

Concern momentarily diverted me. "Have you been shot?"

"Not recently." Nate rapped his knuckles on his armored suit. "This stuff might not do a lot of good when a two-meter bug is chewing on you, but in general, it keeps you alive around humans. He'll be fine. It'll make a nice story to not tell his family when we get back."

His statement made no sense.

"I brought this on them, Nathaniel," I said, clarifying neither antecedent. "I could not even activate Lorik's drone."

"So the drone doesn't work, which is a topic for later, but they *chose* to come with you."

"At my instigation."

"At Jackson's." A muscle in his jaw ticced. "Believe me, I'll be talking to a couple people about that later."

"Those marines . . ." I closed my eyes for the count of three seconds, not wanting to hear the worst, but needing to know. "Do they live?"

He nodded. "Max and Williams have both men stabilized and dosed up pretty well. Lytwin took a nasty bite through his armor. Lost his leg and nearly bled out. The other—"

"Patterson," I interrupted, feeling compelled to name him as well, as if doing so granted him a closer hold to life.

"He's better off, but they're both running high fevers."

"Max and Kyleigh need that equipment." My hands balled into fists. "But I could not control the drone."

"Sweetheart, it's not your fault"—his green eyes held mine—"not unless you're a roach. Or you've been designing bioweapons in your spare time."

"I understand as much, but Nate, how can I be of use when I need help walking a short distance? When I struggle to recall a simple sequence?" I rambled on, and he listened to my incoherent explanation about my weakness, my uselessness, my inability to carry out the reactivation of a drone, my difficulty concentrating.

His forehead creased, and when I finished, he held up a hand. "We're all doing our best, and you're going above and beyond. As to the marines, Max and Williams are both working on a treatment. Whatever I think of Clarkson as a human being, she has a stellar reputation as a scientist, and she and her crew are hammering away at the problem with all the resources *Thalassa* has available. I'm going to choose to hope this time."

The talkative Recorder's statement from the previous ten-day reverberated in my heart: *While I realize the thread is thin, I hold to hope.*

How did one hold to a thread?

Nate's tone gentled. "You need rest, and this doesn't qualify." When I did not respond, he gently lifted my head until my eyes met his. "You've got that virus swimming in your veins, and while I'm thankful you're able to be up and walking, you need to heal before you go charging around to save the system by fighting off viruses, drones, roaches, and genocidal humans."

"Nate, I cannot do nothing when people are at risk."

"I know." His expression softened. "And that's one of the reasons I love you."

His words washed over me, scrubbing away some of the fear that gathered in the recesses of my heart, but I could not summon my own voice to respond.

Nate slid his fingers between mine. "Come on. There's another gurney waiting in the hall. Let's get you a ride out of here."

11

"You brought a second bed?"

"We knew about Lars, and you shouldn't be on your feet yet," he said. "It makes sense. Don't want you to overdo it more than you already have. So, either you use it, or I carry you. While I wouldn't mind holding you, it's been a long day."

I would not burden Nate.

He helped me to my feet and switched on my communications link, and I did not protest. The marines' orders, responses, and quips filled my helmet, and the influx of sound made me flinch.

James followed Kyleigh out the door, and when Zhen activated the microantigravity devices, she and Daniel accompanied the drone into the hall. By the time Nate and I crossed the threshold, everyone else was waiting. Zhen shut the gouged door and locked it from the outside before whipping out the datapad. The drone floated through the knot of marines, who edged away.

Lars craned his head to look behind him. "Not sure I want that thing where I can't see it."

"Nobody wants to see it," someone responded. "No offense, Recorder."

"She isn't a Recorder," Zhen retorted.

My failure and my uselessness ate at me like acid, but I said, "I am not offended."

"Then let's go." The tall marine medic patted the empty hover gurney.

Nate lifted me before I could climb onto it, and the medic grabbed the three-centimeter-wide straps to secure me, as she had Lars.

I panicked.

The last time I had been strapped down while wearing a suit, fire and carapaces had rained down on me, and the memory engulfed me as flames had filled the hangar. Oxygen came in shards, like the broken lamp, and I batted her hands away. Words of protest rose in my throat, but all that emerged was a strangled, "*No.*"

The marines' comments faded to dim threads of sound, then disappeared as Nate moved between me and the medic. "Hold up, Ramos."

"Safety regs require—"

"He said to hold up," Zhen flung at the medic as she, too, inserted herself between us. "She knows the regs better than you ever could."

"We run into more trogs with guns or more bugs, and she'll fall. 'All persons being transported—'"

"Stop it." Zhen lowered her voice, as if doing so would prevent me from hearing her. "You'll agitate her, and she could start hemorrhaging again."

The woman stilled.

"It's okay," Nate soothed. "We won't tie you down."

"James and I will walk on either side," Kyleigh volunteered, and my first friend nodded in agreement.

The medic pursed her lips. "I'm on record as not endorsing this."

Zhen and the drone appeared at the foot of the bed. "Feel free to disagree, if that makes you happy."

"None of this makes me happy," the medic said. "Fine, I won't tie you down, Recorder. When we reach the quarantine room, I'll see if you need any pain meds, but since the point is to get you there safely, lie still."

I nodded.

"Can you untie me, too?" Lars asked.

"No."

"At least give me back my weapon," he protested. "I can shoot just as well on my back. I've practiced firing prone—"

"Not if I'm standing in front of you," a woman quipped.

Lars groaned.

"Save the chatter," the medic ordered, though I did not know what gave her the authority, especially when she had chatted only moments prior. "Move."

Nate tapped my arm. "I'm right behind you."

And he disappeared.

Once more, exposed ductwork, conduit, and fire suppression

systems seemed to glide overhead, until we came to a stop. Most of the marines left us when we passed the laser barricade, but the remaining few accompanied us to the temporary infirmary first. One marine guided Lars's gurney through the door, and ten meters away, the light over the quarantine room's vestibule shone a steady green.

My bed came to a stop, but Daniel and Zhen continued down the hall. Still held aloft by the microantigravity units, the drone followed almost as closely and obediently as it would have for a member of the Consortium.

Thwarted responsibility prompted me to ask, "Where are you taking it?"

"Somewhere it can't torment anyone," Zhen said over her shoulder.

"The other drones have been secured in a storage closet," Daniel added. "No one wanted them lurking in the control room, and keeping them together is reasonable."

"Perhaps," I said, "Lorik's drone will be safer in the quarantine room."

Zhen snorted. "I don't think so."

"Not that I would mind all that much"—Kyleigh eyed me closely—"but why?"

Zhen did not grant me the opportunity to respond. "Why doesn't matter because it's not going to happen."

"And Max is waiting for you," the medic said as she lowered the hover gurney's railing. "Timmons, take her in."

Kyleigh raised her hand. "I'll do it. I'm going in there, anyway."

"You're not in much better shape, Tristram," the medic said. "He'll be able to catch her if she wobbles."

James cleared his throat. "I shall wait with you, Kyleigh Tristram."

"Thanks." She offered him a wan smile. "Though, you need to rest, too."

"There will be time to do so before we attempt the use of another drone in the morning."

The vestibule door slid open, but I placed a hand on Nate's arm. "Wait. James, to whom do you refer when you say 'we'?"

"Daniel and I have discussed reactivating our drones, but he has found a place. I shall leave my jamming device behind after breakfast and reconnect."

A chill swept over me, despite my suit's thermoregulatory design.

My Nathaniel crossed his arms. "That isn't an option, James."

"We have not decided who goes and who stays," Daniel added.

"And I told you back in Christine's office that there has to be a better way." Kyleigh flung out the words as if doing so could create a shield to keep the men safe. "Neither of you will even *look* at those drones."

James raised his chin. "As I said, Daniel Parker has a purpose now. I do not."

"Of course you do," Kyleigh argued. "Besides, you're officially dead. If you go and plug that thing back in, you'll be caught and taken back to the Consortium. They'll put you in a tank and kill you before you could snap your fingers."

I grabbed the railing and slid to my feet. "They are correct. Neither of you will activate any drone. In the morning, I will try again."

"I don't think so," Zhen said.

"If either of you reactivates your drone, both of you will be exposed." When neither answered, I continued, "Which will bring the Consortium's scrutiny on everyone here. Everyone."

"You're putting yourself in danger again," Nate said quietly.

"I am putting my training to use. But this is more than protecting Daniel and James. More than protecting each of you." I resisted a wave of dizziness and squared my shoulders. "You have forgotten the terminal sequence of my designation number: 9545E. They were training me to act as an Elder, and as such, I can serve. I know the codes—"

"Then you shall tell me, I shall do it, and you shall heal," Daniel said.

"Tell *us*," Zhen added.

"That might be a good plan tomorrow, but not right now. It's almost midnight, and we all need rest," the medic said firmly. "Recorder, you need sleep, food, and meds. In."

Nate locked gazes with James. "The marines are stable. We'll discuss this tomorrow."

Though James nodded once, Daniel only grunted. That concession would have to suffice.

Nate led me into the vestibule. The door shut. We stood in silence as our suits were scrubbed clean, and Nate braced me whenever my balance faltered. When we entered the quarantine room, Max greeted us with a tired smile. My navy-blue datapad rested on my pillow where I had left it, and the air filtration units hissed, as if nothing had happened.

After removing my helmet, cap, and lightly armored suit, I crawled onto my bed, and the monitor's steady beep indicated that my cardiovascular system functioned within acceptable parameters. Nate collapsed in a chair at my side, his elbows on his knees.

"You should rest," I told him, but he shook his head.

"In a bit."

"Thank you for trying." Max handed me a cloth to clean the dried blood from my upper lip. "You're doing much better, but no one should have asked you to go."

The door opened again, and Kyleigh entered alone. Her eyes went to Max, who offered her a smile.

"I'll need to check your vitals, too, Kye."

She trudged to her computer and removed her helmet and cap, setting them next to the old-fashioned keyboard. "James wanted to make sure I was all right, even if I'm not the wobbly one. I convinced him to rest."

"Good." Max reviewed the data on her hoverbed. "You're doing well. Have some water and a snack, then get some sleep."

"Max?" She chewed her lower lip. "I didn't say, exactly, but in a way I told him."

Angled eyebrows pulled down. "Told whom what?"

"Before Zhen showed up, when he brought us dinner, I called him James, so he asked how I knew—how we all seemed to know—his name. I didn't say who you were."

Max dropped heavily onto the foot of her bed.

Kyleigh watched him. "He doesn't know?"

He did not look up from his interlocked fingers. "I don't think so."

"Why, Max?" she asked. "You need to tell him."

"We haven't solidified a way to get him out of the Consortium. Telling him who he is, that I've been searching for him his whole life, that his mother gifted him and his sister without my consent . . . Doing so would put him at greater risk." He glanced at me. "I know you'll do your best, but I can't condemn my son. And the longer I wait, the harder it is."

"Deferring the conversation will limit the time you have to know him better," I said.

"But is it truly necessary?" His hands fisted on his knees. "I don't want to force a bond on him that would make escape more difficult."

"I would want to know." All three turned to me, but I focused on Max. "Before I left *Thalassa*, I had the chance to search for my mother. I did not take it. Discovering why I was unwanted would be a burden I could not bear. Her files might contain evidence she changed her mind, but reading those files would be an invasion of privacy. But if she regretted her choice, if she or my father still wanted me . . ." A lump formed in my throat. "If they changed their minds, I would want to know."

Nate's eyes caught mine. "I want you."

A flicker of warmth tried to melt that lump.

Kyleigh sniffled. "We all do. You matter."

"Thank—" A yawn interrupted me.

Nate squeezed my hand. "That's my cue, isn't it? Max, you're dead on your feet. You coming, too?"

Max adjusted something on Kyleigh's monitor and glanced at mine. "You two are as settled as you're going to be, but if anything changes, comm me or Williams." He patted the foot of my bed, then walked to the door, pausing to switch the full-spectrum light to red.

Nate leaned down and touched his helmet to my forehead. "Good night, sweetheart."

"Good night, Nathaniel," I whispered.

The vestibule door closed behind them both. Kyleigh rolled over to face the wall and gave me a muffled good night.

Quiet settled about the room. I stared up at the ceiling, both full and empty, the antipodes of emotion mingling with questions, all churning in an exhausting vortex.

What had made this time with Lorik's drone so different from when I had controlled the drones on *Agamemnon*? When I had used the dead Recorder's drone to take down the roaches?

Again, I saw Nate's face soften and heard him say he loved me.

The nightlight's red bathed the room, its warmth softening the incomplete mural, and I remembered Freddie, his thin face furrowed as he studied the wall but smooth and relaxed as he painted. I identified Kyleigh in his broad brushstrokes, but his ultimate goal in those faces was forever lost, though the foundation had been laid. I would not let him be altogether forgotten, no matter that he had asked to be.

Fatigue swelled, but resolution gripped me.

No matter how I had failed before, in the morning, I would try again. Somehow, a solution would present itself. Somehow, I would find a way to convince them all to allow me to reactivate a drone on my own. Somehow, I would keep them safe. Max would save Lytwin and Patterson, and I would save James and Daniel. Then, together, we would find a cure.

In the quarantine room's gentle red glow, hope expanded from a thread to a rope, and I clung to it.

After less than six hours of sleep, I jolted awake, clearheaded, with both the solid conviction that I needed to access Lorik's drone and the knowledge of how to control it.

Quietly, so as not to disturb Kyleigh, I tiptoed to the water closet. After I washed my face, the mirror caught my attention. My reflection seemed hollower, my cheekbones more pronounced, my brown eyes shadowed. While nothing could be done for those, I ran my fingers through the curls in an attempt to control them, and the underlying welt-like scars made me shudder. I dipped my head to the side and checked. Dark curls hid the raised skin. Relief belied my lack of vanity. The scars were immaterial, except as evidence that Max had removed my neural implant. Even so, I tried again to smooth my hair, then straightened my tunic and slipped back into the room.

Two prepackaged meals remained on Williams's desk, and I opened one with care, casting glances at Kyleigh when the wrapper crinkled. She made a tiny noise, rolled over, and curled into a fetal position.

While I choked down most of the underseasoned beans and rice and the monochromatic, cooked fruit salad, I duplicated the information from my blue datapad to the former station Recorder's green one. Setting my meal and the datapads aside, I searched the cupboards for pyrimethamine and analgesics but could not find any. Medication would have to wait.

Instead, I retrieved my armored suit and, for two minutes, stared at the mottled grey-and-black. It provided no true protection from the roaches, but it would keep others safe should the virus in my blood be airborne after all. And if Skip and his allies appeared . . . After yesterday's incident, the suit's benefits outweighed its restrictions, so I tugged it over my leggings and tunic.

My nose wrinkled. Despite the specially designed antibacterial lining, the sharp tang of human stress tainted the material. It would need a thorough cleaning once we returned to *Thalassa*. At least, I told myself while tugging the beige cap over my head, the filtration system would purify the air in the helmet.

Although there had been no reason to doubt them, I silently conceded that James and Zhen were correct: consuming adequate calories had made a difference. After sleep and a meal, I was not unsteady on my feet, even when I shoved them into the heavy boots. I donned my gloves and gathered both datapads, storing them in the slim outer pocket on my thigh.

Pausing at the door, I pulled out the navy blue one to message Kyleigh regarding my intent, lest she worry. A soft ping sounded from her computer, and confident of the message's arrival, I returned the datapad to my pocket. Tucking my helmet under one arm, I palmed the door's access panel.

It did not open.

My brow furrowed. Locking us in the quarantine room was a safety hazard, given potential malfunctions and possible intrusions. My skin prickled at the thought, and I glanced at the vent. The thick metal plate seemed secure enough to prevent insectile invasion. Although, with terrorists skulking in Pallas Station's darkest passages, perhaps the decision to lock the door made sense.

The panel must have been coded to require specific identification bands. *Thalassa* had similar systems, and I smiled briefly. Whoever *they* were, if they thought to confine me, they had erred. Without a drone, the standard, well-hidden slot for Consortium access was unusable, but the keyboard was not. I set the helmet at my feet and waggled my fingers before attempting to crack the code. My first seven assays failed, and frustration had me tapping my leg twice. Circumventing security should not have been so difficult.

"What do you think you're doing?"

I spun around.

Kyleigh glared at me from under a halo of tight, untidy curls, and unexpected guilt sparked through me.

"You're trying to sneak out to mess with that drone again." She pushed aside her blankets and hopped from her bed. "The answer is *no*."

"I am not sneaking." I waved an arm at her computer. "I sent you a message relaying my intent."

"Bet you didn't tell Timmons, Jordan, or Max."

I opened my mouth to rebut her statement, but she was correct.

"Or Jackson," she added.

Indignation prompted me to protest. "I do not report to Kyle Geoffrey Jackson."

"Down here, we all do." Her huff reminded me of Zhen. "Especially given that the marines are our best chance of getting out of here alive."

My mouth twisted. "I concede your point."

"Of course you do." She tapped her chin. "So. The drone. That's your plan, isn't it?"

Chagrined, I could but nod.

Kyleigh padded to the door on stockinged feet and, when I moved back, inserted herself between me and the exit, hands on hips. "What makes you think that six in the morning will be any different from ten last night?"

I pulled out my datapad. "This does." She did not ask for clarification, but I gave it anyway. "Each time I have interacted successfully with a drone, even the rogues on *Agamemnon*, which is a Consortium vessel, there was a connection with our network."

She eyed the datapad.

"Yesterday," I continued, "with the jamming devices operative, the drone had no external connection to the Consortium."

"So it panicked when it woke up in a vacuum?"

"That is possible, in a manner of speaking." When one of her eyebrows rose sharply, I added, "Even probable."

"And your datapad will help?"

"If I wire it into the drone's access panel and utilize the codes Lorik gave me, it should be enough to allow control."

I did not tell her that when it was active, it would remain at my side, nor did I confess that usurping an Elder's drone would anger the Eldest. With lives in the balance and my own fate predetermined, what did that matter?

Briefly, the thought of holding Nate's hand and the memory of his repeated assertion that he loved me warred with my decision.

My jaw tightened. This was more important. The lives of those injured marines and thousands, perhaps millions, of people depended on gaining access to Dr. Georgette SahnVeer's equipment. We needed that drone. It was not that I had no choice or that my short life held no value. Rather, my decision was driven by the weight of souls.

"That seems—" Kyleigh smothered a yawn. "Tell you what. I'll call to see who's on duty and get an escort. You aren't leaving alone, not while roaches and those horrible people who shot Lars are out there."

"I would prefer to endanger no one else."

"Well, I prefer that you don't die," she countered. "I'd prefer that no one does." Her voice grew firm. "Here's what we're going to do. You'll eat something while I get ready and swallow some food. Then I'll ask for someone to come with us, and we'll face the drone together."

"Kyleigh—"

"Because if you don't cooperate, I'm calling Jackson, Jordan, *and* Timmons, and they'll lock this room down so fast that you won't be able to brush your teeth without a marine present."

"You are being unreasonable."

"Unreasonable or not, it's what you get." She regarded me steadily. "Do we have a deal?"

"This is not a deal. It is coercion."

"Good. I'll take that for a yes." She glanced at the leftover beans and rice that glistened in an unappetizing fashion on my bedside table next to the two datasticks. "Go finish that, and we'll be out of here before you can recite the Founders' oath three times."

I had no desire either to recite the oath or to eat more bland food but finished my breakfast, nonetheless. She hurried through her morning ablutions, pulled on her suit, and tore open her own prepackaged meal.

"Stars, but it'll be good to get back to *Thalassa* and real food." She hesitated, a forkful of rice halfway to her mouth. "You don't suppose it went bad when the power went off, do you?"

The thought gave me pause. "Nate did not tell me it spoiled. A journey to New Triton with nothing but meals like these . . ." I grimaced. "I hope it did not. The freezers would remain cold for many hours, and the nonperishables would be unaffected. They would have brought additional supplies for the added number on board, from scientists to marines."

Her eyes widened, and she gulped down a bite. "Marines! I forget everything." After guzzling some water, she tapped the link on her wrist. "Kyleigh Tristram, here."

Jackson's gravelly voice came thinly over the external links in our suits. "Go ahead, Tristram."

She cast a glance at me and drew in a deep breath. "The Recorder-who-isn't wants to try accessing a drone again."

"When?"

"Now—or as soon as possible."

"Is she up to it?"

"I am," I said as firmly as I could.

"You sound better, Recorder, but I'll send someone to verify that." A brief click, and he continued eleven seconds later. "Glad you'll try. Don't want to lose Daniel."

Kyleigh's thin face pinched. "Like we need to lose her? Or James?"

"Didn't say that," he stated. "But we need that drone. Now."

Kyleigh lowered her voice. "Something happened."

"Lytwin."

The beans and rice clumped in my stomach. "Is he . . . did he die?"

"No, but he took a turn for the worse. Maxwell and Williams are with him and Patterson right now, so our medic is on her way to check the Recorder's vitals. Can't afford another collapse like yesterday. Sending someone to escort you as well."

Jackson clicked off without a word of closure, but Kyleigh did not seem offended. Perhaps his abrupt conclusion was for efficiency's sake.

Kyleigh moved her food across the small tray. "I guess it's a good thing." Before I could ask her to explain her meaning, the light over the door went red. "That should be what's-her-name. The medic."

I choked down my last bite, and we fell silent, Kyleigh to her breakfast and I to my thoughts. I mentally reviewed my past mistakes and their potential corrections, setting aside the intrusive images of Lars doubling over and the tendrils snaking past me toward my friends. Lars was fine, and the drone had not harmed anyone. I disposed of my breakfast's wrappings and utensils in the biohazardous waste container. Kyleigh finished her meal and was cleaning her area as the door slid open and the medic entered.

Though it was not my concern, I blurted, "Is Lars well?"

"That isn't—" The medic's mouth pursed. "He's taped up. Wicked bruising and a cracked rib. He's lucky those trogs are bad shots and didn't get him in the throat."

Kyleigh paled. "Were they caught?"

"No. Trogs got away." The woman frowned. "I don't like this, not after yesterday, but Lytwin's fever is too high. Intravenous antibiotics, pain meds, and fever reducers aren't making a dent. I've told them he has to go in the tank, but"—she turned from Kyleigh to me—"if you're right, that'd seal his fate sure and certain."

Anxiety and determination filled me simultaneously. "This is why I must activate the drone."

For five long seconds, the marine medic regarded me closely, then crossed to my bedside. "Not if I say you don't. You look better than last night, but looks can be deceiving." Her faded bag, marked with a peeling red-and-white medical emblem, thudded onto the foot of my bed. "Jackson thinks it's worth a shot, but I don't know that it's a good idea. You were sick as all get-out twenty-five hours ago, and sure didn't handle pressure well last night."

"I feel much stronger today," I said, hoping I did not sound as defensive as I suspected I did.

She searched the bag's sections. "You ate something?"

Kyleigh spoke up. "We both did."

The medic raised her head. "You aren't coming, Tristram."

"Oh yes, I am. You might know medicine," Kyleigh argued, "but I know nanotech, *and* I have the right retinas. As soon as that drone is ready to go, we need to head to the lab to get that equipment. If those two marines are as sick as you say, we don't have time to waste. I need my lab set up last ten-day."

"Jackson didn't say anything about you."

"So?" Kyleigh shot back. "I'm right. Check in with him, sure, but I'm going, like it or not."

I did not like it, but she was not incorrect.

The medic scowled as she switched off her external speaker.

"Two can play at sneak-talking." Kyleigh hit a button on her wrist. "J?"

"Kye?" Venetia Jordan's alto sounded from Kyleigh's suit's speaker.

Kyleigh glared at the medic. "J, I need backup."

"What's going on?" All fatigue vanished from Jordan's voice. "What do you need?"

"The Recorder-who-isn't needs to access that drone—"

"After yesterday's episode, that's not—"

"Lytwin's dying," Kyleigh interrupted. "Jackson already approved her going because they need that equipment, and the medic is here checking her out."

There was a brief pause. "Jackson's sending an escort?"

"Yes, but I don't know who. That's not the problem. The medic says I won't be going, and I have to." Kyleigh reiterated her reasoning.

"I'll see what I can do. But Kye?"

"Yes?"

"Don't be rash." A click sounded, and the connection was gone.

"I won't," Kyleigh whispered to the silent link.

We both watched the medic. Her expression darkened while her inaudible discussion continued for two more interminable minutes.

". . . sir," she finished, then turned to us, eyes narrowed. "You can't go running to Jordan and undermine my authority like that, Tristram, but you won this one. Jackson says you'll both need medtrackers." She huffed, then pulled two microdatacards, less than a centimeter square, from a pouch in her bag and said to me, "Look up."

I obeyed.

After a brief snap of sound and pressure on my collar, she said, "You, too, Tristram." She inserted a microdatacard into a slot on Kyleigh's neckband. The medic dusted her gloved hands. "That will connect your suits' readouts directly to mine." She surveyed us. "You're both good to go. Vitals are fine today."

Kyleigh stared at her. "You can do that? Why can't Max and Williams? It would save lives."

Behind her faceplate, the medic smirked. "Proprietary tech."

I intervened before an argument ensued. "May we leave?"

The medic nodded. "The vestibule holds two people, but Quincy will be waiting for you in the hallway. Recorder, you go first. We'll join you. I'll have a word with you, Tristram, without a Recorder present."

Kyleigh winced.

It was my turn to narrow my eyes. "Medic, I find your statement suspicious."

A spot of color appeared on the medic's cheeks. She glowered down at me, but although she was indeed much taller, I had been trained by the Consortium. She looked away first.

"I'll be fine," Kyleigh said in an undertone. "Do you have everything you need?"

I checked for the datapads. "Yes."

Whoever Quincy was, he waited in the hall, and Lorik's drone waited beyond that. I fastened on my helmet and entered the vestibule.

13

I emerged from the vestibule to the sight of a single marine, who rotated from scanning the hall to study my face.

"You are Quincy," I said, though there was no reason for my surprise.

"Always have been." A smile appeared behind the bearded marine's familiar stubble. "You look better."

"I am much improved," I began, but echoing footsteps stopped me.

The marine's attention zoomed up the hall, and anxiety imprisoned the air in my lungs. He hit a different channel, spoke, then relaxed visibly. "It's all good, Recorder-who-isn't."

Four armed and familiar figures in mottled grey-and-black suits turned the corner. My heart both rose and fell. My friends should not have come, for if I was incorrect, my miscalculations would again place them in danger. Even so, their presence strengthened me.

"Overkill, Jordan," the bearded marine said. "We're just going down the hall."

Venetia Jordan's voice arrived before she did. "Being prepared, Quincy. If this goes well, we head out immediately to get that equipment. If it doesn't . . ." She drummed gloved fingers on her weapon as my friends came to a stop at my side.

The bearded marine—Quincy—asked, "Recorder-who-isn't, you sure you're up to this?"

"I believe I am."

"I don't like it," Nate began, but Alec interrupted him.

"Tim, we talked about—"

"I know," Nate said, his tenor lower than usual. "The thing is, I . . ." He closed his eyes for a moment, and when he did, it seemed the light had dimmed. When he opened them again, they locked onto my own, and the hall narrowed until all I saw was Nathaniel. "Last few times, when you figured out what needed to be done, I wasn't there."

Uncertainty puckered my forehead.

"You were right about Ross," he clarified. "When we reached Lunar One and you called me and J, I didn't understand the urgency. I should've known. I should have dropped everything."

"You could not have known, my heart," I said, even though they all could hear us, "since I did not explain."

"You weren't right about running off to find Kye and Freddie without backup," Zhen stated. "That was a blasted stupid thing to do."

The bearded marine grunted his agreement, and I could not dispute their assertions.

Zhen scowled. "We wanted to find Kyleigh and Freddie, too. You should've trusted us. We can't show up if you don't say anything."

My thoughts thickened into slush. Had there been a solid reason for my impulsive actions in leaving with Lorik without telling anyone? I could not remember.

"But this time"—Nate's voice drew my focus—"we're here when you call."

I opened my mouth, then clamped it shut before I confessed that I had not contacted the marines myself. Only Kyleigh's sudden wakefulness had prevented me from acting without them.

"But I still don't like it," Nate added.

"None of us do," Alec put in.

"Thing is, sweetheart, I trust you. As much as I dislike that drone, if things go sideways, I want to be there."

Shame at my omitted truth silenced me momentarily, but when I regained my voice, all I said was "There will not be much you can do." My gaze left his to meet the others'. "None of you."

"We know," he said.

"We'll make it work," Jordan stated.

For the next ten minutes, while we waited for Kyleigh and the medic, the bearded marine and my friends discussed the most direct route to Dr. SahnVeer's laboratory from the storage room. When the topic of conversation strayed to sporting events, my attention wandered, finally landing on the light over the door. The others, however, remained alert, scanning the hall's ceiling and corners.

The light turned green, and the medic exited the vestibule, Kyleigh, her face flushed, following in her wake.

Jordan's golden-brown eyes focused like lasers on the medic. She asked, "Is everything all right, Kye?"

Kyleigh's mouth pinched, but she nodded.

I did not believe her, but Jordan gave a crisp nod. "Then, Quincy, lead the way."

Though he had asserted that he trusted me, I expected Nate to argue when I told them all to wait in the corridor while I entered the small storage room alone to activate the drone.

Instead, he touched my hand. "I'll be here waiting, sweetheart. You do what you . . ."

"What you need to," Jordan finished for him.

The bearded marine tapped a sequence on the numerical pad and pulled the door open. Motion detectors triggered the single overhead light. It flickered, casting puddles of shadows under the shelves and the drones, which huddled along the walls like giant mechanical eggs. My mouth went as dry as Pallas's red surface dust.

The marine checked the small room, which was barely bigger than the holding cell on *Agamemnon*, then set his gloved hand on my shoulder. The expression on his face was reminiscent of the one he had when he told the others that Kyleigh and I were his daughters' ages and he did not approve of us being on Pallas.

"It's clear, Recorder-who-isn't. Be careful."

"If you aren't out in five minutes, we're coming in after you," Alec said.

"It might take longer. I cannot know." I tapped the side of my helmet. "I shall relate any pertinent information and return as soon as I can."

"If it—" Kyleigh hesitated and gulped a breath. "What do we do if it goes crazy and hurts you?"

I gestured to the medic. "She is watching my vital signs. You will know if the situation devolves. Should I lose consciousness, do not open the door. The drone is not fully charged. Without additional demands, it should power down in two hours, three at the longest. Do not retrieve me until then."

Nate blanched.

"However, should the drone function within acceptable parameters, given adequate power, we should be ready to access the equipment at once."

"There are portable chargers in the closet." The bearded marine's glance darted sideways into the room. "We filled them up as soon as power came back on. Had a few arguments about whether or not it was safe to keep the drones in there with them, but Daniel said they wouldn't charge themselves."

"Once inert, they cannot," I confirmed. "Even when active, they do not have the self-determination to seek power unless so commanded. If—when—I emerge with the drone, please remember to refrain from mentioning either former Recorder's knowledge of the Consortium. If you must mention them, be careful to use their new names. Do not allow either man near the drone as long as it is active. Guard your speech on all channels and frequencies, as the drone might pluck your words from the air."

"Right." Alec gave a sharp nod.

I paused by the room's access panel. "Notify Jackson that communications will be compromised if this works."

"Right away. Good luck." The bearded marine flipped a switch on his wrist, and his mouth moved silently.

Nate's voice was steady. "I'll be here."

The lines around Jordan's eyes seemed at odds with her light tone. "Come back in one piece."

"I will do my best." There was naught left to do but cross the threshold. I closed the door behind me, and my helmet's communication system magnified the lock's click. As a precaution, I activated my external speaker, though I left the link to my friends open.

The drones crouched on the floor in even intervals. Ignoring the other four, I knelt by Lorik's. The power indicator light blinked dull orange. I pulled my navy-blue datapad from my pocket and opened the drone's panel. My breath came unevenly as I slid the datapad into a slot beside the black one that must have been Lorik's own, closed the panel, and activated the drone. Even before it rose into the air, the drone's orange-framed screen brightened.

As though from a distance, I heard the medic exclaim about fluctuating heart rate and blood pressure and a spike of cortisol. ". . . need to get her out of there—"

Jordan's voice was brittle. "Step back from the access panel."

>>*Network not detected. Assigned Elder not detected,* trailed across the screen.

External sounds faded as a sudden chill swept over me, as if my suit had malfunctioned. Had the drone not read the information on my datapad? The screen flashed again, and I held my breath.

>>*Consortium device accepted. Enter CDN.*

I exhaled with such force that my faceplate fogged, then entered my designation.

>>*Unauthorized. Aberrant. Under supervision.*

My skin prickled in anticipation of punishment, but I managed, "Yes."

>>*No chip detected.*

"No."

>>*Aberrant, locate Elder Eta4513110-0197E.*

"Deceased," I said clearly.

The screen went blank, and the drone rose, though its arms remained in their folded cubes.

"What does she mean, 'yes, no, deceased'?" the medic demanded over the communications link.

"Quiet," Jordan said.

Unwilling to risk further confusion, I entered Lorik's codes.

A rapid series of numbers and letters crossed the screen much too quickly for me to comprehend their meaning. The drone shot to shoulder level. A tendril unspooled and reached toward me. My hands shook as I pulled out the green datapad and accessed the data I had transferred, asserting the same information I had stowed inside the drone's internal slot. The text slowed, and the tendril twined around my arm.

>>*Codes accepted. Temporary access granted. Welcome, Aberrant Zeta4542910-9545E.*

A cold knot formed in my stomach as I reread the screen. How long was temporary access? Whenever that time ended, the drone would be out of my control, and I had no way of discerning what that meant, either.

"Are you all right?" Kyleigh asked over the communications link.

"I am." Surely they understood that I could not say more. When the drone and I emerged, at least, they would see liberty was no longer mine.

>>*Power low.*

"I know," I told it aloud. Once the green datapad was safe in my thigh pocket, I added for the benefit of my people in the hall, "The drone has informed me it needs charging."

"How is she talking to it without a chip in her head?" the medic said, and someone shushed her.

"You managed it?" Jordan asked.

"Indeed."

"Charging units are on the back shelf." Quincy's words were abrupt and crisp.

"Release me so I can locate a power source," I said to the drone, and it did.

Ignoring my friends' protests over the communications link, I located the units and used spare cabling from a small box in the top corner to hook one to the drone. Its screen pulsed, and its orange border brightened as its depleted batteries filled. I searched the shelves again until I found a box of ropes and secured the charging unit to the drone itself. Not knowing how much power the unit would impart, I took two more, tying them together as well and creating a harness which I slung over my shoulders.

"Come," I told the drone.

>>*Not fully charged.*

"I have reserves."

A tendril lifted lethargically and drifted over the unit secured on its superior surface, then trailed over the two units strapped to my shoulders.

>>*Verified.*

Its large silver shape climbed through the air to hover by my shoulder. A single tendril wrapped about my arm again. I fought down panic. The drone's need for a physical connection was understandable when it did not have access to a neural chip. It had done so when the Elder, Lorik, had lost access upon entering the jamming field. I glanced at the screen.

>>*Proceed.*

Not wishing to display my ability to open locks in front of the drone, I said, "Jordan, I am ready. Please unlock the door."

Before Jordan responded, however, the drone shot another tendril to the access panel, deactivated the lock, and opened the door.

Everyone sprang back, weapons instantly trained on the jellyfish-like shape at my side, and their action did not go undetected. The drone rose above my head. Its remaining tendrils snaked around my shoulders, but when I held up both arms, it loosened its grip.

"It is well," I said firmly.

Slowly, my friends lowered their weapons. The drone settled back by my shoulder, as it was programmed to do.

My pocket—no, the datapad—buzzed. I pulled it out and read the message.

>>*Aggression.*

"None intended. They anticipated a threat."

>>*No threat.*

For a fraction of a second, memories of reprimands and the dead man on *Agamemnon* flashed through my mind. "I know."

>>*Untruth.*

"Yes," I told it, though whether it referred to its own motivation or responded to the lie inherent in my previous answer, I could not say.

"Stars," the medic whispered. "You *are* a Recorder."

I raised my eyes from the messages on the datapad to meet hers, which had gone wide as they shifted from my drone—Lorik's drone—to me.

"Indeed." Afraid that my connection to my friends would be obvious, my glance skimmed past Nate and settled on the bearded marine. "If there is naught else to do, we should proceed to retrieve Dr. SahnVeer's equipment."

He nodded. If his jaw was as tight as his eyes, I could not tell, for his grizzled beard hid it.

"Alec, you know the way," Jordan said. "Zhen, Quincy, with him. Tim and I will take the rear. The rest of you, stay with . . . the Recorder and drone."

Somehow, my old title from Jordan's mouth felt like a blow. It was who I had always been, who I had chosen to be when I had reactivated the drone. I swallowed. The title was immaterial.

Without another word, we set out.

When we approached the marines guarding this sector, they deactivated the lasers protecting the secured area from roaches and enemies alike. The two men in blue moved to allow us to pass. Eleven steps down the hall, I glanced back. They had resumed their positions, and the station's ever-present dust ignited when it drifted into the web of light.

We turned left, heading down an unfamiliar hall. The sprawling base had been formed inside Pallas's extinct lava tubes, and though some halls had been drilled to connect with others, this one meandered. Pallid light fell over us from above, where metal fittings encased fluorescent lights. Ductwork, cables, and pipes ran down the raw ceiling's center, but the floor was level and smooth. Only the faintest trace of dust rose at our footsteps, and nothing obscured the blue emergency lights along the bases of the walls.

There was no sign of roaches.

Even so, I entered a command on the datapad.

A response appeared on the drone's screen. >>*Elder's scan active.*

"Insufficient," I said, then typed, >>*Use adjusted parameters.*

The screen pulsed, then read, >>*Activated. Scanning.*

I sent my thanks, and the drone did not respond. Of course it did not. A drone was not human, so courtesy did not matter.

Three more junctions—left, right, right—and we stopped before a paneled door without hinges. A pale-blue screen gleamed from the back of a small, recessed panel a little lower than my shoulder height. The hall turned right into darkness. A dull metallic echo sounded from the ductwork above. I glanced up uneasily but saw nothing unusual, then checked the datapad.

>>*Roach activity?* I typed.

>>*None detected.*

The statement was not as reassuring as it should have been.

Alec broke the silence. "This is where we need your eyes, Kye."

She shot me a tight smile. "Don't worry. This is probably the easiest thing to do on the whole station. The trick is to keep your eyes open until the red light comes on. Well, and to be close enough with all this." She rapped her knuckles on the helmet. "Like I said, not hard. It isn't like wrestling roaches or facing down terrorists."

"I am not concerned, Kyleigh," I said, though perhaps I should not have called her by name.

She stood on her toes to set her chin in the small alcove. The panel changed from blue to red, and after light traced the outline of her helmet, the door slid into its pocket with a dull grinding noise. Alec motioned Kyleigh back and stepped into the corridor beyond. Dust lay in two-decimeter-deep drifts and wafted through the air like smoke. The skin on the inside of my arms prickled, and the pitch of the drone's whir rose. Zhen and Quincy followed Alec.

Jordan spoke, followed by Jackson's gruff acknowledgement, but the sound blurred.

How many insects would have lived and died in this hall in order to leave this level of debris? Calculations cluttered my mind. The only answer that came was *too many*. My pulse thudded unevenly at the thought, and dizziness threatened to buckle my knees.

The drone wreathed a tendril around my neck, near where the medic had inserted her microdatacard. Without warning, a painful jolt of electricity shot through my suit.

I gasped and dropped the datapad, sending clouds of particulates into the air. Nate caught my left arm before I crumpled, and Jordan grabbed my right. My headache came rushing back, and I closed my eyes to block the way the hallway tipped.

The medic exclaimed, "Stars! What the void was that? Clear back, Jordan."

Hands grabbed my shoulders.

"Recorder," the medic demanded. "Hey, let's see your eyes."

It was difficult to pry them open, though the reprimand was a small one. Infrequent discipline—or was it punishment?—and illness had chipped away at my body's ability to process what had once been an expected, even daily, occurrence.

"I will be well. I allowed emotion to color my perceptions and will do my utmost to prevent future episodes."

"That thing shocked you?" The marine medic's eyes moved back and forth as if she were reading something on the interior of her faceplate. "From watching Parker and her drone, I thought . . . But someone else's drone can punish you, too?"

I stepped away from the medic, and Nate steadied me when I wobbled.

"Yes." Nate's harsh tone contrasted with his comforting presence. "All drones can."

"Thank you—" I caught my error before I used his given name and condemned us both. "Timmons." I edged away from my Nathaniel. He had been punished before, and now there was no Elder to cancel any discipline. With the drone active and recording, I could not afford weakness, for doing so would endanger all of them.

The bearded marine scowled in my direction. "If she's good, we need to get moving."

"Unless we want to wait for backup," the medic said.

Jordan's eyes narrowed. "Jackson knows what we're doing, where we are."

"Right, then," Alec said. "Exec decision to go on."

"I don't like it." The medic turned her back on me. "Soon as that door opens, we need to get the civilians out of here. Tristram has done her share. Escorting her to safety is—"

"Unwise," Kyleigh interrupted, her focus on the silt hiding the safety lights along the hallway's floor. "Sorry, but the doors lock as soon as they close. You need me to get out, and besides, no one knows what equipment we'll require better than I do."

"Kyleigh is correct," I said. "And the drone will improve our chances of success."

"Of course it will," Zhen snapped while she checked her weapon. "That's the only reason you're here."

Without answering her reminder that my questionable health made me a liability, I added, "I will take a moment to communicate with the drone, to be certain that it can scan the area for insects."

"Last time, the drone couldn't pinpoint the bugs," Zhen stated flatly. "What can it do this time that it couldn't last quarter?"

Chagrin took hold of me. "Again, it appears I erred."

"You had a concussion." Alec spoke softly, "Your body was tearing itself apart."

"Neither the Consortium nor I should overlook such mistakes." I stooped to pick up the fallen datapad, brushing away powder and checking for damage. No cracks marred its smooth green surface.

"You're too hard on yourself," Jordan said. I glanced up when the weight of her hand on my shoulder registered in my mind. The drone sent an additional tendril around my neck, and Jordan's gaze flickered to it. Her delicate brows drew together, but she did not move away. "You wouldn't judge us that harshly. Don't forget you're human, too."

"With all that entails." For a moment, I rested in that fact. "I adapted scans to detect movement through visual and—"

"When?" the medic demanded.

"Shortly after entering the halls. When the drone is fully charged, I shall program it to detect pheromone levels."

The medic hummed. "Using sensors to find breeding areas could be handy if we are stuck in this rock. Maybe we could eradicate the spacing bugs."

"If you can use that thing to see farther than we can, do it," Jordan said.

No one spoke while the drone's external cameras activated. Its power levels plummeted.

"The scans draw too much energy," I announced.

"Then turn them off," Jordan said. "Our eyes will suffice for now. We don't know exactly what we'll need when we reach those additional security measures that—" She pinched her mouth shut, and her nostrils flared. "The ones Dan Parker discovered."

We filed into the hall, and the door slid shut behind us. The situation's familiarity struck me. Once again, a drone was at my side, and I walked through drifts of silt and cracked carapaces, surrounded by Jordan, Nate, Alec, and Zhen.

The memories were not entirely comforting.

Kyleigh trudged beside me, clouds rising with each step. "The hall comes to a sort of twisty *T*. We'll need to take the right-hand turn. There's a lab at the end of that branch, and that's where the equipment will be."

When we reached the junction, motion-activated lights already illuminated the curving halls. Dark, ovoid shapes lay in and on the mounded silt.

"Not good," Alec muttered.

The medic hefted her weapon. "Where does the other hall go?"

Kyleigh sidled closer. "Phycology."

"We're on the other end of the station from the medbay," Jordan said. "The algae feedlines wouldn't run the whole way, would they?"

"Not the central algae tanks." Kyleigh's stare fastened on the drifts and the droppings. "The experimental ones."

Nate offered me and Kyleigh a half smile. "Not much to do but go on or go back. We can't get out without Kyleigh's eyeballs, so we might as well stick together. I vote we get this over with. Get the equipment and these two back to safety and sleep."

Jordan grimaced. "Onward."

We turned right, but the knowledge that a long, hopefully empty hall stretched behind us weighed on me. When we reached the laboratory, however, neither the drone nor I were needed after all.

The door stood open, and darkness gaped beyond it.

15

"I really don't like this," Alec muttered.

Someone grunted in agreement, and the weapons' targeting beams lanced through the dark beyond the open door. Jordan sent a short communication to Jackson, but my heart thundered so loudly that if the marine responded, I did not hear him. I braced myself. The drone, however, either did not detect my elevated response or did not judge it worthy of discipline, for no reprimand shook me.

"Zhen—" Alec nodded to the right, then at the bearded marine. Without further communication, the three of them entered the room.

"Manual light switch not working," the marine reported from inside the laboratory.

"Freddie used to tease me that I knew my way through that room blindfolded." Kyleigh's voice wobbled. "But I really don't want to know if he's right."

The room was a maw of inky black, yawning to swallow us.

"Jordan?" I asked. "Regardless of power status, I believe it might be beneficial to utilize the drone's lights and also scan for insectile intrusions."

"Do it. We don't know if there are bugs or not, but that kept them back in the hangar first time down here," she replied. "Tim, keep an eye on that hall. Can't have things creeping up on us."

I pivoted to look behind me. Nothing.

Nate caught my eye and flashed a smile. "Got it, J," he said.

The drone at my side, I stepped through the laboratory's door. Our shadows left blotches on the uneven rectangle of light cast from the hall, and I squinted at the datapad while typing commands. The drone's intense full-spectrum light flared.

"Hey!" the medic protested, and the bearded marine cursed.

Bright spots drifted over gathering dark. I blinked several times, but when my vision returned, the orange around the drone's screen had deepened to dull red. Appendages spooled into interior pockets, and the drone drifted to the silty floor, blocking the doorway.

"That wasn't helpful," Zhen snapped.

"Just a miscalculation." Jordan touched my shoulder. "Do what you can to get that back on." She turned to the medic and indicated Kyleigh and me. "Keep an eye on them and keep the hall clear."

With that order, Jordan dodged around the drone and disappeared into the laboratory.

I removed the rigged harness and lowered the remaining chargers to the floor. Shoving the green datapad back in my pocket, I dropped to my knees while Kyleigh disconnected the nearly depleted charger. To my left, four narrow rays of light pierced the dark. The hair on my arms rose uncomfortably inside my sleeves. Turning from the possibility of creatures I could not see, I plugged a new charger into the drone, hesitating but a moment before adding the second one.

The red encircling the drone's screen brightened. Once the chargers were securely tied to the drone's metallic upper half, I looped the empty one over my shoulders, then reentered my designation number and Lorik's codes. It welcomed me back. I peered past it into the dark.

"What do you need me to do, Jordan?"

"Be ready to move. As soon as that thing is on, get it airborne and out of the doorway. Activate the scanners, if you can."

My attention flickered from the drone to Nate and the dust-filled hall, then back to the laboratory, where targeting beams slid over the ceiling and walls. Askew desks and fallen chairs cast distorted, angular shapes before the rays moved on, and dark consumed the furniture again.

The drone remained stationary.

"We left it tidy." Kyleigh edged closer and peeked around my shoulder. "And I don't see how the roaches got in. Christine's regular old insects were down the hall. Freddie's were in another section." Her voice lowered. "I should have killed them all before we went into stasis."

The medic cautioned, "Later."

A blast of light and sound from the far side of the laboratory startled me. Kyleigh jumped back, nearly knocking me off-balance. Dull orange smoke spiraled into a beam of light.

Salty saliva filled my mouth.

The bearded marine—Quincy—said, "Heard something over there." The ray of light left the smoke and darted to the far corner, illuminating a dim, two-meter, oblong shape. Another burst, and it stilled.

"That it?" The medic's voice seemed distant in my ears.

"Hard to tell," the bearded marine responded. "Let's get that equipment."

"The far-right corner." Kyleigh's hand trembled when she pointed. "The bottom cabinet on the left."

Light skimmed the cabinets, furniture, and walls.

The bearded marine said, "Looks clear."

"It shouldn't take long." Kyleigh blew out a long breath. "Like I said, I know this room inside out."

The urge to forbid Kyleigh from entering the laboratory swelled, but I said nothing as she and the medic edged into the gloom.

"Hall's still clear," Nate reported.

I turned back to the drone. Its screen flashed orange, and it rose into the air and blocked my view of the room. A tendril encircled my neck, but I did not flinch as I input the command to emit light.

>>*Charging.*

A clatter made my pulse accelerate.

"I tripped is all," Kyleigh called. "I'm fine."

I reiterated my order.

>>*Inadequate power. Activating light endangers functionality.*

"Comply," I demanded.

"Is that thing going rogue?" Alec's voice carried an edge I had not heard since our first trip underground.

"The drone is under control," I replied, and he grumbled an indecipherable response.

>>*Not rogue.*

"Indeed," I said, almost truthfully, though fear warned me of the potential falsehood.

>>*Not rogue,* it repeated. >>*Situation?*

A frisson of cold unrelated to my suit's homeostatic controls crawled down my back. The drone had heard Alec's comment. Nothing anyone said was secure, as I had warned my friends when the drone and I had first emerged from the storage closet. So why was I surprised—and why did it frighten me?

Wetting my lips, I reassured it. "I know."

"You know what?" the medic snapped.

I ignored her and craned my neck to peer around the drone's waving arms. Two beams still moved around the room, while the other two illuminated Kyleigh's hands as her fingers danced over numerical locks.

"The locks aren't responding."

"Makes sense. No lights, no power," the medic said, and her beam slid over the panel.

"Stop!" Kyleigh held up her hands. "Don't try to shoot them out!"

"Give me some credit," the medic protested. "Science lab. Probably flammable things all over the place."

"Right. Though . . ." Kyleigh darted out of the light.

"Kyleigh!" Zhen exclaimed.

A sharp crack sounded, and metal clattered.

Two beams danced over surfaces until one found the young woman digging through a tall, evidently unlocked cabinet.

"Don't you dare run off like that!" the medic ordered.

"Ha!" Kyleigh lofted a metallic canister with a thin nozzle.

"Oh," the medic said. "Cryo gun? Is it full?"

"Yes and yes." A hint of confidence and energy returned to Kyleigh's voice. "If I freeze that lock, you can shatter it with a chair or something."

"Worth a try," Alec muttered.

The drone shifted to block my view again.

The canister hissed, then a targeting beam danced on the ceiling. Metal pinged on metal.

"Hurry up, Kye," Zhen urged.

"Take this." More shuffling noises sounded, and Kyleigh grunted. "I need the trolley in the corner—no, the one with three shelves." A wheel squeaked. "Thanks."

Jordan's voice held steady, even as she reiterated the command to hurry.

"Think I've found where they're coming in," Alec growled. "Ventilation grate's been chewed off. Upper left."

The bearded marine swore with a fluency I had never heard before. "Without knowing which direction it runs, blasting could make it worse."

"It's just a lab. It doesn't make sense why they'd gnaw their way in here," Zhen put in as she helped Kyleigh with the trolley.

"Bugs, DuBois." The medic huffed. "They don't make sense."

"We had a refrigeration unit with food and another with agar and things like that," Kyleigh said. "Georgette was notorious for working through meals. I used to bring snacks, in case we worked late."

"Maybe you could get a move on," Nate suggested over the communications link. "I like my suspense in vids, not in—"

A heavy, organic thud interrupted him. The scritch of insectile feet on the floor carried through my helmet's external speakers. Percussive sound echoed, and light flared inside the room, reflecting off the drone's silver surface. Stunned by noise and lumens, I could not discern whose boots pounded through the subsequent darkness.

"Activate lights," I barked like a marine. "Now!"

Immediately, red-spectrum light flooded the room, not enough to drive back any intrusion, only enough to gloss the surfaces with scarlet. I ducked past the dangling tendrils into the laboratory where two-meter, red-highlighted shapes hurtled across the floor toward the open cabinet.

Kyleigh screamed.

16

Weapons' fire reverberated like a physical blow, and though I squeezed my eyes shut, the flashes of light pierced my eyelids. Sound thrust me against the drone, and all its appendages lashed out. Its thicker tentacles wrapped around my hips, waist, and shoulders. When the blasts' echoes faded and light stopped pummeling me, I squinted into the afterimage-speckled dark.

Dust glittered and sparked like embers around two mounds of smoldering carapaces near where Kyleigh pressed herself against a cabinet. An alarm's sharp beep cut through the air, and liquid misted from the ceiling. When the smoke dissipated, the alarm shut off, though the fire suppression system continued to sprinkle fluids.

The medic lowered her weapon, but from the edges of my vision, a shadow separated from a crooked desk on my side of the room. My drone's light dimmed, and its whir deepened as it lifted higher into the air, tugging at me. Despite the steady flow of oxygen my suit provided, I struggled to breathe.

"Jordan," I gasped. "The desk by the door!"

Scarlet-edged compound eyes gleamed as the roach reared up on its four hind legs, antennae lashing at my friends.

The drone shot into the air. My feet left the floor, and my helmet bumped the ceiling.

Below me, weapons fired, hitting the insect's lower wings, but it dropped onto its front legs and rushed forward. A brief explosion of matter—and the roach skidded to a stop.

My ragged breath and the drone's mechanical whine were all I heard. Two and a half meters from the laden trolley, Jordan, Zhen, and the medic braced themselves like a shield in front of Kyleigh, who clutched the cryo gun and a handful of pipettes to her chest. I scanned the room. Nothing twitched. Anxiety loosened its tendrils. The drone did not.

"Jordan!" Had Nate been calling the whole time? "Status!"

"We're good, Tim."

"Hall's still clear," Nate said. "Might be a good idea to leave."

"I'll second that." Alec's tone gentled. "Kye?"

"I . . . I'm fine." Her voice quavered, and the metal canister and the pipettes rattled onto the trolley's top shelf. Liquid dripped from Kyleigh's helmet as the suppression system trickled to a stop. "Stars, but that's enough to wake anyone up. I don't think I'll have coffee this morning."

Over the communications link, Nate said, "Always choose coffee."

Kyleigh uttered a weak laugh.

The drone tightened its hold. I could feel the pressure through my suit. I tried to reach the datapad and order the drone to release me, but tentacles made it impossible to access my pocket.

The medic patted Kyleigh's shoulder, then turned around and said, "Recorder, your heart rate . . ." Her sentence trailed off. "Where the—" She released a string of obscenities that surely would merit a fine if documented.

Multiple targeting beams slid over me and past my helmet to the drone. I whispered, "Stop."

Jordan and Alec lowered theirs at once, but the medic, the bearded marine, and Zhen did not.

"Her heart rate what?" Nate's voice sharpened. "Where is she? She's not out here."

"The spacing drone has her," Zhen snarled.

Bootsteps echoed from the hall, and Nate's voice rang out. "Put her down."

The drone did not obey.

Abandoning the trolley, Kyleigh darted forward, slipping in the insects' ooze and the sludge created by water and dust, righting herself on a stray chair. "Zhen, Quincy, please! Shooting drones does no good! Remember what Tia said happened when that one broke Eric's arm? You have to be calm, reason with it."

The room dipped as the drone's antigravity faltered, but the tentacles lifted me higher, once more banging my helmet against the ceiling. I winced and closed my eyes.

The medic hissed. "Stars! It's going to give her a concussion."

"The one in the hangar melted before it exploded," Zhen reminded them. "The underbelly is its weak spot."

"You can't!" Kyleigh's protest rose in pitch. "You'll hit her."

"No," the bearded marine stated, "I won't."

"Please—" My voice sounded unfamiliar in my ears. With as much calm as I could muster, I added, "The insectile threat is over. Set me down before all power is drained." When I opened my eyes, double vision blurred the room beneath me. I could not see Nate—he must have been by the door—so I met Zhen's dark eyes. "I am unharmed. You must stop threatening it."

"Do it," Nate said, and Jordan added, "Now."

Slowly, the three of them lowered their weapons, but their pronounced scowls were obvious even in the dim red light.

The drone eased down, and my soles touched the floor. Three tentacles withdrew, so I rotated in the fourth's grasp to read the screen, which was edged with yellow, despite its bizarre actions.

>>*Complied. Complied. Complied*, scrolled in a steady stream.

My forehead knotted, but I merely said, "Acknowledged."

>>*Charging. Not at full power.*

"I know." I turned away from the drone and found Nate. His tall form remained in the doorway, but with the light behind him, I could not see his face clearly. "I am well."

The drone's glow brightened slightly, touching Nate's features with red. His jaw ticced, and his eyes bored into mine before darting to Jordan. "Like I said, J, it's clear."

Jordan made no comment about Nathaniel forsaking his watch over the corridor. "Then let's get out of here before that changes. Kye, get that cart. Quincy, Alec, watch that grate."

"Right." Kyleigh stepped backward, tripping over a long, hooked hind leg. The medic caught her arm.

While the others kept watch, Kyleigh tugged the trolley's handle, circumventing the closest roach, where fluid oozed and mixed with dust to create something like paste. The three-shelved cart's wheels caught on something I could not see. Kyleigh gagged and turned her head to the side.

"You'll be all right, Tristram," the medic said. "What we need, though, is microAG. Wheels are going to be difficult in that debris."

"Probably, but you won't find any. There wasn't a need for antigrav carts in a room this small. Whenever anyone suggested it, Georgette would tell them not to be lazy." Kyleigh gave the trolley a yank.

The front wheels clunked over something, but the back wheels caught on whatever it was. I tried not to imagine antennae.

Jordan lifted them clear and asked, "Still bug-free?"

"So far," Alec said tersely as his targeting beam skimmed the cabinets below the broken grate, then traced the room's perimeter again.

The bearded marine—Quincy—swore, and four beams zoomed back to the gaping ventilation shaft. A shot reverberated in the laboratory as he moved between Kyleigh and the broken vent. Another shape emerged. Too close—the moving silhouettes that pressed against the floor were too close.

"Get them out, Jordan," Quincy said sharply.

Zhen grabbed the trolley's handle. The medic grabbed Kyleigh's arm and tugged her into the hall while Zhen wrestled the trolley over the threshold. Jordan, Alec, and the bearded marine kept their focus on the dark.

Nate's hand caught my elbow, and we both ran. The particulate remains of decayed insects billowed under our feet, cushioning the sound of boots on concrete, and the empty charger thudded against my back with each stride.

I lost my footing in the silt, but Nate and the drone kept me from falling.

Zhen's voice sounded over the communications link: "Door."

"Won't close," the bearded marine said. "Have to block it."

A masculine grunt replied, and a blast ripped through the air.

Alec's voice scraped between breaths. "Won't work for long."

The corridor stretched before us. Though I tripped more than once, Nate and the drone did not allow me to falter.

"Keep a hold on her, Timmons," the medic panted. "Her vitals . . . off."

I forced myself to keep moving.

As we neared the junction, the drone came to a full stop, yanking me out of Nate's grasp, but his attention remained riveted down the hall, past the turn to the door. He released me, raised his weapon, and fired.

Gasping for air, I lifted my head. Ten meters away, three roaches crouched by a smoking carapace. More antennae twitched from a crack in the ceiling.

"J," Nate warned, "company ahead."

Clouds rose as she thundered to a stop at my side. "Just get them out!"

Jordan braced herself and took aim. Another roach went down, and the remaining insects edged back. The antennae withdrew.

While Nate targeted another one, the drone wrapped its tentacles around me once more and partially spooled in its appendages, hauling me up against its belly. With regard for neither Nate's shouted protest nor my own, it flew down the hall toward the withdrawing roaches, then veered left. Shouts echoed, but the drone kept on. Motion detectors tracked our movement too slowly, and lights flickered on after we passed them. The door and its alcove for retinal scans grew closer.

The drone dipped and released me. Momentum flung me forward, and pain flared as I hit the concrete. The empty charger slammed against the back of my helmet. I hit the wall. Pain fulgurated up my hands and wrists, and gritty clouds obscured my view. I tried to push myself up, but my arms could not support me, and I crumbled back down.

Nate skidded to a halt and helped me to my feet. After a sharp glare at the drone, which had spiraled in all appendages save its four tendrils, he turned about, weapon ready. Within seconds, Kyleigh and the medic jogged up, and Zhen and Alec carried the trolley close behind them.

"J? Quince?" Nate asked.

"On our way," the bearded marine responded.

Barely winded, Zhen ordered, "The door, Kye!"

Kyleigh darted past me to the scanner. A blue light pulsed, and as the door slid open, the medic edged her way through.

"Lights on. No roaches," she announced.

Alec and Zhen shoved the trolley through the door, and Kyleigh, Nate, the drone, and I followed. Jordan and the bearded marine rushed past us, and Kyleigh slapped her palm against a button. As the door eased shut, Alec took something fist-sized from his belt, pulled a tab, and hurled the object down the hall. An explosion ignited the dust. A cloud of burning orange rolled toward us, but the door clicked shut, muting the blare of a fire alarm.

Relief hit me in a nearly physical wave.

Despite the roaches, despite everything, we had retrieved the equipment.

"The suppression system must have kicked in," Kyleigh managed between gulps of air.

A lopsided grin crept across Alec's features. "Figured it would."

"Stars, Alec," Jordan said, "a little warning next time?"

The medic glared at him. "Not a gamble I appreciate."

"But we did it." Zhen tapped Kyleigh's shoulder. "Only lost a couple of pipettes, too."

The bearded marine, however, squinted into the hall before us. "Expected backup by now."

Jordan peered past the activated lights, into the dark. "So did I."

"Probably delayed," the medic said. "Let's hope that we don't run into more bugs. I vote for getting a move on. This had better be all we need, because going back there is a bad idea."

Jordan's eyes skimmed the hall, but her voice seemed lighter. "That's a fair assessment."

Nate, however, frowned at me. "Why did that spacing drone tie you up like a Festival present and go hurtling off?"

"I do not know. I did not program it to do so."

"Tell you what," Alec said. "You can figure that out later, but for now, we need to get you back to rest. You're looking green again."

Before I could rebut his analysis, something clattered at my feet. A sharp pop, and magnesium-bright light assaulted my eyes.

I threw my arms over my faceplate, too stunned to count the seconds. A hand caught my upper arm and drew me back. Dull thuds seemed to come from everywhere at once.

A single shot. A feminine shout. A protest cut short.

"I see you fetched the equipment," a masculine voice said through my communications link.

I pulled my arms down and blinked. Past and around the light burned into my retinas, human shapes dropped from the ceiling. Confusion snaked through me. From the ventilation ductwork? That made no sense, but otherwise, would not the medic and the others have seen them? My drone—Lorik's drone—had told me nothing.

The medic—

I turned to my left. She was gone. Her helmet lay on the ground, two meters away.

Metal flashed through the air. Alec dropped. Strangled gasps filled my ears, and metal rang on concrete. Zhen fell to her knees beside Alec and the knife near his legs.

Nate shifted his weight, moved in front of me, and widened his stance. To my left, the bearded marine stepped in front of Kyleigh. Jordan positioned herself like a guardian over Alec.

Weapons bristled—at us, at them.

A man wearing a respirator and a thick, quilted jacket stepped forward, flipping a knife, catching it by the blade. Past the bearded marine and Kyleigh, a man in an armored suit hauled the medic into the hallway's reaching dark. Her head lolled to the side.

Jordan took aim at the figure holding the medic. "Let her go."

Someone laughed. Why could I not count the attackers? Surely I could count that high?

A man in an armored Consortium suit swung down from the ductwork, landing with catlike fluidity. He straightened and strode toward us. Though bright blotches swam across my vision, my attention latched onto the multiple medical jet injectors he wore like sidearms.

He pulled one out and tossed it to the man holding the medic. The armored man tilted her head back and held the injector against the bare skin under her chin. Delayed recognition struck, and my stomach twisted.

"I applaud your effort," Skip said conversationally. "But I'll take that trolley."

17

"Like blazes you will," the bearded marine growled. "Let her go, and I won't kill you."

The man who held the jet injector to the unconscious medic's throat laughed.

"I don't think so," Skip said. "And where did you get an active drone? You don't have Recorders left, and that Elder should be dead by now."

No one responded. Alec's wheezing continued, and Zhen jumped to her feet, her weapon up and aimed at the knife-man.

Jordan's voice, low and even, came over the communications link: "Easy."

"Ah-ah," Skip said. "Do it, and your pretty girl gets a vein-full of bioweapon. Hand over the trolley."

Jordan flipped a switch on her weapon but said, louder, "We don't negotiate with evil."

"And yet here you are in the company of Consortium tech." Skip pulled out another injector and clicked his tongue. "Cord."

The man holding the medic depressed his thumb, and the subsequent hiss seemed as loud as weapons' fire. He dropped it, then caught the one Skip tossed his way.

"That's part one." The man who had killed Freddie and Lorik and tried to kill me locked his gaze on Jordan. "Cord has part two now. Do you want her to die like the others? Give me the trolley."

"Why?" The question emerged before I could stop it.

Skip moved to the side, his attention skimming over all of us until he found me. "Consortium? How are you not dead? Should've grabbed that one, Cord." He tapped his wrist and spoke over a channel I could not hear.

I sidled farther behind Nate and pulled the datapad from my pocket.

>>*Not Elder Eta4513110-0197E*, cycled across the screen. >>*Citizens are prohibited from wearing Consortium attire, per AAVA section 1.37.11.*

>>*Stolen from Elder*, I typed. >>*Monitor channels.*
>>*Documenting.*
Still fighting afterimages, I ordered, >>*Notify Jackson.*
A second passed, and the drone informed me, >>*Notified.*
Skip's voice resonated through my communications link once more. "Right. So we'll take her, too."
"Over my dead body." Nate's voice was low and taut.
Behind his mask, Skip bared his teeth. "If you insist."
The man holding the medic hit the second injector's button. A nod from Skip, and a knotted rope tumbled from the ductwork overhead. As the knife-man shimmied out of sight, a storm of weapons' fire filled the hall. Echoes masked the number of shots.
I cowered behind Nate as projectiles hit the drone with sharp, metallic pings and exploded into the wall beside me.
My Nathaniel held fast, his shoulders jerking in time with painful spurts of noise. Shards of glass flew from the cart.
Nate staggered, knocking me against the drone. Something flew at me and chipped my faceplate. I lost my balance. The charger crunched against the wall.
Too many—too bright—too loud.
Zhen cried out and crumpled. Did she roll to her back and raise her weapon, or was I imagining it?
The man was dragging the medic away. The hall's stark light illuminated the sole of her right boot, where the tread had worn unevenly, primarily on the outside and back of the heel. That meant something, though what—
But these men could not be allowed to take her.
The drone.
More debris pinged off my suit, but I ducked between the drone and the wall. I checked its screen: power levels had faded to red-orange.
Skip snarled an order in my ear—no, in the communications link—and the trolley exploded. The fire alarm blared. Water sheeted from sprayers above, beating down the flames.
My hands shook as I typed the command: >>*Retrieve the medic at all costs.*
Metal struck against my upper arm, and the datapad crashed to the floor.
The drone turned sideways, unspooling and unfolding all twelve appendages. Tendrils-first, it flew out of the fire suppression's downpour at the man holding the medic. Tentacles encircled his helmet. A scream

tore at my ears stopping abruptly as a sickening crunch echoed, even in the chaos. The medic slammed onto the ground, and the man crumpled next to her.

Bile rose. I had not meant—

Descending on the medic, the drone cradled her in its jointed arms, but after a few meters, it slowed, lowered her to the ground, withdrew all appendages, and settled daintily beside her bare head.

Another curse, another shout. Skip and his men ran. One of them tripped, his unsecured sidearm skittering across the floor. He abandoned it and pelted after the others. They disappeared down the hall, leaving the two injured and the one Skip had called Cord. How many had there been altogether? I could not remember.

Motion-activated lights flickered off behind the fleeing men, enclosing the hall in shadows. The alarm stopped abruptly, and the water slowed to a dribble, dripping down my faceplate like tears.

For the second time in my life, I was sick inside my helmet. Despite the virus's threat, I tugged it off, wiped my mouth, and raised my face to the ceiling. Droplets fell from the sprayers, dampening my cheeks and gathering on my eyelashes.

Voices sounded in my communications link, but I did not wish to hear them. I pulled off the cap as well and tossed it aside. The water had not completely purged the pungent odors of chemicals and smoke from the air, and fumes singed my nostrils.

Nate remained at my side, and a quick glance showed that Jordan and Quincy stood alert, weapons ready. Kyleigh huddled in fetal position, her gloved hands over the sides of her helmet. Zhen knelt beside Alec, her attention flickering between him and the ductwork above.

Alec's writhing stilled.

When I wiped my face again, what might have been red glinted on my gloved fingers. I crawled away from the wall, away from the destroyed trolley's debris, then stopped, unsure of where to go. To Zhen and Alec, or to Kyleigh? Or to the medic? Or to . . . or to the man who lay beyond my drone?

Kyleigh slowly uncurled, then picked up the medic's helmet and clasped it to her chest. The blue safety lights along the base of the wall reflected eerily from her faceplate.

Slick with chemicals, water pooled on the floor, glimmering with out-of-place beauty in the midst of ash, splinters of glass and metal, and the crumbled concrete from the damaged walls. Jordan, Nate, and the bearded marine still stood, weapons out, scanning the area, but Zhen lifted Alec's head onto her lap. When his fingers curled around hers, my heavy heartbeats calmed, if only a little.

Footfalls sounded again. Too numb to move, I did nothing when Jackson's marines arrived.

Two faced the dark hallway down which the men had fled. One knelt by the medic, and another crouched next to Zhen and Alec. The other trained her weapon on the round holes torn through the metal ductwork.

Nothing dripped through the perforations. The knife-man must have escaped.

Another storm of boots thundered, and more people arrived with hover gurneys and platforms.

The marine near the medic waved an arm, but I did not watch them lift her carefully and strap her down. Nor could I watch them secure Alec, though a sliver of guilt told me I should.

Instead, an endless cycle of the drone grabbing the man and his subsequent death replayed in my mind. I wrapped my arms around my legs and set my forehead on my knees.

"Sweetheart?" Nate did not say anything else, only raked gloved fingers through my damp curls, then cupped my chin. Fingertips whispered over my lips, wiping away whatever stained them. Then he crushed me close with one arm, and I buried my face against his scratched armor.

Time lost all its minutes and seconds, becoming both instantaneous and eternal, as the marines loaded the fallen attackers onto platforms and affixed microantigravity devices to the drone and what remained of the trolley. Nate released me and helped me to my feet, and Kyleigh handed me the green datapad. I slid it into my pocket, ignoring its pitted and scratched screen.

Once Alec was buckled down, Zhen retrieved the fallen knife and slipped it into a strap on her thigh. Her eyes burned like dark fire when they met mine, and she nodded tersely before returning to Alec's side.

The marines escorted us to the . . . to whatever that section was. I walked under my own power the entire way back, surreptitiously wiping my nose lest Nate worry. Concern for the way he cradled his arm nagged at me.

We left Kyleigh and the medic at the quarantine room and continued to the storage closet, where Nate and the others waited in the hall while Jackson's marines and I secured Lorik's drone. I found a receptacle in the back of the closet and plugged in the two undamaged chargers, leaving the scuffed one unplugged, since charging a damaged device could be dangerous.

Once the marines left, I stood alone in the closet, staring past the drones at the bland grey wall. The equipment Kyleigh required had been destroyed, and I had no idea where we must venture to find replacements. Against my will, the events in the hall replayed in my mind: my inexact command, the drone's compliance, the sound—

My stomach clenched, but so did my fists.

Despite my part in a man's death, Lytwin and Patterson remained in danger and needed Kyleigh's help. The moment they located the equipment, Jackson would give the command and we would leave. Lorik's drone must be charged. I bit my lip because ready power meant nothing without instantaneous control, even if I only had temporary access. How long did that status last? Surely it was days rather than hours. It had to be.

Resolution steadied my hands as I attached the cables and activated the drone. I answered its appeal for identification, then shut the door and left it to charge where it could harm no one else.

Nate escorted me back to the quarantine room before leaving to have someone check his injuries. I removed my suit and set the helmet aside to be cleaned. Teeth brushed and face washed, I exited the water closet to find Kyleigh staring blankly at Freddie's murals.

Williams had trundled the medic onto Freddie's bed, and the young woman answered Williams's calm questions in a strangled undertone. Snatches of their conversation penetrated the fog obscuring my thoughts: *good as dead, medication, don't care.* Williams uttered soothing responses as she gave the medic water and pills. After checking Kyleigh and me, Williams left us to assist Max with treating the others, and time continued to have little meaning.

No news came about Alec or anyone else.

At length, Kyleigh said, "What do we do now?"

Wordless, I stared at the metal plate over the ventilation shaft until my eyes burned, but all I saw was the drone grabbing the man's helmet.

The hiss of the air purifiers answered her. I did not.

Steam rose in delicate wisps over the disposable cup Kyleigh offered me, and the gentle scent of lavender momentarily tinged the air before the filtration units stole it away. I accepted the tea and thanked her before taking a tentative sip. The tisane's soft, dusky taste soothed my nerves.

Kyleigh hopped onto the foot of my bed, resting her elbows on her knees. "You saved her, you know."

My attention flitted to the sleeping medic.

"I'm glad you did. Whatever happens next, you kept them from stealing her away and locking her in a closet to die, like they tried to do to us."

"That is not all I have done." The bitterness of the memory overtook the tisane's sweetness. "I killed that man, Kyleigh."

"*You* didn't," she said carefully. "The drone did."

I nudged aside the glass with the datasticks and set the cup on my bedside table. "I sent that drone. If I had been more precise, had thought through the commands . . ."

"I don't know how anyone thought straight. I certainly didn't. I didn't even think to drop until Jordan shouted at me."

"You were not armed. You could have done nothing."

"I guess." She shifted her weight. "You, however, saved the medic from being a hostage and an experiment. There's an access hatch to the tunnels around the corner. If you hadn't acted, she would've been gone, impossible to track without some high-end SAR tech. I mean, no one found us. Besides, with the roaches on the loose, those people might not have made it back to their hideout."

"A hypothetical evil does not negate facts," I murmured.

"I'm not saying it does." She leaned forward to set a hand on my arm. "Look, I know you. You never meant for him to die, just to protect her. And you did. That matters."

My fingers knotted and unknotted around each other. "Death without the opportunity of change . . . It is too final, Kyleigh, and it is my doing."

Kyleigh's usually soft expression hardened. "They didn't think about it when they injected Freddie or the Elder or you. That man had no compunction about murdering people. Jordan is right to call them all genocidal maniacs."

Her brittle tone changed the course of my thoughts. "Kyleigh, you are . . . angry?"

"Yes, but not at you. You did what needed to be done." She pulled her knees closer and rested her chin on them. "Some help I am. I just curled up and did nothing. The point is, you took her back from those murderers. What they're doing is against the laws of God and man."

My forehead bunched. "You are not incorrect about the laws of man. But what of Max's assertion that all people are unique and valuable? What of your unquantifiable God?"

Kyleigh unfolded her legs, stood, and brushed invisible dust from her leggings. "How are you feeling, other than being riddled with guilt?"

Her refusal to discuss her beliefs was not my concern, but a trace of disappointment wound through me, nonetheless. I paused to take an internal inventory before responding. "My headache has subsided, though my joints ache."

"Your nose isn't bleeding, so that's good. Stars above, though. What are we going to do now? Alec—" She shuddered. "Alec lobbed that explosive charge through the doors just before they closed. The hall could've collapsed. At the very least, it's probably damaged, and who knows if the bugs are actually gone. I don't want to go back there, but I will, if they need me."

"I will not allow it," I said.

"*You* won't be making that decision. And if I don't go back, how are we supposed to save Lytwin and Patterson?" Kyleigh nodded toward the medic. "And her. And us, for that matter."

"Although I know for a certainty that you will do your best, the burden is not yours alone." I glared at the computer's speakers, from whence had come my sole interaction with the virologist. "Dr. Clarkson must do her duty. Her refusal to comply is akin to—" My mind went blank, and after digging through my vocabulary, I finally ended with the closest, yet incorrect, term. "Mutiny."

"I don't like her much, either." Kyleigh's nose wrinkled. "Are you going to reactivate the drone?"

Afraid to close my eyes and risk seeing the drone fly at the man, I stared at the dried ooze of sealant under the plate covering the ventilation shaft. "I have already done so. It is charging."

"Well, I'm going with you when you retrieve it." When I protested, Kyleigh held up her hand. "You were one hundred percent right about how to manage it. I'm not concerned about it going rogue."

"It is not that I fear for your safety this time," I said, though I recognized the statement as a lie.

Her gaze flickered to the medic, then back to me, and a crease appeared over her nose. "Fair warning. You're getting a hug today, whether you want it or not."

I hastily grabbed the tea as if doing so would shield me.

A hint of a smile appeared. "You can hide behind that tea, but eventually it'll be gone or cold, and you'll be fair game."

I did not recognize the idiom and tried to quirk a single brow, though as usual, both rose.

Kyleigh lofted one in response. "Don't think raised eyebrows will stop me, either. Or maybe I can convince Timmons to hug you instead." She grinned. "I suppose he wouldn't mind."

Heat suffused my cheeks.

Across the room, a thermal blanket rustled, and the medic croaked, "How long have I been asleep?"

Kyleigh's grin vanished. "Not long enough. About two hours. Someone is supposed to bring us lunch soon."

"Has anyone come up with a cure for concussions and viruses while I was out?" Before I could tell her that no one had done so, the medic rolled onto her side. "Any news on Lytwin and Patterson?"

"Not yet," Kyleigh said quietly. "And none on Alec, either."

The medic shifted to rest back against the wall. "What's wrong with Alec?"

Kyleigh's voice faltered. "We don't know, exactly."

"He was hit in the throat with a knife," I said.

"What?" The medic shot upright and winced. "Even in a suit, a blow to the throat could kill him, let alone a knife!" She proceeded to fire questions at us as rapidly as the weapons in the hall. Had his chin been down or had it hit the less armored joint? Had it hit blade first or butt first? Had it bounced off or penetrated his suit? How was his breathing? What had been done?

"They said they'll let us know when they have more information." Kyleigh glanced at the red light over the door, then back at the woman on the other bed. "It's a matter of hurry up and wait, though I suppose that could be Max coming with news. In the meantime, do you need a drink or something?"

The medic snorted. "Yes. But not the kind Maxwell has in here."

"We have lavender tea," I suggested.

"I didn't mean . . ." The medic sighed. "Sure. Thanks."

"I'll get it," Kyleigh said when I began to get out of bed. She padded across the room and plunked a packet of tea in a clean cup.

"Stars." The medic swallowed visibly. "Only two hours? I didn't realize how horrible it is, waiting to find out when you'll die." She fell silent for five seconds. "Tristram?"

Kyleigh paused in the act of pouring hot water. "Yes?"

"I shouldn't have scolded you this morning."

A flat smile flitted across Kyleigh's face. "It's all right."

She brought the medic her tea, and while they conversed in undertones, I sipped my rapidly cooling tisane until the light over the door switched to green. I swallowed the remainder and set the empty cup aside.

Nate entered, and eschewing protocol, I ran to him. He held out his right arm, and I slid close. The scratched suit hid his heartbeat, which was another loss. I needed to hear his heart again, for I could not quite recall its cadence.

At the moment, however, his presence was balm enough.

19

Lars followed Nate in and deposited a small bag on Kyleigh's desk before offering greetings.

"You're both okay?" Kyleigh demanded. "And Alec?"

"Alec is . . . stable." Nate cleared his throat. "Max needs Edwards to run some scans to check for blood clots, but as far as they know, his trachea isn't damaged. He's got pretty deep bruising, though."

"They're taking him up to *Thalassa*?" Kyleigh asked, and I was glad she did, for my throat had tightened.

"Shuttle's leaving in a couple hours to take us up for treatment," Nate said. "They're cautiously optimistic, yes. The rest of us will be fine. J's untouched, which is standard. Only time I've seen her scuffed up is after sparring."

"Don't fib, Timmons," Lars said. "You've got a hairline fracture."

I pulled away, and the movement caused his mouth to tighten. "Nate, is this true?"

"Sure it is. Clavicle." Lars cautiously lowered himself onto Kyleigh's stool, which creaked alarmingly under his weight. "Maxwell and Jackson want him back on *Thalassa* for treatment, same as me, though I'm pretty sure I could tough it out like I've done before."

My heart pinched. "Nathaniel!"

He glared at the marine. "Not the way I wanted to break that news, Lars."

The taller man cocked his head. "Don't see that hiding an injury makes it better." He turned to me. "They've got those red-light things in the infirmary. Used them on that kid's broken arm when he shunned nanites."

Concern and confusion laced through me. "What do you mean? Which child?"

"It's how Max treated Eric's broken arm when he first came on board," Kyleigh explained. "Advanced infrared light therapy."

Nate brushed a gloved thumb over my cheek. "Max, Williams, and Edwards know their stuff. Like I said, I'll be fine. Alec will, too. Zhen and Quincy are only bruised."

Kyleigh's eyes closed and her mouth moved silently, then she said, "What about Lytwin and Patterson?"

"Lytwin looks real bad," Lars said. "Bad as Westruther from what I've heard, but Patterson is better. He ate breakfast and everything. The real good news is Michaelson's out of the tank. Not up to much yet, but they're sending him up to *Thalassa* to have the medicomputer check out his missing arm."

"How or why would anyone examine an amputated arm?" Kyleigh asked.

"Ghosting," the medic answered. "Checking for nerve damage, though my guess is they'll send him to South Brisbane Research Hospital once we reach New Triton."

"Well, I'm glad he pulled through." Kyleigh glanced at Freddie's mural again. "I'm tired of people dying."

"I do not like death, either," I said.

"No one does." The medic shivered. She tugged her blanket off the bed and draped it around herself. "It's why I chose field medic as a specialty. Do what I can while saving the system. Never thought I'd be the one in a quarantine room."

Kyleigh rubbed a hand over her sternum. "Death is inevitable, but stars above, it hurts."

A deep crease appeared across Lars's forehead. "Sorry. About Freddie, I mean." He reached in the bag and pulled out a prepackaged meal. "I . . . James made sure you didn't get fish."

I could not see any connection between the prepackaged meals and Freddie's death, but Kyleigh said, "Thank him for me?"

"I will." He grimaced. "Freddie was a good kid. It was downright decent of him to give up his name for James."

The medic peered at Lars from her blanket-tent. "You really don't mind that a Recorder is going to take that boy's identity? I mean, it's one thing for Dan. He earned it, and we all chipped in. No one will be erased."

Kyleigh's shoulders stiffened, and she crossed to the wall and leaned against the broad, black brushstrokes.

Lars grunted. "Nah. I don't mind. From all I can tell, Recorders are basically good."

"Not in my experience," the medic began but stopped abruptly and looked at me.

Kyleigh whirled around. "How *dare* you say that? After she saved—"

"Kyleigh," I said. "Please."

"She needs to know."

"Know what?" the medic demanded, her gaze darting between us.

Nate's chin rose. "How you made it out of that hallway."

"No," I pled. "Not . . . not now."

The air purifiers hissed in the brief silence.

"Don't see why not," Lars remarked, "but I guess it can wait."

Anxiety gave way to relief, and I slumped back against Nate, though when he muffled a moan, I straightened.

"Anyways, I'm not saying Recorders are perfect, not any more than most of us." Lars gestured broadly around the room. "But a lot of 'em stand up for what's right. For the little guys, you know? Even the big ones."

Kyleigh frowned. "What do you mean?"

"Well, when I was in school, I didn't get the highest marks, and some of the kids teased me pretty bad."

"Hate bullies, myself," Nate said mildly.

"Not my favorite, either. Being bigger than other kids has its plus side, but big plus low marks paints as good a target as any shooting range."

Indignation rippled through me. "Such behavior is unacceptable."

Lars grinned and pointed in my direction. "See?"

"Yeah." Nate's voice softened. "I know."

"So, right after we got a new Recorder at our school, some of the older kids were picking on me, and the Recorder pulled me aside and said I had two choices." Lars shifted his weight, and the stool creaked. "'You can be bitter, or you can be better,' she said. So I decided to find the good things. Be thankful. Not always easy, you know?"

"No," Kyleigh said slowly. "It isn't."

The medic fingered the spreading bruise under her chin where the man had injected her. "I don't know if I can do that."

Though my experience verified Lars and Kyleigh's claim, the medic's statement resonated with an ache in my chest. Nate took my hand and did not let go.

"Yeah." Lars cocked his head in the medic's direction. "Sometimes looking for good isn't easy."

Her hand still on Freddie's wide brushstrokes, Kyleigh pivoted toward him. A single tear on her cheek shone like mercury. "Sometimes you can't find them on your own."

"What do you mean?" the medic asked.

Whether she addressed Kyleigh or Lars, the towering marine answered first. "For me, it meant Clarissa." The overhead lights' glare on his faceplate partially obscured Lars's grin. "Met her when I was in my last year of school. Best girl in the system. Smart, pretty, a year younger. Don't know why she took a chance on me."

Kyleigh grabbed a tissue and scrubbed her face dry. "She sounds lovely."

"She was—still is. Anyway, I broke it off when I turned eighteen and finished school, since she's younger. I knew she could go on to university and do something with her life more than get stuck with someone like me, so I joined up with the marines."

"Excuse me?" The medic glared at Lars. "Joining up isn't just an option for people with low marks."

"No one said it was," Nate interposed. "Did four years myself after university before J, Alec, and I saved up enough to start freelancing." When I looked up at him, he winked. "Got shot at a lot less. Maybe I should join up again."

"Nate," I protested.

He squeezed my hand. "It'll be okay."

Kyleigh kept her eyes on the tall marine. "But what happened with Clarissa?"

"Soon as she turned eighteen, she tracked me down. Before she was even out of school. I was back on New Triton, and she took an express from Destiny to Albany City to give me a right sharp lecture about never giving up on people." Lars's smile radiated, as crisp as starshine. "Worst fight of our lives."

Not wishing to interrupt his narrative to ask why an argument would make him happy, I glanced at Nate instead. He was grinning, too, reaffirming my suspicion that citizens frequently did not make sense.

"She went on to the teaching college in Destiny, and I went back to work. Kept in touch long distance, and I was a little scared she'd find someone better than me. Saved every credit I could while she finished up." Lars's smile broadened. "Never been as nervous as I was, asking her to contract. Figured she'd say no. Stars, I think I'd rather face roaches than go back and ask her again."

Kyleigh darted Nate a look, and his hand tightened around mine.

"But she said yes?" she whispered.

"Said she'd never wanted anyone else. Bought a ten-year contract, even though everyone thought it was foolish—two kids tying themselves up long-term, but it was the best decision of my life."

"So she's all right?" Kyleigh asked. "Is she waiting for you now?"

He jabbed his thumb at the door then winced and blew out a slow breath. "Yep. She wants me to stick around more, but problem is, I'm not much good at anything else. Most of the other jobs I'm qualified for are on the belts. Not taking Clarissa there. She's back in Albany City, teaching little kids. Like I said, she's the clever one." His expression faltered. "Clarissa wasn't too thrilled I was going on this trip, and if she knew where I was, she'd really worry. Doesn't like tunnels, germs, or bugs at all—she washes her hands an awful lot." He studied the wall behind me. "Might not tell her."

The medic rolled her eyes. "She'll know soon enough. It'll be all over the news vids."

Lars's expression fell. "True."

Kyleigh glared at the medic. "She'll be proud, though, Lars, won't she?"

He brightened. "Yeah, I think so. She says she wants me to quit, but"—he lowered his voice—"I think she likes the uniform."

Nate let out a crack of laughter, then stopped abruptly. His hand rose to his shoulder. I moved closer, hoping he would lean on me, if needed. He did.

"Got the call to report while I was washing breakfast dishes. Tell you what. I was downright excited about this gig, myself. Good danger bonus. It might cover that permanent contract we've been talking about for the past few years."

The thermal blanket crinkled as the medic snugged it closer. "Why would you saddle yourself to one person forever like that?"

"Because I learned my lesson." Lars turned suddenly serious eyes on Nate and me. "When you find the best prize in the system, you don't let go."

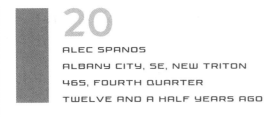

The orange stain over the sink had crept further since Alec had been home last. How he hated that stain. His jaw clenched, and he looked away, though the next thing that caught his gaze was the lumpy sofa that hid its equally uncomfortable rollaway bed. Such an ugly old thing. He'd been sleeping on it—or its rollaway when Nate stayed with them—for years now, ever since he'd convinced his mother to listen to reason and take the bedroom.

Mama deserved better than this busted, one-bedroom flat, but she wasn't going to like his solution. Neither would Nate, but that couldn't be helped.

Her chuckle brought Alec's attention back to the kitchenette where she and Nate were finishing up the dinner dishes. Ages ago, Alec had been a little jealous that his best friend had been the one to make Mama laugh, but all that really mattered was that she did.

"Nathaniel," she was saying, "if I didn't know better, I'd say you were the one who spilled whatever it was on the magister's desk."

"Nitrogen triiodide." Nate placed his hand over his heart and sighed dramatically. "Must've been an accident. They never figured out who threw the paper airplane that set it off. Stars, but that purple cloud was stellar."

Mama twisted the towel and snapped it at Nate, who dodged it with ease.

Alec frowned. "It's a good thing Magistra Jones never found out."

Both turned to him, and Alec forced what he meant to be a smile. Nate grimaced and went back to rinsing the dishes, but Mama dried her hands and crossed back to the table, taking a seat on the wobbly chair next to Alec's.

Her brown eyes fastened on his. "Is something bothering you?"

His hand sought the worry beads in his pocket. "Just thinking."

"About?"

"University."

She beamed. "I am so very proud of you, son, for working so hard. Magistra Jones told me what a rare accomplishment it is to double up on classes and still win a scholarship. When you—"

"I'm not going," he blurted.

Mama's smile vanished.

A dish splashed back into the sink.

Alec clenched the smooth olive wood beads.

"But you," Nate sputtered. "We're supposed to—we start classes after Founding ten-day. You can't back out now."

That little upside-down *V* of worry appeared over Mama's nose. "Son."

"I . . . I'll take out the dinner scraps." Nate grabbed the small composting bin from the counter and left. Fled, really. The door clicked behind him.

Mama leaned back against her rickety chair. "Alexander, what on New Triton are you thinking?"

"One of the mining corporations is hiring. Job auditions start tomorrow."

"That is *not* an option."

Indignation straightened Alec's spine. "I've finished secondary, and I'm old enough to make my own decisions."

Her eyes bored into his. "You're sixteen."

"Almost seventeen." The beads dug into his palm. "Mama, I can't run off while you're stuck here."

She reached across the table, and after a moment, he took her hand. The skin on her swollen knuckles was chapped and papery thin.

"You're not drinking enough water," he said.

A faint smile crept up. "Are you worried that I'll dehydrate and waste away?"

"No."

"You can't turn down this opportunity," she insisted. "This isn't about here and now, son. This is about your entire life."

"I can't afford to go," he insisted. "I've been talking to recruiters, Mama. The mining office is hiring for the heavy metal processing plant outside the southern buttresses. Second-tier pay, with living quarters provided on rotation. You can move to a better, safer place. One without a stained ceiling."

Her fingers closed around his. "This is your chance. Without it, you'll be facing a life of hard labor, stuck at the mercy of the mines' whims. Think, son, think. An education will allow you to write a pass to another place, better pay, better future."

"I'm not going to dishonor Papa and Aria by leaving you to rot here."

"It isn't dishonorable to think of the future, Alec, and this isn't forever. Just for now." She released his hand. "Alec. I need you to escape all this."

"Second-tier pay," he repeated.

"But at what cost? You can't trade your best hope for momentary gain."

The knot in his throat threatened to choke him. "Papa would've wanted me to take care of you."

"Your father wants—" She caught herself when she used present tense, like she did sometimes. "Would want you to have a future."

"A future the Consortium ruined."

She shot a glance at the open window. "Don't even think that, Alexander, let alone say it aloud. That's why your father . . . why he's gone. Why we have such a debt to pay. Don't draw their attention. Be better than we were."

"No matter what I do, Mama, I'll never be better than you."

"Alec—"

"You have to understand. If I can get that job—good pay and a quarterly rotation, maybe even a part-time job on the off-quarters—I can get you out of here. Let me. Let me pay off Papa's fines."

"I'm working on that already. Your father—" She took a long breath. "The debt is being paid down as quickly as possible. My wages will be garnished for a few more years, and . . ." She released his hand, sat straighter. "I'm not the only one contributing. With that help, there are just sixteen years left."

"Sixteen *years*. That's almost as long as I've been alive." Alec narrowed his eyes. "And whose help?"

"It's complicated."

The room suddenly seemed very hot. Alec jerked backward, and his chair squeaked in protest. "You're not seeing someone, are you?"

Her mouth dropped open. "What? Oh, stars, no."

Alec swallowed. He wasn't being fair, and he knew it. "I mean, Papa's been gone for four years, and you would've told me, right?"

She crossed to the window and slid the curtains shut. "Maybe it's time you know."

His stomach plummeted. She *was* seeing someone.

"I'll be right back." Moments later, she emerged from her bedroom with a small blue box, which she set in front of him. "Go ahead."

He eyed it, then her, suspiciously. No dust dulled the keepsake box's glossy paper sides. Metal rivets reinforced the corners, but it had no lock. If she meant to keep it a secret, she'd need a different one altogether, though secure boxes cost credits, and those were scarce. Strange, really, that she'd even purchased this one.

He lifted the lid.

Printed pictures of his parents and him and his sister, copies of Mama and Papa's contracts, a sketch of her holding Aria as a baby with Alec at her side. Letters. Even four years later, he instantly recognized Papa's scrawl.

She reached over, shuffled through the papers, and pulled out a damaged envelope. "You need to read this."

"No, Mama." He hastily put the lid on the box and shoved it back to her. "I won't read letters Papa wrote you."

"You need to."

"It's wrong," he protested. "It's . . ." He couldn't bring himself to say just how uncomfortable the thought made him.

She held out the letter.

"It's all right," Alec said softly as the realization hit. "I don't have to read a love letter to know you loved each other. I didn't mean to question that."

"That isn't the point." She threw another glance at the curtained window, then held the letter to her heart. "This isn't something I feel safe saying aloud. It's bad enough that I keep this. But someday, you'll need to know what's in this letter and how it pertains to your future, especially if anything happens before those sixteen years are up." She carefully placed the letter back into the box and closed it again.

"Nothing's going to happen." Another sixteen years and he'd be thirty-two. The same age Mama had been when their world came crashing down.

"Processing ore is rough work, Alec," she pressed. "Don't sell your future for your present."

"For yours, too," he countered. "I can help you pay that debt down faster."

"I can't have you trapped in a job that will eat you alive. Paying it off faster is not worth your life, not worth some mining corporation owning your soul. Don't you see? That would make everything we've gone through meaningless."

Memories flashed past. Those kids, years ago, calling his mother names, calling him a miner brat. The review board questioning whether or not the disappearance of his father made Alec unfit for schooling. Those same doubts cropping up this ten-day when he sat through the interview for the accelerated study plan at university.

"The best victory is success," she whispered.

His determination wavered. Was she right? Would refusing his scholarship fulfill everything those people had said? Would it justify the Consortium's claims? Take away any future of fighting back against the ones who had let his sister die and stolen his father away?

"Only sixteen years, Alec. We've already paid off five."

We? But she'd said she wasn't seeing anyone.

"Do you know how lucky I am?" Mama offered him a wan smile. "Maybe blessed is a better word."

Alec glanced around the flat, at the stain on the ceiling, at the covered sofa he slept on, at the pots that held the struggling ferns. "How is any of this lucky?"

"Do you remember the night we moved in, and I cried about that hideous stain on the ceiling?"

Alec frowned. "I don't see any blessing in that."

"We stretched out on the floor and stared up at it. Made it into a map from another world where no one ever disappeared except the villains."

"Your stories—"

"No," she interrupted gently. "Yours, like your father's. My brave son took a stain in a dilapidated flat and made it so much more." Her eyes softened. "You protected me with your father's fairy tales and brought the drab, lonely world back to life. You faced down bullies to protect my name. Studied to get through school faster than anyone expected, even me, and I think you're brilliant. *You* are my blessing, Alec." She inhaled and finished, "I need you to go to university."

"And you're mine." The old clock he'd bought for her at the open market a few years ago clicked in its uneven, irreparable way. He heaved a sigh. "You win."

"So you'll go?"

"I will," he promised. "Maybe I should've thought it through more."

"Good." She glanced at the broken clock, then at her black-and-metal identification band. "It's getting close to curfew. Go find poor Nate, who is taking way too long to get rid of food scraps." She tapped the blue box with a thin finger. "Bring Nate back for cake while I put this away again."

"You shouldn't have made a cake, Mama."

"Nonsense." Her smile returned. "When my son and his best friend pass their entrance exams, a celebration is in order."

He headed for the door but turned back when she called his name. Brown eyes bored into his. "You will need to read these letters."

Alec made a noncommittal noise instead of a promise and closed the door behind him. "Nate?"

No answer.

Alec jogged down the stairs to the community compost vat and winced at the sharp stench of methane. Sure enough, Nate was leaning against the faux brick wall that separated the slowly rotating barrel from the walkway while he chucked pieces of debris at the neighboring building.

Nate's glare pinned Alec like a biology lab specimen, all the little needles flaying it open, then he looked away and lobbed another pebble. It bounced back, sending up a tiny cloud of dust. "Should've told me."

"I know."

"Thought we were friends."

"We are," Alec said. "I just wanted to get Mama out of here. Getting a job instead of a degree seemed like the fastest, best way."

"It's a stupid—" Nate raised his head. "Wanted. Seemed. That's past tense. You change your mind?"

"Yeah. I guess I spoke too soon. I'm going after all."

"Good. I mean, I get it. I want to help her, too. Your mom's closer to a mother to me than anyone else. Better than my family, for certain."

"She calls you her second boy." Alec blew out a long breath. "Stars, Nate. I about spaced everything."

"You trying to make it worse? Your mom hears you swear like that, and you'll be in a freighter load of trouble."

A reluctant grin spread over Alec's face. "True enough."

"Tell you what," Nate said. "I'll help, too. We'll get internships or something, and between the two of us, we'll get her out of here."

Alec stiffened. "She's not your responsibility."

Nate stooped to pick up another piece of crumbled concrete. He threw it hard, and it pinged off the composting vat. "Thing is, you're right. She deserves more than this stupid flat. If the universe really was fair, it'd kick my grandfather—"

"Who's voided dross." When Nate raised an eyebrow, Alec added, "She met him once, remember? She'd agree."

"That's probably true. Wish I could kick him out of his fancy place and set your mother up there." He gestured. "You attached to hanging out next to the compost?"

"Not really," Alec said. "You're the one who chose it."

Side by side, they retraced the path to the flat.

"Alec?" Nate's voice grew quieter. "I couldn't have gone with you, not after working in the mines killed my mother."

They reached the stairs, and Alec paused at the bottom step. "I didn't expect you to."

"My grandfather tells people that mines are all I'm worth. I can't make that true."

Don't let them win, reverberated in Alec's mind. "Mama says the best victory is success."

Nate stared up at the riveted dome. "I think she's right."

"I suppose the one way to know for sure is to succeed."

The curfew signal sounded its first warning.

"We'll show them," Nate said as they climbed the steps. "Know what? I'd trade places with you if it wouldn't mean sticking you with my family. You're lucky."

The truth of the statement settled in Alec's bones, and he almost smiled. "I know."

Before they reached the top step, the chipped green door opened, almost as if Mama had been watching for them. "Well, are you two going to stay outside until you're arrested, or are you coming in to have some dessert?"

Nate's expression brightened. "There's dessert?"

"Cake. *Real* cake," she clarified. "With proper flour, not beans."

Nate whooped and darted past her.

"Wash your hands, young man," she reminded him. "Alec?"

"In a minute, Mama."

She studied him, then offered a faint smile. "We'll wait for you."

The door clicked shut, and he leaned against the frame. Overhead, a dim, dim blur told him that New Triton's moon had risen.

Mama was right. Nate was right.

But no matter what, he'd see that his father's debt was paid off.

Alec set his jaw, nodded goodnight to the distant moon, and went inside to join Mama and Nate. To join his family.

We had finished our unpalatable lunches when Nate's communications link crackled, and a feminine voice sounded over the external speaker. "Osmund's prepping the shuttle. You and Lars need to head over."

After Nate's affirmative answer, the link chimed without a farewell.

Lars braced himself on Kyleigh's desk and stood. His face tightened, and he exhaled slowly. "Right then. Get this over with. Sooner we're there, sooner we're back."

He was not wrong, even if a few seconds would make little difference.

I reached out and took Nate's hand. "Nathaniel? Will you keep me informed as your treatment progresses?"

He promised, and then they were gone. The door closed behind them, again leaving me—and the other two—in temporary confinement.

"He'll be fine," Kyleigh said. "They all will, especially Alec. They have to be." She trudged to the stool Lars had vacated and collapsed onto it with a groan. "Stars, but my legs ache."

My breath caught. Was that a symptom? No one had complained of that before, that I recalled.

"My abs, too." My concern dissipated, however, when she added, "Who would've thought that escaping roaches would use stomach muscles? That was more running than I'm used to."

"If you were more diligent in your exercise . . ." My words tapered off when Kyleigh glowered at me.

She turned to the medic. "This is a bit awkward, but I don't know your name."

The woman on Freddie's hoverbed spoke to the ceiling. "Yrsa Ramos."

"You are twenty-four?" I asked.

"Almost twenty-five." She squinted at me. "How did you know? Did that drone-thing tell you?"

Slightly affronted, all I said was, "No."

"Well, Recorder-that-isn't, I suppose I shouldn't be surprised by a level of borderline omniscience."

"Yours is a preposterous conclusion, Yrsa Ramos," I retorted. "The name is simply one of the most popular female names the year I was born."

"So we're the same age? Huh. Never thought of Recorders as having birthdays." The medic's expression twisted, as if she smelled something sour, but the air filters remained operational. "We're going to die in the same year, too."

"You can't know—" Kyleigh began, but her computer chimed. The stool squeaked when she rotated to the screen and projections. The uneven taps on her antiquated keyboard sped, then slowed, then stopped altogether, and her hands fell to her lap. "Lytwin is dead."

A lump swelled in my throat. Lorik would never have wanted death as his legacy, yet that was what the roaches had spread.

"Patterson?" Yrsa Ramos asked.

"Williams said he's holding," Kyleigh said quietly. "They've delayed the shuttle to take him, in case there's anything Edwards and the researchers can do."

"That's it, then." The medic flopped back onto her pillow, and her hand covered her eyes. "I'm dead, too. Walking dead."

She was not walking, but I understood. "If I have not succumbed, nor has Kyleigh, we all have a chance."

She lowered her hand and glared at me. "Don't be stupid. I've seen the numbers. Just because you two haven't died yet doesn't negate the fact that once you're sick, the fatality rate is almost one hundred percent." The medic's gaze drifted back to the ceiling. "But sure, I'll shun reason if you say so."

Determined to alter the conversation's course, I attempted to change the subject. "Yrsa Ramos, how do you want to be called?"

"Does it even matter now?"

"Yes." The word shot from me without forethought, straighter and truer than almost anything I had ever said.

The medic rounded on me. "How can you say that, Recorder? You don't have a name, not even—"

"Stop!" Kyleigh demanded. "I won't let you sit there and spout rubbish like that when she's gone through so much. Stars, she saved your life!"

My heart thundered. The idea someone would recite the events in the hall sliced away any calm. I beat a rhythm on my thigh.

"Did she? I hadn't noticed," the medic said through clenched teeth. "It seems to me that we are all trapped in a quarantine room in varying stages of death."

"They were going to take you. They were dragging you away—" Kyleigh broke off, then took a breath. "And she stopped them."

"Stopped them?" The medic flopped back onto her pillow again. "Dying here, dying there. What does it matter?"

"Fine," Kyleigh snapped. "You go ahead and quit. We won't. We'll figure it out without you." Her hazel eyes turned to me. "So what can we do?"

My heart's uneven rhythm slowed. Kyleigh was correct about quitting, though loss of the equipment hampered our ability to detect nanotechnology. "I need the drone." I held up the damaged green datapad. "I might require another one."

"Does it work at all?"

I powered it on, and it flickered unevenly. "It seems to, but the pitting on the surface may impair my ability to communicate properly."

"I'll track down another one," Kyleigh said.

My attention fell on the datasticks again. I set down the datapad and spilled the mismatched datasticks into my hand. Freddie's and . . . why could I not remember?

It seemed important. Something about tunnels? But why would tunnels matter?

"You know what I don't get?" the medic asked the grey ceiling. "How did they even know we were there? Spying on the door the whole time isn't likely."

Kyleigh glowered. "Julian Ross would've known where the equipment was. He worked on nanotech stuff with Dr. Johnson and my dad."

I flipped the datasticks over and over in my palm, struggling to recall what Ross had told me quarters past on our trip to New Triton, before he had tried to kill me. The words played in my memory in patchy bursts. "He was working with Dr. SahnVeer to combat the mortality rates in the miners in the outer belt. Ross used viral therapies to trigger immune responses to autoimmune disorders, and he and the doctor designed nanotechnology to deliver medication directly to the tumors themselves without damaging surrounding tissue."

"Not a bad idea," the medic said.

Kyleigh set her fists on her hips. "No, but he used that mechanism to hide his murder weapon."

The medic tucked one hand under her nearly bald head. "Maybe it would have been better to work on preventative methods. Better respirators and suits. Still doesn't tell us how they knew."

As if in a memory download, I saw Skip and the knife-man in the hall. The knife-man's respirator gleamed, reflecting the overhead lights as he ducked behind Skip, who had been clad in the mottled grey-and-black of Consortium—

"Oh!" My fingers tightened involuntarily, and the datasticks dug into my palm. "Suits!"

At my exclamation, both women asked simultaneously, "What?"

"That is how they knew," I said in a rush. "Skip was wearing Lorik's suit! And that woman, the one who stole your necklace, Kyleigh, she was wearing yours when I found you. Someone must have Freddie's, too. They must have accessed the communications links to monitor our channels."

"Stars," the medic hissed.

"And that means . . ." I tapped my thigh. "How could I have forgotten?"

"Forgotten what?" Kyleigh asked.

Ignoring her, I dropped the datasticks onto my crumpled bedcover and snatched up the damaged datapad. My fingers flew over its pitted surface.

I sank to my bed when its response scrolled across the screen.

>>*Continuing temporary access granted, Aberrant Zeta4542910-9545E.*

"What is it?" Kyleigh demanded.

I held up one hand for silence, then resumed my query about access to the main channels through the Elder's suit, but the drone's answer was garbled. Or was it my question? I retyped the same request. The drone asked for clarification.

With a groan of frustration, I dropped the datapad and pulled my suit from under my bed.

"What do you think you're doing?" Kyleigh demanded.

"I need the drone."

The medic pushed herself up on one elbow. "Why?"

"In the hall, it was both monitoring channels and recording their transmissions."

"Documentation," Kyleigh said in a hushed voice.

"Blasted Consortium spying machine," the medic growled.

"They are listening to us, but with the drone, we can now spy on them." I checked the light over the door. It was still red. The men were not through.

The medic, Yrsa Ramos, pulled herself upright and blinked hard, as if to correct double vision. "Could it be used to triangulate their position so we can find those spacing trogs?"

"It might. I must get to my drone, and I must warn Jackson."

Yrsa cursed. "And we can't comm Jackson without them hearing."

"They can't know that we know that they know." Kyleigh blanched. "Stars! Can they access the data about the virus we've been transmitting up to Dr. Clarkson and that she sends here?"

"I do not know, but I fear we must warn *Thalassa* as well."

"Right," Kyleigh said as she pulled out her suit.

"Both of you should stay here," the medic stated. "I'll go."

"Don't be stupid, Yrsa," Kyleigh said sharply. "You've been drugged, dosed with a virus, and dropped onto a concrete floor. If you don't have a concussion, I don't know who does."

The medic tried to stand. She grabbed the railing and lowered herself back onto her bed. "You're right. What good is training when I can't use it? You need protection, but I'm seeing double." She groaned. "Void take it. It isn't safe. Even if we've kept these hallways clear of roaches for the most part, there're still vents."

"Yrsa, someone needs to remain here." I fastened my boots. "If anyone returns, you must explain our theory, should we—"

"Don't you go saying you won't make it," the medic snapped. "Blast. Sending civilians into this disaster isn't right." She slumped back onto her bed, her hand over her eyes. "Just make sure someone goes with you once you pass the barricade. And for Founders' sakes, keep an eye on the ceiling."

Kyleigh stomped her feet into her boots and turned to me. "What do you think? You're faster, but I'm steadier. Who goes to the hangar, and who goes to the control room?"

"I shall inform the shuttle. They can take the information to *Thalassa*." I slid the datapad into my pocket, hesitated, then added the datasticks and the communications link Nate had given me.

"Can you get the drone before they leave?" the medic asked. "Otherwise we won't know for sure that's what they did."

My jaw tightened. "I must."

The light over the door turned green. Kyleigh entered the exit code at the panel.

I checked the chronometer over my bed. Sixteen minutes since Nate and Lars had left. Kyleigh and I would spend fifteen waiting in the vestibule. The timeline was too tight.

I paused at the door. "Rest, Yrsa Ramos. Rest and heal."

"Be safe," she countered. "And be fast."

Kyleigh and I entered the vestibule and left the quarantine room behind.

22

When the vestibule door finally opened, Kyleigh and I rushed out into the deserted corridor, she to the right and I to the left. Air burned my lungs as I ran, and by the time I reached the storage room, a stabbing cramp in my side made opening the door even more difficult. It unlocked, and the drone hovered where I had left it, still tethered to the wall by its charging cables.

>>*Power level, 37%.*

For three seconds, I stared at the words, but the image that played before me was the drone in the hall, its tentacles squeezing—

No. I pushed away the memory and pulled the drone free. "Come. I must reach the shuttle before it leaves."

It complied, keeping even with me as I dashed down the hall. When I reached the barricade, a single marine stood at attention.

"Recorder?" she exclaimed, her eyes darting from me to the drone to my helmetless head.

"Let me pass."

She centered her weight. "Can't do that."

"I must get to the hangar before the shuttle departs."

"Not without armed escort you don't. Besides, the shuttle will be leaving any minute now."

The skin on my neck prickled. Captain Archimedes Genet needed to be informed about the probable corruption of our communications system. If this woman would not let me pass, she left me but one choice. Refusing to allow fear of past actions to influence my present ones, I sidestepped to enter commands directly into the drone.

Her voice tensed. "Move away from that thing!"

Its appendages unspooled.

"Deactivate the lasers," I countered while I finished entering commands. "I do not have time for your games."

"This isn't–" She broke off as the drone reached toward her. "Stars, Recorder. You going to kill me, too?"

My mouth went as dry as Pallas's surface, but I straightened my shoulders. "Lower the barricade."

She held her ground. "Orders–"

The drone wrenched the rifle from her hands, and its attached tether yanked her off her feet. While the drone kept her away from her weapon, several tentacles connected with the access panel. The barricade vanished.

Unleashing a flurry of imprecations, the marine fumbled with the tether. She broke free and pulled out her sidearm, aiming it at me, but before her action fully registered in my mind, my drone intervened, all tendrils and tentacles splayed. Panic rose as appendages twined about her neck and captured her wrist.

"No!" My cry echoed back at me. "Drop it! You must drop the weapon." I backed into the corridor. "Please."

Her sidearm clattered to the concrete floor, and she cursed.

"Do not use your communications link. Do not notify Jackson. Doing so is unsafe," I warned, then addressed the drone, "Come."

My footfalls and labored breath muffled all other sounds as I ran, the drone at my side. When we rounded a corner, however, it raced in front of me, but I dared not waste precious seconds to read its message.

"Later."

In answer, the drone grabbed me in all four arms, hauling me from my feet. Ignoring my winded protest, it accelerated and turned corners with a precision that did not alleviate my fears. The bland hallways became a grey blur and the emergency floor lights a searing blue streak. Air whipped past, and my short hair lashed my face. I pulled one arm free and covered my eyes with my elbow.

Someone shouted, and the drone slowed. I cautiously lowered my arm and craned my head. The open door to the hangar loomed, and two figures in marine blue aimed rifles in my direction.

I gulped down air and called, "The shuttle–has it left?"

A tall figure strode between them. "Recorder, get back to quarantine."

"Jackson?" I asked. "You are not in the control room?"

"Obviously." Behind his helmet's faceplate, Jackson's steely grey eyes became slits. "That thing brought you here. It can take you back. Now."

"Release me," I said to the drone, but it did not comply. Instead, the arms tightened, making it difficult to breathe, but I managed, "Jackson, has the shuttle left?"

"Not your concern." His words ground over each other like rocks. "I don't know what stunt you're pulling, but if you don't want to be locked in that storage closet with the rest of those things, you get that monstrosity out of here."

"Jackson, you do not understand. Communications have been—"

"You threatened my people." He tapped his link and said something inaudible before tapping it again. The marines behind him shifted in front of the hangar's laser barricade.

The barricade . . .

"That marine." I gasped as my mind belatedly caught up with the situation. "She notified you."

"Spacing right she did."

My hands fisted. "I warned her! Communications are being monitored."

One of the marines scoffed, but Jackson stilled. "How?"

"The suits," I said. Surely, he heard the desperation in my voice? "The stolen suits must be how they knew where we were, that we were retrieving the equipment. Why you did not receive Jordan's call for backup."

He spat out an uncouth epithet. "Should have opened with that."

"Stars," one of the marines breathed.

"I was to warn the shuttle and thus *Thalassa*. Kyleigh ran for the control room to tell you—"

A short pattern of sound—perhaps an alarm or a signal—blared down the halls.

"Looks like Tristram made it. The shuttle had to have heard that. They'll know not to trust comms." Jackson strode toward me. "No need for you to come this way, especially without escort or helmet. Don't think we won't address that later."

"Set me down," I repeated.

The drone finally complied, and my knees hit the floor. I gracelessly forced myself to unsteady feet, but it twined a tendril around my waist, rotating me away from the marine and rising until its screen was directly in front of me.

>>*Located Consortium suit.*

I blinked. "What does that mean?"

"It means once we're secure, we'll discuss how your reckless behavior endangers my people and yourself," Jackson said.

>>*Located stolen Consortium suit belonging to Elder Eta4513110-0197E.*

A chill swept over me. "Where?"

>>*Ventilation ductwork and fissure twenty meters southeast.*

Which way was southeast? Every nerve tingling, I spun to face the hall, studying the ductwork as if I would be able to see through the metal.

"In the quarantine room where you belong," Jackson said behind me. "I'll get you an escort—"

"Alone? Or with others?" I fumbled for the damaged datapad on my thigh.

>>*Two biosignatures from previous encounter. Two unknown.*

"Yes, others," Jackson said. "I can't take you myself."

"I did not say you would, Jackson," I told him, my focus shifting from the datapad to the ductwork and back. Not wanting to risk input on the damaged screen, I asked aloud, "Can they hear us?"

>>*All communications monitored,* flickered across the pitted surface.

"Yes, we can all hear you." Jackson said more slowly.

"She's lost it," one of the other marines hissed. "Want us to take her straight to Maxwell?"

I backed against the drone, its familiar surface an uneasy comfort. "Then they know?"

>>*Uncertain.*

"Recorder," Jackson began.

The drone shifted behind me and twined two tentacles around my waist and neck.

Jackson grunted, and something thudded to the floor.

"Recorder!" someone barked, and another voice shouted, "Call it off!"

I spun in the drone's grasp.

Jackson was on his knees beside me, shaking and gasping, a tendril wrapped around his throat.

Dropping the datapad, I rushed to Jackson's side and tugged on the drone's appendage. "Release him!"

The tendril whipped loose but did not spool back inside. Jackson did not raise his head. All other thoughts dimmed, and I tried to brace his weight.

"Stars, he was trying to help you, Recorder," the second marine said. "No reason to try to kill him."

"Jackson," I urged, "you must breathe through it. The pain will subside." I glared at the drone. "He would not have harmed me."

The drone pulsed red.

"There is no excuse," I continued as if the flash of light had been an apology, though a drone did not have that capacity. "Unless directed, drones are not to harm citizens save in protection of members of the Consortium." I lifted Jackson's head—his helmet seemed heavy indeed—and studied his unnaturally grey face. "Can you stand?"

He nodded once and shoved off the floor, using my shoulder as a prop.

The drone's red deepened, and one thin tendril handed me the green datapad. A new crack spread across the lower left-hand corner, but its response was clear.

>>*Protection.*

"Protection from these marines is unnecessary. They are my—" I stopped myself before the word *friends* emerged. "Allies. They are allies, here to assist in tracing the virus, which threatens the Consortium. They mean me—us—no harm."

>>*Delaying access to shuttle.*

"Without malicious intent."

>>*Unsafe. Leave Pallas. Others closer. Safety on shuttle away from terrorists.*

Which way was southeast? "Where are they? Is their intent confirmed?"

>>*Monitoring channel.*

"Void it, Recorder," Jackson growled through gritted teeth. "You've been talking to it? Those terrorists are coming?"

The first marine whistled. "That's what she meant by others listening."

Before I could respond, the drone issued a low buzz of static, then a muted conversation played under the noise.

"*. . . armor holds up pretty well. Didn't take down that big guy in the hall first time.*"

"*She has a drone again,*" a woman said. "*But the grunt at the gate reported that she doesn't have a helmet.*"

A dull chuckle made my flesh crawl.

"Her head's the target," Skip's voice declared. *"One clean shot, and we're good."*

"Serves her right after what she did to Cord. And we don't need the murderer anyway. Ross just needs a few cc's."

The hallway seemed to spin. Jackson touched my shoulder, and the drone sent a short reprimand, snapping me upright. Jackson cursed. He released me and shook out his hand.

". . . don't want the sample polluted. I still say we grab her instead."

"Right, but we should be able to get enough," a different man said. *"The drone's the problem. Can't have it going rogue and taking out our people. Let them deal with it. We do this right, and we'll have what we need."*

"Fair enough. Linda, fall back," Skip ordered. *"Risking a fight with that many grunts is stupid."*

"Don't know which way they'll take her back."

A resounding boom emanated from the hangar as the seal on the doors unlocked.

"She won't be out without a helmet again. Can't miss the chance. We'll have to split up."

"Shuttle's leaving," said the second marine.

Jackson nodded. "That's our safest bet."

Both the eavesdropped dialogue and the static disappeared.

The first marine pounded a code into the panel, and the barricade flickered off.

"Drone," Jackson ordered, "get her out of here."

Though it should not have responded to a citizen, the drone grabbed me around the waist and towed me into the hangar, its speed increasing with every meter. I glanced back. Jackson and the marines shrank, then disappeared as the drone raced around the second shuttle. Shouts echoed, but the cavern and the growing rumble of the shuttle's engines swallowed the sounds.

The drone stopped so suddenly that I slammed into it, and a blast of cold air slapped my bare cheeks and burned my eyes. To my right, the hangar doors crept open, and beyond them, I caught the faintest glimpse of stars. The drone lifted me through an opening hatch. A tendril shot out to a control panel, and my ears popped as the hatch shut.

Noises swirled and blurred. Nate's tenor broke through insistent and emphatic conversation, and I latched onto it.

Whether the drone dropped me or the floor rose to meet me, I landed on my hands and knees, and the engines' growl rumbled through the antistatic flooring. My stomach lurched in time with the small craft. The drone withdrew to the single Consortium alcove, anchored itself, and shut off external sensors to charge more efficiently.

Voices raised in protest as hands lifted me, then secured me in a safety harness in the seat across from two hover gurneys. The one closest held Alec. Though still in his suit, an extra canister of oxygen fed directly to the small filtration unit, and a monitor beeped steadily at his head. The second gurney bore a large black bag, sealed with biohazard tape.

Skip, not I, had destroyed the equipment needed to save Lytwin. So why did my conscience nag me?

I leaned against the headrest while Nate settled on my left and Lars on my right. The others who had come to my assistance hurried through their own safety routines. The general scurrying and shuffling disappeared under the engines' dull roar. I closed my eyes as forces hurled me against my seat. Weightlessness took hold, then gravity switched on. The engines settled into a steady thrum, and my drone hummed in its alcove.

I stole a glance at Nate, and worry threaded through me again. His face had drained of color.

"Quite an entrance, sweet—" He stopped abruptly, then concluded, "Sweet stars above."

The marine in front of us grappled one-handed with his safety harness and glanced over his shoulder. "Timmons is right."

"Michaelson," I said. "I am glad you are well enough to travel."

He grimaced, then his gaze flicked to the drone before boring into mine. "It isn't that we don't want your company, but we have ninety minutes until we reach *Thalassa*. Why don't you explain why on any known planet you chose to join us in such a dramatic fashion."

23

I kept my eyes on Nathaniel's while I explained that our communications had been compromised. Guttural murmurs rose until Michaelson motioned for quiet.

A young woman added, "That doesn't explain why that thing dragged you here like you're my two-year-old niece throwing a tantrum."

"Jackson told the drone to bring me."

"Since when does any Consortium tech listen to a regular marine?"

"That's not the real question," Nate said.

Michaelson frowned. "No, it isn't. Jackson told it to bring you. Why did he decide to risk your life by having that drone break open the hatch when the shuttle was spooling up?"

My words collapsed in my throat.

If I told them, Nate would be angry. Eight days before, he had risked the Elder's ire by interfering and grabbing hold of a drone. This morning—how could it have been this morning?—Nate had asserted that Skip could only have me over his dead body. I could not bear it if his hands went as cold and limp as Rose Parker's had. If Nathaniel were in a black bag with biohazard tape . . .

The idea made me flush with cold.

"Look at me." When I shook my head, his voice dropped low. "What happened?"

I hesitated, but hearing the story later from someone else would be as bad as hiding the truth. Lifting my gaze to the beige ceiling, I garnered my courage and related the conversation the drone had played.

A general uproar ensued. Nate said nothing but captured my hand in his. Still, I did not allow myself to look at him.

Michaelson raised his arm, and the shuttle fell silent. A pang shot through me. I had insisted on bringing back the station Recorder's body, and Michaelson had paid for my error with his arm. That insect had bitten him—

But, for once, my tumbling thoughts latched onto something else. The Recorder who was now Daniel Parker and I had acted in concert. Armed with drones and a torch, we had pulled Michaelson free, and Jordan and the marines had come to our aid. A weight lifted, for the loss of his arm was not, truly, my fault, any more than his rescue had been entirely my doing.

"Well." Michaelson's sandy brows lowered. "We're not letting them have you. Period."

His assertion warmed me. "Thank you," I began. "When I return to Pallas—"

"Not with those trogs down there," the young woman announced. "Not if we can help it."

"Drone," Michaelson said, and the marines fell silent, each casting glances at the charging station near the hatch.

Fatigue overtook me, and though the drone occupied the alcove, Nate did not let go of my hand while I dozed. My helmetless head drooped against his arm, his armor again cool and reassuring against my cheek, and my eyes drifted shut.

Osmund's announcement that we could unbuckle jolted me upright. No one else spoke. Two marines, one limping heavily, departed with Alec's hover gurney. After another fifteen minutes, Michaelson and another marine left, taking Lytwin's remains.

The blue-eyed marine who had assisted Michaelson stepped in front of us. "Timmons, you and Lars are up next."

Nate finally released my hand. "They won't let you off the shuttle without a helmet. I'll track down a spare before I head to the infirmary."

"Nathaniel," I protested, "you must prioritize your own well-being."

Behind his faceplate, his green eyes softened. "Looking after you is good for my health, so finding that helmet is arguably self-care."

With that, he left.

Others did as well. Finally, the last two people emerged from the front of the shuttle. I did not recognize the woman carrying a small chest sealed with biohazard tape, but Osmund slunk past me, studiously avoiding my eyes and casting furtive glances at the drone.

The shuttle's emptiness rang in my ears, and though I tried, I could not relax. I fidgeted in my seat, jumping when my communications link chimed.

"Left a helmet for you in the tent," Nate's voice said. "Took me a while to find a replacement. Not sure where they want you to go next, but I suspect Archimedes will want to talk to you."

"Very well."

"Edwards is busy at the moment, so if I can sneak off, I'll join you."

Concern clenched at my chest. "You should not sneak, Nathaniel Timmons."

He chuckled. "Try to stop me."

Once he had signed off, I turned to the drone. Despite the more functional charging station, it had barely reached fifty percent. I tapped the external screen, and it followed me out.

A replacement helmet was indeed waiting for me by the door. It clicked into place, but an unfamiliar, unidentifiable odor was a constant reminder that it was not my own. The drone and I stepped into what Nate had called a tent. Thick, semitransparent sheeting fastened to the ceiling, floors, and walls, while fans and sprayers roared, making the sheets rustle and snap.

Nate was not waiting for me. Neither were Edwards nor Captain Archimedes Genet. Instead, two university students and a cat greeted me when I stepped through the curtains secured to the ceiling and walls.

Grins stretched across Cameron Rodriguez's and Eric Thompson's faces, but Bustopher sat, surveying me with what might have been disapproval.

The cat's glossy black fur had grown even thicker since I had seen him last, and the white splotch on his throat was striking. Despite his aloofness, I smiled. This was how I had expected cats to look, not like hairless mythological monsters. When the low whir of the drone sounded, however, Bustopher jumped to his feet. His back arched, and his ears pressed against his head. His low growl made the hair on my arms rise. Surely the drone would not see Bustopher as a threat, but for his safety, I placed myself between its long tendrils and the cat.

Eric's expression changed. "We're here to take you to meet with the captain, Zeta. Maybe you should leave that thing behind?"

"There is nowhere I could leave it. I have no quarters and no way of securing it."

Cam's laryngeal prominence bobbed. "You probably need to keep it close at hand in case it goes rogue since you're the only one who can control it."

Eric grunted and rubbed his left arm. "True enough."

The young men accompanied me down the hall, the drone trailing after us and the cat slinking several meters away, his tail low.

"You should not have brought Bustopher," I said.

Eric almost laughed. "Bustopher does what he wants."

The cat paused to glare at me, as if he knew I had spoken of him, then disappeared around a corner with a twitch of his tail.

Every familiar scratch in the paneling, every ugly, unframed piece of art seemed to welcome me, though I did not allow even the hint of a smile to cross my face.

Thirty-seven steps later, I asked, "Have you fared well?"

"We're all right," Eric said. "It's been more interesting than classes."

Nate's earlier concern for Tia prompted me to ask, "All of you?"

Eric's jaw ticced. "For the most part. Sorry about Freddie."

"We all are." Cam motioned at the green-and-white mourning bands they both wore. "I hope Kye is doing all right." He paused, but when I did not answer at once, a small sigh snuck out. "I'll ask her myself, I guess, when she's back up here. Timmons told you that the ship's Recorder is down, right? Losing her drone knocked her sideways."

"Since Miller's out of the tank, Edwards sedated her and shoved her in. Dr. Clarkson was right upset about it. That old—"

"Eric," Cam warned.

"She's as bad as Kavanaugh was, Cam, and you know it." Eric rubbed his jaw and huffed. "Though I guess Tia would scold me for speaking ill of the dead."

Cam made an indeterminate noise. "It isn't entirely unfair, though. Dr. Kavanaugh wasn't exactly amiable."

"She was not," I said. "I have not yet met this Dr. Clarkson in person, though I have spoken with her once. She, too, does not seem amiable."

A grin creased Eric's face. "We heard you put her in her place."

The memory did not grant me the pleasure it evidently granted him. "Tia said you were tempted to speak against her, but you must not." The drone's whir reminded me to be cautious, but I risked, "Nathaniel Timmons expressed concern about Tia's presence on *Thalassa*."

Eric's grin vanished. "He's right. She should've stayed behind."

"Be reasonable." Cam's voice dropped, as if lowering his pitch would keep the drone from recording him. "What else would she do? Stay quarantined with Watkins, Bryce, and Foster?"

"Yes," Eric snapped.

I halted, and when they did as well, I studied their faces. Eric's mouth pinched in a tight line, and Cam's dark brows bunched together.

"What is wrong?" Dread overtook any caution of the drone, and I touched Eric's arm. "We were all aboard *Agamemnon*. Has the virus—has she fallen ill?"

"No."

Eric's imprecise and terse answer was unhelpful, so I turned to the taller young man. "Cam?"

He puffed out a breath, but before he could answer, Eric did. "Oh, Cam's known this whole time. And said *nothing*."

"Her decision, Eric," Cam said quietly. "Zeta, the captain is waiting."

"You have not answered me," I said more sharply than I should have. "Tia—"

"Isn't sick. She'll be off duty in a few hours. Maybe you can talk to her later." Cam held up a hand when Eric sputtered. "Her tale to tell, Eric."

"It's not only that, Cam. She didn't tell me until I . . . Like I wouldn't care? Like I'd offer just for—" His attention snared on the drone, and color rushed to his cheeks. His chin jutted up. "I care. And I'll keep asking." Eric pivoted on his bootheel and stormed down the hall.

"He's worried is all, maybe a little hurt that she didn't talk to him before." Cam exhaled. "Don't worry, Zeta. She'll be fine. Eric's just afraid Tia will either get shunted from university or . . . or worse." He waved at the hall. "Shall we?"

We followed Eric, but my mind raced.

One could be removed from university for several reasons, but . . . Nate had seemed concerned for her health. Pregnancy without a contract or support system was the only reason for removal from university that posed any sort of health challenge. Tia had spoken of betrayal by someone she had thought loved her and had mentioned consequences. Her questions from nearly four ten-days ago ran through my mind: *Zeta, what was it like, growing up at a Consortium training center? Do you regret being gifted?*

A chill swept over me as I envisioned a small Tia, bald and eyebrowless, in Consortium grey, a drone wrapping a delicate tendril around her to reprimand—

I stopped myself. Wild suppositions were akin to gossip, and I would allow myself neither to speculate or to pry. She would tell me when or if she needed to.

Cam shortened his stride to match mine, and the drone resumed its place near my shoulder.

We had not caught up with the other young man when Cam broke the lull in our conversation. "That's the Elder's, isn't it?"

As if on cue, one of the drone's tendrils encircled my neck. Cam edged away.

"Yes. It was Lorik's."

"Who's Lorik?"

The memory of the Elder tipping his forehead against mine in the darkened hall raised my chin. "It was his chosen name."

"The Elder?" Cam's steps faltered. "He had a name?"

"Indeed. He found his name and held it in secret." I swallowed past a knot in my throat. "Lorik means freedom."

"An odd choice, given some of the stuff he pulled. Have you—" He glanced back at the drone.

Anxiety gripped me. How had I spoken so when it would be recorded? I fisted my hands. No, Lorik was gone, and there was nothing the Eldest could do to him now.

Cam cleared his throat. "Never mind."

We sped up. The remainder of our short walk passed in silence, and we reached the conference room in which I had met with Jordan, Nate, Alec, Zhen, and the now-deceased Captain North before our first trip to Pallas. The young men took up positions outside the door, shifting over to avoid the drone.

"We'll wait for you out here," Cam said as I reached for the access panel.

The door slid into its pocket, and I entered. Archimedes Genet stood, his eyes steady on mine, then crossed the room and extended his arm. After a moment of indecision, I held out my own, and he clasped my wrist. A hint of a smile crinkled the corners of his eyes.

"Recorder, you had us worried for a while, though barring your repeated trips to the infirmary, you do seem to have remarkable luck in adverse circumstances." Archimedes Genet's baritone was as soothing as always. He pulled out a chair for me. "I've been informed about your unexpected trip and your news, but I need to hear it from you."

"I will do my best."

My drone took a position opposite the painting of an old-Earth ship, its white sails full as wind propelled it inexorably forward. Ceres' skies were lavender blue, but I would have liked to see that sky as well, to feel true wind on my face.

Archimedes glanced at the drone, but his expression never changed. "I realize the Consortium processes records before citizens have access, but if it's possible to share them, we could use every advantage we can get in order to protect our people and find a cure."

I sat, my back to the drone, and avoided the captain's eyes. "I am more than willing to divulge what I can."

He rounded the rectangular table and lowered himself into the chair across from mine. "What happened?"

My mind went blank. What had he been told of Freddie? Of the Elder, James, and the talkative former Recorder whose name was . . . was . . . I could not recall, but neither could I afford to err.

The captain rested his elbows on the table and interlaced his fingers. "Start with anything that might help us track the perpetrators down."

Instead of the whole story, I recounted the events of the past twenty-five hours, avoiding all mention of Freddie, James, or the talkative former Recorder. The captain listened attentively, though his frown deepened when I told of the failed attempt to retrieve the needed equipment, and when I continued with Alec's injury and the subsequent exchange of weapons' fire, he straightened in his chair, even though he must have been informed, since Alec was in the infirmary now. I choked out what had happened in the hall before the marines arrived.

Archimedes Genet frowned. "Do you regret your actions?"

"I do not regret stopping them from abducting the medic."

"And you shouldn't. Whether or not she knows it, Yrsa Ramos owes you her life," he said gently. "Sometimes in fulfilling our duty to protect those who cannot protect themselves, unintended consequences occur."

"She cannot owe me her life, as you say. Her discontent is understandable. I prevented them from taking her, but she has the virus in her veins."

He tapped steepled forefingers to his chin. "You kept them from using her for experiments, which is no small thing. You gave her as much of a fighting chance as you have yourself."

"That man . . ." I shuddered. "I should have thought. Should have—"

The door opened, and startled, I sprang to my feet. The drone whirred behind me, appendages spreading over my head like floating tree roots, as a middle-aged woman in an orange biohazard suit, but no headgear, stormed in. She smacked a large, reinforced datapad on the table.

"You're a hard man to reach, Genet," she snapped, and I thought I recognized her voice. "Not on the bridge, not answering comms? I've been trying to contact you for five whole minutes."

The captain leaned back in the chair. "What is it, Clarkson?"

This was Dr. Imogene Clarkson? This slight woman with a sharp, thin nose? Her soprano was weedier without the static, and she was within two centimeters of my height. I had thought she would be taller.

"None of you believed me." She flipped sparse braids behind her shoulder. "Even when I told you it was something here on the ship. And I was right, even if I don't know what it means yet."

The drone hovered over my left shoulder, a tendril twisting from my wrist to my neck.

Archimedes Genet responded with greater patience than I felt. "Your assertion of self-confidence doesn't justify barging in here to interrupt an official interview."

She huffed. "You're lucky I convinced Shiro to upload the grunts' medical records before those trogs hit the ship. And it's a good job I shut down the computers after we got half of them into memory, or we would've lost everything when *Thalassa* lost her files."

"As I have already said, Clarkson," Archimedes observed.

"Yes, yes, but if Shiro hadn't taken all the time in the system, we'd have more data." The woman thrust a finger at the large datapad. "I've checked Lytwin's medical records over and over. Read that."

Archimedes Genet skimmed the data. "This hardly indicates—"

"Of course it does. I *told* you there was a link." Dr. Clarkson raised her nose in the air and announced, "Lytwin was allergic to cats."

Their uneven, almost incomprehensible conversation swirled around me. Imogene Clarkson ranted on, emphatic and frequently rude, while Archimedes Genet's comments remained measured and thoughtful. My headache struck like a reprimand, constricting around my temples, stabbing through my right eye, obscuring the discussion of cats and potential links to viruses.

I asked, "Do you have proof of a connection?"

Dr. Clarkson glared at me. "It's clear enough for anyone with half a brain. You really should have stayed on Pallas." She pursed her lips. "Genet, I warned you about bringing carriers onboard, but no one listens to me. Autopsying Lytwin's shell is one thing, but there was no need to bring her or that bite victim."

The captain stood. "Shiro's research says otherwise."

"Shiro is overly optimistic."

"We've had this discussion before, but I'll state this one more time"—he slanted a glance at me and my drone—"for the record. The other researchers have shown that the virus is not communicable save by bodily fluids. We're honoring your concerns by keeping all potentially infected people in quarantine and suits until cleared by the medicomputer."

"She's contaminated. A public threat."

Archimedes Genet's voice grew crisp. "Cowardice is not a virtue, Clarkson. We need the Recorder's help, and we are here to research a virus, which can't be done without a degree of risk." An emotion I could not parse flickered in his eyes. "Millions of lives depend on getting this right. While you have the right to personal opinions, Consortium-based bigotry has no place here."

For approximately eleven seconds, they locked eyes.

Her nostrils flared. "Whatever."

Despite the pain in my right temple, or perhaps because of it, her insolent remark summoned my training. "Drone."

It hummed.

"Record Dr. Clarkson's disrespectful attitude."

Silence wrapped the room while the drone rotated so they, too, could read the word flashing across its screen.

>>*Documenting.*

"I treat everyone with the respect they deserve." Dr. Clarkson sucked air between her teeth. "Well, at least since you're here I can get good samples. Keep that drone out of my way."

The contrary desire to send it to record every single thing she did—from researching RNA to braiding her hair—hit me like a solar flare.

"What matters is that I was right," she added, pointing again at the datapad in front of the captain. "As usual. Good thing for that medic, too. What's her name?"

Archimedes Genet crossed his arms. "Yrsa Ramos."

I should have remembered that.

"Right, right. She's the one who was contaminated next, if reports are accurate, though no one verifies anything. I have to do all the work around here." She stopped suddenly and scowled at the door.

"About Ramos?" the captain prompted.

"Oh," she said with a vague wave of one orange-clad arm. "She'll be fine."

"But that man, the one I—" I bit my lip. "He injected her with the virus."

Dr. Clarkson shrugged. "He could have been lying, but if he wasn't, and if I'm right—I usually am—his little stunt won't be a problem. It's the cats, I tell you. Lytwin avoided them like the plague I thought they were. I was wrong about that one thing, mind you. You didn't avoid them. Tristram didn't. Patterson didn't."

"Patterson is here?" I asked while I searched my memory for any reference to holding the shuttle for him. "He is the bite victim you mentioned?"

Dr. Clarkson rolled her eyes. "Stars, for a Recorder, you don't notice anything. Yes, they sent him up here on that shuttle, too. Ramos should be safe enough. She grew up on Ceres. On the southern continent's central plains, on a farm." She folded her arms and glared. "With cats."

The image of fields of felines momentarily confused me. "A cat farm?"

"Don't be—"

"Clarkson," Archimedes warned.

She glanced at him and modified her statement. "Of course not. Her family grew winter wheat, barley, and beets, but they had cats to keep down Rodentia. And goats," she added, momentarily confusing me. Surely she meant neither that cats suppressed a rampant goat population nor that the addition of ruminants would increase the credibility of her cat-theory. "My point is, she was exposed to them her whole childhood until she signed her life over to be a marine."

Hope slivered through me.

"Have you shared this with Shiro?" Archimedes asked.

"Of course. But we need more help." The woman tapped her fingers on the table. "Since they went and ruined the proper equipment, you might as well send Tristram up here. You'll have to do without her retinas on Pallas, because she has to focus on nanoencapsulation." She side-eyed me. "Even if I don't like having carriers running loose."

A frown crossed the captain's usually neutral features. "We'll send for Tristram in the morning. Anything else?"

Clarkson snatched up her datapad. "Blood, I suppose. Hers. Better have Edwards take care of that. He might be Consortium staff, but he understands the integrity of samples."

Without another word, the woman stomped from the room, and I fought the desire to tap my thigh.

Archimedes Genet stared at the door through which Dr. Clarkson had left. At length, he said, "Recorder-who . . ." His gaze shifted to the drone, then back to me. "You look exhausted, though we probably all do." His forehead creased. "I trust you understand why you'll remain quarantined until we clear you."

"Yes, but I must keep the drone with me."

As if I had summoned it, the drone rose slightly and wrapped a tendril around my arm.

"The only place with a vestibule and a charging station is the Elder's quarters."

I managed a smile. "That will suffice. However, I have much to accomplish, so my first stop should be my computer laboratory, if it is available."

"I'm afraid not. Your primary goal right now is rest." He cocked his head, and previously unnoticed traces of silver in his dark hair caught the light. "You aren't immortal, you know." I opened my mouth to protest, and a smile touched his eyes. "Don't make me summon Edwards to issue a medical order."

Edwards must be overworked; I would not add to his burden. I braced myself on the table and stood. "Then I shall take my leave."

He accompanied me to the door and ushered me out, nodding at the three men waiting in the corridor. "Rodriguez, Thompson, Timmons."

Archimedes continued speaking, but his words washed over me incomprehensibly. All my attention centered on Nate, who pushed away from where he had been leaning against the wall. His face was paler than usual, and blond hair drooped over his forehead and over his jacket's collar. All I wanted was to fall against him and hear his heartbeat.

"... escort the Recorder to the Elder's quarters," Archimedes finished.

"What?" Nate exclaimed, his green eyes flashing to the captain.

"It is well, Timmons," I said quietly. "His room has a charging station for the drone, and I can be quarantined there." I matched his frown with one of my own. "A better question would be why you are not under medical care."

"Bit of a backlog at the infirmary." Though Nate's words were casual, his tone held an unfamiliar sharpness. "Thought I'd stop by, make sure you're safely ensconced in a place you can rest. The Elder's quarters doesn't fit the description."

I wanted to touch his arm, to make him listen and take care of himself, but did not allow myself that luxury. "Ignoring a fractured clavicle is unwise."

"I'll be fine."

"I'm sure you will, Timmons," Archimedes Genet said, "but you'll head straight to Edwards after you see her to the Elder's quarters. Recorder, someone will be stationed outside. You are not to wander the ship, but when you do leave those quarters, you'll have an escort."

Nate's eyes narrowed. "Why?"

"Patterson is quarantined as well. Until we have confirmation from the medicomputer that neither of them are contagious, they will remain under watch."

"We heard Clarkson ranting." Eric glared down the hall. "Her tantrums about Zeta staying on the moon are ridiculous. The other researchers insist the virus isn't airborne."

"She can't go down there again," Nate all but growled.

Cam demanded to know why I could not return, but Nate did not explain. Neither did Archimedes Genet.

"Recorder?" the captain said as we turned to leave.

"Yes?"

"While the situation is less than ideal"–his expression softened– "welcome back."

25

Warm, red light greeted me when I woke the next morning. For uncounted moments, I blinked contentedly at the wall, which was a comfortable rose-pink in the gentle light, while a vaguely familiar rhythm pulsed below my range of hearing, like an external heartbeat. I stretched between soft sheets and under the soothing weight of a heavy blanket. The familiarity of being back in Consortium quarters—

My heart jolted. Behind me, a medical monitor squawked, then beeped in time with my heart.

"Lights." I forced the command from a suddenly dry mouth, wincing as the monitor grew more insistent. The room sharpened around me as the light shifted from warm red to full spectrum.

My communications link chimed on the bedside shelf. I pushed myself up on one elbow and fumbled for it.

"Recorder? Recorder!" Edwards. Nothing was amiss. It was only Edwards.

I licked my lips. "Yes?"

"Your vitals went—" His sudden silence added to my disorientation. "Are you well?"

My gaze swept over the room. Everything was as I had left it the night before after I had showered and donned a clean, Consortium-sanctioned nightshirt brought up from the laundry. The small cleaning unit that held my suit and the borrowed helmet had finished a sanitation cycle, and a thermos of water still sat on the Elder's desk beside a sealed container of breakfast bars, the damaged datapad, and the datasticks I had stowed in my pocket before my precipitous flight.

"I am well. I had not remembered where I was."

"Ah." Three seconds ticked past. "I am not yet able to leave the infirmary to check on you."

"I shall wait."

A soft chuckle sounded over the link. "Yes, I suppose you will."

"The captain said the shuttle would be departing this morning. Has . . . have they . . ." But I could not bring myself to ask if Nate had left without saying goodbye.

"Osmond and Johansen took off a while back." Edwards paused, and the centrifuge's click sounded in the background. "I have been busy, but we shall get you out of there as soon as possible."

A chill swept away any residual comfort. I bolted upright. "How is Alexander Spanos?"

"Alec is doing well," Edwards said. "He has deep bruising on his throat. Give him a while to rest, and he will be as good as new."

"Blood clots?" I asked. "With severe bruising, clots are possible."

"We are keeping an eye on him. The machine that synthesized your pyrimethamine is working on his medication. But Timmons," Edwards volunteered, "is well. He and the marine have started red-light treatments, and yesterday the research team certified that the bone treatment jet injectors are clear of Consortium technology. Given the minor nature of the damage, their bones shall be knit together in two days at the longest, and their pain levels have improved already."

Relief swept through me. I wanted to thank him for telling me, but the words snagged in my throat.

His mild voice lowered. "*Thalassa*'s Recorder is fading. She needs her neural chip removed, if she is to survive. And the bite victim, Patterson, he has had a setback."

"I am sorry." The inadequacy of that response made me cringe.

"Thank you," he said. "I will need you in here for a scan this afternoon."

Though he would not see me, I nodded. "As you say."

"Be sure to eat," he reminded me.

The link chimed, leaving me alone in the nearly empty Consortium quarters, and my monitor's beeps slowed, then faded away when my heart rate normalized.

I scooted against the wall. Without the ability to see invisible light, I could neither read the daily thought over the desk nor see the designs that surely edged the ceiling. Without my neural implant, I had lost the ability to discern sounds beyond the range of human hearing, so a subsonic canon only pulsed rhythmically in my chest. For a second, I longed again for the strains of music only a drone and neural chip could translate. Here, however, nothing spoke of individuality, which was as it should be for a child of the Consortium, though perhaps not for a child of humanity.

All my life I had lived in rooms like this, in apparent sterility, yet in such a short time, the need for color had replaced the safety of white, grey, and burnished metal. The desire to fight for both color and friendship swelled, and I stood.

The ever-present rumble of the engines was faint beneath my bare feet. Too faint. My forehead wrinkled. *Thalassa* had not yet recovered from the damage wreaked by Skip and his associates.

Tea. I needed tea, so I padded over to the desk and poured the flask's tepid water over ginger-turmeric, then dropped into the Elder's uncomfortable chair. The solid white surface was cold against my bare legs, so I pulled the nightshirt down and tucked the fabric under my thighs. I had work to do. The green datapad and the two datasticks were yet in my possession. Moving aside the food bars and weak, lukewarm tea, I reached for the datapad. Its battery was nearly drained, but I did not seek a charger. Nor did I inspect the damage itself.

A whir behind me indicated the drone had left its alcove, but I did not turn toward it.

Questions dueled for predominance. Firstly, if the Elder had linked his personal drone to the one I had left in the control room, would it be possible for *Thalassa* to communicate with Pallas without the insurgents' knowledge? Secondly, would his drone remain linked to the Consortium itself? That second thought splintered further. Would the potential connection betray me, or could I utilize it to save James and Daniel?

My mind could not settle on the appropriate question, but regardless of which line of reasoning would be the most relevant, I needed to replace the damaged datapad in my hands. The surest way to do so would be to retrieve my navy-blue one from inside the drone.

I swiveled the chair around and, as authoritatively as I could while in a nightshirt, demanded that the drone power down.

It rose several decimeters, as if in defiance, though I knew full well that an emotional reaction would never have been programmed.

I held up the damaged datapad. "I cannot afford to be without a clear method of communication. Verbal commands could be inappropriate, if I am to protect Consortium interests in front of citizens. Without a neural implant, I must have a functional datapad. Focusing on a drone's screen to the exclusion of my environment is unsafe. There are adversaries who would utilize that deficit to kill me, which could leave Consortium equipment in the hands of those who wish us ill. Having handheld access is vital."

>>*Defend. Protect.*

An odd statement, but one I did not wish to argue. Keeping my eyes on the drone, I continued, "I must replace this datapad with the one currently transmitting Consortium codes." I paused, then added with an involuntary smile, "Since I do not wish to be electrocuted, power down."

The drone slowly lowered.

"Here." I set the tea and bag of food on the floor, put the chronometer and datasticks on the chair, then patted the desktop twice. "After switching the datapads, I shall investigate any potential corruption of *Thalassa*'s communications systems."

The drone spooled in all appendages and rotated so its screen faced me. >>*Ship-wide network damaged.*

Distracted from the idea of investigating the connection with the AAVA drone, I asked, "Will I be able to reach the Elders and inform them of the events and losses? They must know of the virus and the way Consortium technology has edged its way into the citizenry."

>>*Delay.*

Though the drone's response was unclear, I said, "Noted."

The drone settled on the reinforced desk, and the green datapad joined the chronometer and datasticks on the chair. The Elder's drone maintenance kit was in a desk drawer, and after opening the drone's access panel, I peered into its innards. There. The comforting blue of my old datapad peeked back at me beside the one I assumed to be the Elder's. I glanced at the thin, black datasticks, then at the damaged green datapad beside them.

"I am ready to make the switch."

>>*Neurochip faster.*

Attempting to mask both nervousness and impatience with a degree of levity that was surely wasted on a drone, I said, "Yet while I cannot replace a chip inside my brain, I can replace a datapad."

>>*Restart enabled to allow extension of temporary access.*

"Yes."

Without another comment, its screen went dark. I should have inquired about the length of time I had remaining. Since nothing could be done now that the drone had powered down, I removed my blue datapad.

Eyes still on the drone—for I did not completely trust it—I reached behind me for the damaged green one on the chair's seat, but my fingers curled around a datastick instead.

Freddie's information. James.

With the drone unaware of my activity, this was my unplanned opportunity, my accidental cleverness. So, I set the datastick aside and inserted the green datapad. A quick search of the Elder's desk yielded spare cables, which I used to attach my blue datapad to the drone, creating a passive link to view the information that would save James's life. Once that link had been confirmed, I studied the drone itself. Several datasticks jetted from interior slots, and if my memory served, the third from the right provided the arms' secondary controls. Before doubts overturned my decision, I drew a deep breath, then removed that datastick and jabbed Freddie's in its place.

My datapad's screen flickered, but what appeared was not Fredrick Westruther's biographical and medical information. It was information about the virus.

I forgot to breathe. How did I have—

"*Recorder, I copied what I could. Do what you can,*" Elliott Ross said in my memory.

He had handed me this datastick in the passages of Pallas Station, before the Elder, Kyleigh, Freddie, and I had fled into the roach-infested corridor.

"Moons and stars," I whispered.

Though I read much slower than usual, and though letters raced past in unfamiliar words, I understood enough to know this might make the difference. There was, of course, nothing about Dr. Clarkson's cat theory, but this data might tip the balance, might save the bite victim and the medic, not to mention citizens and members of the Consortium on New Triton.

But . . . *James.*

I would not have the excuse to disconnect again. When the drone powered back on, everything I did would be recorded. James might never be free. Freddie's sacrifice of memory would be for naught. But someone else's son, someone else's daughter . . .

Chills swept over me. I was wasting time, yet I could not move, could not decide. How long until the drone restarted? Or was there another way?

Each life was valuable. Each one was unique. Each . . .

The skin on the back of my neck tingled. I pulled out the datastick and inserted the other one.

James first.

Images, letters, and numbers swept across the linked datapad's screen, and though I closed my eyes against the onslaught, they burned in my mind.

Freddie as a child in a hospital bed. Freddie learning to write and draw after receiving his new eyes. A small Freddie playing catch with a younger and happier version of his father. Freddie, his father at his side, as his mother's remains moved down the conveyor belt in a Center for Reclamation and Recycling.

How could I erase the importance of this one bright life? And how had the weight of doing so never mattered to me?

My sole focus had been on saving my first friend, but now the pressure in my throat made it difficult to draw air. I made myself remember the young man who had given me the datastick. His insistence that saving Max's son was what mattered. His belief that he was not dying but going home. His face, streaked by bloody tears—

That brought the virus to mind again. My concentration splintered.

But perhaps the two tasks were not mutually exclusive. All I needed was for the researchers to examine the datastick, and that could be done here on *Thalassa* while I saved James and the talkative Recorder. It would take but moments to turn over the information. I had that much time, did I not?

I tapped my communications link, demanding to speak to virology.

"Dr. Clarkson," I began when she answered, "I have—"

"Recorder? What can *you* possibly want? Bother Edwards instead. I've got work to do."

"Which is why—"

A snort interrupted me. "Stay where you are, plague take you."

"Enough!" I snapped, and she fell quiet. My fingers curled around Elliott's datastick. "I have information about the bioweapon."

She clicked her tongue. "So I've heard, but you're not a virologist, Recorder. What makes you think you could come up with—"

"From the people who released the virus." Interruption had been frowned upon in the Consortium, but she showed no signs of stopping.

"What?" After a brief pause, her words unleashed in a torrent. "Void it, why didn't you say so yesterday? Were you withholding it on purpose? What information?"

I ground my teeth. "If you could display but a modicum of manners, I could better complete my sentences. As you noted, I am no virologist. The information was given to me by the young man who helped us escape. Elliott Ross—"

"The one who assaulted you? I find it hard to believe someone like him would give us reliable data."

Never before had I felt such a rush of violence toward someone who was not a criminal. "Elliott Ross downloaded information to a datastick. Without a computer in the Elder's quarters, I cannot transmit the information through the ship's network."

"No computer? Oh, right. There'd be no need for one with drones and all," she said. "Fine. Call Edwards. Tell him to get the stick with your supposed information. And your blood, while he's at it."

Eyes on the frozen images of Freddie's past, I disconnected her link. *Call Edwards*, indeed. I should have contacted him first, save that I wanted to get the information to virology as soon as possible.

When Edwards did not answer, I left a message, then attempted to contact Archimedes Genet. He was also unavailable, and chasing people to get them the information was stealing valuable time. If they received their messages right away, Edwards or whomever the captain sent could arrive in as little as fifteen minutes. That had to be enough time. If they did not receive the messages, however, I needed someone who would listen.

Nate. I needed Nate.

I chided myself for not contacting him first, for though he was not a virologist, either, I knew he would answer. He did.

"Nathaniel, my heart—"

He inhaled sharply. "Careful now."

I gestured at the drone, belatedly realizing he would not receive visual cues over the communications link. "I must get a datastick to Dr. Clarkson."

His voice pitched low. "That doesn't mean you need to be reckless."

"I am not." I did not waste time clarifying. "But I need you."

He immediately responded, "On my way," and the link ended.

Even if Nate took the datastick to the virologists, I could—should—transmit the information over the Consortium network. I inserted Elliott's datastick into my blue datapad and copied the information, pacing the room while it loaded. When it finished, I ran a check to verify that it had transferred properly. It had.

While swallowing the remainder of the weak ginger tea, I pulled up James's biomedical information from the Elder's files and switched it with Freddie's, then duplicated it onto my blue datapad. I could not recreate their ancestry, but their Earth ethnicities were a close enough match that perhaps no one would notice. Their ages, however, were a different matter. No one would mistake James for a young man of twenty-one who had wasted away to skeletal levels after two years in a medical pod. His shoulders were too broad, his muscles too well defined. For a moment, I stared blankly at the data, then I shrugged. There was nothing I could do. If Julian Ross had not become gaunt, perhaps my friend had not, either.

As I altered Freddie's educational records to match James's experience at university, a pang rippled through me at the diminishment of Freddie's art. His handiwork should not be lost. That had to be his memorial. I falsified a surge in the medical pods from his time in stasis, emphasizing system glitches to explain any discrepancy in artistic abilities.

I dove deeper, replacing pictures and images, merging documentation for both Freddie and James, inserting the merged images into data I would somehow transmit over the Consortium network once the drone reconnected.

The words swam before me, and my headache spiked. I poured the last of the warm water into my cup and swallowed it before checking the chronometer.

Nineteen minutes had passed. Nate had not arrived.

One last adjustment: I altered Frederick *Standon* Westruther to Frederick *James*. At least in this small way, my first friend had the option to go with the name he had accepted as his own.

I tugged on my nightshirt's hem, tempted momentarily to gather a blanket from the bed to wear as a cape against a chill that might have been imagined. What else? The talkative Recorder, the AAVA drone?

The door sprang into its pocket, startling me, and Nate entered. His green eyes, bright against the biosuit's orange, darted from me to the drone, and his shoulders lost some of their rigidity.

He let out a breath. "The drone's off? Don't go scaring me like that, sweetheart." His gaze drifted from my eyes to my bare legs, then shot back up. His lips quirked into a smile that showed his dimple. "You look nice."

Attempting—and failing—to raise a single brow, I said, "It is but a nightshirt, Nathaniel."

His smile broadened. "Sorry I'm late. The marine at the door made me change. Told him orange wasn't my color, but he insisted."

"He was correct." After a moment's consideration, lest Nate believe I referred to his obscure remark about owning the color orange, I clarified, "You cannot be in my quarantine room without protection."

His expression softened. "I'm pretty sure Shiro is right. I'll be fine. Haven't caught anything yet, and neither has Kye. She'd be down for the count if you were contagious, especially after Freddie . . ." He cleared his throat. "Besides, I'll be going back through that cleaning thing on my way out. The ship and I will be safe enough."

I bit my lip.

Nate crossed the room in three long strides. Instead of immediately telling him why I required his assistance, I buried my face against his chest. His arms encircled me, and his cheek rested against my head, the face shield's rigid sides uncomfortable on my scalp. Though dimmed through the suit's stiff material, the music of his heartbeat felt like home. I closed my eyes and rested against a rhythm that surpassed the resonant beat of the subsonic canons.

This. This is the music for which I had longed.

He eased back and lifted my chin. "You said you needed me."

"I do."

"Don't get me wrong," he said, his voice thicker than usual, "because I'd stay here in an Elder's room with a disemboweled drone, if that's what you wanted, but I know you wouldn't have commed me if you didn't think it was important. You mentioned a datastick."

I jerked backward, drumming my thigh. He caught my hand.

"Ease up, sweetheart," he murmured.

Pulling free, I skirted the chair to place it between us so I would not allow myself to listen to his heart again. Lifting the datastick from the seat, I said, "This."

He accepted it, but his eyes remained steady on mine. "That's the datastick you had on Pallas, isn't it? Freddie's?"

"Yes, and no. Elliott gave it to me."

All gentleness disappeared from Nate's face. "When?"

"He loaded it with information from Ross's computer."

Nate's eyebrows disappeared behind his orange hood, and his fingers fisted around the black datastick.

"I contacted Dr. Clarkson, but she would not come to get it," I admitted. The confession did not ease the sudden pang that he still thought I had called for him on Pallas when, in fact, Kyleigh had contacted Jordan. "I should have known to reach out to you first."

He merely nodded.

"The researchers and authorities must have the information. It might save Patterson or the medic. Or others." I tipped my head to study his face. "If I am not to leave the Elder's quarters without permission, I need help."

His eyes held steady on mine, but his perfect brows met over his nose. "You only just remembered you had it?"

I ducked my head.

"Don't worry," he said. "I'll get the information where it needs to go, and you're going in that medicomputer first chance we get."

All at once, I saw around me the walls of the medicomputer, heard the door lock, heard men arguing. I shrank into myself.

"Hey. Look at me."

I shoved my panic aside and raised my head. "I am looking, my heart."

"You'll go in the medicomputer, right? For me?"

"For you," I whispered, "yes."

He backed to the door, his eyes on mine, then it closed Nathaniel into the vestibule. For uncounted seconds, I watched its unmoving surface before turning back to the drone. Allowing emotions to cloud my reasoning was unsound.

The talkative Recorder—Daniel Parker. I had to save him, as well.

My nose tickled. I dashed to the water closet in search of a tissue, but the nosebleed was of short duration. I disposed of the reddened wad and forced my mind back to crafting an alternate life—and death—for the talkative Recorder.

Falsifying the deaths of both Recorders was simple enough, though I would need to alter the marines' logs as soon as the opportunity presented itself. I disliked saying that either man had been killed and devoured by insects. It felt as though I were making an evil prediction, that I would murder them by accident, even as I had killed the man Skip had called Cord.

My hands shook when I finished and again saved the information to my datapad, and I closed myself in the water closet and doused my head in the sink, then leaned against the wall. Water ran in rivulets down my neck. But the scent of soap did nothing to clean the splotches on my conscience. My lower lip quivered.

Prime numbers: two, three, five, seven, eleven, thirteen . . .

As I listed them, the water ceased to drip like tears from my short curls, and slowly, I pushed myself away from the wall. After eliminating Recorder Mau4531809-3423R and Recorder Gamma4524708-3801-1R, I could save Daniel, too.

Adjusting James's identity had been easy enough, but Daniel's? Uncertainty nagged at me. I had little experience with fiction, but if I remembered correctly, fiction was most believable when it bore a kernel of truth. But which truth? I tapped my thigh. At the very least, I could retain Daniel's birthday, for like all Recorders, his CDN was based on the date of his retrieval from the tanks and the center where he had been donated.

But what had been his education? He had worked in a governmental center. Perhaps a dual degree in liberal arts and political science would serve? Had he told me his middle name? I could not remember. After scrounging through my memory, I settled on the middle name of a marine who had vowed to give up his identity to keep a former Recorder safe. It seemed a fitting honor.

All I had was a name, a birthday, a college degree, and the falsified marine service record. As insufficient as it was, I copied everything onto Freddie's datastick as well as my blue datapad. At least, it was a beginning. I would need to access the ship's records, as well, to be certain that the information I transmitted matched any surviving documentation in *Thalassa*'s computers. My old computer laboratory would have to be my next destination.

I reinserted the datastick with secondary arm control and slid the green datapad into place. Then, I hesitated.

My heart thundered, and the burden of risking two more lives— lives far more precious to me than Cord's had been—made my hands tremble. There was no one to double-check my workmanship, and the consequences of any mistake could destroy those two men and all who endeavored to free them.

Yet, this was what they wanted.

The realization selfishly brought my mind back to my own predicament, and cold seeped through me.

For another three minutes, I stared at the door through which Nathaniel had left, torn between hope and resignation. Whether or not the cure existed or would be found in cats or on a datastick, the Eldest had announced that I must return. My escape would endanger Daniel and James. After all, a mission wherein all aberrations mysteriously disappeared would be highly suspect and call for closer scrutiny. Conversely, a trip in which an Elder and only some of the expendable Recorders and their drones were destroyed by mammoth insects, but one aberrant survived would be believable.

"It is well," I said quietly, though no one was there to hear, and no record was made.

The drone's screen pulsed twice, and I turned away. Once it powered on, there would be nothing else I could do.

Consortium grey filled my hands when I removed a clean tunic and leggings from the closet. The deep rhythm of music beyond human hearing was beautiful, as were the bold yet delicate colors of infrared and ultraviolet. However, the color that mattered most was the green of Nathaniel's eyes. The music that mattered most was his heart beating beneath my cheek.

Sickness, reclamation, death . . . Too many endings. Past and present twisted around each other like DNA into an unfathomable future, one in which freedom seemed unlikely.

I dressed slowly, clasped my hands together to keep from drumming my thigh, and waited.

Perhaps . . . perhaps it was not wrong to look for freedom, for despite the endings all around me, there might be beginnings, as well.

Once the Consortium's network registered the new information, it would take a fraction of a second for Recorders Mau4531809-3423R and Gamma4524708-3801-1R to cease to exist. Whether or not they liked their new names, Daniel Geoffrey Parker and Frederick James Westruther would take their places.

As they should.

27

Elliott tried to ignore the camera mounted over the door. Two days before, when he hurt so bad he could scarcely sit up, Cord had climbed a ladder to aim the blasted thing into the utility closet. Its glassy eye continued to glare balefully. Watching, waiting, though for what, Elliott couldn't tell. Nothing would happen until they let him out, if they ever did. Nothing had happened since he'd been locked in here, except Cord dropping off food and water once in a while, and Skip coming in person to gloat that Freddie was dead.

Elliott's jaw tightened. That lunatic could keep repeating that lie till he rotted to nothing. Words were only words. They didn't prove Freddie was gone.

It couldn't be true.

Elliott paced the closet's length one more time, if it could be called pacing when he could barely limp three full strides. Exhausted, he leaned against the wall and slid to the floor.

Should've taken them all the way back to Pallas Station proper. Should've made sure Freddie had the care he needed.

But he *had* led them the long way to the station proper. No matter how bad off his friend had been, Freddie knew the tunnels and halls as well as Elliott did. Even as sick as Freddie had been, he would have gotten them to safety.

That little voice nagged at him again: *Shouldn't have come back for Julian.*

Except he'd do it all over, given the chance. He meant his promise, years back, that he'd always be there for his brother.

Returning to convince Julian to sneak away hadn't done either of them a micron's worth of good, though. It had been another spectacularly stupid idea in Elliott's long string of stupid ideas. Skip had been waiting to pummel him for stealing Linda's human petri dishes. In front of Julian, too, punishing them both. The anger and anguish in his brother's shouts had almost been as bad as the blows. Elliott rubbed his jaw. The bruises had to be edging from black to green.

Not that he didn't deserve it.

The door flew open and hit the wall with a sharp crack, but Elliott didn't startle, only raised his head.

Kirk stood there, fingering one of his voided knives. "On your feet."

"Why?"

"You want me to make you?"

No, he didn't. Kirk made a big show of practicing with those knives in front of everyone. How far he could throw, how fast. How deep the blade bit.

Elliott drew himself upright and hobbled out the door. After a dozen meters, he slowed, but Kirk punched his back. He tripped as pain spiked.

The tunnel brightened as they approached their control center. If Skip was really as smart as he thought he was, they would've moved deeper into the lava tubes, farther from the station and its roaches, closer to their small ship. Not that Elliott would suggest something that'd help.

They wouldn't listen, anyway.

"Company's here," Kirk announced before muscling Elliott past the woman standing guard.

Elliott saw Julian first. His brother sat at a makeshift desk near the center of the room, well away from any exit, staring unblinkingly at the small screen, occasionally stopping to make notes on his datapad. He looked almost as rough as Elliott felt. The circles under his eyes were as livid as the bruises on Elliott's arms and chest, and Julian obviously hadn't shaved in a couple days. Despite the beard, his cheeks seemed hollow, though maybe that was the lighting. Those lanterns around the room's perimeter threw weird shadows over everything.

Skip spun on his heel to face the door, and for a moment, confusion overrode Elliott's other emotions. If Skip hated the Consortium so much, why would he be wearing that Elder's suit? But, no, an Elder would have a top-of-the-line model. Of course Skip took the best. He had, however, painted over the Consortium eye with red. Probably used Linda's nail polish. She always looked like her fingers were dripping with blood.

Cord left the knot of people sitting in the corner and sauntered to Skip's side. "Been expecting you, roach-boy."

That brought Julian to his feet, his chair scraping against concrete. If looks could kill, Kirk and Cord would have been burnt to ashes.

Skip leaned against the wall's unfinished surface, while Cord widened his stance. The man was living proof that flunkies didn't need brains. Linda, who still wore Kye's stolen suit, glanced up from her computer, bumping a datapad in the process. Its corner hit a delicate gold chain, which spilled unnoticed to glisten on the floor. *Kye's necklace.* He should've taken it back for her, but it was too late now. She was safe in the station, and he was . . . here.

"I told you I'm doing all I can," Julian growled. "Elliott—"

"All you can?" Skip scoffed. "You were supposed to create something that targeted Consortium trogs, not killed off innocent citizens."

Elliott couldn't suppress a snort.

Linda scowled. "You have something to add, miner-boy?"

He shook his head. Maybe if he had the barest hint of a backbone, he would've reminded them that they all—himself included—were scarcely innocent.

Stupid, spineless, weak.

Guilty.

"We'll deal with him later, Linda." Skip's beady eyes stayed on Julian. "You said the tech would lock onto Consortium nanodevices and was transferable by blood."

Julian's nostrils flared. "That's true."

"Actually," Elliott clarified, "saliva—"

"Shut it." Skip dismissed Elliott's comment and glared at Julian. "Little Tristram nearly confirmed it before your brother stole our best chance at unraveling the problem. And now I find out that her files mysteriously went missing?"

Elliott froze. Had he ruined the files when he'd transferred the data? No one had said anything about a missing datastick or disordered information. He couldn't have made a mistake like that, could he? That would've made Julian look guilty. Elliott fisted his hands—surely he hadn't been that sloppy.

Julian's chin lifted infinitesimally.

Sure, his brother had messed up records on *Thalassa.* Had he found out what Elliott had done and deleted things to throw the blame on himself? Stars, Julian wouldn't have—

Elliott's stomach plummeted.

He would have.

"You don't need Tristram anyway, because it isn't the tech," Julian said through clenched teeth. "I told you. Somehow North had Consortium nanites in his system."

"Greg wouldn't have any Consortium filth in his blood." Linda skewered Elliott with a glare. "He hated them all, even before his son was removed, even before his heart attack."

Had Captain North ever owned a heart? Kirk's knife reminded Elliott to keep that nugget to himself.

"Unless *someone* put it there," Linda continued.

"Maybe that's why your pal died," Kirk said in Elliott's ear.

Elliott held absolutely still, reminding himself that Julian's *friends*— what a misnomer that was—had no way of knowing what was going on back in the civilized section of the station. They were baiting him, baiting them both. That was all. Trying to make him pay for smuggling out their prisoners.

His friends *had* to have made it to safety. Freddie would have led them true, and that Recorder had seemed pretty determined when she'd taken the datastick.

Skip was right about one thing, though. Kye was brilliant. Once they reached safety, she'd figure it out. And they probably had researchers up on *Thalassa*. Best in the system.

That was where Julian ought to be, not here. Void it, what a mess.

Skip motioned, and sharp metal suddenly pricked the skin at the base of Elliott's skull.

Kirk's voice went taut. "People—citizens—are dying, Ross. We need that cure."

"If you want to save your brother," Skip added mildly, "you'd better work harder."

Julian's jaw ticced. "I'll cooperate. Let him go."

"Let him go?" Linda sneered. "So he can run to his Consortium friends?"

"Consortium's dead," Cord interrupted. "Bugs. Found part of a tunic in the dust. Showed you."

The Recorder, dead? Or that Elder?

Linda laughed. "Right. I forgot."

What if—

What if they hadn't made it? Bile rose in Elliott's throat at the thought of Freddie or Kyleigh or even the Recorder and that Elder caught by roaches. He'd seen what they'd done to that man who tried to access the computer cave. Cord's statement had to be a lie, too.

Except something told him that it wasn't a lie after all.

"Slouching is a bad habit." Kirk's knife bit a little deeper, and a warm trickle ran down the back of Elliott's neck.

Skip hadn't taken his eyes from Julian. "Prove your commitment, Ross."

Julian slammed his fist onto his crate-desk. "Void it all, Skip, can't you see I'm working on it? What else do you want?"

If Julian caved, more people could die. Elliott drew the deepest breath he could without provoking Kirk to use his knife. "Julian, don't."

"Shut up," Linda snarled. "It's all your fault anyway. That Recorder you mauled probably got her blood on North somehow, and that's what killed him."

Skip glared daggers at Julian. "Your brother needs to face the consequences of burning out hallways to hide which way he went when he kidnapped our guests," he said. "And you need motivation."

At least Elliott had done that right, since Cord's and Kirk's teams hadn't been able to track the escapees down. Despite the metal point between his neckbones, Elliott raised his chin. "Only consequences I see are that you're out people to experiment on."

A hollow grin appeared on Skip's face. "Then it's fair you make up for that, isn't it?"

The knife tip left the back of his neck, and the blade was across his throat as the bite of an injector hit his carotid artery. Cold lanced through him, and his pulse roared in his ears, drowning Julian's cry. The knife disappeared, and Kirk shoved him against the wall so hard that lights flashed like flares. His lip split when his face hit the concrete.

Julian and Skip were shouting at each other, but their words ran together like that time Elliott had fallen into the deep end of the pool and water rushed over his head. That time, Julian had pulled him out. Not now.

He had to stand, had to tell Julian it wasn't worth it. What had Freddie said? To stop hiding behind others? To face his own mistakes? What he wouldn't give to have Freddie tell him one more time.

Ears ringing, Elliott pushed himself up onto his hands and knees, then he used the wall to force himself upright. "Julian."

The room fell silent, and suddenly Julian was at his side, bracing him. And somehow, just then, it was like Elliott saw his brother for the first time. Like they were equals or the same age, despite the eleven years that separated them. He met his brother's eyes, blue locking on blue.

Sudden understanding washed over Elliott. How had he misunderstood that pinched look? Fear practically bled from his brother's face.

"Don't do it, Julian," he pled.

"I have to."

"That isn't true, and you know it, deep down." He swiped at the blood trickling down his chin. "It'll be okay."

Julian's hushed answer seemed too loud. "I can't see how."

"Then I'll see it for you. Just, don't."

"You're my brother." Julian's voice cracked. "Family first."

Cord stormed over and yanked Julian back, but neither spoke. Kirk dragged Elliott over to Linda's computer and threw him against a crate.

"Well." Skip rubbed an invisible smudge on the back of his glove. "The fever hit North in a matter of hours. You had better get to work if you don't want your brother to die like my friend—or like his."

Silence crept through the room.

Julian marched around the crates to his computer, and complex helixes spiraled before him, a translucent barrier of amber and cyan edged with red. Things Elliott had never understood. Never would. Not now.

Time oozed past, and a dull ache filtered through Elliott's bones. Fatigue pulled at him, and his gaze dropped, catching on the gold chain by his feet. When no one was looking, he bent and snatched it up. The cross's sharp edges dug into his palms.

Chills shook him, but he held fast to Kye's necklace, as if it were a lifeline. Maybe it was. Maybe someday he'd be able to ask her about it.

Why was he so voided cold?

A cough scraped from his chest and drew Julian's attention from the spinning display. The lines around Julian's eyes deepened.

No, Elliott didn't understand the helixes and equations and how machines could be as small as molecules. But he did understand this.

He mouthed, *"Don't,"* and then did the one thing he could.

Holding fast to the necklace, Elliott forced his shoulders straight and smiled for his brother.

Once the drone again informed me of my temporary access, I held my breath and typed, >>*Available networks?*

Its screen went blank, then, >>*Internal network acknowledged. Ship-wide network damaged. Consortium network disabled.*

I dropped into the chair, and relief swelled in my chest. No one had witnessed my efforts. James and Daniel were yet safe. I could feed the information as slowly as I needed, hiding it within—

My thoughts crashed to a stop. The Consortium network had been disabled?

>>*When?* I typed. >>*By whom?*

>>*Clarify.*

I bit my lower lip. >>*Who disabled the Consortium network? When?*

>>*Elder Eta4513110-0197E disabled the network on 478.2.5.06 at 15:47.*

"The Elder himself?" The words slipped out, unintended.

>>*Confirmed.*

"But . . ." Why eight days ago? I mentally reviewed the events of last sixth-day. That would have been . . . Rose Parker's death. I caught myself before I uttered her name. "When the first shuttle returned from Pallas?"

>>*Thirty-seven minutes after.*

But what had happened? "Show me."

>>*No neural chip.*

I blinked at the drone before I realized what it meant. I snatched up my blue datapad. "Show me. Utilize visual records of events."

Without any other acknowledgment, images sped past. I watched on my datapad as Jordan escorted Rose Parker's hover gurney onto *Thalassa*. A small monitor at the top of the image displayed Lorik's vital signs. His heart was already racing when he arrived, but when Jackson called the Recorder *Parker*, the Elder's stress hormone levels shot up beyond normal parameters. A spike of self-administered neurochemicals brought his responses under control. With what I knew now—his apology, his name, his concern for the people under his care—his actions took on a different light. He had not been solely concerned for himself, but also for the Recorder. For Rose Parker.

The records lost a degree of dimensionality when they split. A tiny image from his slave drone showed Rose Parker, Cam, and me on our way to the quarantine room, while the second image showed the Elder refusing to comply with Jordan's and Jackson's demands to release the Recorder into Max's care. My focus darted between the two scenes, lingering in the quarantine room. The recorded, miniscule version of me turned to the door as the drone locked Cam out, and he shouted for me. While recorded-me turned to fetch the dying Recorder a drink of water, my attention flitted back to the Elder. Hormones indicating fear and anger surged. Lorik sprinted to stop me from harming her, checking the few working cameras as he ran. He had known Jackson was on his way when he had issued the command to leave the door open.

The perspectives united again, and there, on the screen, I saw myself, aghast at the Elder's apparent lack of concern. A blip in the record verified that Lorik had lied, had tricked the marines into promising not to reveal how Rose Parker had died. His threat to withhold medication to ease Parker's pain was that—merely a threat.

Lorik had hidden his reaction to the subsequent reprimand well.

On my datapad, tiny-Jackson's eyebrows slammed together, his anger evident to Lorik and noted in the record. The marine held out his hand to apply his thumbprint and sign the nondisclosure agreement. His words sounded with unusual strength for the miniscule images, as if the Elder had granted them more weight than they should have had: "I'll do it. We all will."

The documentation ceased.

My datapad's screen flickered. >>End of transmitted records. Network disabled.

I sagged against the wall. Lorik might have watched through the camera, but he had told the truth. No one else had seen Parker die or witnessed the marines' farewell. Or had they?

"Access ship's records," I said. "Display documentation of the Recorder's disposal."

The drone showed me official documentation of death and cremation, such as any Center for Reclamation and Recycling might issue.

"Insufficient," I protested. "Play records from the event itself."

>>*No record exists. Certificate of Disposal available.*

Impossible. "How?"

>>*Camera not functional.*

There was one more place to check, so I typed, >>*Transcription of personal record for Elder Eta4513110-0197E. Date 478.2.5.07.*

I skimmed the files. The Elder had neither recorded Rose Parker's death nor prioritized the repair of *Thalassa's* Consortium devices. In fact, his last log entry stated that transmissions from Recorders on Pallas had ceased, that he suspected accidents. The official message had been transmitted to the Consortium over the ship's communications links.

He had never reactivated the network.

I dropped down onto the unmade bed, the datapad clasped to my chest. The marines were safe. Every marine who had sung as Rose Parker was cremated, every marine who had shaved his or her head out of respect for the Recorder called Parker. *Safe.*

We were all far safer than we had thought.

Lorik would have been sentenced to the Halls for interfering with the record, but according to his personal logs, that decision had been made long before he had faced the roaches.

A knot formed in my throat. I had not known. No one would have known, if I had not accessed his logs. Shame trickled like water.

"I am sorry," I whispered to the man who had died so I would not.

The datapad buzzed in my hand.

>>*Reenter security codes to access files.*

Had I not already viewed the files? My forehead scrunched, but I again input Lorik's codes. Once more, the screen blurred with letters, numbers, and images, but these did not belong to the Elder.

"Stop!"

The images and letters froze, and the skin on my neck prickled.

"These personal records belong to the Recorder assigned to Pallas Station?"

>>*Recorder Eta4311101-1348R.*

The answer was as uninformative as it was meant to be, since

Recorders had no names. "I do not recognize that number. Was she stationed on Pallas as Recorder?"

>>*Yes.*

Her datapad, the damaged green one . . .

When I had opened it for the first time, there had been no layers of security. Instead, a small recording had played in which she explained her suspicions of conspiracy to create a bioweapon. She had supplied an index of materials that had disappeared, including medication that may have ended her life. I had believed that the lack of evidence was to protect potentially innocent citizens, though, if memory served, she had mentioned Parliament's fear of potential corporate espionage. Or had the lack of information been based on her inherent distrust of citizenry?

I tapped my leg.

Anyone could have found the datapad, but not everyone could have found her files. Only an Elder would be able to open her personal records.

For three seconds, I hesitated. My original goal outside my assignment from the Elders had been to track down Kyleigh's father's murderer. This . . . this might help me do so.

"Play the recordings."

>>*Datapad insufficient.*

"Other than a neural implant, what will suffice?" I stood, staring at the empty frame across from me. I held up a hand. "No, do not answer. Reserve VVR."

>>*Power restrictions prohibit unauthorized usage of VVR. At current rate of repair, next available VVR slots will be 478.2.8.09. Reserving first slot at 04:30.*

Two and a half ten-days?

"There must be a way to display partial records." I pursed my lips. "Create index and display on the linked datapad. Add alarm for VVR reservation."

I set the datapad on the chair again and turned to the drone, but before anything flashed across its screen, my communications link chimed.

"Got the datastick to Edwards," Nate said without preamble. "We copied it all and sent it both to Archimedes and to the virologists. Took longer than I thought."

"Thank you," I said, though I watched the datapad, which continued to say nothing.

"That drone on?"

"Yes." The delay in his response drew me from my introspection. "Timmons?"

"Still here." The communications link magnified his exhalation. "Look, I—we—need you to suit up."

"Why?" I asked, though I was already crossing to retrieve the lightly armored suit that was not entirely mine.

"You're heading down to Pallas."

"I do not understand, Nathaniel." I hastily added his surname. "Timmons. Nathaniel Timmons. Yesterday, you and the captain were adamant that I remain on *Thalassa* for my own safety. What has happened?"

"We're expecting company."

I turned as if I would see Nate, my hand on the cleaning unit's door. "Clarify." Perhaps I had been spending too much time with the drone. I modified my query. "What do you mean by 'company'?"

His voice sounded tight, even over the communications link. "The Consortium is on its way."

I pulled the suit over my Consortium tunic and leggings by rote, nearly unaware of the room about me, seeing instead the holding cell on *Agamemnon*. If the other ship arrived before I returned to Pallas Station, I would not endanger my friends by resisting arrest. Another holding cell would be my fate.

Nate had assured me that the other ship would not arrive for several hours, but fear for my friends and fear of confinement sped my movements as I tugged on the skullcap and fastened the helmet. Then the drone's statement flashed through my memory, and momentary relief flickered.

The network was down.

If it had not been and I had attempted to upload new identities when the Consortium was this close, they might have witnessed the switch. I would have condemned us all in an attempt to create safety.

My fist tapped my armored thigh.

If I could . . . but could what? If I returned to Pallas, would I not lead the Consortium straight to James? If they knew I had Lorik's drone, would it not be worse? And even though both former Recorders had jamming devices, the range was small. Unless they, too, hid, the Consortium could find them.

My stomach churned as I proceeded through the vestibule. When I exited, I had found no solution, though I had wrestled my fears to manageable levels.

Cam waited for me outside the door, but his salutation died on his lips when he saw the drone. He wiped his palm on his pant leg and said, "The captain wants to talk to you."

"Very well."

"I suppose you know you're going down to Pallas later?"

"Yes. Timmons informed me."

"Tia got the incoming message last night." Cam's attention ranged the empty hall, as if he scanned for adversaries. "The busted comm array garbled it, and Smith couldn't–Eric says wouldn't–figure it out."

Pride lifted my heart. Tia had done well.

Cam's lips pinched, then he asked, "What did Timmons tell you?"

"That the Consortium is on its way."

"It's not their ship, though, not like *Agamemnon*. Marshalcy. SGS *Attlee*, out of Krios Platform Forty-One." His jaw tensed. "But Tia says they have Elders and Recorders onboard."

I suppressed a shiver.

"Evidently, they knew something went wrong days ago. Authorities suspected pirates, which is why they're sending *Attlee*." Cam exhaled heavily. "I don't know if I should say this in front of a drone or not, but I rather wish that when they show up, they blast those murdering, genocidal terrorists into atoms."

I did not tell Cam that a murderer walked beside him.

We continued to the meeting room in silence, and when we reached it, people were dispersing into the hall. The marine from the shuttle nodded at me as she jogged past, but when Nate followed her, dressed in his usual black but with a green-and-white mourning band on his upper arm, he did not greet us. Archimedes Genet exited the room beside a woman in engineering blue, and inside the room, Edwards himself gathered a stack of slim datapads.

"All I can say is that if they have parts and food, they're more than welcome." The woman's jaw muscles jumped. "Without assistance, we'll be luck to limp back to the closest Krios platform, never mind making it all the way to Lunar One."

"I'm well aware of that." Archimedes frowned. "And yes, *Attlee* has technicians and parts."

"And more Recorders." The woman shot a glare in my direction, then nodded at Archimedes. "Captain." She strode away, already discussing repairs over her communications link.

Datapads cradled in the crook of his arm, Edwards emerged into the hall. "I am certain this will be a good thing."

The datapad in my thigh pocket buzzed, and I pulled it out.

>>*Suspected untruth.*

Nate raked his fingers through his hair, which flopped back down over his eyebrows. A lump rose in my throat. I wanted to touch his hair, to hold his hand, to hear his heart again, but the virus, my gloves, the drone, and the constant threat of event after event prevented those small acts. For the space of two seconds, the inequity of our situation blazed.

"Ah, there you are," Edwards said, bringing my attention back. "Did young Rodriguez inform you that a tribunal of Elders assigned to the closest mining platform noticed that the Consortium network went down nearly a ten-day ago?"

"He told me that they knew."

"They'll be here in about six hours." Nate's jaw tightened. "But you won't."

I straightened as indiscernible emotion hit me, though whether it was selfish hope for myself or fear for his defiance, I could not tell.

Archimedes Genet inclined his head. "Unfortunately, as Timmons and I were discussing, you won't be here to greet them."

"It is entirely my fault that you must return to the surface," Edwards put in, but his pale-blue eyes twinkled. "I will need someone with a scientific background to take medical supplies to Dr. Maxwell and relocate equipment, allowing further research into the virus's origins."

I did not comment on the flimsiness of his excuse. The datapad in my hand buzzed again, but I ignored it.

"The shuttle will be arriving in an hour and a half. I want you on it," the captain said. "However, Nathaniel Timmons has brought it to my notice that we need some information from you."

"She's done more than comply," Cam interjected. When Archimedes Genet quirked a brow, Cam flushed. "Sorry, sir. Out of line."

"She has, but we do," Nate said, following up on the captain's comment. "We need a full medicomputer scan."

Archimedes nodded. "Since you were exposed to the virus but haven't succumbed, you'll head to the infirmary for that scan and to have blood drawn. They need more samples."

I opened my mouth to protest. Nate's compressed but indecipherable expression stopped me.

"When you board the shuttle," the captain continued, "any and all Consortium tech will remain behind." A thin tendril twined around my neck, and his face grew taut. "Whomever the Consortium sends will collect it when they arrive to take the incapacitated Recorder from the infirmary–"

"I still say we send that Recorder to Max." Edwards straightened to his full height. "If they take the ship's Recorder back–"

The captain said, "No," and the datapad buzzed simultaneously.

"She'll die," Edwards argued.

"For those few moments she retained her faculties, she demanded to be returned." The captain shook his head. "We not only have to acknowledge her final wishes, but also that she's Consortium."

"But"–Nate's eyes focused on me–"*you* aren't."

Archimedes Genet glanced at the drone. "You'll leave that tech aboard when you head down to Pallas."

"I will not."

The drone eased what would have been a stranglehold, save for the armored suit, and rose several decimeters to hover directly over my head.

Nate's jaw ticced, and Cam sucked in a breath. Even the captain took half a step back. Only Edwards had no visible reaction.

"I cannot," I said more gently. "We have work to do."

"We?" Edwards asked.

I did not answer. If they insisted that I relocate to the surface, I would. Whatever they thought, however, I could not abandon Lorik's drone on *Thalassa* where the Consortium representatives would retrieve it. My discovery of personal logs within the drone's memory made it more dangerous than my friends believed, for I had not deleted Lorik's records.

Beyond that, somewhere, deep within the station Recorder's logs lay the possibility of evidence regarding Kyleigh's father's murder. I could not walk away from that small favor, not when she had already lost even more with Freddie's death.

My head throbbed. I did not have enough time, and concentration grew harder and harder. It was then that, like a lead weight in heavy gravity, my stomach seemed to drop.

"Zeta?" Cam asked. "You went white as a sheet. Are you all right?"

The corridor blurred before me, overlaid with a memory of the cavernous Hall of Reclamation. In addition to all else, all records of James and Daniel must be cleared from *Thalassa*'s databanks. It was absolutely necessary to ascertain that the ship Recorder's drone carried no information that would contradict the falsehoods I had created to facilitate my friends' escape.

The drone sent a mild reprimand, merely a hint of pain, sufficient to pull me back.

Nate tapped my shoulder. "Hey, look at me."

I raised my eyes to his, despite the drone's presence. "I am looking."

His mouth opened, but he clamped it shut, as if to halt words that could not be unsaid.

"Timmons. Rodriguez," Archimedes said.

"Sir?"

I, too, turned to the captain.

His forehead creased. "Get her in that scanner as soon as possible."

"Yes, sir," Cam said.

Nate's jaw muscle pulsed, but he made a sweeping motion, almost like a bow. "Shall we, then?"

Nathaniel's gesture nearly brought a smile. Then, realization struck, and I sobered. My friends were risking themselves to save me.

I, in turn, would bear anything to save them.

Cam and Nate escorted me into the infirmary, where Alec waved from a hoverbed by the door. I left the drone outside the temporary vestibule beside the medicomputer and removed my suit. Edwards donned his orange hood before joining me in a small area sectioned off with sheeting. I heard Cam and Nate speaking to Alec in undertones while Edwards drew several vials of blood.

As it had last time, the sight of the closet-like medicomputer's metallic door sent a trickle of fear down my spine. Feeling oddly exposed, I padded on stockinged feet into its red-lit interior, reminding myself that the medicomputer itself was not a threat. No one here—not even the drone—intended me ill. I whispered to myself that all would be well, that there was no danger, but my fingers tightened around the bed's railing.

Edwards closed the door, and the lock clicked.

I focused on the warm red light and began reciting prime numbers, but when the machine's clicks began, panic jabbed sharp claws through my chest. Oxygen seemed to vanish. Each gasp burned my throat and brought another clash of pain. The machine's alarm blared in my ears, and beyond that, men shouted.

The alarm ceased abruptly when the door flew open. Long tendrils grabbed me and pulled me out of the narrow closet and into the air. I struggled, but the drone's grip grew tighter. It lofted me higher. Sweat beaded on my upper lip, and tears oozed down my face. The room swam, dizziness engulfed me, and I clamped my eyes shut.

Sound edged past the roar of my pulse in my ears and the drone's whine.

"Put her down," Nate demanded crisply. "No one is going to harm her."

Edwards echoed Nathaniel's assertion, and strangely, the drone complied, lowering me to the floor. I huddled in a fetal position while a rush of air and sound told me the drone shot its arms around me like a cage.

"What is that drone doing?" Cam seemed to choke on the words.

"I do not know. Neither do I know what went wrong. She did not have a problem before that Elder took her away." Edwards's voice softened as he added, "I apologize, Recorder. I forgot that you had a difficult time the last time we used the medicomputer, but I assure you: nothing has gone amiss."

I peeked through damp lashes. Edwards crouched near me, Nate behind him. Cam stood rigid at Alec's bedside, and Alec's gloveless hand gripped Cam's arm, while his bed sang gentle alarms.

Edwards glanced at the drone. "Release her so she may have treatment."

One long arm retreated, opening my cage. When Nate took a step forward, however, it pounded back down.

"Wait, Timmons." Edwards held out his hand, and his pale-blue eyes found mine. "I know you know, deep within, that it is well. Perhaps, if you could tell the drone?"

Recognizing the truth in his request, I tapped the drone's polymer underbelly, and two legs retreated. Ignoring the proffered hand, I scooted out, but when I stood on wobbly legs, the world spun. My vision blurred. Tendrils reached for me, but someone shoved them aside and caught me when I dropped. My fingers curled around black fabric as a jet injector popped, and the scents of lavender and pine washed through me. My eyes closed, my breathing slowed, and my muscles relaxed.

The belief that everything would be—already was—fine wrestled with the knowledge that something was wrong. The scent of pine, internal and external, began to override the panic lodged in my chest. Someone was in danger, but either lassitude or contentment—perhaps both—stole the impetus to act.

"Over here, Timmons." Edwards's voice echoed as if he spoke through a long tube.

I was lowered into a chair where I slumped against the armrests.

Men continued to debate my state of being and possible overmedication, but I simply did not care. The whir of a drone approached, but the warm, strong hand that held mine did not let go. I forced heavy lids up to see Nate kneeling before me.

"What's going on?" He gave my fingers a faint squeeze.

Warm haziness kept me from answering, but my Nathaniel was here. Everything would be fine.

"I think I know, sir," Cam said hesitantly. "There was an . . . incident on *Agamemnon*."

"What happened?" Nate asked, his gaze still holding mine.

"One of the engineers locked her in the medicomputer. He thought she carried the virus, so he tried to override safety protocols to start a cleaning cycle."

Nate pivoted toward Cam. Even though Cam's stammered recitation of the events seemed to be about someone else, my apprehension flared. Had that truly happened? Would I not be more concerned, if it had?

Alec growled a curse.

"And you never thought to tell anyone?" Edwards demanded.

"You're right. I should have. But when we came aboard, the processing officer in the shuttle said not to talk about *Agamemnon*, that the information was the Consortium's. We all had to sign waivers," Cam explained. "The man died back on *Agamemnon*. It's on record, sir, since the Elder was there."

Nate cupped my face with his hand, his thumb lingering on my cheekbone, and for a moment I leaned against his palm. He growled, "I suppose that's something to be grateful to the Elder for."

Footsteps approached, and Edwards asked me if I thought I could manage the medicomputer again. "We'll talk you through it, like Max and I did last time."

Summoning all my energy, I forced out, "Not alone."

In near unison, Alec, Cam, and Nate said, "You aren't."

The effects of whatever medication Edwards had given me receded while I was in the medicomputer, but it was not until I was on a hoverbed that I realized I was not in a suit. Panic chased away rest. People had touched me, and sheeting no longer separated me from the rest of the infirmary. Additionally, I had held Nate's bare hand with the drone present. Our interactions had been recorded.

Too late, my insufficient hands covered my mouth.

Edwards turned abruptly from his computer. He glanced at my bed's readout, then slid a datapad from a capacious orange pocket. "You are awake, finally."

Nate shifted in the chair beside my bed, and on the other side, the drone rose seven centimeters at his movement.

Alec rolled over to watch me. Next to the infirmary doors, Cam grinned. No one save Edwards wore orange, and not even he wore headgear. I could not understand such laxity.

"Edwards, it is unsafe. I am not in my suit." My voice, muffled by my hands, faltered.

"You are not." A half smile flashed briefly. "The medicomputer declared you virus-free."

Relief hit me in a wave, and my hands dropped. "I am not contagious?"

"Indeed not. Your symptoms are not due to the bioweapon." Without making eye contact, he tapped a few notes on the datapad.

Nate studied his fingers. "You've been out of it for a while. You'll need to suit up again once the shuttle arrives. *Attlee* should be here in about four hours, and we need to get you well below the surface if we're to keep you safe."

Uneasiness edged through me, but the timeline was not my primary concern. "Edwards," I began, "to what are my symptoms due, if not to the bioweapon?"

Nate leaned forward, elbows on his knees, and his eyes rose to Edwards. "It's a good question."

"Not to the virus." Edwards heaved a sigh. "But when Kyleigh gets here, I'm having her take a look at your blood."

That was as forthcoming as he was, no matter how Nate or I pressed for information. Edwards handed me another vile, green, fizzy drink, even though I told him I would rather take my calories and nutrition through protein bars and supplements. I tried not to gag as I drank as fast as I could.

"Alec," I ventured after finishing the beverage. He looked over, but no smile lit his features as he stared past me at the drone. "You are healing?"

"Yeah." His hand rose to the deep black and purple bruising showing above his medical gown's V-neck. "Swallowing hurts a bit, but I can breathe, which is always good."

"It is."

"Been thinking a lot about things I should have done." His chocolate-brown gaze drifted from me to Nate to the ceiling. "At least between Archimedes and that rotted Elder, Zhen and I renewed our contract before we left. Should have taken a longer one, but I also should have made sure that my father's debt wasn't linked to her. She shouldn't be burdened with it if I . . ." His focus latched onto the light fitting in the center of the infirmary. "That box. Should've opened it years ago. Could've died without knowing what's in it."

Though I had no knowledge of any box, I protested, "But you did not die."

"No." He fingered his blanket's hem. "Nate."

Beside me, my Nathaniel startled but said nothing about Alec's use of his nickname.

"I want that box, the one I've been carting around since my mother's accident. Zhen's on the shuttle, right?"

Nate nodded.

"Once everyone finishes debriefing, can you bring her here?"

"I don't think I'll have to force her to come," Nate said with a lopsided smile. "But sure."

Alec regarded him steadily. "I should never have stopped calling you *Nate*. Mama never did, and she was usually right."

"Yeah. She was."

Alec turned to me. "Someday, I'll show you a picture of my sister."

A knot rose in my throat. "Arianna."

"You remind me of her, once in a while." His long exhale was almost a sigh. "Stars, but I miss her."

The infirmary's quiet was undergirded by the circulation fans' thrum, the centrifuge's click, the medtanks' burble, and the constant whir of the drone.

The drone.

It would document Alec's regret over his shattered family, which could place him at risk. I pushed away the thin, white cotton blanket and swung my legs over the side of the bed.

"Where do you think you're going?" Nate asked.

"You said the shuttle will arrive soon."

"There was a delay. Issues in coordinating departure and arrival without comms. It's about thirty minutes out."

"When it arrives, we will leave immediately?"

"As immediately as possible, yes."

I could not tell him the whole truth, which was not, I assured myself, the same thing as lying. "I have work to do, and the best place to do it will be my old computer laboratory. First, however, I must return to the Elder's quarters to leave it tidy and retrieve equipment to repair the drones on Pallas."

"Repair the . . ." Nate studied my face. "Let me guess. You don't need my company for that."

"Indeed."

"Too bad." Nathaniel grimaced as he stood. "Cam? You ready?"

"Yes, sir."

"Nate," Alec spoke up again. "You'll get Zhen? And that box?"

"I promise."

"If you are carrying off linens and clothing, you will need this." Edwards handed me an empty duffel bag.

We left the infirmary, Nate on my right, Cam on my left, and the drone behind me. They remained outside while I changed the sheets and removed every bit of evidence that I had been in the Elder's quarters, including the microdatacard in the headboard and any information saved in the headboard's memory. After verifying that the network remained down, I took Lorik's repair kit, but paused at the door, eyeing the empty frame.

"What does it say?" I asked aloud.

The datapad buzzed, and I read, >>*Clarify.*

"The daily aphorism."

>>*Shed the past as a snake sheds its skin, and so conquer the inner chaos that breeds fear.*

"That is hardly helpful," I protested.

>>*Interpretations available upon request.*

"I do not need one."

It would have been injudicious at best to tell the drone that it was shedding the past that provoked my fear.

31

The Elder's door closed behind me with a click, and Nate and Cam escorted me to my computer laboratory. They waited in the hall, and for five seconds, I stood in the doorway and studied the room.

The destroyed Consortium computer had been replaced with a standard public-usage one, and patchwork antistatic tiles marked where someone had replaced the scorched and peeling flooring. The charging station that had electrocuted both me and Julian Ross had been repaired, but the same workplace safety posters stared back at me.

I crossed to my favorite computer station and commanded the drone. "Over here."

It complied.

While my fingers summoned information, my mind wandered back to the exceedingly unclear aphorism in the Elder's quarters. The definition of irony eluded me. Was it ironic that the Consortium's daily saying told me to shed the past?

"Everything okay in there?" Nate called from the hallway.

"Yes."

I drew a deep breath and attempted to obey the aphorism in the way least intended: erasing records.

But when I opened the proper programs and checked *Thalassa*'s footage, my concern about records was proven unfounded. The EM cannon's damage to the ship's records was more extensive than the damage Julian Ross had caused before he, Elliott, and Captain North had fled *Thalassa*. It even exceeded the damage I had done when I destroyed what he left untouched. Though I could do nothing to further obfuscate the information, I frowned all the same.

While nothing remained to betray us, hiding new identities in these shattered records was impossible. Unable to transmit the data from the network, unable to sneak information into the ship's records, I was at a loss as to how to save the two men.

The other Consortium access point would have been the injured Recorder's drone, but if she had been incapacitated by the EM cannon, it must have been destroyed. I rubbed my temples, but doing so did nothing to summon new ideas.

A communications link sounded nearby, and Nate's muffled voice came from the hall. After several seconds, he appeared in the doorway.

"You about done? We're running out of time," he said. "Engineering needs me to check the chem system before I get that box and find Zhen."

"It is well. Go on."

His mouth quirked to the side. "Don't think so."

"It is well," I repeated. "I must check on the ship Recorder's drone. Cam can escort me, if he has not been assigned elsewhere."

After a short, muted conversation with the younger man, Nate said, "I don't like it, but that'll have to do. Not sure if Archimedes will let me go back to Pallas until my clavicle's healed up, but I'll see you before you board that shuttle."

His boots beat out a steady rhythm as he left.

I turned to the drone and used the first excuse that came to mind. "I must ascertain that the Recorder's drone is secure. Remain here and safeguard the computers until I return."

>>*Acknowledged.*

Leaving all else, I picked up the repair kit and the duffel bag containing my laundry. The computer laboratory door closed behind me with a click.

Cam accompanied me to the Recorder's quarters, which I opened with relative ease. The drone had fallen on its own arms, crushing them beneath itself. There was no power, no way of turning it on, and black singed the sides of its access panel. I pried it open. Just as the fail-safe had destroyed the computer in my laboratory those ten-days ago, this drone was beyond recovery. No amount of forensic research would dig through its chemically disintegrated innards to discover Consortium secrets or records.

A rush of conflicting emotions hit me. Gratitude, that although the Elders had programmed a self-destruct sequence for EM cannons, they had not done so for the impossible, unforeseeable chance that giant roaches would tear drones apart. If they had, I could not have made the jammers. Relief, that I did not need to search through data and remove evidence. The twins of fear and self-doubt, for no drone, indeed no one at all, would be able to assist me as I tried to hide my friends.

I closed the panel, repacked the tools, and joined Cam at the door.

"Edwards commed me." He hoisted my laundry bag over his shoulder. "Everyone's waiting in the infirmary."

"Very well." I refrained from pointing out that *everyone* was a misnomer.

Neither of us spoke as we traversed the hallways. We had not reached the lift to the lower level when Cam's communications link chimed.

Tia's disembodied voice sounded. "Cam, you're requested in meeting room B17."

"I promised Timmons I would take Zeta to—"

"Edwards cleared her. She'll be fine. Meeting room B17." Tia paused, then whispered, "Cam, you have to go. Not only did the captain request it, but there's talk of sending you back. I don't know why, but you need to make sure they don't. Who knows where you'll end up."

Cam paled.

"It is likely for your safety," I said.

"Then why not me and Eric, too?" she demanded.

Cam's mouth pulled to the side. "Eric's useful. You are, too, even given your situation."

She huffed. "B17." The link stopped abruptly.

He rubbed his palm on his pant leg. "Zeta, you good with going on without me?"

"It is *Thalassa*." I held out my hand for the laundry, and he looped the handle over my arm. "Additionally, Nate understands orders."

"I don't like it," Cam said before he strode away.

Seven seconds ticked past as I stood in the hall, concern for Cam—for them all—tumbling through my mind. If I could somehow upload the new identities without betraying my friends, James and Daniel might be able to walk away, but I would not. The idea that I was bound for destruction in the future, however, did not alter the fact that I needed to go to the laundry room, the infirmary, and then retrieve Lorik's drone.

The circulation fans brushed air against my skin. Pressing needs came rushing back, but I continued, bag in hand. My mind raced exponentially faster than my feet trudged.

Lorik's last words to me had been to have faith, though he had not specified the foundation for his admonition. The concepts of hope and faith blurred in my mind, their meanings overlapping, melding into something beyond the unreasonable optimism I had always believed they implied.

Even though anticipation of my friends' freedom carried no guarantee, it was what I worked for. Though based in my limited abilities and despite my failures and the life my mistakes had cost, was that hope? To work toward a goal despite uncertainty?

I had no reason to be optimistic about my future, and the good in my present was unmerited. My past and my present were my only certainties. I could not assert with finality that James and Daniel would be free, that I had not assigned all of us to removal and the Halls. Did any of us have a future? Not one of us could secure days yet to come, so was claiming it an act of . . . faith? Kyleigh's confidence in her unquantifiable God seemed to have wavered, but perhaps she was incorrect. Perhaps the very immeasurable nature of such a God made its acts unfathomable to finite creations.

My footsteps slowed, for intricacies upon intricacies seemed to speak to something beyond mere reason.

The gifting of Max's unborn twins shaped his life, enabling him to save my own. I had not died, and my specific training had led me to discover the bioweapon and alert the Consortium. I had suggested the Eldest send condemned Recorders to Pallas, and when she authorized their presence, she had saved Max's son.

Coincidence seemed an insufficient explanation, but did that point to something beyond my understanding? I stopped in the middle of the hall, and people dodged around me, offering low, polite excuses.

Like the promise of delicate wings inside an ungainly caterpillar, a chrysalis of hope—and perhaps faith—dissolved who I was in order to shape me into something else.

Or, not *perhaps* after all.

I squared my shoulders and changed course, heading for the laundry before collecting the drone. While I needed to return the bedding, more importantly, I needed something to wear that was not Consortium grey.

32

Last quarter, when I had traversed *Thalassa*'s corridors, crew members had gawked at my unsanctioned hair and attire. This time, greetings and occasional smiles bolstered my fluctuating confidence. The cumulative weight of the microdatacard, Freddie's datastick, and my datapad pulled at my thigh pocket. My black pants and jacket felt more natural than my greys had. I had considered asking for a mourning band—for Freddie, for Lorik, even for Lytwin—but the words had stuck in my throat. It was as well. My friends would understand that those lives weighed on me, with or without any braided fabric.

The deep green of my shirt, however, pleased me even more. Every swish of fabric as I walked proclaimed, *my shirt, my shirt*, though with the jacket properly fastened, no one knew of my small rebellion.

The infirmary doors parted, and when Nate saw me, his mouth quirked into a brief smile. Edwards was entering data at a medtank's terminal, but when Kyleigh rotated away from her old computer, her faint, welcoming smile seemed heavy, as if it took enormous effort. Jordan arced a brow. Zhen waved me forward but remained at Alec's bedside, while Alec himself studied a cerulean box.

The doors clicked behind me, and I approached the foot of Alec's bed. He turned the box over in his hands. Its blue shone in the infirmary's bright light.

"Well, she's finally here." Zhen eased onto the bed beside him and tucked a loose curl behind his ear. "You've delayed long enough."

He had waited for me? The thought sparked a burst of warmth in my chest.

Alec inhaled. "I know I have." He set the lid aside.

Rare enough in their own right, a stack of paper envelopes filled the box to the top, but they were more unusual since, despite their tattered appearance, no Consortium-approved stamp certified delivery.

"She numbered them." Alec sifted through the letters until he found an envelope with the numeral one circled on the lower right-hand corner. He opened the envelope's flap and removed the contents as carefully as if he handled explosives. "Am I doing the right thing?"

"You are doing what your mother asked," Zhen whispered. "Go ahead, babe."

He began to scan the document, his forehead creasing as he read. Within seconds, he stopped. His face went suddenly and utterly pale. His hoverbed beeped, pulling Edwards from the medtank, but Alec batted everyone back and read it again.

"This . . . this is from my father."

Jordan's brows met over her nose. "We knew as much."

Alec's hand trembled as he held out the letter.

Zhen snatched it away, then gasped. "Alec, this is dated sixteen years ago!"

Seconds of quiet were shattered when Nate whooped. Alec dumped the box onto his bed and dug through the papers while I tried to remember why sixteen years mattered.

"The most recent one," Alec croaked. "I need the most recent one!"

Multiple hands pushed papers aside, scattering them over the bed. Multiple voices called out numbers. A picture fluttered to the ground, and I picked it up without a glance at the image.

"Twenty-nine!" Jordan held an envelope above her head. She shoved it into Alec's hand. "Open it!"

He tugged the letter out and skimmed the handwritten words as the headboard continued its mild alarm.

"Alexander Spanos," Edwards commanded, "you must remain calm."

"You don't understand. My father"—Alec's chest rose and fell quickly—"my father is alive, or was four years ago."

Kyleigh sprang to her feet. "He wasn't removed?"

"He was. My sister was dying, and he'd blamed the Consortium too loudly and too often. A man in green came with a Recorder, and the next day, my father left. He never came home. I assumed—I thought they'd killed him."

"Stars above." Jordan beamed. "This is the best news of the year!"

Suddenly, her breath caught, and she spun to face me, her braids fanning around her shoulders. "A man in green said that's what happened to my cousin. Is there a chance Gerry's alive, too?"

"I do not know for certain. It is possible." A ripple of guilt mocked my previous contentment. I should have checked.

Jordan sank onto the foot of Alec's bed. Her beads clattered as her head slumped into her hands.

"Moons and stars." Zhen's eyes widened. "Your cousin, too?"

"They notified her family during her graduation party," Nate said.

Zhen fingered the end of her blue plait. "Intimidation?"

"From what I remember, I'd say so."

Jordan raised her head, and her golden-brown eyes shone. "Gerry, not dead. Stars."

"Even so, that's a decade at least for Gerry, and"—Nate glanced at the letter in Alec's hand—"another four at least for Alec's dad. My mother didn't last four years in those mines."

Zhen speared Nate with a glare. "They'll be there. They'll be fine."

"The first letter—I put it down right here." Alec scrabbled through the envelopes, pictures, certificates. "He was pressed into service to pay off fines for speaking against the Consortium. Wound up on a planetoid orbiting Krios. Which one? Blast it, Nate. I *knew* those fines should have been larger. The pittance we've paid shouldn't have made a dent." He found it, and his eyes darted across the page, then rotated it to read the crossed lines. "Someone in external processing knew a freighter who smuggled letters in exchange for food and medical rights."

Zhen made a peculiar noise. "He gave up food and medical to get this out?"

"Which mine?" Nate demanded. "How did your mom contact him?"

Alec shook his head. "This doesn't—wait—no." He squinted at the page and marked a place with his index finger. "Krios-A137, Mining Site 12. He says she can send a reply care of"—he glanced at the page—"someone named Swokowski. On MTS *Ibis*." He slung the covers away and tried to stand, but Zhen stopped him.

"What do you think you're doing?"

"I can't sit here."

Protestations tumbled over each other, and finally, Jordan's voice rose above the rest.

"You don't have a choice," she said almost roughly. "I'm sorry, Alec, but we're stuck. I want to find him and Gerry, too, but we're tilapia in a pond here. Even when *Thalassa* regains functionality, we have to get the cure back to New Triton."

Before Zhen could snipe an answer at Jordan, Alec spoke. "Then I'll track down *Ibis* and whoever Swokowski is." He groaned. "But that EMP fried the memory banks."

I should have searched for Gervase Singh and Alec's father. My attention dropped to the picture I held. A handsome little boy with deep-brown curls held the hands of a laughing toddler above her head as she took a flat-footed step.

Alec and Arianna.

The unfairness of what terrorists and the Consortium had stolen from Alec and countless others smote me again. When the Consortium network reactivated, I could redeem some of the damage my people had done, but doing so would betray my usage of Lorik's drone, which would betray James and Daniel. My stomach twisted.

Nate touched the back of my hand. "You've got that look on your face, sweetheart. Have you thought of something?"

All conversation ceased. All focus shifted to me.

"Yes, and no." I dared not drum my thigh with Zhen present. "If I used the Consortium's network—"

"It's running?" Alec interrupted quickly.

"No." The medtanks burbled in the quiet while I studied the twenty-nine envelopes and the family pictures scattered on Alec's white cotton blanket. "But theoretically, I could utilize the Elder's drone to search for your father. I believe I can hide the former Recorders' identities safely in other data, but I am not . . . confident. Reactivation might lead the Consortium straight to me and betray both James and Daniel."

"Recorder-who-isn't-and-needs-a-name," Alec said as if it were a name in truth.

I blinked back moisture and met his gaze. "Yes?"

"Even though your guesses are more reliable than most people's facts, don't do anything to put yourself or anyone else at risk." The letter crinkled as his fingers clenched. "And it might."

The only protest I could muster was "Alec."

"There's been enough hurt from seventeen years ago. Let it stop now." He swallowed, then added, "If I'd listened to my mother when she insisted I read these, years ago, everything might be different." His gaze fell to the letter in his fist, and he laid it on his thigh and attempted to smooth it out. His voice dropped. "Stars, what a stupid kid."

"You're not stupid, Alec," Nate said firmly. "Never have been. A bit hardheaded from time to time, maybe. But I promise we'll figure this out."

In that instant, I wished with all my heart to find the people my friends had lost. Perhaps a trace, like the one I created to find Max's son and daughter, would suffice, for even though their names and numbers had been removed from public records, the Consortium must have tracked their movements. I handed Alec the picture. Stillness settled over his features as his fingertips brushed the laughing toddler's face.

"I hope so, Nate," Alec murmured. "I hope so."

We gathered the letters and documents in silence, but before we finished, Edwards tapped my shoulder. "Despite my protestations, Clarkson took all your samples. I will need a little more blood."

Nate handed the last letter to Alec. "Why? You said she's clear."

Edwards shook his head. "This is not your concern, Timmons."

"The void it isn't," he growled.

"It is well." I touched his forearm. "I will comply, Edwards."

Nate bit back his response when the infirmary doors parted and Dr. Clarkson herself strode in. Kyleigh moved closer to me, as if her small form would protect me from the virologist's ire.

"I'll be glad when that other ship shows up and fixes this one," she complained. "Your commlink isn't working, Edwards, just like Genet's wasn't yesterday."

A hint of pink tinged Edwards's cheeks, and his weak explanation made me suspect he had been avoiding Dr. Clarkson.

"I see you haven't even been working." Dr. Clarkson glowered. "Founders' sakes, no one takes his job seriously around here."

Jordan narrowed her eyes. "Hardly the way to ingratiate yourself, Clarkson."

"I'm no sycophant, Jordan, and you know it," the virologist began, but what I suspected would have grown into a tirade was curtailed by a chime from the computers.

Edwards held up a hand for silence, then hit a button.

Max's deep rumble sounded over the speakers. "The shuttle hasn't left, has it?"

"Not yet," Jordan said. "If you—"

"Maxwell!" Dr. Clarkson interrupted. "You haven't been answering, either."

"I've been busy," Max said tersely.

"That's all well and good, but Genet and Edwards don't understand the importance of what I'm doing. You're as good as I'll get."

Jordan stiffened.

"Your point?" Max said without emphasis.

The virologist *tsk'd*. "Among other things, I need to run some simulations in VVR, but engineering says there's not enough power. I need the generator Edwards is using for that medtank."

Everyone froze.

"If you are referring to the tank holding the Recorder, no," Max said with unusual sharpness. "Taking that generator is akin to murder."

"She's already as good as dead. The Consortium doesn't like people messing with their own." Dr. Clarkson affixed her glare on me, and anxiety scritched up my spine as if on insectile legs. "You can't play favorites with lives on the line, Maxwell. We all know you've got a son in that group. Though maybe you've got more than one."

Max did not respond.

My heart thundered, and Nate caught my arm. She knew who James was? Had her use of the communications link revealed his presence to Skip?

"Enough." A vein in Jordan's temple pulsed. "You have your answer: he said no."

"We need to focus on the greater good here, which means giving me that generator," Dr. Clarkson said, as if killing someone meant nothing.

How could she not see the value of a life?

"No," I said.

"Stars, Recorder, it's not up to you. And I'm merely pointing out that Maxwell's biases are interfering with developing a cure."

Jordan's nostrils flared. "You won't steal that generator and kill that woman. Nor will you undermine Dr. Maxwell again." She pointed to the door. "Now."

For eleven seconds, they faced each other. With a snort, Imogene Clarkson pivoted on her heel and stomped out of the infirmary.

The door closed, and I sank against Nate, whose heart hammered in his chest.

"I told you she was abrasive," Edwards said.

Zhen glowered at the doors. "Abusive is more like it."

"Max," Jordan said softly.

The sound of a throat clearing came over the computer's speakers. "I'm here."

"Don't worry about what she said."

"Easier said than done." Max exhaled. For five seconds, no one spoke, then he resumed in a tight voice. "Edwards? Did you finish synthesizing those antibiotics?"

"I did. They are packed and ready to go."

"Good," Max said. "Someone should keep an eye on the generator. I don't trust Clarkson."

Jordan scowled at the door. "I don't, either. Tim, we need to talk to Archimedes about posting a guard."

"Consider it done," Nate said. "It's not like you can lock people out of the infirmary, Edwards, but with only one of you here—"

"I'll stay," Kyleigh offered, "if you want the company. I'm neither a nurse nor a marine, but I can change sheets and wake you up if there's an emergency." When he did not respond immediately, she gestured at a computer. "Besides, I can work on the nanoencapsulation here, just like I did on the trip to New Triton."

Edwards studied her for a moment longer. "That could be helpful."

"I don't think she'll attempt to steal the generator." Max paused. "Thank you, Venetia. I must be tired to let her get to me."

I could not decipher her expression when she said, "You're exhausted, Max. You need to rest."

"No time," he began, but the chime of four communications links interrupted him.

"Shuttle is loaded and waiting," Communications Officer Adrienne Smith twanged, her nasal voice setting my teeth on edge. "You have twenty minutes, or you won't make it."

The link ended.

"Moons and stars," Zhen snapped. "Maybe Archimedes can leave her and Clarkson on the moon together, and Tia Belisi and I can take comms."

Max chuckled. "That might not be a bad idea."

"Two hours, or so. Hold out until then," Jordan said.

Zhen shot a peculiar look at her as the communications link cut off.

I buried my face in the hollow of Nate's good shoulder, and he held me close.

"It'll be okay," he said.

Zhen bent over and kissed Alec. "Behave while I'm gone."

"I don't like this." Alec's brow furrowed. "You'll be careful, babe?"

"I was born careful." She pulled out a pack from under his bed. "Got my knives *and* my knitting this time, so I'm set." She pivoted to me. "While I like the new outfit, you'll need your suit."

Edwards handed me a bag with the suit I had taken off when I had first entered the infirmary.

"I must retrieve the drone, Edwards," I said. "There is no time to draw more blood."

He did not meet my eyes. "Williams can send it on the next shuttle."

"I can't go down to Pallas until Max clears me," Nate said. "But don't worry. Jordan, Zhen, and I talked to Genet about keeping you safe."

"I will have the drone."

"We talked about that, too." Zhen huffed, then tossed her long blue plait over her shoulder and grinned. "Like it or not, I'm your double."

"And I'll be watching both of you," Jordan added. "We don't have long before the shuttle departs, and I want you as deep in Pallas as possible before *Attlee* shows up. We're already cutting it close."

Kyleigh darted across the infirmary and threw her arms around me. "I need you to be safe." I nodded, and she stepped back and patted my arm before hugging Jordan and Zhen as well. "All of you."

"You'll be safer there with J and Zhen than here," Alec said.

Nate was silent as he and Edwards walked us to the double doors.

Edwards placed a hand on my shoulder. "Little one," he said, as if I were a child. "Tell Williams I have left her a note."

"A note?"

"To be on the safe side." He gave me a brief hug, then backed away quickly. "You do not have a name yet, do you?"

I glanced up at Nate, then away.

"Ah. You are correct. It is unsafe," Edwards said. "Perhaps when I see you next?"

"Perhaps."

Nate traced my cheekbone, then pressed his lips to my forehead. "Don't worry about us."

I dared not look back as Zhen, Jordan, and I took the hall to the computer laboratory, where I rushed to gather the drone and the equipment I had left behind. Ignoring the buzz from my datapad and with Lorik's drone at my side, I walked away from the room where I had first kissed my Nathaniel, leaving *Thalassa*—and Nate—again.

34

While Jordan, Zhen, and I sat without speaking, the others returning to Pallas argued with great intensity over which adversary was worse, roaches or humans. Their debate circled around facts and fictions until Osmund's voice sounded over the speakers.

"Hitting a dust storm. Descent might be bumpy," he announced. "Stay buckled in."

Only I seemed bothered by the craft's lurching, though I spent the rest of the trip with my eyes shut, so the veracity of my assumption might have been incorrect. We landed with a graceless jolt, and I waited for my stomach to settle.

Warmer months produced more turbulence, but if Pallas's thinner atmosphere meant lower wind speeds and decreased severity of atmospheric disturbances, I never wanted to travel to Ceres, where the storms were more severe. Roiling nausea finally under control, I leaned back into the synthleather seat. Had Nate been piloting the shuttle, I did not doubt the trip and landing would have been smoother.

While the marines pulled on skullcaps and helmets and waited by the door, I awkwardly donned my suit. The drone left its secured station to hover at my side, and conversations petered out. Jordan twisted her braids into a knot and tugged on her cap, then her helmet. The hatch opened, but after the others filed out, I stopped her. Behind her faceplate, one slim brow rose.

"What is it?"

"Have Jackson and his marines been informed SGS *Attlee* is inbound?"

Zhen's voice sounded behind me. "Osmund knew."

"Do they know of my arrival?"

"Probably not," Jordan said. "Jackson was pretty explicit about you staying on *Thalassa*."

"Without secure communications, would it not be preferable to send warning?" I glanced over my shoulder at the drone. James and Daniel must avoid its presence, but speaking circumspectly proved difficult.

"Go on," Jordan prompted.

I cleared my throat. "It is unwise to . . . endanger the drone. Drones have malfunctioned on Pallas before."

The datapad in my thigh pocket buzzed, and I ignored it. There was no reason to read the drone's assertion of *suspected untruth*.

Jordan shot a sideways glance at the alcove. "Right. Zhen, stay with her. I'll talk to whoever's in charge." She turned and strode down the ramp.

"Moons and stars," Zhen said as the echoes of Jordan's bootsteps disappeared, "but you would've made a lousy agent."

I studied her for a moment. "An agent of what?"

"Of anything." She rolled her eyes. "You have all the subtlety of an earthquake."

The drone's presence reminded me of the proper response. "Subterfuge has no place among the children of the Consortium."

Another buzz issued from the datapad. I suppressed a groan.

Before she made any rebuttal, however, Osmund slunk from the front of the shuttle, avoiding both the drone and me.

Zhen smirked. "Nice landing."

"Shut it, DuBois," he all but snarled before he disappeared through the hatch.

"Your passive-aggressive dross won't go unreported, Oz," she muttered. "Odious man. I should've called him out on not powering down properly. I'll have to do it myself, and he knew I would."

"But should there not be a . . ." My mind fumbled for the correct term. "A copilot?"

"Yes, but Johansen's still down here, and Tim and Alec are on *Thalassa* . . ." She huffed. "I'll go check. You stay put until I get back."

"Where would I go?" I asked, but I lifted my hands when her glare turned on me.

The lights flickered, and Zhen and I spun to face the front of the small craft. The drone unfurled its tendrils.

"Oh, good!" Eric Thompson exclaimed as he stepped into the main cabin. "I thought you might still be here."

"Eric?" Zhen glanced between him and the hatch. "You're shadowing Osmund?"

The young man grinned. "Yep."

"And he left you to power everything down?"

"I have experience," he protested, his lilting inner-belt accent more obvious than usual. "Freighter brat, remember? I flew with my uncle for years. Last few times we had small deliveries to Krios-A137, as well as Platforms Seventeen and Twenty-three, Dad let me take *Gryphon*'s shuttle." His chin lifted. "Bet I coulda handled the turbulence better than Osmund. I don't think he's done much atmospheric stuff before." He hesitated, some of his confidence fading. "Would you mind?"

Zhen smiled at him, scowled at me, and pointed to the floor. "Wait right here."

Fatigue nagged that I should sit, rest, but I fought the suggestion and remained standing, though I wavered several times. Bootsteps jarred me fully awake when Jordan returned before Zhen and Eric, and I received yet another frown.

"Where's Zhen?"

I shoved aside the errant thought that if I charged a fee for the frowns people threw at me, I could pay off my gifting with credits. I only said, "She is assisting Eric Thompson."

"About time, J." Zhen returned from the cabin, Eric at her heels. "So what's next?"

"Had a couple runners take off to inform Jackson and the others of our arrival. They'll be ready in the control room. Eric, you're with us for now."

The drone and I waited in the hangar while the other three made quick work of securing the shuttle and speaking with the marines near the barricade.

Two armed men joined us, and we had traveled thirty-seven meters when I realized Zhen DuBois was unarmed. Jordan had a long, thick, heavy-looking rifle, as did Eric. Zhen caught me staring and mouthed the word, *"No."*

My datapad buzzed, and this time I pulled it out. In my peripheral vision, Zhen mimicked me and removed a datapad very like my own from her thigh pocket. She entered information manually in a mirror image of what I was doing, which I found unnerving.

>>*Citizens are prohibited from wearing Consortium attire, per AAVA section 1.37.11.*

I responded verbally. "There is no need—"

"Keep it down," the shorter, thicker marine barked.

Taken aback by his rudeness, I inhaled deeply and entered, >>*Yes.*

>>*Citizens are prohibited from wearing Consortium attire, per AAVA section 1.37.11.*

Was the drone damaged?

It was only when Zhen turned her attention to her datapad that I noticed the patch on her shoulder: a triangular Consortium Eye, exactly like mine.

Realization hit me. *My double.* Zhen was a decoy. She had placed herself at risk from the people who wanted to destroy the Consortium and had killed Freddie and Lorik, but that was not all. The drone would be recording her flagrant defiance of official AAVA codes, and if it connected with the Consortium network, she faced stiff penalties for masquerading as a Recorder. Suddenly, my mouth tasted of ash.

The datapad buzzed again, repeating section 1.37.11.

I had to rebut its persistent recitation, but my fingers shook. I entered the eight characters a second time. >>*Protect.*

>>*Clarify,* scrolled across my datapad's screen.

Somehow, I managed to enter, >>*The citizen wears Consortium suit to protect.*

>>*Clarify object.*

"Me," I whispered.

>>*Acceptable, per additional directive from Elder Eta4513110-0197E. Violation noted and waiver granted.*

Relief and confusion blurred together. I typed, >>*Explain additional directive.*

>>*Elder Eta4513110-0197E issued additional command to protect Consortium members, technology, and interests.*

>>*When? What was the order?*

>>*478.2.5.07, 15:37. Rescue from any threat, insectile or human.*

I counted back. Lorik must have issued the command before the shuttle left *Thalassa* to bring him to Pallas, but while the command could explain the drone's abnormal behavior, drones were linked to their specific, assigned member.

>>*I am not Eta4513110-0197E.*
>>*Affirmative. Identified as Aberrant Zeta 4542910-9545E.*
I refrained from tapping my thigh. I knew who I was.

It continued, >>*Directive expanded on same day at 21:33, to include any Consortium personnel and interests.*

I could not remember the exact time, but it must have been close to when Nate's shuttle had gone dark.

Which meant that carrying me away from the cockroaches and away from the people planning on killing me was in obedience to Lorik's command.

>> *Defend and protect,* the datapad read. >>*Rescue.*
>>*Thank you.*

The datapad's screen flashed purple once, then I placed the unit back in my pocket for the remainder of our walk, which was mercifully short. Despite the previous night's rest, I was exhausted.

Double doors slid apart, and the six of us entered the cavernous control room. A small group of marines gathered around the communication console under the ceiling's fang-like protrusions. Jackson moved to meet us.

"*Attlee* showed up over an hour ago, so it's a good thing you brought her back here." He eyed the drone. "The trick now is to get her to disappear for a while until things blow over."

"That'll be a magic trick with drones reporting everything to the Consortium," one of the two men accompanying us quipped.

"Why?" Eric asked. "I mean, not the drone, the marshals. They ought to be able to patch *Thalassa* up and get us out of here, right?"

"That's the plan," Jackson said. "But there have been . . . complications."

My gaze flickered to the middle of the room. "Whatever the complications are, I must check on the drone."

Jackson stabbed a finger at the one at my side. "I'll give you ten minutes. Go ahead."

"The AAVA drone." I gestured to the solitary drone which seemed to crouch over the main console like a spider over its prey. "I need to ascertain it was not corrupted when the . . . when *Thalassa* went dark." I tapped my helmet over my communications link to indicate I truly meant that Skip could listen in.

It seemed my attempt failed, because Venetia Jordan tilted her head to the side. "They checked already. You hooked it up properly. We've been trying to figure out how to use it for communications, but with *Attlee* here, doing so might be unnecessary."

"*Attlee*'s probably listening in on whatever that thing's trying to send up," one of the marines said.

"When we first entered the control room, I linked the AAVA drone directly to CTS *Thalassa*," I said. "SGS *Attlee* should not have access."

The overwhelming urge to check my work was unreasonable, but denying it hurt almost physically. Parliament had wanted the information. I had not compromised our network then, for while I might have become a traitor to the Consortium, that had not always been the case.

Sudden apprehension blocked my throat. Surely the Elders on *Attlee* could not remotely activate the network on *Thalassa*? If they utilized the AAVA drone's connections, would small jamming devices be sufficient to keep James and Daniel safe? Or would the tiny moving pockets of nothing betray my friends? The Consortium's knowledge could jeopardize every marine on Pallas.

If, if, if all spun into a disaster I might not be able to avoid, a disaster that could very well engulf us all. Everything I had done to protect my friends would be for naught. *Check the drone* vied with *already secured.* I rubbed my chest plate over my sternum, but the pain did not dissipate.

"Good," Jackson was saying. "We need to find a place to stash you."

"Why?" Eric asked.

Jackson growled, "Because when they showed up—"

"I need a datapad," I interrupted.

They all turned to me.

"You have one," the short marine stated. "Saw you playing games on it while we walked."

The other one elbowed him. "Recorders don't play games, stupid."

But Jordan understood. "A datapad like Kye's flowered one?"

I swallowed. "Yes."

She rotated toward Jackson, her back to me and the drone.

The marine's eyebrows rose, and he clicked a button. "Dan, we need one of those extra datapads . . . Right. Thanks." He paused and motioned to the taller of the two marines. "Dan Parker says there's an extra one on the console next to comms."

The marine took off at a run.

"As I was saying," Jackson continued, "*Attlee* showed up early, about sixty-five minutes ago. The Consortium wants their property back. They took *Thalassa*'s Recorder and her drone."

My focus drifted to the marine who jogged up with a lavender datapad in hand. Lorik's drone flicked its tendrils as the jamming device disconnected it from all networks and signals. It spun in slow circles, and the appendages stretched like roots. The citizens backed away. Despite the threat of the network activating, and despite the Consortium taking the Recorder, a small part of my tension dissipated. The jamming device still worked.

"Nothing Genet could do," Jackson said, then his voice hardened. "They took Edwards."

I dropped the datapad, and a tendril snatched it before it smashed on the floor. Stunned, I gaped at the tall marine.

"What?" Zhen spat out. "Those voided—they have no right—"

"He's Consortium staff, DuBois," Jackson said tersely. "He's a good man and would be a good doctor if they'd let him, but he's theirs until he pays off his gifting."

Eric sputtered, "That's not fair."

Zhen folded her arms. "Well, we have to get him back."

"There's more." Jackson's steely grey eyes held mine. "They're demanding you're turned over as well."

Jordan's hand clamped my arm, as if she had the slightest chance of winning a discussion with an Elder. "Not an option."

"This is why you want me to disappear." My voice sounded distant, even to me. I had known they would make the demand, but for the minute, all I felt was an overwhelming numbness.

Caught between worry for Edwards and dread for myself, I had not noticed the drone approaching Zhen. One wandering tendril wrapped around her waist. Her cry rang over her external speaker, and she grabbed the appendage to pull herself free before I could warn her not to resist. She went rigid, and all color drained from her face.

"Founders—" Eric went as pale as Zhen, but he darted toward her. "Don't fight it!"

She shuddered and released the tendril. It rotated around her once, and when it let go, she slumped.

Eric caught her. "Breathe," he said, voice low. "You'll be fine."

Appendages flailing, the drone seemed to feel its way across the floor. Eric pulled Zhen back a meter, and everyone else jumped away. Tendrils encircled my waist, and the drone rotated until I could read its screen.

>>*Protect.*

It took a moment for the word to register.

Protect, indeed, though how I would protect Edwards when he had been removed, I did not know. But I did know what I needed to do, how I could use the very equipment they demanded that we return to protect those I had to save.

The drone rose to hover beside my head.

"In that case," I said, and their attention shifted from the drone to me. "I know exactly where to go."

Jackson's gravelly baritone grated through the quiet after my statement. "Which would be?"

"Past the feeding frenzy Jordan, Timmons, and their team discovered." I raised my chin and turned to Jordan. "Take me to the lower levels and Pallas Station's main data storage."

>>*Connection lost. Connection lost,* scrolled over the drone's screen.
>>*Suspected interference.*
 >>*Utilize video and auditory processors to remain in contact,* I entered.
 >>*No neural chip.*
"I know." Braving potential intrusions might be safer if the drone could assist, so I entered, >>*Continue visual monitoring and pheromone detection. Connect with datapad.*
 >>*Protect.*
"Indeed," I said aloud and inserted a tendril into my datapad, and the drone's writhing slowed. It unspooled the tendril about my waist, allowing me freedom to move, but remained hovering two meters overhead, so I set Edwards's pack down and lowered myself next to it. Jackson returned to the communication console to call for supplies and escorts, and the other two marines departed for whatever duties they had.

Zhen dodged under the drone to crouch in front of me. "You need rest."

"We all do," Jordan observed, "but real rest or even instant coffee will have to wait until we're settled."

"So . . . Timmons said there was a feeding frenzy outside deep storage." Eric shuddered. "Do you suppose the bugs have moved on?"

"Probably, though I'm more concerned that no one outside our group heard about our arrival. We've been careful enough, so Ross"—Jordan spat his name—"and his cronies shouldn't know where you are."

"I studied the schematics," Zhen put in. "The room is located at a dead end. It feels like a trap."

"Maybe it's a good place for that very reason?" Eric asked. "Defensible? Like having high ground in a fantasy vid?"

Jordan did not answer, and though I was inclined to agree with

Zhen's concern over Eric's optimistic supposition, I remained silent. Tucking my knees to my chest, I rested my head against the wall. The drone's grip slid down my arm.

"Zhen," I said while staring up at the shadows pooling awkwardly around the stalagmites, "did the drone harm you?"

She lowered herself to sit at my side. "I'm all right, but my insides are still buzzing. I don't think it approves of me in general and wearing the suit in particular."

"It does not, but your violation of the AAVA code has been—" What was the word? Excused? Absolved? "Dismissed."

"Hardly seems likely, but I'll take your word for it."

I kept my eyes on the ceiling. "It is more likely your attempt to free yourself provoked the reprimand."

"It was bad," she said slowly, "but yours have been worse."

In the powerful floodlights, one of the rounded formations in the far corner resembled a nose. It made me uncomfortable that a large nose protruded into the control room, as if the moon could smell the drone and me and would inform the Consortium of our location.

"Perhaps."

"That's dross. This particular monstrosity nearly killed you at least once."

Zhen's rudeness lifted my spirits, but my thoughts drifted to my other friends: Eric's distrust when he met me, then Tia's personal questions on *Agamemnon*.

A thread of worry turned me toward her, the drone's tendril tugging on my arm. "You are not pregnant, are you? I do not know if the reprimands would damage—"

She flushed. "No."

Eric coughed. When I looked over at him, he shook his head.

My faulty memories of social etiquette rushed back. "I apologize. I should not have asked such a personal question."

"It's all right," she said after several seconds. "You were concerned."

"I still am." I folded my arms on top of my knees and studied the ceiling again. "You should not pretend to be me. Inherent dishonesty aside, it is unsafe."

"Easy decision," she said.

"It was her idea," Jordan added quietly. "You're close to the same height, and the suits mask any difference in weight."

"Not that there is much after you've stopped eating."

"Ease up, Zhen," Jordan said.

"What?" Zhen protested. "She can make personal remarks, and I can't?"

"Don't worry. We'll fatten you up on the way back," Eric put in, earning a glare from Zhen.

"You'll be safer with a double," Jordan said with an air of finality. "Keep your head down, and no one will know the difference."

"I do not like it."

Zhen nudged my shoulder. "Don't fuss. It's the obvious choice, even if finding another navy datapad was a challenge. The difference is that thing."

I followed her gaze to the drone two meters in front of me. "The drone will be too much of an identifying mark. The people who want to kill me and my people will simply . . ." I hesitated.

"Simply what?" Jordan prompted.

I sighed and, against my better judgment, explained, "Eventually you and I will separate, and the drone will go with me."

"Of course it will." Zhen jumped up and pointed to the side door opposite the communication console. "Why do you think we asked for those?"

Six marines escorted the four undamaged drones across the open floor, the hum of microantigravity devices approximating their whir. My mouth fell open, and I clambered to my feet.

"Zhen's idea again." A slight smile appeared on Jordan's face. "By your own account, she manages the controls pretty well."

"I loaded them on microAG before J and I went up to *Thalassa* so we could hide them, if we needed to," Zhen said. "I guessed that if the Consortium showed up, which seemed likely, you wouldn't want them to have the drones."

An unfamiliar marine guided a small platform loaded with bags and equipment. "That should be everything you need. Jackson's not thrilled about having a parade when those trogs could be watching, but if you're gonna hole up, you'll need all this."

Gratitude brought heat to my cheeks. They had anticipated my needs as if those requirements had been their own, and even with the Consortium overhead, I felt safer.

"So we leave now?" Eric asked.

"Not quite." Jordan motioned at the backpack against the wall. "Max wasn't fudging his request for antibiotics. They've run low, after everything."

The final drone reached us, and a marine handed Zhen a holster and sidearm. The man hesitated before offering a second one to me. I shrank back against the wall. The drone dropped closer.

"I do not know . . ." My mouth went dry. "I cannot take the weapon."

"Can and will," he said.

"I cannot."

All I heard was the echoing crunch as the drone killed that man. Cord. His name had been Cord.

The marine's reply slurred together in my ears.

"No!" If I had caused death with a drone, how much more dangerous would a sidearm be? "I have no training—cannot—"

"It's not loaded," Jordan said, though sound lagged behind as she pushed the drone aside. Tentacles wrapped around her neck and arms. She swallowed, but kept her eyes on mine.

The drone lowered, and its screen flashed red. >>*Protect.*

She caught my gloved hands in hers. "Listen to me. You can't hurt anyone with it."

>>*Protect.*

"Zhen needs a weapon," she said calmly, oblivious to the drone's continuing directive. "She can't wear one if you don't. You won't match."

I gulped down air and nodded.

"Void take it," someone said. "This is such a bad idea."

"For Zhen." My voice wobbled. "I will take it for Zhen."

I reached past Jordan and entered directly on the drone's screen, >>*Protected. Release her.*

Tendrils and tentacles lashed away from Jordan and retreated into interior pockets, all save the one coiled about my torso.

>>*Well done,* I typed.

I took the holster and strapped it to my left leg so it would not interfere with my ability to reach my datapad. Zhen ducked under the tendril to adjust it.

"It'll be all right. I promise." She stepped back and set a hand on my upper arm. "You're holding my spare, in case I need it later."

"Spare," I repeated.

"Right."

The control room's double doors slid apart, and Max strode in, flanked by the bearded marine—Quincy—and another one.

Max's eyebrows became a thick line at the sight of me and my double, at the drone, at the holster at my side. He half turned to Jordan. "Venetia, are you sure this is wise?"

It was not, but I did not say so.

"It's our best option for keeping her safe." The rest of Jordan's low reply was hidden by footsteps as Jackson jogged up.

"Get going," Jackson ordered. *"Attlee*'s sending a shuttle. Consortium's inbound."

"But James," I began. "And Daniel—"

"Not your problem." He turned to Jordan. "Get out of here and as deep as you can."

One terse nod was her sole answer, and as if she, the bearded marine, and five others communicated telepathically, they gathered weapons and started to the door.

Jackson touched my arm and said with unusual softness, "Don't worry. We've got it covered."

Max moved aside. I pressed the backpack into his hands, though a part of me wanted to keep it. It was all I had from Edwards, and he was gone.

"Thank you," Max said gently.

Zhen shooed me along. Before the doors closed, I glanced back to see Max standing alone, the backpack dangling from one hand and the other raised in farewell.

Jordan led the way and the bearded marine—*Quincy*, I repeated over and over in my head—followed behind, so I was as safe as possible, given the circumstances. The trek was silent and uneventful, though each step had me checking the ceiling for cracks and listening for the faintest sound. My head ached from the effort.

We wound through clean, dust-free corridors to a lift and a ladder reminiscent of the ones in ships. I held my breath as Jordan descended the ladder, then Zhen, the drones, and I took the lift next. Jordan awaited us at the bottom.

Dust was thicker on the lower level, with occasional ovoid shapes and remnants of exoskeletons littering the halls and hiding the blue safety lights. We passed one half-eaten carcass, larger by a third than the live ones I had seen, though why the insects would abandon a food source, I could not guess.

I pulled my datapad over and typed, >>*Insectile presence?*
>>*None detected.*

"None present" would have been preferable, but the answer sufficed.

On and on the hall twisted, meandering unevenly. Dark passages yawned on either side, and the metallic clicks of the marine's equipment kept startling me. Tracks laced drifts two decimeters deep. Motes sparkled in the tracking beams, and clouds rose at our feet. When we reached the door, only a few scraps of synthetic material, one boot, and a face mask testified to the reported frenzy.

I motioned the others to stand clear as the drone and I moved forward. Once it adequately handled security measures, Jordan and three others entered, emerging within minutes. She beckoned to me, so I followed her straight through the room to an inner door. Again the drone handled the locks with ease, and again, Jordan investigated the interior room before she gave an all clear.

>>*Lights,* I ordered.

The drone glowed, illuminating a large, sparsely furnished but not unwelcoming, paneled office, which was unlike the grim computer cave I had expected. A center console faced the back wall lined with monitoring equipment. The room must have been designed with Consortium presence in mind, for a drone alcove was embedded in the wall to my left beside a charging station for smaller equipment. A small VVR unit occupied the far corner.

Jordan leaned in. "Does the monitoring equipment work?"

"I shall attempt to find out." Ignoring the bustle of marines, drones, and supplies behind me, I manually attached Lorik's drone to the computer. Static screens lit, displaying the hallway outside the rooms with its half-buried scraps, dust, and tracks. The hangar flickered on another screen, then the control room, and more. I found the link to the AAVA drone and snuck a look. I exhaled. It was indeed secure.

Once that was completed, I ordered Lorik's drone to dock in the alcove and power off to conserve energy. It complied.

Jordan patted my back. "Good job."

"All documentation ceased when Westruther activated the self-destruct. I am setting it to monitor but not document, though we do not have sound."

"That presents a challenge." Quincy's words made me jump, and I spun around to face him. His frown gentled. "Don't worry, Recorder-that-isn't. We'll figure something out."

"Are you sure this is the right place?" Eric peered at the screen in front of me. "The whole setup is pretty fancy for a computer cave, and I don't see any computers. It's just monitors and entry pads. Besides, that VVR display is older than the one on my parent's freighter."

"It's even bigger than this," Zhen said. "When they built this place, they dug out a large enough space for this room and added extra seismic reinforcements. The main units are protected beyond those panels, and geothermal power keeps the units cool and dust free."

"Good thing, too, with all this tech in here," said a young marine with a moustache struggling across his upper lip. He handed his scanner to the bearded marine. "The air in both rooms is cleaner than on most ships."

Quincy grunted. "Hodges is right, but we'll still leave the air filters, in case something goes wrong."

Eric tapped a panel on the wall, then crossed to examine the VVR unit. He hit a button, and it flickered on, showing nothing but a transparent version of the room in which we stood. "I don't get it. VVR on *Gryphon*—my parent's freighter—was old, but this one?" He knocked on the control panel, making the image jump. "It's an antique."

"Probably didn't need anything fancy down here," the bearded marine answered from the other room. "Might've been for entertainment if the assignment was long."

"Lousy quality for vids," the young marine said.

"Older technology is frequently inaccessible without specialized equipment," I added before turning back to the displays, but a yawn hid the monitors for three seconds. "I might need to rest."

For the first time in what felt like years, Jordan chuckled. "That was the plan. I suggest we send the extras back home, secure the door, and set up camp."

"Extras?" quipped the young scanner-marine. "We risk baddies and bugs to get you all here, and we're *extras*?"

A guffaw sounded from the antechamber, drawing my attention back through the door.

Powering the computers on had turned on the lights, so the room was no longer the dark void I had traversed. Whatever I had expected to find in the bowels of Pallas, the small, comfortable antechamber was not it. Landscapes of Ceres' rocky northern beaches hung over the two squat, surprisingly aubergine sofas facing each other from opposite walls. A small white table with two matching chairs and an empty decorative bowl stood in the corner closest to the inner door. Lined paper rested on one end table under a lamp, and opposite the end table, a door led to a small water closet. Two cleaning bots blinked quietly in their alcoves. The room felt almost welcoming.

"You're set?" Quincy asked.

"Set?" The young marine with the thin moustache answered on our behalf. "This is nicer than my flat at home."

"Except for the neighbors," someone quipped. "I'll take loud music over bugs."

Several of them laughed. When another marine made an unkind remark about bugs being the only neighbors who would want to live near him, more laughter ensued.

"Contact us if you have to, Jordan." The bearded marine turned to me. "You stay tight until we say so."

"If there's any news, Quincy, let us know," she answered.

"Will do. Thompson, you're with us. Can't leave our newest pilot behind. We'll see the rest of you later." A tight grin snuck past Quincy's grizzled stubble. "Don't forget to lock up."

Since the scanners declared the rooms clean, we removed our helmets and gloves, though we left our suits on. After a heated debate over who should sleep on the sofas, Jordan and Zhen conceded, and I unrolled a thin mat in the computer room with the drones, which I insisted did not bother me.

Though exhaustion pulled at me like heavy gravity, and I could have done nothing to protect them, I needed to know the marines returned safely. Before they reached the control room, however, the monitor displaying the hangar showed the arrival of an unfamiliar shuttle. Five marshals, two Elders, and six drones descended on Pallas Station.

My mouth went dry, and I croaked, "Jordan. Zhen."

Together, we watched Jackson escort the new arrivals from the hangar to the control room. When the Elders left the main group to study the AAVA drone, unnecessary fear coated my throat. The group left for other areas, and as Jackson led them in a circuitous route, I skimmed ahead to watch the hallways. My heart skipped a beat, and an exclamation escaped involuntarily. I could not warn the marines of the two roaches blocking the hall.

The three of us watched with bated breath as marines and marshals both fired on the behemoth insects. Jordan's gloved hand tightened on my shoulder when the first cockroach fell but the second charged. Incendiary rounds flared brightly, and the second roach skidded to a smoking stop three meters from the Elders.

Oddly, Jordan laughed. "I should have known. There are always bugs that close to the algae tanks."

"Then why did he not go another way?"

"To make a point," Zhen said.

The newcomers returned directly to their shuttle after the encounter, and Jackson stood near the back of the hangar as they departed. The doors shut, and the marine beside Jackson pounded him on the back.

I fell limply against the chair. Somehow, two meters seemed even larger on a small screen. But, no one was injured. Neither Elder had lost control of the drones, so they would not die. We had seen neither James nor Daniel, and neither had the Elders.

"We're safe enough in here for now," Jordan said. "Get some sleep."

She was correct. I did not even remove the suit before collapsing on the mat near the other four drones.

Despite the certainty that the Elders would return, and despite witnessing the confrontation with the roaches, I slept well that night, though drowsiness clogged my mind upon waking. Jordan pressed me into eating a packaged meal—overprocessed protein blocks were as unappealing as ever—and I returned to the monitors. *Attlee* remained in synchronous orbit, and no shuttle arrived from *Thalassa*.

I stared blankly at the monitors. "Do you believe Nate is safe? And Alec? Without Edwards—"

"Timmons will be fine, and Alec was recovering well enough when we left," Jordan answered. "Between the Consortium on *Attlee* and ongoing repairs, Archimedes will need both of them on *Thalassa*, not on Pallas."

"Doesn't make it any easier," Zhen said. She was correct. "So what do we do while we wait?"

I glanced at the drones to double-check that they remained silent and dark. "I believe I can utilize these computers to feed information to the AAVA drone, which will transmit it to *Thalassa*."

"We knew that," Zhen said.

"I can use that to insert James's fictional past into the record."

"That would be safer than only having an ID bracelet." Jordan drummed her fingers. "What about Dan?"

"Inserting Daniel Parker's story might be harder, but since James is taking Freddie's place, his information would be here, in these databanks."

Jordan bared her teeth in a tight smile. "Do it."

I pulled out my datapad and Freddie's datastick, and after discussing modifications with Jordan and Zhen, I spent the next several hours tucking James's altered identity into the station's databanks. When I reviewed the talkative Recorder's falsified history, however, I stopped and tapped my thigh twice.

"Something bothering you?" Jordan asked.

"I am concerned about the talkative Recorder—Daniel."

Jordan chuckled. "Talkative Recorder? That fits. So what's the issue?"

"Why would his information be in Pallas Station's databanks and nowhere else?"

"Point." Her lips pursed. "What do you have so far?"

I explained, and Jordan, Zhen, and I wrestled with the problem for the next two hours. Zhen's knitting needles whispered against each other as she continued the intricate variegated blue pattern, and Jordan's knives took on razor-sharp edges.

"That's it!" Jordan sheathed her knife with a snap. "That storm—what, four years ago? On Ceres. It pummeled the entire northern coastline, but Trinity North was hit hardest. They had to evacuate. Remember?"

Zhen's gaze grew distant. "The one people took up collections for?"

"Exactly. The storm was so bad the Consortium lost a bunch of patrollers and a section of their Hall of Records when their storage facility flooded."

Something about that storm . . .

The memory teased me, as if it held deeper significance than Jordan's summary, but I gritted my teeth and shook off my uneasiness. What mattered now was not the cumulative effect of my difficulties with names and information. To dwell on a faulty memory only obscured the true task: keeping Daniel and James safe. Forcing my mind back onto the problem, I asked, "You are suggesting we falsify the records to indicate that he came from Ceres? His accent will be incorrect."

"We'll tell him to practice a few phrases. No one will think much of it if he learns some regional idioms."

"After years away, it's reasonable that speech patterns change," Zhen said without looking up from her stitches.

I jolted to my feet and clapped my hand to my forehead. "Moons and stars! How did I forget?"

"Simmer down," Jordan said. Once I sat again, she added, "What's wrong?"

"The marines' logs! They must be altered to verify that both Recorders were destroyed by roaches, and I cannot do so from here—"

"Easy enough," Zhen said. "J, you and I will make sure they tweak a few facts."

Her assertion did not allay all my concerns. "Additionally, Daniel and James need identification bracelets." I glanced at the silent drone, the discomfort of anxiety seeping through my chest like steam from a damaged vent. "I cannot add the security layers and details until I have access to the Consortium network, but we must have the bracelets."

"James can have mine—"

"He'll have Freddie's," Zhen said. "Either man will look downright silly in yours."

"Right." Jordan added, "But not the gold and amber one, Zhen. The black one."

"Two. I forgot." Zhen muttered something about upper tier upbringings. "Your wrists are thinner, though."

"It's adjustable." Venetia Jordan turned to me. "You say you need a drone to fix them, but the first step is his history. I think that the Ceres story will work."

With their assistance, everything clicked into place. Daniel Geoffrey Parker had been born on Ceres in Trinity North. After studying political science and liberal arts at the local university, he accepted an assignment on Pallas as a technical writer on the strength of his exit exam for language. Guilt twinged when I relabeled some documents with his new name. I had not only erased Freddie's past, but now I lessened Alicia Brisbane's accomplishments.

He had left the station and joined the marines on a supply trip right before the first people had fallen ill. I slid the information in and sighed.

Zhen's knitting slowed. "What's the problem now? We figured it out."

"There is none." I could not find the words to explain that the inherent dishonesty of my actions weighed on my mind, or perhaps I did not want to call attention to it.

Her yarn resumed its steady dance from needle to needle. "You're not a very good liar."

"Which isn't a bad thing," Jordan said.

She would have been correct, if fewer lives depended on it.

I leaned back against the sofa cushions and stared at the clouds churning on the horizon, muting Ceres' lavender skies and the ocean's surface tossing beneath them. Craggy cliffs anchored the nearly one-sided coniferous trees that leaned away from the water, as if years of wind had taught them to protect their branches from storms by turning inland. In the upper right-hand corner, a solitary bird rode the winds, but the fine brushstrokes did not make it clear why the bird flew. I knew the painting by heart after twenty-three hours in the two rooms, from the obscuring clouds down to the hidden signature: F. Westruther.

There was no one to ask if the bird ever made it home.

The turbulence depicted in oils was too similar to the turmoil in my heart. I moved to the other sofa to avoid seeing it and settled at the opposite end from Jordan, who was flushed from doing calisthenics in the center of the room. Facing the other painting's calmer images did not still my racing thoughts. Light sparkled on deep waters of blue and aubergine. The barest hint of Nivien, Ceres' smaller, slightly uneven moon, showed above the horizon.

"I should have written a list," I said to myself.

Zhen stuffed her knitting into her bag and gestured at the end table. "Paper's right over there. Knock yourself out."

"With paper?" I asked.

She rolled her eyes. After perhaps seventeen seconds, she added, "Moons and stars, but waiting is hard work. I keep coming up with new things to worry about."

"The Consortium might have taken Edwards, Zhen, but they won't—can't—leave *Thalassa* without a doctor."

My self-centeredness hit me again. Alec. Preoccupied as I had been with saving the other men, with Nate's absence, and with Edwards's arrest, concern for Alec's health had receded from my mind.

"I know." Zhen rubbed at her eyes, then leaned back. "Regulations.

Those Elders must have left someone else. Good thing Williams and Max are down here. They've defied the Consortium to its face more than once."

My stomach grumbled, and Jordan searched through the stack of supplies by the door. She tossed a prepackaged meal at Zhen, who caught it one-handed, and a second to me. I left mine on the table, then washed my hands in the small water closet.

Jordan and Zhen had started eating by the time I settled in one of the chairs. Again, my stomach protested, but after I tore my package open, I stared with revulsion at the food inside. The label clearly stated it was a pasta and vegetable dinner with dried fruit, yet the contents bore little resemblance to the promised items.

Zhen did not seem as repulsed by her food. "At least they sent a variety this time. The work-study trip right before I met Alec, they sent a crate of nothing but fish loaf and isopod stew."

Whatever my meal was, it was not fish loaf. I stiffened my resolve and took several bites.

"They did that on one of my cousin Gerry's tours." Jordan took a swig of bottled water. "But he's allergic to isopods, so he lived off dried tilapia. Never touched the stuff afterward." She studied the bottle as if doing so would reveal her cousin's location. "I hope he's still out there somewhere, avoiding fish and isopods."

"We'll find out," Zhen said.

I sipped my water before attempting another unappealing bite of my rations.

"So," Jordan asked, "what sort of list?"

"There are several things I need to do while we have access to those computers." I toyed with the pale lumps of pasta, then set my utensil aside and twisted a disposable napkin into a knot. "They seem, however, to have fled my mind."

"Not surprising," Zhen said. "You're tired, and there's been a freighter-load of things happening." She ticked each item off on her fingers. "Saving people, check. Securing voided AAVA drones, check. Keeping an eye on the monitors to make certain no voided Elder messes—"

"Zhen!" I protested. Suddenly, the computer room's open door, where the drones waited silently, seemed a maw threatening to swallow us whole.

Jordan waved a fork in Zhen's direction. "Add *work on good habits* to your own list."

Zhen rolled her eyes and attacked her pasta.

"I cannot remember," I said cautiously, "which is an uncomfortable feeling."

Jordan finished her meal and threw away the empty container. "Don't worry about Alec or Tim. I'm certain they're fine." Pointedly ignoring the open door, she asked, "Are there penalties for staff who disobey? Like the way they murder Recorders?"

I shifted uncomfortably. "Staff, while also members of the Consortium, are in a separate category, somewhere between Recorders and citizens. Disobedience is met with increased fees, making it more difficult to pay off gifting. Staff may be reassigned so Elders can closely monitor their behavior. Only the most extreme actions—murder, assault, or insurrection—are met with extreme penalties."

"So they won't kill him," Zhen said, "just sell him further into slavery?"

I bristled, but there was truth in her analysis. "I would never say that."

She snorted. "I bet you wouldn't."

"Ease up, Zhen. I don't like waiting, either." Jordan took the chair across from mine. "*You* need to actually finish a meal."

I grimaced and rotated the container to sample the fruit. It was edible.

"*Ease up?*" Zhen skewered the last of her vegetables with such force that her disposable fork broke. She stomped across the room, threw out the whole package, and dropped onto the sofa, her arms folded tightly across her chest.

"Hold onto the knowledge that it will be all right," Jordan said. "Those Elders on *Attlee* make me uncomfortable, too, but repairs will be underway. We won't be stuck here long. And whatever her flaws, Clarkson is good at what she does, and with the information on the datastick you"—she nodded at me—"and Nate got to the researchers, we'll be out of here soon enough. Besides, as soon as we're back on *Thalassa*, Max will check on Alec, and we'll be underway."

"You can't know that," Zhen argued.

"Of course I can." Jordan caught my eye and mouthed, *"Back me up."*

I blinked rapidly, my mind a blank, before repeating her assertion that Max would indeed see to Alec.

Zhen turned her glare from Jordan to me.

"Both Alec and Tim will be fine," Jordan soothed. "Max is the best—"

"Moons and stars!" Zhen shot to her feet. "I'm sick to death of that."

Jordan raised one delicate eyebrow in response.

Zhen stabbed a finger in Jordan's direction. My heart accelerated, and I fisted my hands to keep from tapping my thigh.

"There you go again"—Zhen's dark eyes flashed—"and I've had enough."

Jordan remained calm. "Enough of what?"

"'Max is the best and kindest man in the system,'" Zhen mimicked.

Why would his goodness be a cause for argument? I managed, "No one disputes the fact."

"No one?" Zhen's chin rose, and she glowered across the room at Jordan. "What about you, J? You keep saying it, but you take up with complete dross like Julian Ross? Quit lying to yourself and everyone else, especially Max. He deserves better."

Jordan's drumming fingertips slowed to a stop.

"Best man in the system," Zhen scoffed. "Maybe Tim ought to add another two points to the stupid tally you two keep. You ought to be penalized for such an abysmal level of self-awareness."

Jordan's scowl reminded me of the storm clouds on the painting above the sofa, but before she responded, Zhen spat out, "Julian. Voided. Ross."

I wanted to protest that his middle name was actually Meredith, but wisdom kept my mouth shut.

Color tinged Jordan's cheeks. "People make mistakes."

Zhen hissed like a cat. "Any other justification you want to offer for *that* mistake? If Max is the best and kindest man in the system, why didn't you ever notice?"

"I noticed," Jordan said flatly. "In fact, I could scarcely have said that without noticing."

Zhen's long, deep-blue braid fell over her shoulder when she leaned over the table and punctuated her remarks with jabs at the inoffensive white surface. "Nesmith, Copperfield—*Ross*. And all the while the 'best and kindest man' is always there? Every time? Looking to you first when there's a question, making sure you're all right?"

Jordan's heightened color disappeared, leaving her ashen. "Of course he did. He's thoughtful—"

"Remembering your birthday, your favorite color, your favorite dessert? Let me guess." She flipped her blue plait to her back and splayed her fingers over her heart. "You're *friends*."

Jordan's chin came up. "Yes. Friends. Even Tim—"

"Tim is probably more aware of your feelings than you are." Zhen waved a hand. "And no, we don't run around gossiping about you behind your back. You even lean into Max's hand when he touches your shoulder. You're that obvious. Or rather, Max is. Stars, J. He calls you Venetia, when no one else does, and you let him."

Golden-brown eyes widened.

Zhen's whole frame drooped, like a drone when its power ran down. "Look, I know Alec will be fine. If I didn't, I wouldn't have left *Thalassa*. And Max would risk the Consortium and removal if he thought Alec needed him." Her voice gentled. "Max deserves a bit of goodness back in his life." Zhen took hold of my elbow and raised me to my feet. "The two of us are going to join those spacing drones and figure out what she's forgotten."

She guided me to the door, but I peeked back at Jordan who seemed to have withdrawn into herself. I wanted to say something to bring color back to her cheeks, but nothing came to mind. Zhen turned in the doorway.

"Think about it, J. For your own good. For both of you."

The second morning, I regretted insisting I take the mat in the other room, for when I woke, my right side tingled, and my headache had returned with its full disruptive power.

Jordan and Zhen were still asleep—Zhen's light snores were a rhythmic purr—so I lay there several minutes before getting up. Once on my feet, I attempted a kata learned as a child to drive off the discomfort. Instead, I lurched over. The words *semicircular canals* chased each other through my mind, though the reason for that particular phrase eluded me. I pulled myself to the chair, falling heavily upon it.

Jordan's sleep-laced voice croaked, "Everything all right?"

My answer must have been insufficient, for seconds later, two images of Venetia Jordan leaned over me. "What was that?"

I blinked, and the images resolved into one.

"What's going on?" Zhen called from the antechamber.

I forced syllables over my uncooperative tongue. "Nothing. Slept poorly."

"Anyone would with an army of drones around them," Zhen muttered.

"Had"—what was the word?—"a degree of para . . . pares . . ." I could not finish.

Jordan worried her lower lip, then finished for me. "Paresthesia?"

I nodded.

Zhen's soprano sharpened. "What?"

"Her arm fell asleep," Jordan explained.

Tousled blue hair entered my field of vision. "That wasn't what I meant, J. My grandmère had . . . Never mind."

Jordan studied me. "Can you tell me what happened?"

"Tried . . ." My left hand tightened around the arm rest. "Exercise for blood flow. I fell." Heat crept up my neck to my cheeks. "Is nothing."

Zhen spun my chair around toward her, and the room swam. She tilted my face up. "Your leg was affected, too?"

I nodded, though my brain felt as if it sloshed in my skull.

Jordan put her hand on Zhen's shoulder and knelt in front of me, her eyes searching mine. "Headache?"

Her frown deepened when I grimaced at her question. "For days."

"Comms, J?" Zhen asked. "Or not?"

"Not."

"Right." Zhen ran her fingers through her hair, twisting it into a knot. "I'll do it."

"We should have taken her to Max as soon as we landed."

Their words flew too fast, but I managed, "No."

"She's right," Zhen said. "Those rotted Elders would have snatched her away. Besides, he might be the best in the system, but he doesn't have a medicomputer down here."

Jordan leaned back on her heels. "There should be supplies in the medkit. If he didn't send jet injectors because of nanites—"

"I know, I know. Acetylsalicylic acid is the next best thing." Zhen tugged on her cap. "I'll be back with Max or Williams in an hour."

She meant to leave?

"Must not!" My response erupted with energy that startled even me. "Will be—am determined—to be well."

"Doesn't work that way." Zhen tugged the skullcap over her tangled bun.

"You must not." I turned too quickly, and dizziness overtook me. I concentrated on enunciation to prove nothing was wrong, though my speech sounded odd in my ears. "Jordan, not with roaches and people who would kill me for my blood. She is dressed like me. And what if they return?"

"They don't know where we are," Jordan said calmly.

Had I been unclear?

"No, no. The roaches. That carcass, half-eaten." I jerked upward, stumbled through the antechamber to block the door, and turned to face the room.

Jordan and Zhen stood side by side, watching me.

"Don't worry, my friend," Jordan said slowly. "Zhen will stay here with you. I'll get Max."

My heart roared like a shuttle engine. I said something, and whatever it was, they both stilled.

"J, we can't let her get worked up," Zhen said in an undertone, as if I would not hear.

I held my position. Potential attacks by roaches or murderers were too possible. They could not leave. A tear trickled down my cheek.

"Calm down." Zhen pulled off her skullcap. Her hair fell from its knot and tumbled over her face. She tucked it behind her ears. "I won't go."

"We'll both stay with you. The roaches won't get anyone." Jordan spread out her hands. "Simmer down, my friend. Everything's fine."

"Promise," I demanded. "You must promise."

"Founders' oath," Zhen declared. "But you promise to ease up."

My body sagged. "I will."

"We'll see to your headache," she continued, "then you'll eat and rest."

A dim sense of urgency prompted me to say, "Something else."

"Something else what?" Zhen asked as she guided me to the sofa under the stormy painting and Jordan dug through the medkit. "Water, J."

"I cannot . . ." I obediently swallowed the pills. Jordan gave me food, but rather than eating, I leaned forward to rest my forehead in my hand. "Yes, the drones. Charles? I think . . . And Kyleigh. Yes, Kyleigh."

"My friend," Jordan said softly, "you aren't making any sense. Rest for now. Whatever it is, it can wait."

They layered blankets over me, and as sleep took hold to drag me under, my final thought was that Jordan had twice referred to me as her friend.

Snatches of conversation intruded on dreams, which I forgot upon waking. I stretched. The blankets crumpled to the floor as my stocking-clad feet slipped from underneath.

Zhen was at my side before I stood. "Feeling better? Tingling gone?"

After a brief internal inventory, I nodded.

"Don't worry," she said proactively. "You haven't missed much. Sit. Eat."

Jordan's tall form filled the doorway. "We've been keeping an eye on the halls upstairs. You can join us after you eat something."

My attempt to raise but one brow failed again. "And where else would I go?"

Zhen's smile flickered then vanished, and I choked down three food bars while she watched me as intently as a drone witnessing a contract. When I left the table for the other room, Jordan stood, spun the chair at the console around, and motioned to it.

I accepted the seat with thanks. "Is everyone well? Did *Attlee* send another shuttle?"

"Yes, but the one Elder and his drone-minions stayed close to it the whole time. Like glue." She smirked. "It left pretty soon afterward."

Confusion blurred my reasoning. "What do you mean?"

"That Jackson's plenty smart," Zhen answered. "He must've had your jammers nearby. That Elder wouldn't risk losing control."

Jordan tapped a monitor. "And from what we can see, everyone's fine down here. We've only seen one roach the whole time."

I sank back into the chair. "Good."

"Earlier you said something about Kyleigh and drones," she continued.

"Did I?"

"Moons and stars." A touch of Zhen's usual asperity returned. "On and on about those blasted drones. We dealt with them yesterday."

"I had forgotten."

A frown flitted over Jordan's face. "My guess? You wanted to check the backup files, then investigate Kyleigh's father's death."

Kyleigh's tear-stained face flickered in my memory. "Yes."

Jordan's expression lightened. "It seems you've forgotten Zhen DuBois is good with computers. She's already pulled them up and loaded them on datapads."

I felt as if I had lost mass and could hover like a drone. "Thank you both."

"Once we're back on *Thalassa*," Zhen added, "we can go on a crime-solving spree."

Her use of first-person plural further lifted my spirits. "I could start now."

"You need rest," they responded in unison.

"If my headache returns, I will lie down." When they began to protest, I added, "Not that either of you are licensed physicians with the authority to tell me what I may or may not do."

Jordan's eyes bored into mine. "If you have any symptoms of anything at all, you stop. I need to eat, but Zhen will keep an eye on you."

"There is no need," I said to her back as she left the room.

"Too bad," Jordan answered over her shoulder.

Zhen inserted her datapad into a slot at the VVR and settled on my sleeping mat, which had been neatly pulled smooth. She took out her knitting. "There. Everything's loaded onto that pathetic piece of equipment."

I thanked her and propelled the chair to the antiquated station where I sorted through records from right before and after the time of Charles Tristram's death. Kyleigh, Freddie, and Elliott were easy enough to find. They had been in class at the time, but I frowned.

Where had Julian Ross been?

Behind me the sound of knitting needles tapered to nothing. Zhen called out, "J, can I borrow your whetstone?"

"Why?" Jordan asked, but I heard her shuffling through a pack. "Thought you said you were taking your knives to be sharpened when we get back?"

"Not this one." Zhen grunted thanks, then steel swished on stone. "And don't stand there judging me, J. I'm no thief. It's not like I'm keeping it."

"That's not—"

"I'm planning on giving it back in *very* good condition."

The tightness in Zhen's voice pulled me around. She was carefully and precisely sharpening the blade that had struck Alec. Something in her movements chilled me, so I refocused on the documentation, but for the first time, the sound of someone sharpening a knife was not relaxing at all. The angry whisper of knife and oiled stone crept up my spine.

Ignoring the repetitive rasp, I poured all my efforts into my search until I found him. Ross had been in his laboratory all the way across

Pallas Station from the room where Charles Tristram died. He peered into microscopes, ran calculations, wrote a report—which I verified—and would occasionally drop to do push-ups before returning to his computer. When the station's alarm sounded, he tapped his communications link. I checked the logs. He had contacted his brother and Gideon Lorde, in that order. The hallways around his laboratory and Georgette SahnVeer's never flickered. Never disappeared.

Julian Ross had not lied.

It was anticlimactic, to be truthful, and moreover, I was irritated at my relief. "Jordan, Zhen."

The knife stopped its incessant threats, and Zhen and Jordan were at my side.

"Another headache?" Zhen asked sharply.

"No." I pointed at the images. "I have proof. Julian Ross was indeed in his laboratory the entire day. He did not kill Charles Tristram."

Zhen scowled. "He probably faked this."

I shook my head. "His alterations of *Thalassa*'s records proved he lacks the skill."

"Maybe, but it doesn't absolve him from trying to kill you," Zhen growled. "Or from trying to kill the Consortium, or being a lying, deceitful—"

"I do not deny his other actions, but he did not murder Kyleigh's father."

Zhen's scowl deepened. "Whoever did is long gone."

"True," Jordan said. "But it had to be someone Kyleigh knew, someone she considered a friend." Her expression darkened. "Kye deserves a measure of peace over the whole thing."

Which had been my point all along. "There is also the death of the Recorder and the sudden death of nineteen people."

Zhen cracked her knuckles as she studied the monitors. "It's the right thing to do, and we've got the time. What do you need?"

Julian exited the provost's office holding the verified, recorded assurance that, in defiance of regulations, he would receive guardianship of his younger brother.

He'd done it. He'd walked in and confronted Provost Humphreys. And if she didn't want news to go public about her drunken behavior, broken contract, and bigotry, she'd continue to cooperate. She'd keep her promise. And void take it, if she decided to reveal Julian's methods, fight him, or try to take him down, he'd pull her with him as relentlessly as a singularity.

The point was Elliott would be safe, even if the cost was a sliver of Julian's soul. No, that metaphysical rubbish of souls was an old-Earth relic of whatever religions the Founders had fled. The word didn't even belong in modern society. Except it felt true. It felt like he'd betrayed himself and a part of what made him Julian was gone.

He hadn't made it past the library, though, when the impact of what he'd done hit him like a city tram gone off its rails.

Blackmail.

A crime that would mark him—on the right cheekbone, like his father's sentencing tattoo—as someone with a debt to society. Blackmail was a crime that would pack him off to the inner belt or even LaGrange clusters around Krios, where his father had been sentenced. And unlike his father, he'd be guilty.

He ducked behind the bushes to try to get his racing heart under control. With no Consortium spies watching, he pressed back the onslaught of nausea. He couldn't be sick—wouldn't. Not if any shred of willpower would prevent it.

Elliott was just a kid, he reminded himself. Julian knew what it felt like to have his world destroyed. So, he forced down the fear he'd be caught. Ignored the nagging voice telling him he should have found another way and the persistent whisper that Mum and Dad would be ashamed of what he'd done. But space it all, what else was he supposed to do? Let Children's Services keep Elliott in some rotting dorm on the belt? He compacted those thoughts and fears deep inside, hid them with the tight ball of grief at Dad's death.

But as Julian made his way across Albany City University's campus, it didn't feel the same. Or he didn't.

The same dome soared overhead. The same mimosa trees littered the science quad with the same tiny leaflets. Other students rushed past him to lectures, while he watched—as detached as if from another planet, one with no connection to Ceres or New Triton. He sat through Molecular Genetics, but whatever Dr. Jimenez droned on about was as unintelligible as the opera he'd saved up credits to take Medea to last quarter.

After the lecture, he made his way toward the café near the gymnasium, where he and Medea had breakfast every ninth-day since their first date almost a year ago. The promise of spending time with her usually centered him, but this was different. He couldn't flub this up. Medea was smart. He had to figure out how to convince her the provost had declared he could have custody of Elliott even though the university prohibited uncontracted, underage parenting and guardianship, but he also couldn't let her get trapped in his—in criminal behavior.

She'd understand, though. She had to. She'd like Elliott, and her gentleness would be what Elliott needed. They'd be a family.

The door slid open, and the warm scents of cinnamon, nutmeg, and coffee tumbled out. Medea was already at their usual table, though she was sipping lemon water instead of her typical latte. Her quick smile patched the part of him the morning had damaged.

"Morning, Julian."

"Medea, my lady." He tucked his pack under his chair and skimmed the menu out of habit. Once they'd placed their orders, he held out his hand. She took it. "Dee, I have to—"

"Would you still love me if I got fat?"

That came out of nowhere. His brows twisted. "But you aren't."

"If." She studied the lemon water.

"You won't. But I'd love you whatever."

"My mother got fat, and my father canceled their contract."

He frowned. "That's pretty low."

"Yeah."

Their food arrived, and Julian stirred cream and sugar into his coffee and offered to pour Medea some.

"Not today." She took a dainty bite out of the lemon thing she'd ordered. "Julian? When you asked me something a while back, did you mean it?"

He cocked his head. "A little vague."

"You asked me to contract."

He choked. Void it—had she decided to answer after he had gone and blackmailed the provost? All the same, she wouldn't have brought it up if she was going to turn him down, would she? He wiped suddenly sweaty palms on his pants.

Pink suffused her cheeks. "Did you mean it?"

"Yes. I wouldn't have asked otherwise." He straightened. "Do you have an answer?"

She glanced at the window. "Not yet."

"Oh." Deflated, he finished his bagel and poured a second cup of coffee.

Her eyebrows arched. "You never have a second cup."

"Busy morning."

"Your genetics class was that busy?" she asked dryly.

Don't mess up, Julian. "I had a meeting."

"With?"

All the practiced threats he'd laid out hours ago were easy compared to this.

"Julian." Concern laced her features, and she slid her tiny fingers between his large ones, her thumb rubbing his knuckles. "You look like one of those dust storms that has the city scrambling to replace panels in the dome. All towering and dark. Are you all right?"

Get it over with. Void it. She was the best thing to happen to him since he'd reached this ugly planet.

He met her gaze. "I met with Provost Humphreys, Dee. I convinced her to let me have Elliott."

"Elliott? Your brother?" She lowered her voice. "No one can have a kid unless they have a contract. Regulations."

"I can."

She jerked her hand away. "That's impossible. People get booted from uni if they're pregnant and uncontracted. You can't have a kid or a guardianship and attend classes."

Be nonchalant. "She sent the official documents to a Recorder and had them verified, then contacted Children's Services. They already sent out an emergency request. He'll be bound out on the next transport."

She gaped.

"I think she knew I can handle it. Maybe she felt bad that a little kid with family would be shunted into the system."

"Provost Humphreys has all the compassion of a meteorite. There's no way . . ." Her deep-blue eyes narrowed. "Julian Meredith Ross. What did you do?"

He chugged some coffee, scalded his throat. "I presented my case and—"

"Stars," she hissed, as she shot a glance over her shoulder. "You have something on her, don't you?"

"What?" His face heated. "No."

"Don't you lie to me, Julian. I can take a lot of . . ." Her face drained of color. "That's why you asked."

"What?"

"You didn't ask because you loved me." Medea's voice broke. "You were using me so you could keep your brother."

"Don't be ridiculous. I asked you before my father's accident. Remember?" Under his eyes, she shrank down into herself, and his panic reared up. "I brought a picnic to the top of the biology building, where there aren't any spying Consortium cameras, and—"

"You . . ." Her pupils grew so wide they almost hid her blue irises. "You knew no one would see—no one would hear."

"You think I wanted anyone else there? I wanted me and you. That's all—"

"You wanted your brother."

"Elliott was fine, Dee," he protested. "He was with our father. And although you've always known I wanted both of them out of the mines—"

"I should have put it together."

"You don't get it." He tried again. "I asked you because you've been the best thing that's happened to me since I can't say when."

"And I fell for it. Stars. I really thought you loved me, or I wouldn't—"

"I do." Desperation set in. "Medea, look at me."

She turned her head away.

"He's only a kid," he pled. "Not even as old as I was when we lost everything. No kid should be shoved into a system when someone can come to their rescue."

"And you wound up on an asteroid with him and your father. You never told me what your dad did."

His temper flashed. "Nothing. He didn't do anything at all."

"Because innocent people are always sent to the mines to pay off their debt to society." She put a hand to her head and groaned. "No, I'm sorry. I shouldn't have said that."

Spacing right, you shouldn't have.

"Fine. You want to know? Mum died when Elliott was about one, and—no!" he said quickly when her face drained of all color. "Dad didn't kill her. It was established in court. It wasn't his fault, but my aunt pressed for negligence charges. Recorders came and testified against him."

She gasped.

He picked up his coffee mug and turned it around and around in his hands. "In a way, it's my fault because I petitioned to keep us together after Mum died. I persuaded the courts my father was competent. And no one else wanted us. No one, not even Mum's family. Don't you see? With our father gone, my little brother will be caught up in the inner belt Children's Agency's machinations. They were spacing bad enough back on Ceres."

"That must have been so very hard."

She spoke so gently that his hope sparked, but he didn't let himself reach for her hand again.

"Dad let his grief eat him up for a third of my life. He didn't snap out of it until I was accepted here. A third of my life, Dee. His grief and the mines destroyed my childhood, and I can't abandon Elliott." He clamped his mouth shut before he revealed how he convinced Provost Humphreys to let him have custody of his brother.

"It doesn't matter to me that your dad was a convict." Her words sank down like lead. "But Julian, I need your honesty and your trust."

"You have it, Medea."

"But you're lying about something—or hiding something. That's as bad."

"I—" Void it, she'd be as complicit as he was. He wouldn't put her in danger. If anyone was going to be sent to the belt for this, it wouldn't be Medea. They'd eat her alive out there. She wouldn't last a ten-day. "I can't tell you."

She clenched her small hands into fists. "And therein lies the problem. If I believed you really loved me, I know we could be happy."

"I do. You're the first thing I think of every day. I can't prove *that*, Dee, but I do love you."

"More than your brother?"

That was the radiation burst he'd been afraid of. "Medea."

"You have to love me if you want me to stay. Thin or fat. Better or worse."

"I do."

"Above all others."

His heart slammed in his chest. "Dee, please. Don't make me choose."

Her tears spilled over. "You already did."

She rounded the table and stood before him, ran her perfect hands through his hair and kissed his forehead.

"I love you, Julian."

And she was gone.

Around him, customers finished meals, then left. Finally, the café manager tapped his shoulder, told him they were closing up.

That late? He'd missed Intra-system Economics.

Julian trudged out, his hands stuffed in his pockets.

Well, he'd survived losing Mum. He'd lost Dad twice, once when Mum died, then a few ten-days ago he'd lost him forever. Medea was safer away from him and his splintered soul anyway. He'd paid for his brother's safety with a part of who he always claimed to be, but there wasn't any other choice. Whatever happened, Elliott was family—Julian tried to expunge his thought that Medea could have been family, too—and family comes first.

Always.

Frustration built to surpass weariness when, the next morning after breakfast, the translucent images in the small VVR had not proven anything other than Ross's innocence, although at least I remembered what I had meant about *drones*. Any and all documentation needed to be purged from the Recorders' individual drones, which took several hours. Zhen insisted on saving their personal records on spare datapads, which seemed exceptionally unwise to me.

I returned to my fruitless perusal of records on the antiquated VVR, and Zhen watched the monitors and kept me company, her needles trading yarn like whispers of gossip. Jordan, who had been unusually restless, traversed the other room. Zhen would occasionally call out an update, but when she laughed out loud, Jordan left her pacing to lean over the monitor.

Jordan snorted. "Does Hodges have what I think he has?"

"He does."

"They'll kill him for this." Jordan's low chuckle seemed to contradict the severity of her assessment. "Can you angle the cameras?"

"Hold on," Zhen said.

I frowned. While not displeased she had discovered a solution, I had received training solely for this purpose. Adjusting the cameras should have been simple.

"There." Jordan pointed. "To the right."

Zhen grinned. "Oh good, he left the door—"

They both collapsed in laughter. Curiosity pulled me over, but all I saw was the young man with the struggling moustache running full speed down the hall from the rooms where the marines slept, clutching a—

"Is he holding a cockroach antenna?"

Caught in the throes of amusement, Zhen nodded and gestured at another monitor where a knot of laughing marines blocked a man in his stocking feet from chasing the runner.

There were moments I did not understand citizens. This was one of them.

A flurry of activity on the control room's monitor snared my attention. Marines were jumping to their feet, and at the communications console, the woman's hands flew between knobs, buttons, and switches. Surely a man who was unwise enough to snap off a cockroach antenna had not provoked a response clear in the control room?

"Jordan? Zhen? The control room—is the activity connected with Hodges?"

Their amusement vanished as they watched the other monitor.

While one man dropped to his knees to rifle through a pack on the floor, a pair of marines sprinted from the control room. People throughout the station went still, their heads cocked as if they listened. The hangar began to pulse with activity.

I scanned the images until I found two Consortium-grey, armored suits amid the marines' blue. James and Daniel and three others pushed a hover gurney laden with boxes and bags. They paused for a moment, then sped up, taking the second turning, but away from the hangar. James and Daniel proceeded another fifteen meters, then the shortest marine patted their shoulders. Daniel hefted his weapon, and they both turned right and disappeared from our view. The other three marines continued with the material-laden gurney and turned onto more frequently used passages.

"Jordan?" I asked. "I do not understand."

Her forehead knotted. "Still no sound?"

Zhen shook her head. "Not unless you want to start recording everything."

I added, "Which is not worth the risk."

"Quincy!" Zhen pointed at the monitor showing the control room. "Good man! He remembered we can't hear. Hold on, I'll zoom in."

I might not have recognized him without Zhen's identification, but indeed, a tiny, clean-shaven Quincy raised his face so the camera had a clear view of his features. He stood by the communication console holding a large datapad over his head with one hand and waving with the other.

The letters on the datapad blurred and danced, though whether due to poor resolution or a vision issue, I could not tell. He lowered it, typed, and gave the datapad to another marine before jogging over to Jackson. Not realizing where the camera was, the woman slowly rotated, only facing the camera at random.

I squinted at the screen. "What does it say?"

Jordan huffed and rubbed her eyes. "I can't tell. Zhen?"

After a moment, Zhen, too, jumped to her feet, embraced Jordan, then enfolded me in a hug. "They have it! They have a treatment!"

Surprise at Zhen's quick hug delayed my comprehension. "The virus?"

She beamed at me. "Yes!"

Hope hit me like a shock wave. I dropped into the chair, and tears welled up. This would prevent deaths like Freddie's or the ones on *Agamemnon*. The promise felt too overwhelming and grand.

"How?" I asked, my voice shaky. "Do they have an antivirus or simply understand the mechanism?"

"Can't know unless they write it down. Move," Zhen said, but not roughly.

Jordan helped me to my feet, and we watched the screen as the woman typed something else and again showed Quincy's datapad to the entire control room.

"Datapad says—" She growled an unkind description of the woman. "Just a moment. She took it down to write something else. There's no way to pause what we're seeing," Zhen protested. "Wait . . ." Her voice brightened. "The datapad says, '*Attlee* leaving supplies, departing for NT. Stay put.'"

"That makes sense," Jordan said. "Even with *Thalassa* fully operational, *Attlee* is faster, and the information has to get to New Triton as soon as possible. We'll fix up *Thalassa* and follow. Any idea when we can get out of here?"

Zhen spun the chair around and lofted her eyebrows at the taller woman. "Moons and stars, J, how am I supposed to know?"

Jordan grinned. "Well, the marine put the datapad down. I say we break out the instant coffee to celebrate, since that's as fancy as we'll get."

My thoughts crystalized, and I blurted, "Will they keep Edwards?"

Both of my friends' smiles evaporated.

"They ought not keep him," I pressed when neither replied. Panic punched tiny fists into my lungs. "He has done much to assist us, much to, to . . ."

Zhen stood abruptly, caught my arm, and lowered me into the chair.

"They probably will. We'll find out soon enough." Jordan settled in a crouch in front of me. "We haven't forgotten him, and we won't. And we haven't forgotten you, either. Daniel and James have new identities now. You still need one yourself."

I resisted the urge to tap my thigh. "I cannot."

"Dross," Zhen said rudely. "You can so."

Jordan, however, asked why, and I gave them the muddled explanation that my disappearance would call attention to the men's.

"Wait right here." Zhen retrieved her pack from the other room, then placed the black-and-silver identification bracelet that had once belonged to Alec's mother in my hand. "I've carried this since you left. I knew you'd be back. That you'd need it."

"Did you ever pick a name?" Jordan asked.

My gaze shot to the drones, and my respiration sped up.

"I know," she said, as if she read my thoughts. "It feels all wrong to talk in front of those things, but you turned them all off, remember?"

"I had forgotten," I confessed. "As to a name, I have one in mind." I caught myself before I said more, before I told them something that could draw them into danger. "As Edwards told me long ago, it is not a decision to make lightly. He never told me what he chose." I sighed. "I will keep it as my own secret and hold fast to the truth."

Jordan cocked her head to the side, and her braids clicked. "Which is?"

"Love." I would not say family. "Sacrifice means nothing without love. And that every human in this system is unique and valuable."

"Including you," Jordan said softly.

I closed my eyes and claimed her assertion: "Even me."

Silence crept around us, filling gaps with larger gaps, until Zhen said abruptly, "We're still going to celebrate finding whatever they found so they can save the system and *Attlee* taking off. You don't like coffee, do you?"

I blinked. "Pardon?"

"I'll look for tea."

"We won't forget you," Jordan said quietly.

"I know." I stood. "I will shut down the VVR. Eric Thompson was correct about its inadequacies."

"I'll do it." Jordan's expression softened. "You haven't recovered from your headache yesterday. Have some tea and then a lie-down. Work on it tomorrow." When I sputtered another protest, she added, "Please."

I acquiesced, and Jordan settled in the chair, her focus flitting from screen to screen. I turned off visual records and settled on the sofa with a cup of lavender tea.

Even if I never claimed a name legally, I would hold one as my own. After all, Lorik had done so. I reviewed the names people had called me, from Izzy to Zeta. Choosing a name that was an abbreviated form of either *Recorder-who-isn't* or my Consortium designation number did not feel like who I was, who I was meant to be. No, I lingered over my favorites, from ones offered before I left on *Agamemnon* to the one offered here on Pallas. Then, deep in my heart, I repeated the one that felt like home.

I drifted to sleep, content that *Attlee* would carry whatever knowledge the researchers had uncovered to New Triton. The scent of lavender lingered in the air, both a memory and a promise.

40

Jordan whistled.

When I looked around from the antiquated VVR, she tossed me a water bottle and a food bar. I caught the first, but the second skidded under the chair. My lack of coordination brought heat to my cheeks. The package proved difficult to open by hand, and I was close to swallowing my pride and asking for Jordan's knife when the packaging split on the third attempt. The scent of blueberries and oats wafted free.

I left the antiquated VVR flickering and took the seat at the monitor while the other two chatted quietly, but when there was a lull in their conversation, I confessed my lack of success uncovering the perpetrator who had made Kyleigh an orphan.

"Not quite an orphan. Her mother lives on Ceres." Jordan stabbed her fork into her rice and beans.

"And there is no one to bring to justice." I carefully folded the wrapper into a tidy cube.

Zhen frowned. "Not knowing would bother anyone, but as if grief itself isn't hard to bear, she knew whoever it was. Talked with them, had meals with them. She doesn't talk about it much, but I bet it's eating at her. Who can she trust; who can she not?" Her eyes flashed. "Especially after Ross and Elliott. She took it personally that her friend was in league with genocidal monsters."

"The station's security chief," Jordan began. "What was his name?"

"Gideon Lorde," I offered.

"Right." Jordan nodded. "He didn't figure it out, but he was one of those nineteen who died after Kye's dad, if I remember correctly. Maybe he didn't have time." She scraped the last bite from the dish. "I'd want to know, if only so I could properly hate the person who did it."

Zhen's glare eased. "Kye's not quite like that. I think she'll want to know so she can forgive them or something."

Jordan gestured with her empty fork. "Point."

Therein lay my secondary problem. "And yet she did not seem to feel forgiveness before she left Pallas. It was as if she had forgotten who she was."

The inactive drones seemed to grow behind me, looming over our conversation, threatening every word I had not spoken. Even here with my friends, I could not bring myself to admit my concern that Kyleigh might have lost her assurance in her unquantifiable God.

The loss mattered to me, more than I could have predicted. She had held to her beliefs through grief before, and whether or not I—or anyone else—believed them as well, they had provided her a foundation. They offered her a glimmer of hope that the inexorable march of time, coincidence, and human error were inadequate obstacles on a path to something greater. But I could not admit that aloud, either.

I placed the empty wrapper in the portable rubbish compactor.

"She hasn't forgotten." Zhen joined me in the monitoring room. "It's just been a few days since losing Freddie. She probably believes it was her fault—"

"It was not," I declared emphatically.

Jordan held up a hand. "No one but Kye thinks it was."

"Kyliegh's emotions have to be all over the place. She's lost her father, Freddie, and everyone she'd known over the past few years. I mean, I don't think Elliott was a loss, but he was her friend before he joined up with those trogs." Zhen sighed. "I get it. I felt lost when my grandmère died."

Zhen loosened the collar of her Consortium-labeled suit and pulled out a necklace with a small pendant, a centimeter wide and twice as long. She unfastened the clasp and placed the necklace onto my palm. A plain silver casing surrounded strands of white hair interwoven with black, not dissimilar to the roots of Zhen's blue hair. A smooth glass-like substance encased the intricate pattern.

"A memorial pendant?" I asked.

"My grandmère's. I have this physical reminder of her, and some days . . ." Zhen paused, then began again. "It's been four years, but some days it's as raw as it was then. Some days the ache is all encompassing. Others, it's not there at all, which felt like a betrayal at first. Maybe it isn't that way for everyone." She shrugged. "I wouldn't know."

A knot rose in my throat. "Today?"

The corner of her mouth lifted. "Today's all right, though I wish she'd been there when Alec and I first contracted. She would have approved of the strawberry cake. She loved strawberries."

Like a shot fired in an enclosed space, jealousy ricocheted through my heart. I had never had such a person—a mother or grandmother who wanted to share strawberry cake with me. I was a child of the Consortium. I had no other family. My hand fisted tightly around the pendant. But as quickly as it had come, the jealousy fled.

Faces appeared one after another in my mind. Nate. Max, James, Alec, Kyleigh, Jordan, Zhen. And the others: Edwards—though thinking of him pinched my heart—Williams, Cam, Eric, and Tia. For whatever time I had remaining, I had their friendship, which was wealth beyond anything I had dared imagine.

Wordlessly, I returned the pendant to Zhen, who refastened her necklace and traced a fingertip over the surface.

"In those first days, there was nothing at all except the hole left by Grandmère's absence, but Kyleigh doesn't even have a pendant. Maybe it isn't so much that she's lost her faith"—I gasped at Zhen's supposition—"but after losing her father, her mentor, her friends, and the boy she loved, she has to reorient herself. She'll change some. Grief does that. It takes a while for a gaping wound in your heart to heal."

I opened my mouth to protest that loss was unlike physical injuries, but had it not been as painful as any medically treatable injury to be taken away from *Thalassa* and Nate? To lose Lorik as I began to understand him, watch Freddie suffer, or fear Alec might die? Had not my chest ached when they had stolen Edwards? There was no true cure for the hurt, was there?

I wanted to reject the idea that pain was the price of love, and yet . . .

The storm on Ceres caught my eye.

"His paintings," I said. "Can we take them? They could be Freddie's memorial."

Zhen's expression lightened. "That's a lovely idea."

"We can pack them on the platform," Jordan mused. "Stars, what a puzzle we've locked ourselves into." She glanced past me, and her gaze sharpened. "Hangar's opening."

Though Zhen spun around at once, it took two seconds before

I realized Jordan was not implying that the hangar was part of a greater puzzle.

On the central monitor, the hangar doors crept apart, and *Attlee's* shuttle settled. A droneless Recorder descended the ramp, and five alert and armed marshals accompanied a hover platform similar to the one we had used to carry equipment. After a heated discussion we could not hear, one which involved wild gesticulation on both sides, two marines left the small office and led *Attlee's* group down the halls. After they rounded the corner, two more took off at a run toward the control room, while another one opened the tail end of one of the hangar's towering industrial bots and dug through the rubbish it had collected.

"What in the system is that about?" Zhen asked.

Neither Jordan nor I knew the answer.

As the first procession wound its way through convoluted passages, the runners reached the control room. Except for the woman focused on the communication console, every marine shot to his or her feet.

"They're arguing," Zhen observed unnecessarily.

Finally, there seemed to be a resolution, for moments later, the same runners, and two more, dashed out before the Recorder, marshals, and other marines arrived. After a brief discussion, five marines led the way down the hall to the blocked tunnel where Lorik had died. They aimed heavy guns on tripods at the rubble, and I grabbed Jordan's arm.

"They cannot mean to—"

"Oh, but they can," she replied through gritted teeth. "They must be after proof your Elder is gone."

"I do not want—cannot watch. And the roaches." My voice echoed mechanically in my ears, and I waved a hand at the screens. Zhen caught my wrist. Despite my assertion, I could not look away while the marshals set explosives.

"Moons and stars," Zhen hissed, and her grip constricted my wrist. "What are James and Daniel doing back in the station proper with a Recorder present?"

"What? Where?"

She pointed to another monitor, where James, Daniel, and one of the runners hurried down a passage not far from the control room.

The hair on my arms rose. "The Recorder will see them!" My words rushed out in a torrent. "And she will take them, and they will be sent to the Halls."

"Steady on." Jordan placed a hand on my back. "They aren't stupid. There must be a reason that they—"

"Hold up." Zhen leaned forward, and her long, straight blue hair poured over her shoulder. "Isn't that the room where we took your drone?"

The marine exited and dashed back to the control room. On the small screen, my friends peeked both ways and vanished into the unobserved sectors, but their departure did nothing to ease the building pressure in my chest. I pulled from Zhen's grasp.

Two of the monitors flared with yellow-orange and white lights.

I backed away until I hit the wall. My fingers guided me into the antechamber. When my legs bumped a chair, I slid to the floor beside it. I drew my knees as close to my chest as the armored suit would allow, resting my forehead against them.

No. I could not watch. I would not see what remained of Lorik. Moisture leaked from my eyes as I rocked. Dimly, I heard Jordan's husky alto and Zhen's smooth soprano, but their words were naught but noise. I wanted to uncurl, to stand, but it was as if I stood far away and called to myself, and the self on the floor refused to listen. A hand tapped my shoulder, but I curled into a tighter ball.

Their conversation resumed, but all I could discern was *too much, do something, consequence, risk.*

I thought I heard Max's voice, but he was not present, was he?

The pop of a jet injector on my neck stilled my thoughts with the memories of lavender, pine, and cinnamon. My respiration slowed. When internal tremors ceased and I raised my head, Jordan's golden-brown eyes stared into mine.

"You with us again?" she whispered.

I licked my lips. "Yes."

Her eyes closed briefly. "Good."

"They retrieved the station Recorder's damaged drone but had to run for it when a small army of bugs showed up." Zhen appeared and knelt beside Venetia Jordan. "Everything's all right. They loaded it on the platform, along with some scraps."

The scent of lavender intensified, enabling me to ask calmly, "Scraps of what?"

Jordan shot a glare at Zhen, then cleared her throat. "No one was hurt."

"They retreated and resealed the corridor," Zhen said. "That Recorder is almost as good with explosives as Alec."

"They're loading the shuttle now," Jordan said. "No one found James."

"Or Daniel." Zhen's attention darted back to the small room, and she was on her feet, then at the desk. "We've got another datapad message." She groaned. "Why can't Quincy tell that woman where the blasted camera is?"

Jordan gripped my elbow and brought me to my feet.

"'*Attlee* shuttle departing.'" A quick tap sounded from the other room. "Well, we knew that, thank you very much. Right here on the screen."

Once I was ensconced on the sofa, Jordan brought me a bottle of water and some medication. Too tired to argue, I simply swallowed the pills.

"Wait, she's—oh good, she's turning this way first. '*Attlee* to depart once the shuttle returns.' About time."

"Any news on *Thalassa*?" Jordan asked.

"She's typing again." After another minute or so, Zhen appeared at the door, a tight smile on her face. "They're almost done on *Thalassa* and are starting to pack up here. Won't take long, so don't get too comfortable on that sofa. Looks like we're leaving."

Jordan, Zhen, and I remained in the computer room much longer than we had anticipated. Although we were prepared to return to the upper levels after *Attlee* had finally departed, the roaches and another power fluctuation conspired to keep us locked in the underbelly of Pallas Station. Insects had massed near the hangar while the marines loaded the shuttle. Even after the marines drove them away, discouragement and regret pinned down my spirits.

My headache returned, and Jordan insisted that I sleep on the aubergine sofa instead of the mat. I conceded. Zhen brought out another jet injector, and by that point, the discomfort had grown to an unbearable level. I accepted it. Her face pale, she settled on the floor beside me, the sound of knitting lulling me to sleep.

I woke but once that night. Zhen still sat beside me, staring through the doorway at the monitors, her grandmother's pendant in her hand and her cheeks streaked with tears. I debated rising and bringing her a blanket, but witnessing her tears felt like eavesdropping. I closed my eyes and faced the wall.

In the morning, when the only communication from the control room was a note from Quincy, telling us to hold tight, I insisted we reconfigure a communications link to listen in on their chatter. After all, I reasoned, if Skip and his ilk could do so, why should we not?

We did, just in time to listen to a call for backup, as somewhere on the station, unwitnessed by the monitors, the marines stumbled across a knot of the terrorists. We listened to shouts and the percussive cracks of weapons' fire. Jordan nodded to Zhen, who walked me back to the sofas and stayed with me, where we could barely hear the external speakers. After an eternal minute or two, the terrorists scattered. The marines apprehended a man, but he swallowed a pill and died before relaying any information. When Zhen informed me that the two that had been captured after the drone killed that man had done the same, Jordan appeared at the door and shushed her. They both fell silent, casting furrowed glances in my direction.

When *Thalassa's* shuttle landed, Zhen was knitting in the chair, and Jordan stood behind her. I squeezed between them in time to see Nate's tall silhouette disembark. Hope lifted me, but though I thought I recognized Lars, I did not see Alec. I glanced at Zhen, whose knitting needles clicked instead of shushed. Muttering imprecations, she scowled at the yarn and unraveled several rows.

Before anyone gave us a signal that our escort was coming, a flurry of activity in the control room combined with chaos over the communications link. A small ship had lifted off from a cave seven kilometers away. All marines took defensive positions, in case the ship fired upon us. Though truly, there was not much we could have done, deep underground, and when I said as much, Jordan's expression tightened.

The small ship simply . . . left. Chatter over the communications link verified that the craft had even avoided *Thalassa*.

"Good riddance," Zhen muttered.

We pulled on our caps, but as I did, my gaze drifted to the five drones.

"I do not wish to reactivate the Elder's drone," I said.

"Then don't." Zhen folded her knitting into her pack, which she stuffed between the blanket-wrapped paintings.

"We do not have enough microantigravity units to carry it." I bit my lip. "I should activate a drone for you, Zhen."

"There's no need now that the criminals have left." Jordan squinted at the door, then said, "Actually, I don't see why we need to take any of them out of here."

"No, without the need to deceive anyone," I began, but an idea flashed so brightly that I exclaimed, "Oh!"

Jordan raised a brow, and Zhen demanded, "What?"

"Has my AAVA drone finished transmitting all information to *Thalassa*?"

Zhen lifted a shoulder. "I think so."

"Double-check." I yanked off my cap and gloves and dashed to Lorik's slave drones.

"Moons and stars, what are you doing?"

My fingers flew over panels and through commands as if I had never had a headache, flawed memory, or tingling hands. "I *am* leaving drones here, Zhen, as Jordan suggested."

A slow smile curved Zhen's lips. "Good."

I held up my hand. "Wait." Without a single glance at the monitors, I ran back to my pack and pulled out the tools and wiring. "Jordan, I need your assistance."

"What do you need?"

"Fetch the lavender jammer. *Attlee*'s Elders have left, and with no further need for the AAVA drone, with Zhen's help I can turn Lorik's slave drones—the larger ones—into jamming devices. The other three can remain here, hidden, and the Consortium will not find them, for without a drone, no one will be able to access this room."

Zhen's expression shifted. "So, bugs aside, the station will be safe."

I smiled. "Exactly."

"And any Recorder who wanted to flee the Consortium could hide here. Having met a few dissidents lately, I'm pretty sure there are more than three of you." Zhen was already tugging off her cap and gloves. "Tell me what to do."

The next hour flew past. Jordan listened to communications and watched the monitors as Zhen and I created the safest place in the system, right in the middle of a moon that would kill the unwary. It was the best gift I could give to others like me, though it was unlikely that anyone would ever find it. Still, creating a sanctuary seemed the right thing to do.

My contentment was compounded when Jordan called out, "Company incoming," for in my heart, I knew it meant Nate would be here soon.

"I'll be glad to be done with this place," Zhen said. "When?"

"Quincy said they're gearing up to come and get us in half an hour, so we've got time to eat first."

"That's a lot for a small, hard-to-read datapad, J."

Jordan tapped her ear. "Ross and his ship left, so things are back to normal."

"About time." Zhen opened a container and tossed each of us a package.

As loath as I was to eat another packaged meal, I peeled back the wrapper, but when I saw the contents, I reread the label. It was not a mistake.

So *that* was what fish loaf was.

I moved the bland vegetables away from the alleged fish. Beans should be green, not a dull brown, but in comparison to the grey block of protein, they seemed a gourmet choice. I ate them instead and, thinking no one would notice, slipped the remainder of the meal into the rubbish.

Jordan eyed me.

I rechecked the water closet and under the sofas to confirm we had left nothing behind when my communications link crackled. My heart leapt in the expectation of Nate's voice.

"Venn?" a baritone asked. "Kyleigh?"

Chills swept over me as surely as if I had been ejected onto Pallas's subzero surface.

Not my Nathaniel.

Julian Ross.

"I need to speak to Venetia Jordan or Kyleigh Tristram," he demanded. "Or that Recorder. Put her on."

"Moons and stars," Zhen hissed.

"Venn, I know you're out there. I don't know about Kye," he continued. "I need to—"

"Too spacing late," Jordan growled.

"Then put the Recorder on. I know she's with you."

"Identify yourself," Jackson barked, startling me further. I had forgotten he, too, would have been connected via communications link.

"Julian Meredith Ross—"

A sharp snap popped in my ears, and the link went silent.

Jordan's jaw was taut, and her eyes were like lasers. "Looks like the departure was a decoy."

"Two can play the decoy game." Zhen turned to me. "Sorry, but we need drones after all."

Jordan's tone gentled. "I know you don't want to carry a weapon, but you're going to have to do it again to keep Zhen safe. And you need the Elder's drone."

All peace forgotten, I somehow managed a weak acknowledgment before turning to the drones resting on the floor and in the alcove.

"I will need to ensure that a short-range connection allows for communication, since we have created the jammer. Zhen, give me your blue datapad. And Jordan, yours as well."

They handed them over without complaint. I copied mine to both, opened the access panels, and inserted them into interior slots. I held my breath and activated the drones.

The power level on the Recorders' drones had plummeted, but the marines had left small charging units, like the ones I had used on Lorik's drone earlier. I attached the cables and lashed the units over top.

"Zhen, do you have a preference?" I asked.

For five seconds, there was silence, then she said, "That's a joke, right?"

"Indeed, it is not."

She poked her head around the corner. "I don't have a favorite drone. You go ahead and pick the best one."

"The one that belonged to James is a more recent model. I believe that they simply reprogrammed a previous Recorder's drone for Daniel, which though older has more extensive capabilities. Its programming, however, seems—"

"Void take them, I won't be *using* it. It's a prop." She withdrew into the other room again. "They look exactly the same to me."

Unable to decide, I activated both and tied them to my datapad using an uncommon frequency, then adding and expanding Lorik's directive and verifying it with his codes. They hovered at eye level while I added an order to remain in close proximity.

Having done all I could, I checked the time. I had procrastinated long enough. Jordan watched from the corner of her eye while I slid my navy-blue datapad into my pocket and reactivated Lorik's drone.

>>*No network detected. Assigned Elder not detected. Consortium device accepted. Enter CDN.*

Once more, I entered my designation and Lorik's codes.

>>*Codes accepted. Temporary access resumed. Length of time remaining, three hours, thirty-one minutes. Welcome, Aberrant Zeta4542910-9545E.*

Less than four hours? That gave me pause. Angling my back so neither of my friends could see the drone's screen, I asked, >>*Consequence of temporary access ending?*

>>*Illegal access punishable to the fullest extent of law, per AAVA section 41.7.13B.*

Removal for citizens and reclamation for Recorders.

"Very well," I said aloud.

>>*Power low.*

"Power will be sufficient for the task at hand," I said, ignoring the look Zhen threw at the drone and me.

>>*Protect.*

For a full minute, I stared at the single word on its screen, at its threat and its promise.

Well. I would have full control of an Elder's drone for over three full hours, and we would reach the upper levels and relative safety before then. I would simply shut it down before it turned on me.

Jordan straightened on her chair, squinted, and pinched the bridge of her nose. "Blast it—I should have—Zhen! I need you to read this for me."

Zhen strode in, leaned over the screen. "They're on their way. We need to be armed and ready to go."

"Helmets on." Jordan tossed me mine.

Zhen blanched when James's drone encircled her arm.

"It is merely mimicking mine," I reminded her.

"The Elder's." Zhen's sharp tone snapped over the external speaker. "Not yours."

"As you say." I fidgeted, adjusting the drone's tendril around my arm. "Why would Julian Ross wish to speak to me?"

"Don't know," Jordan said tightly. "And I don't care if I never find out."

My communications link clicked loudly.

"You'll need to open the door from the inside," Nate said, "since we don't have a drone."

Like a weighted blanket, an out-of-proportion sense of safety settled over me. Nate was here, and between him, Jordan, Zhen, and the drone, I knew I was safe.

Julian Ross could not harm me.

Jordan raised her weapon. Zhen unholstered—was that the word?—hers as well, which made little sense if she was to be my double.

"It is Nate," I objected.

"Most likely. Stay as far back as you can and keep the drone between you and the door for good measure."

At her warning, tension percolated underneath my layer of trust, but I did as she bade me. Zhen strode forward, the drone trailing behind her, and touched the panel that opened the door. Nate stepped through, and though I was behind the drone, as Jordan had wished, his eyes found mine. "You're okay?"

"Nathaniel Timmons." A smile bloomed on my face. "Yes, I believe we all are."

One corner of his mouth lifted, but he turned to the others. "Nice bracelet, Zhen, but Alec would like your gold one better." He grinned. "He's back in your quarters, out of the infirmary. Wanted me to tell you to be careful."

Her face lit up, and for three seconds, she closed her eyes and breathed out.

"Ready to roll, J?"

Jordan quirked a small smile. "As ever."

Nate met my eyes again. "We're splitting up once we reach the upper levels, so stick close to me."

"I will," I said, inwardly applauding myself for the self-control in not adding that doing so was all I wanted.

"We've got people waiting, so after you." Nate made an old-fashioned bow in my direction.

Targeting beams lit the hall. It was difficult to see exactly who was present, but a flat, rectangular shape surprised me.

"Nathaniel Timmons. You brought a hoverbed again."

"You don't have to use it," Nate said. "Walking is good. It's just in case."

My cheeks heated. "I am not an invalid."

The bearded marine's—no, his name was Quincy—voice sounded over his external link. "After Jordan and DuBois contacted Maxwell, he insisted we bring it as a precaution."

I spun back to Jordan. "You did not . . . This was when I—before using communications links were—"

"Later," Nate said gently. "Fuss at them when we're back."

"They were worried," a young voice added.

A sliver of anxiety supplanted indignation. "Eric Thompson?"

I could almost hear a smile in his voice when he answered, "The same."

"You should not be—"

"He's good," Lars interrupted.

Lines of concern, annoyance, and gratification intersected in my heart. "Has the entire station descended to escort us from the lower level?"

"Nah," Lars said. "Not everyone. Jackson asked for volunteers, but he said half his people was too many."

"Chat later," Quincy ordered. "We need to get her to Max."

"If you'd lock up, sweetheart," Nate said, "we can move."

I bit my lip at his endearment, but since I planned on shutting down the drone, there would be no need to worry. We could damage it, destroy its innards, and no one would be able to retrieve its information.

The door closed, and the locks snapped shut. No one would undo what Zhen and I had done. The station—and its jamming field—would be safe. Even if no one ever used it, it was here, a hidden sanctuary. The thought brought a layer of peace.

I turned back to the dim hall full of marines. "I can request the drones to provide light."

Nate and Quincy gave simultaneous negative answers, but neither explained why. It could not have been for secrecy's sake, since the targeting beams lacing the hall were anything but stealthy.

Clouds of silt drifted with every step and billowed softly under the drones' trailing tendrils. We walked silently past the dead roach, its desiccated frame casting shadows that grabbed the uneven light. I snuck a peek at its head. Both antennae had been snapped off, though there was nothing to indicate the perpetrator.

When the first group reached the ladder, Quincy climbed up and sent down a hushed summons that it was clear and to use the lift. Zhen and the drone moved to enter, and I left my spot to grab her drone-free arm, though I could not think what to say. Her dark eyes met mine, and the hint of one of her fierce smiles touched her lips. Both drones followed her obediently, and Eric and two others joined them. The inner and outer doors clanged shut. When I stepped back, Lorik's drone bumped my shoulder.

Nate's voice sounded low over his speaker. "She'll be fine."

"I know," I lied.

When the doors flew open, startling me, Nate guided me into the lift. Lars followed us. My stomach dropped as the lift shot up, then stopped abruptly. We exited into a hall mercifully clear of roach debris.

"See?" Lars said. "Everything's fine."

In very short order, Jordan, the platform, and the remaining marines joined us.

"We split up at the next junction after the hall turns right," Nate said.

Zhen's group led the way. Bootsteps, the whir of drones, the platform's microantigravity, and the jostling of weapons and equipment could not fill the hallway's emptiness. Instead, the small noises somehow made the stillness even more daunting. The floor's blue safety lights combined with the targeting beams to create eerie shapes that moved like awkward marionettes over the people in front of me.

When we neared the turn, however, the baritone I had been dreading echoed down the hall: "Recorder?"

Weapons rose around me, and the hair on the back of my neck stood on end. Ahead of me, Zhen's fingers twitched over her sidearm, but she fisted her hand and tapped her thigh instead. The marines gathered tightly around her and the drone, hiding her from view. Nate moved in front of me, and Lars disappeared behind.

"Drop it!" Quincy barked, and something clattered. "Hands in the air!"

"Elliott's in trouble," Julian Ross begged. "Recorder, I know you're there. I see the drones."

The marine to my right shifted closer.

"Please?" Julian Ross's voice carried the same emotion I had heard when Elliott was waking up. "I have to find him."

I set a hand on Nate's back and whispered, "Something is wrong."

"Please," Ross begged. "They shot him."

Someone spat out an epithet, and the datapad in my pocket buzzed. I ignored it.

"Venn? If you're there, you have to listen. I'm—"

"Leave her out of it," Nate growled. "Where are your *friends*?"

"They aren't my friends!" Ross's voice sharpened. "They blame me for North's death."

Nate squared his stance. "Sounds like a personal problem."

"They shot Elliott! They injected him with that virus and shot him!"

My stomach twisted, and in a flash of memory, I saw Elliott carrying Freddie through the tunnels. Elliott, apologizing before he sealed the hatch to go save his brother.

Acid burned my throat. I leaned my helmet against Nate's back.

"Liar." Jordan's alto scraped through the hall.

"Nate, please," I said, and Nate stiffened.

A shuffling noise, then Quincy barked, "Back on your knees!"

"Recorder!"

I set a hand on Nate's arm and slid past him.

"Get back," he ordered, but I did not listen.

The drone rose, its tendrils writhing. My datapad buzzed again, and the drone zoomed in front of me. >>*Protect.*

"I know." I pushed the tendrils aside.

The drone and I maneuvered through the marines, Nate and Lars at my side, and drew even with Eric, whose face was pale. Before us, Julian Ross knelt on both knees, his hands high above his head. His right hand was swollen, his fingers bent at unnatural angles. Bruises marred his symmetrical features, and blood trickled from the corner of his mouth. Ice-blue eyes latched onto mine, but that sneer was gone from his face.

"Recorder, Elliott's out of time." Ross's voice cracked. "They beat him, then injected him with the virus. I tried . . . Then they shot him, dragged him off, and knocked me out." His eyes still on mine, he held out his hands before him, palms up. "Recorder, I swear I'll tell you anything—everything—just find my brother."

"Whatever El's done, we can't abandon him to be roach fodder," Eric said, though he kept the muzzle of his weapon pointed at Ross's bare head. "Please, if not for *him*, if not for Elliott, for me? He was my first friend."

His first friend.

Those three words solidified my determination.

"No," I said. "We cannot."

"Oh, yes, we can," a marine said. "A terrorist who attacks innocent women? Part of a group who's already killed how many and planned to kill millions more?"

Someone else added, "It's their fault Parker's dead."

"Venn, Recorder," Ross pled over the marines' rumble of agreement. "Please. The roaches."

Bile rose as I turned to Quincy and Nate. "If we do not help Elliott, how are we any better than those who would kill us?"

"It's a matter of scale," Quincy stated flatly. "Two monsters versus an entire group of people? No comparison."

I touched his arm. "But, Quincy, your daughters. What would they think?"

Behind the stubble, his jaw ticced.

"Whatever else," I pressed, "we cannot let the roaches have Elliott as they took Lorik."

"Timmons?" Quincy asked.

"Stay in line, Ross." Nate glared at the man before us. "One single stunt will be reason enough. Trust me. I'd welcome a reason."

"Then, yes?" I asked.

He nodded so slightly that if I had not known him well, I might have missed it.

Heart pounding, I asked, "Julian Ross, where have you searched?"

"I can't remember." He scrubbed his uninjured hand over his face. "They pulled us both through some hatch, shot him, then knocked me on the head. The roaches—"

"Are traceable," I interrupted as the thought occurred to me. "Nate, are you with me?"

At Nate's quiet affirmative, I interrupted the drone's continual decree of protection. >>*Roach activity nearby?*

>>*Several.*

>>*Is there a convergence?*

>>*One-half kilometer northeast.*

It was as good a chance as any, but it was far, and at my current speed, I could be too late.

>>*Take me.*

>>*Danger. Protect.*

I did not have time to argue. >>*Protect there.*

The drone thrashed its tentacles as if in protest, then its arms shot out. Ross flinched as the jointed appendages wrapped around me. I summoned the other two drones while Lorik's rose into the air.

"I will do my best, Julian Ross." I flashed Nate a half smile. "Nathaniel Timmons, my heart, try to keep up."

Blue safety lights blurred into a solid line as the drone's speed increased. Behind me, footfalls faded until only the drones' whirs remained.

I pulled out my datapad. *>>Faster.*

The drone complied.

>>Ease from red-spectrum to full-spectrum light.

>>Complying. Danger.

"I know," I said. "Stay the course."

The drone took the next turn too quickly, and my datapad flew out of my hand. A sharp crack echoed as it hit the wall. I cried out, but it was gone. Before I had too much time to regret its loss, the drone slowed. The other two caught up. Moments later, the scritch of insectile feet on concrete and the hollow tap of limbs on ductwork echoed.

"Down," I ordered.

It did not obey. I twisted and tried to enter the command but could not reach the panel.

When the drone tugged me tighter against its underbelly, I realized the noise of the insects' movement had stopped. I craned my neck to look up.

Perhaps nineteen meters ahead, a man lay in the middle of the hallway. A large roach stood over him, its head raised, its multifaceted eyes seemingly fixed on me.

"Get away from him." My mouth was too dry to do more than croak the words, even though it was irrational to expect an insect to listen. "Elliott!"

One foot twitched, and horrified relief tumbled like rocks in my stomach. He lived.

The roach touched his head with its antennae. The others—How many? Why could I not count that high? Surely no more than a dozen?—cocked obscenely large heads in my direction. One jumped from ceiling to the floor with an awkward thump and scurried closer.

In the space of two heartbeats, the drone raised me overhead. The drone's screen remained a fingertip out of reach.

>>*Danger: Protect*, scrolled continually.

I squirmed, straining to enter a command.

A nauseating crack reverberated through the hall. I could not see Elliott, but I could see the wings of the insect nearest to him.

Bracing both hands on the drone's arms, I pulled myself forward two centimeters. My fingertips brushed the entry pad. >>*Donw.*

>>*Reenter command.*

Mercifully, it lowered me to allow me to enter, >>*Down.*

>>*Compliance violates Elder Eta4513110-0197E's directive.*

"Put me down!" I cried. "They killed the Elder. We cannot allow them to kill Elliott, too!"

The screen went blank before the drone acknowledged my statement. >>*Roaches destroyed Elder Eta4513110-0197E.*

My vision blurred as tears splashed from my eyes to the faceplate. "Yes. They *ate* him, drone, and you were not there. You did not save him."

>>*Failure noted.*

But it did not release me. "We must stop the roaches. *You* must. Doing so will fulfill the Elder's directive." Perhaps my logic was faulty, but I demanded, "Set me down."

The drone lowered me several decimeters but kept its tendrils around my waist. >>*Not Consortium.*

How could I get it to understand? "He provided the information that helped stop the virus. He saved us. We must save him."

>>*Reconciling directive to remedy error.*

In another heartbeat, I was on my feet. Lorik's drone released me and lowered itself to eye level.

>>*Will comply.*

A roach scuttled closer. The drone's arms retracted, then shot like spears through the closest roach. Tendrils enfolded it and sent a visible reprimand through the insect. Smoke wisped from the exoskeleton as the drone hurled it down the hall where it collided with the one standing over Elliott.

I stood, temporarily frozen, as the dead roach and the writhing live one skidded to a halt three meters past Elliott's motionless form. The Elder's drone drove arms into one roach after another, electricity snapping like lightning between its tendrils. Blindingly sharp light pulsed. The roaches scattered.

It had cleared a path. The other two drones on my right and left accompanied me as I dashed forward and looped my arms under Elliott's, linking my hands around his chest. Adrenaline granted me strength, and I dragged the young man's limp body down the hall, leaving a trail of bright red from his left leg. Then, my vision fogged, and I tripped.

Elliott's not inconsiderable weight pinned me between a pulsating abdomen and one hideous, jointed leg.

My right arm prickled. I whimpered and tried to push him aside so I could stand and pull him away from the insects. The impact must have pinched a nerve, for this time, I could not lift my arm. When I kicked to get out from under Elliott and away from the roach, my right leg would not respond, either. I tried to call for the drones, for Nate, for anyone. I could not. My mouth did not work.

Down the hall, sparks and the crash of exoskeletons against concrete receded. The abdomen behind me throbbed, and in my peripheral vision, the roach's thick leg twitched as if trying to gain traction.

I could do nothing, and armor was meaningless against the insects. Michaelson's loss of limb had proved that.

Elliott lay, unresponsive, on my chest. I tugged my left arm free, unfastened my helmet, and leaned my cheek against Elliott's bare head and held him close. At the very least, he would not be alone.

A flash of metallic grey descended, and a reprimand tore through me, stealing my breath.

The roach stopped moving.

Elliott's weight lifted, and seconds later, long, mechanical arms wrapped around me as well.

A drone's comforting whine covered the diminishing thuds, and air moved past my face, perhaps like wind. I would not truly know. I had only felt the breezes of fans.

I had wanted to feel the wind, too.

Pounding grew louder. Boots thundered to a stop, someone swore prolifically, and Nate cried out.

"Put them down," Jordan ordered somewhere to my left.

"Wait, I got it," Zhen said.

The safety of tendrils was replaced by strong hands. Gloved fingers touched my face.

"Sweetheart." Nate's voice cracked. "Look at me."

Green eyes glistened behind a faceplate. I wanted to tell him I was looking, but the words would not emerge. Instead, I blinked up at him.

He lifted me against his chest, and he whispered, "Thank you."

"Is she—Elliott!" Eric. That was Eric.

"He's alive, but between the bite on his leg and the bullet . . ." Quincy trailed off. "Stars, I need Ramos here. I'm no good at triage. Put Elliott on the gurney."

I lifted my left hand, which was so very heavy, to Nate's helmet. He clasped it.

"Put her on the platform," Zhen said. "Tuck her between the paintings so she won't fall off."

"No." It sounded as if the single syllable had been torn from Nate's throat.

Jordan appeared beside him and placed a gloved hand on his arm. "You can't carry her all the way back, Tim."

"The void I can't."

"Nate," Jordan said softly. His eyes left mine. "We'll get her to Max sooner."

I wanted to tell them to take Elliott first, that I only suffered from dizziness and a pinched nerve. I would be fine.

Instead, darkness welled around me and carried me off as surely as any drone.

"It is only a headache, Max," I repeated, though my attention drifted from him to the paper envelope on my bedside table. Almost against my will, I reached for it. Once more, I carefully opened the flap and unfolded Nate's note. My fingertips traced his slanting signature and the thick, confident strokes of black ink neatly lining the page.

"You're leaving something out." Max smothered a yawn, and his long cords of hair rustled over his suit. "I need to get you in a scanner, but no matter how much you like charging through roach-filled halls, we're not using the one down here." He flashed a quick smile in my direction. "We'll wait until we're back on *Thalassa*."

"I do not believe it is necessary, Max. After all, though my arm tingles occasionally, I have sufficient range of motion." I hesitated before adding, "I am healing."

The note in my hands bore silent witness that the half-truth itself was but half true, for, Nate's words were not words. While I could read the bold, simple EXIT over the door, the letters in the note slid into and over each other.

I did not—could not—tell Max that I snuck peek after peek at signs, labels, notes, and undulating displays. He was allowed to believe I hid something—anything—as long as no one knew I could not read.

My eyes were tired or dry, I told myself silently. My hand was healing. My eyes would as well.

I hated that I misled Max, but I was afraid—even ashamed—to tell him the truth. And Nate? I could not bear to tell him that I did not know what he had written. Additionally, if I could not read, I could not create an identity for myself. I had not planned to, for my friends' sakes, but having that possibility destroyed was like a physical blow. It was pointless to cause Max and Wiliams—and Nate—to worry over treatments.

There would be no escape from the Eldest.

"I'll be the judge of that," he said, bringing my scattered thoughts to the present.

I startled.

"Of your recovery," he clarified, and his brow knotted. "You're jumpy today."

"Oh," I said, slumping against the pillow behind me.

Max tugged his ear, and the familiar motion calmed some of my tension. "I should scold you for throwing yourself into danger, but I'm proud of you."

Heat rose in my cheeks. "For winding up in the infirmary? Again?"

"No." A smile touched his eyes. "For standing up for what you believe to be right. Repeatedly. You saved his life."

Elliott's, perhaps, but not the other man's, and nothing I did could ever undo that damage. I tried to fist my hand when the desire to tap my leg welled up, but my fingers would not curl properly.

I forced myself to ask, "How is Elliott?"

"Alive." Max's gaze seemed to hover halfway between me and the wall. "Ross said Elliott has already been injected and fought off that infernal virus. I told him the risks, but as next of kin, Ross made the decision to put him in our last tank. Some of his injuries are older, including his cracked ribs, but the nanites should help with that. Elliott had already lost a good deal of blood before the roaches found him, and that bite . . ." Max slumped. "Between the beatings, the virus, the shot, the bite itself, and the infections, risking Consortium tech is his one chance."

"You have done your best," I said.

His nut-brown eyes turned to me. "As have you. Even if you aren't telling me everything."

I stammered a dishonest rebuttal.

"Let's see how steady you are before you have another sleep."

Nagging dread nearly made me refuse, but I allowed Max to support me as I hobbled to the water closet, then across the room to Williams's chair.

"Max, why here? Why not the infirmary?"

He leaned against the desk. "Patching up Elliott before putting him in the tank took a while, and you needed rest. Yrsa was well enough to keep an eye on you. There isn't much I can do until we know what's going on."

"*Thalassa*'s medicomputer cleared me of the virus," I protested. "Edwards said so."

Immediately, I regretted bringing up the friend we had lost.

"Which raises other questions and is one reason you'll need to go back in as soon as you can." Max took a long breath. "Stars, what a mess."

I returned the letter to the envelope and, having hesitated long enough, said, "I am sorry, Max."

"Edwards has been my friend for two decades. There was nothing Archimedes or anyone else could do, not with a shipload of marshals and Recorders at his doorstep, and apparently, Edwards told everyone to remain calm. Resistance would've made matters worse." He lifted his eyes to the ceiling. "I can only pray at this point. Do you know what will happen to him?"

"No."

What an inadequate word.

Max stared off again. "Edwards must have suspected the medicomputer hadn't picked up something when he asked for samples before Venetia and Zhen took you into hiding. If he left notes on your files, I haven't seen them."

I watched him carefully. Did he have more grey at the roots of his hair? "Max, you need to rest."

"I'll rest on the way home. Archimedes's last cryptic message stated that *Attlee* left a doctor, though he didn't say who. He usually would, so something's off." Max lowered himself onto the stool that used to be Kyleigh's, his elbows on his knees and his fingers loosely clasped. "All the same, I'm grateful to have the help. We have Williams, and Yrsa is doing better each day, so she can be of assistance. More hands, less work."

Even though I had never seen James so casual, my heart constricted. At that moment, Max looked very like his son. "Have you talked to James?"

He stared blankly at Freddie's mural. "Not yet. It hasn't been the right time."

"It will never be—" I stopped. How very hypocritical of me to contradict him when I kept my own secrets.

"I'll get to it," Max said. He looked at me. "You need to take it easy until we know for sure what triggered your last episode."

"I have not had an *episode*," I objected. "I fell. I hit a nerve. I am fine."

The door opened, and Yrsa Ramos poked her head around the corner. "Good to see you up, Recorder-who-isn't. Max, Jackson needs to see her in the control room."

His nostrils flared. "No. I told him this morning that she needs to rest."

Yrsa edged her way into the room. "Ross is demanding to have a Recorder present, and she's all we've got."

Max growled an imprecation. "I've had enough of people skirting medical advice."

I stood, trying to balance on my left leg. When I wobbled, I grabbed at the chair back, but it swiveled. Yrsa darted across the room and reached me before I fell. She lowered me to the seat. Heat suffused my face. "Thank you."

Max knelt at my side but glared up at the medic, though it was not her fault. "Tell him no."

All I wanted to do was to hide under the blankets, but I tapped his shoulder. "It is well, Max. Julian Ross promised information, and if it will help us defeat the people who created that evil virus, I will talk to him."

His voice was firm when he insisted I remain in the old quarantine room, but Yrsa Ramos kept her eyes on mine as she backed through the door.

Shortly after Yrsa Ramos left, Max did as well, though he adjured me to rest but to call him or Williams should any need arise.

I lay on the bed, avoiding the note and my communications link, staring at the unmoving mural. It felt like hours, though it was perhaps twenty minutes, when the door opened and two armored, helmeted marines escorted a limping Julian Ross into the room. I pushed myself upright while he settled into Williams's chair.

The marines might have wanted to leave him to the roaches, but they had treated him well. Several medgel bandages hid part of his hairline and the corner of his mouth. His short hair had been recently washed and fell over his forehead in loose, drying waves. His clothes had been replaced by a short-sleeved shirt and a pair of matching blue pants. I caught a glimpse of his right hand, splinted and swathed in bandages, before they secured his wrists behind the chair. They must have jarred his injured fingers, for he blanched.

Eyes like blue ice took in the room and settled on me.

Jackson's gravelly voice arrived before he did. ". . . think so. Like every human on this rotted moon isn't my responsibility?"

The door made a soft click when it closed behind him.

For a split second, I wondered if Ross's ice would split Jackson's granite, or if Jackson would crush him instead.

"There, Ross. A Recorder," the marine said with dangerous calm. "Talk."

But when those pale-blue eyes returned to me, the expression was one I did not recognize. He swallowed. "Elliott?"

"That's not why you're here," Jackson stated. "Information. Now."

The man who had wanted to use me as a biological weapon shrugged off the hand on his shoulder and leaned forward. The marine beside him shoved him back.

Concern? Of course he would worry, so I said, "Not an hour ago, Max told me he lived. This is the truth, to the best of my knowledge."

Julian Ross slowly nodded. "You wouldn't lie to me." For the count of five seconds, he closed his eyes. "Thank you for saving him."

"You are welcome."

"Get on with it, Ross," Jackson ordered.

Julian Ross glowered up at the marine.

"Please," I said, striving to enunciate each sound clearly. "If you have information, share it."

His jaw clenched.

Jackson widened his stance. "We have the data your brother smuggled out. What's different?"

"You wouldn't understand." Ross's upper lip curled. "Above your pay grade, marine."

"Julian," I said softly. His icy glare snapped back to me. "Do not antagonize him."

He exhaled. "It's rather technical."

"It would be." I reviewed all I could summon of my shattered memories. "When we talked on *Thalassa*, you explained you had arrived on Pallas to find treatment for autoimmune disorders, using nanotechnology?"

His face went blank. "Yes. Using DNA, combined with bacterial and viral therapies."

"And you used that knowledge to create the virus," Jackson inserted.

Ross's eyes closed. His short, dark lashes fanned blotches that spoke of poor sleep and a beating. "Christine Johnson and I worked on it together."

"Was that before or after you killed Kyleigh Tristram's father?" the man to his right demanded.

Ross glared up at the marine.

"He did no such thing," I said before an argument broke out. "Julian Ross was at work in his laboratory at the time of the murder."

All four of them turned to me.

"You . . . you believed me?" Ross asked, suddenly appearing closer to his brother's age than his own thirty-two years.

"No," I said bluntly.

His expression fell.

"I searched the records." I faced the tall marine. "But Jackson, whatever else he has done, he is innocent of that. Proof has been transferred to *Thalassa*."

The marine squinted at me. "Do you know who killed him?"

I shook my head. "Not yet."

"Christine did." The two words cut through the air like shards of glass through flesh. "She murdered the station Recorder, too. Christine stole potassium chloride from the infirmary's medical supply locker and used it to stop her heart."

My breath hitched. The Recorder herself had noticed that medication and supplies had disappeared. I had viewed those logs and guessed that the drug had been used to prevent her from investigating what she suspected to be corporate espionage, but hearing the woman's murder described with so little feeling disturbed me.

"You're telling me you knew who killed Tristram's father and that woman all this time and didn't say anything?" Jackson's steely eyes were as livid as any Elder's. "That makes you as guilty as she was. For both murders."

"I think Gideon Lorde was onto her, and she killed him, too, but I'm not sure."

"How many other deaths you gonna blame on her?" the quieter marine asked.

"It's mighty convenient, Ross," said the marine who had accused him of killing Kyleigh's father. "Blame a woman who's dead and gone."

"Of course she is," Julian Ross shot back. "I—"

He stopped, clamping his mouth shut, and a chill ran down my arms. I kept my tone gentle and prompted, "You what?"

He shuddered so slightly that I almost missed it. "I know her connection to the terrorists." His jaw worked, then he met my eyes. "Her brother, Xavier Johnson, is planning on taking down the Consortium no matter the cost."

"We know about your virus, and the researchers figured out your nanotech," Jackson ground out. "You'd better have more information than that."

Ross kept his eyes on mine. "Johnson knows your people isolated the virus and created a treatment, and the plan's failure spurred him into a rage. They were listening in on your comms, which is how they knew when that gun ship left and how they knew it was safe to take off."

"You think *Attlee*'s a 'gun ship'?" The rude marine made a disgusting noise. "Stupid trog. You wouldn't know one if we threw you out its airlock. Probably don't even know what a Sentinel-class is."

Julian winced. "Recorder, whether or not Elliott . . ." Zircon-blue eyes locked with mine. "You saved him. I want to return the favor. You saved my family, now I'll save yours."

The same marine grunted. "Recorders don't have families."

"Enough," Jackson snapped, and the scoffer fell silent.

"This is why I needed to talk to you, Recorder. The Consortium has a network separate from regular comms, right?"

I stiffened. I would not give him that information.

"Even if they don't, you have to listen," he insisted. "If you want to save your people, you've got to warn New Triton." His voice dropped, as if he were afraid this Xavier Johnson would hear his confession. "He's planning on taking out the Consortium Training Centers."

A chill arced through me. The little ones, the giftings, the novices. The Recorders and Elders.

Jackson's focus drilled in on the man in the chair. "*What?*"

Ross again kept his eyes on mine. "They're bound for the New Triton Training Centers."

"But the children," I whispered. "That is where we raise the children."

"I know." Ross exhaled harshly. "Xavier Johnson blames Recorders for his older sisters' deaths. If he can't kill the Consortium with a virus, he'll take out the next generation."

At Ross's statement, I bolted from bed, but my right leg wobbled. I grabbed for the bed rail and misjudged the distance. My knees hit the concrete floor. Gloved hands grabbed me and hoisted me up, and Jackson peered into my eyes.

"Stars, Recorder. What are you thinking? You can't walk from Pallas to New Triton," he growled while he set me on the bed and tapped his communications link. "Medical assistance to the quarantine room."

Shame warmed my face. "You overreact, Jackson."

He ignored my assertion. Behind him, Ross watched me closely, his forehead creased. Within seconds, the door flew open, cracking against the thick wall.

Williams was at my side, bootless, her hair loose around her shoulders, and a streak of paste trailing from her lower lip. Her tunic flared as she spun from checking the medical display on my headboard to the computer, but when she saw Ross, she gasped.

"You!" She pointed at the door. "Get out!"

He shrugged and pointed his chin at the marine beside him.

Williams rounded on Jackson next. "You brought him in here? Were you even *thinking*?"

Before he could reply, she activated her communications link and called for Max, Nate, and Jordan. When Jackson planted his feet and crossed his arms, she did as well, a shorter, middle-aged, ash-brown-haired, unarmed, feminine mirror image.

"Williams," I said. "I am well. It is merely that my leg gave out."

"We will see about that." Still facing the marine, she jabbed her finger at the door again. "Out."

"You do not understand," I continued. "Julian Ross has information."

Before she could protest further and before I explained the threat, the door opened again, and again, and again. The room seemed to shrink when Zhen and Jordan, then James and Nate, and finally a bleary-eyed Max entered, but not even Nate's presence could quell the pressure building in my chest. Arguments swelled around me until a shrill whistle cut through the voices. All eyes turned to Williams, who pulled her fingers from her mouth.

"Get that man out of here," she repeated, and a nod from Jackson had the two marines unfastening Ross from the chair.

"Stop!" he demanded over his shoulder as they guided him past Freddie's mural. "Her symptoms—I know what happened."

Jackson barked an abrupt command, and the marines made a rough pivot so that Elliott's brother faced Max. "You got medical information, Ross, you tell Maxwell. Now."

Julian Ross straightened. Even injured, he towered over the men on either side. "Nothing showed up when you scanned her."

Only the air filtration system answered him.

"Check for shells."

The quieter marine began, "What do dead bodies have to do—"

"Not that kind," Ross said rudely but quickly, as if he were afraid they would pull him out of the room before he finished. "Nanites."

"Nanodevices are small," Williams argued. "The size of a virus. They would be eliminated through normal means."

"Yes, *normally*." Ross focused on Max. "But Christine designed them to link with Consortium tech. You know there were two parts?"

"Go on," Nate said, his green eyes like lasers drilling into the taller man.

"They link up with nanites specific to Recorders. Christine designed them to release the virus when all three nanites are present. It was a safeguard." He lowered his head. "We didn't know that citizens carried the same devices in their blood. I still have no idea why Consortium tech is present."

Max and Williams exchanged glances, and she folded her arms. "Which is why it works faster on members of the Consortium."

"The more nanites," Max growled, "the faster the release."

Ross avoided their glares and focused on me. "I don't know for certain, but after they injected my brother, they made me study Elliott's blood. The nanites keep linking up, even after the virus is free. Theoretically, if you had fewer Consortium nanites, it wouldn't be a big problem because they'd be flushed out in time. You, however, are a Recorder. You must have had enough of them in your system that the clump was big enough to act as a clot."

"The medicomputer cleared her," Jackson argued.

Max's eyelid twitched. "It's a machine, limited by programming. It wouldn't search for nanite shells, only for viruses, bacteria, plaque."

"This," I said, "is not the important thing."

They all turned to me.

Nate's gloved fingers tightened about mine. "How is that unimportant?"

"Julian Ross," I said, motioning to my friends with my free hand, "tell them."

The man held his breath for two seconds, then said, "They're going to destroy the Consortium Training Centers."

The others grew eerily still as Julian Ross elaborated on plans to use EM cannons to disable the drones so it would be easy to murder any Recorders present. To destroy the tanks which nurtured the newest giftings, to eliminate the little ones and novices, and to slip the altered technology into the water supply as soon as they could utilize the adjustments Ross had labored over.

Protests filled the room. James went ashen, and Zhen touched his shoulder. He did not seem to notice.

"You're still working for them?" Jordan demanded.

Julian Ross's brow knotted, and he kept his gaze on me. "Elliott asked me not to."

Williams pursed her lips. "Yet you did."

"You don't understand." Ross's temper flared. "I did my best to disable the spacing thing without them knowing, but I didn't have the right equipment."

Jackson swore.

"I can now, though," Ross continued. "I remember everything I did. If I could have access to—"

"Void take you, you vile, drossing—" Zhen's cheeks flamed. "You think anyone will let you near something as high tech as a *spoon* for the rest of your voided life? I hope they recycle you."

No one contradicted her. Nate's jaw ticced. Max set a hand on Jordan's arm, and she shifted toward him.

I managed, "What matters is that we discover how to protect and prevent attacks. If possible, I recommend allowing Ross to try to undo the damage."

Ross locked his icy gaze on me, but a flush rose in his cheeks. "I've said it before, Recorder, but I underestimated you."

"She's not a Recorder," Jordan said.

James spoke for the first time, his deep, rich voice a heavy monotone. "Jackson. Remove him."

"Oh, he'll be removed soon enough," the marine said with such force that at first I thought he had cursed.

He and the marines tugged Ross away. The door shut, and I slumped back onto my bed.

"So what do we do?" Nate asked.

"We notify the Consortium as soon as possible," I said. "They must have a defensive plan in place."

"Yes, yes, whatever," Zhen said. "But what do we *do*, Max?"

"I don't know yet." Max pulled off his helmet and set it on the desk that used to hold Kyleigh's computer. "The first step will be taking her up to *Thalassa*—"

"Inadvisable," Williams said. She turned to Nate. "Tell them what you told me."

"Indeed," James said.

The door opened again, and Daniel and Yrsa strode in.

"We were delayed," she began. "It seems—"

"Moons and stars." Zhen snorted. "Anyone else coming?"

The latecomers exchanged glances.

"No," Daniel said slowly. "Why?"

"Tell them, Timmons," Williams insisted.

Nate closed his eyes. "When they took Edwards, they left another doctor."

"I don't see how that's a bad thing," Jordan said. "Maybe you can finally get some rest, Max—" Her cheeks darkened, and she stopped abruptly.

Williams wrapped her arms around her waist. "A Recorder."

"A Recorder or a doctor?" Max asked. "Which?"

James answered, "Both in one."

Venetia Jordan's heightened color vanished. "Recorders can be doctors? Isn't that inherently biased?"

"Medicine is science," I said.

"The Consortium has to have medical personnel," Williams explained. "Maintaining the gifting tanks, implanting neural chips, routine health, removal of . . . of organs in the Hall of Reclamation."

Max sat heavily on the stool. "And they don't want citizens to have access to their technology."

"But they have staff," Jordan protested.

Williams gave a short nod. "While we trained with Consortium doctors, staff are not allowed to obtain degrees. We are trained to be outsourced at reduced costs to citizens, enabling us to support the Consortium and earn back our gifting."

"Recorder-doctors are stationed at Training Centers and central hubs," James said. "This one must have been assigned to Krios Platform Forty-One, which I believe to be the closest Center. Sending a doctor would be a logical choice, if there was the chance that any member of the Consortium might require medical care."

Jordan's eyes flashed. "With a Recorder-doctor onboard, she's not going up to *Thalassa*."

"I concur," Williams added. "They will take her as they took Edwards."

"What other option is there?" Zhen demanded.

After a moment of silence, Jordan straightened to her full height. Her jaw tensed, and she said deliberately, "She can stay here."

Everyone except Nate began talking at once.

Zhen's soprano rose above the chorus of protests. "Don't be stupid, J. She *can't*. *Thalassa* will leave, and she'd be alone. She can't even fire a gun. Those bugs would finish her off in no time at all."

"Thank you for the vote of confidence," I said, somehow offended even though she was correct.

"While a station-wide jammer is all well and good for the Consortium," she argued, "it means nothing when the station is overrun with bugs."

"She won't be alone," Jordan said.

Nate tightened his hold on my hand. "No, she won't. I'll stay with her."

Jordan folded her arms. "I don't suggest the solution lightly. I'm staying, too."

"It might not be a bad plan," Daniel said. "The station-wide jammer works."

"It does." James offered me a slight smile. "We turned off the small ones, and I activated my drone."

Max paled, but Yrsa responded before Max. "You didn't!"

James inclined his head. "A calculated risk. We needed to ascertain that the station would be a sanctuary, as proposed."

"So I'll stay, too," Daniel said. "We'll hide her. You can charter a ship and swing back around to pick us up next year. She'll be safer."

Zhen gaped. "Safer? With the roaches? And a rogue drone on the loose?"

"You saw the carnage that drone wreaked." Jordan nodded at me. "It'll protect her."

"Who knows where it is," Zhen snapped. "Sure it took out those roaches, but you also saw the wreckage of the drone she sent to protect Michaelson and Daniel. Besides, its power can't last forever."

For a split second, I had the vision of the Elder's rogue drone hunting roaches, avenging him until every roach was dead and dust. I almost smiled at the thought, but the horror of lying against that pulsing abdomen stopped me. Bile rose in my throat.

"She can't." Max's eyes were like brown lasers. "Staying on Pallas doesn't address her medical issues. Whether or not Ross was telling the truth, we need to get her in the medicomputer."

"Not after Edwards," Williams countered. "She cannot risk returning to the ship."

I squared my shoulders. "I will go."

Daniel straightened. "Tell you all what. I'll go up first."

"You cannot," I objected. "Not if there is a Recorder with a drone on *Thalassa*. The personal jamming field is meters wide, and the field's radius will betray you. You still have a neural implant, and the Recorder-doctor could discover a way to activate the chip and retrieve your memories."

"That's fixable," he said with a wave of his hand. "Recorders rarely get within an arm's length from citizens. You can shrink the radius."

Panic laced through me. I could not alter its range, not when I could not even read Nate's note.

Zhen pulled a navy-blue datapad from her thigh pocket and handed it to me. "He's right about that."

My fingertips traced the three long cracks radiating from the upper right corner.

"I spotted it while we were chasing after you," she said, "and it's a good thing I did. I used it to command the drones to set you both down."

I tilted my face to the ceiling and closed my eyes. "Indeed."

Zhen tapped my arm. "You make that word work too hard."

The datapad was no longer of any use to me, so I extended it to her. "You keep it."

"I don't know your password."

"You should. You gave it to me before I left *Thalassa* the first time." Despite the whole situation—viruses, roaches, the Consortium—a smile tugged at my lips. "*Chrysanthemum.*"

"Moons and stars, Max," Zhen said. "She's handing out passwords like Festival candy. How hard did she hit her head?"

"I took no injury to my head. It is as well that you all know, in case . . ." But I could not finish the thought.

"Fine." Her reply rushed like falling water. "I'll do it, though I still don't see how Daniel going up first is of any help."

"My citizen identity is forged," Daniel said matter-of-factly. "With a Recorder on board, if I don't get hauled off to who knows where, we will know she succeeded."

"That puts you in danger, Dan," Yrsa protested.

He gave her a lopsided smile. "If the Recorder-doctor takes me, they can both stay on Pallas. The rest of you can fake their deaths and smuggle them out later."

James broke his long silence. "You will not be sacrificed on my behalf."

Daniel clapped him on the shoulder in a fair approximation of the gestures I had seen among the marines. "Can and will, but I trust her." He met my eyes. "You've found a way to keep us safe before. My trip will prove James and you can go up. It is one less infraction for you to worry about."

One less thing, indeed. "While I appreciate your offer to hide me, the Consortium must hear Julian Ross's warnings. They must know of the potential attacks. As a Recorder, it is more likely that the doctor will listen to me. I will go."

Not even my Nathaniel could convince me to change my mind.

I stayed in the quarantine room for another two days, with very few visitors. Even Nate had been scarce, since he and the other pilots ran almost nonstop trips to *Thalassa* and back. Daniel left the station, and nothing went amiss. Before James departed as well, he brought me a cane he had fashioned from a wooden table leg, smoothed and polished until it gleamed. Max had paced the quarantine room for hours until Nate returned with the news that James was safely ensconced in the room Freddie had shared with Eric and Cam.

"Go eat something, Max," he said quietly. "Maybe catch a nap."

"We'll have thirty or so days to rest."

"J's in the break room." Nate casually inspected his fingernails. "Just don't let her make you tea. She forgets to take out the bag. Oversteeps it every time."

Max chuckled. "Maybe a bit to eat would be helpful, but I'll remember about the tea."

Nate watched him leave.

His eyes caught mine, but I spoke first. "Nate? I must confess, I did not call for you when I went to fetch the drone. Kyleigh did."

"When . . ." Perfect brows drew together. "Oh. I figured that out a while ago, sweetheart."

"Forgive me?"

"Already done." The wells of green in his eyes darkened. "Did you get my note?"

"Yes."

He searched my face. "What did—what do you think?"

My hand rose to my chest, where I kept the note next to my heart. "I have not read it yet."

Guilt rose up when his face paled, and the scar on his cheekbone grew clear. "You really didn't—not that you'd fib."

His communications link chimed, and Jackson demanded his presence in the control room.

"Be right there." He swallowed visibly, then picked up his helmet. "Don't worry about the note. Just rest, sweetheart."

And he was gone.

I should have explained that I wanted to read it and why I had not, but I had not even explained my lack to Max or Williams. For unmeasured time I stared at the mural until I could see it in negative when I closed my eyes.

In one small way, however, my enforced rest was beneficial. Each day, I felt stronger and more myself, and though I limped, even my headaches receded. I practiced walking with the cane while marines loaded materials and personnel onto the shuttles, until only a few of us remained.

If they dealt with more intrusions, they did not inform me.

Finally, Max, Zhen, and Lars bundled me onto a hoverbed and escorted me and Elliott's portable medical tank to the hangar. Zhen walked at my side, the Consortium Eye no longer adorning her shoulder, and her weapon back on its tether. She did not speak as we joined the short line waiting to board the shuttle. The bearded marine—Quincy, I reminded myself again, frustrated that the condition which had stolen my ability to read made remembering so difficult—inspected each item to be loaded. The line crept forward.

Quincy's sharp "Is that a roach egg?" brought everyone's attention to the front of the line.

The marine in front of Elliott's tank snatched back his duffel but grunted an affirmative.

Color leached from Zhen's cheeks. "Are you insane?"

"What d'you mean trying to bring one of those things?" Lars sputtered. "Don't you ever watch the vids? There are at least thirty-seven about what goes wrong when you bring monsters and their eggs onto ships."

"It's for science," the other man objected. "If we can study shifts in the genome—"

"Stars!" Lars's mouth dropped open. "That's exactly what they say in the vids!"

While I knew little to nothing of entertainment, the tall marine's point about releasing monstrous insects on the ship was valid. "It is highly improbable Archimedes Genet will allow living samples on *Thalassa.*"

Lars crossed his thick arms. "And if the Recorder-who-isn't agrees, you know I'm right."

"They both are," Quincy said. "Authorized specimens only. Live specimens, not at all."

"Fine," the grouchy marine huffed. "I'll freeze it and submit paperwork." Grumbling, he stomped off.

"Some people." Quincy rolled his eyes and gestured to Lars to move Elliott's tank for inspection.

Grinning, Lars complied. "'Preciate you backing me up."

"I might not have seen your vids, but your insistence on leaving behemoth roach eggs behind is well-founded."

His eyes widened. "Not even the classics?"

Momentarily confused by the idea of classic roach eggs, I belatedly realized he referred to entertainment. "I have not."

"We need to fix that," he declared. "I'll see what I can do."

"You've done it now," Zhen muttered, but a smile flitted over her features. "He'll talk Archimedes into horror vids on fifth- and tenth-days."

Quincy waved Lars on and began to inspect my hoverbed. By the time he smiled at us and said, "Get her out of here," I had resolved that even if I could not read, I would be busy on entertainment evenings.

Between Zhen, Lars, and my cane, I made it to my seat and buckled the harness. We three were the sole passengers, but Nate joined Lars in securing equipment and materials the marines had removed from accessible laboratories.

I studied my Nathaniel. Something did not seem right: he was pinched and pale. Sad? Disappointed? I could not tell. He paused by my side and took my hand when I reached for him, but Johansen announced that the shuttle was cleared to depart.

"I'll see you when we get there," he said.

Even with Zhen and Lars, I felt alone when he left.

None of us spoke as gravity shifted, pushed, and pulled. I had been correct that with Nate flying, the trip was smoother, though perhaps

I was unfair. Perhaps there was no real turbulence. I did not ask. I removed my helmet and stashed my cap and gloves inside it.

Lars collected our helmets and gloves, then tucked them into a bag near the medtank, which burbled against the wall. When his back was to us, I reached up my sleeve and removed the black-and-silver identification bracelet I had worn since Zhen had given it to me days ago. My wrist felt empty without it.

"Zhen?" When she looked over, I offered it to her. "I cannot keep this now. If that Recorder finds out, he will steal it from me, and I will never get it back."

She simply held out her palm.

Lars returned to his seat, yawning and setting off a chain reaction that provoked a glare from Zhen. He kicked out his legs and put his hands behind his head. "So, Recorder-who-isn't, did you ever figure out a name? I'm guessing you'll need one." He jabbed a thumb toward the front of the craft. "No way he'll let you go back. Don't know how he'll manage it, but I'm not the smart one."

"Don't say that, Lars," Zhen said.

His face twisted, but then he offered us a half smile. "People think I don't notice, but kinda hard not to. It's all right."

Zhen huffed.

"Daisy's a nice name," he continued, "although I should maybe tell you that Clarissa and me talked about using it if we ever have a kid. A girl. Might not be a good name for a boy."

I smiled. "You and Zhen have something in common, then. She also suggested a flower."

"Solid." Lars grinned. "But, well, been thinking. Izzy's all right, and Zeta is, too. Just . . ." His brow creased. "I don't want to step on your feelings, but I don't know if you should go with Sweetheart. I know Timmons calls you that, and all, but it might be awkward for other people. I mean, Clarissa wouldn't like it if I walked around calling you Sweetheart."

"That had not crossed my mind." Concern for his feelings kept me from clarifying my antecedent. I had no desire for anyone other than Nate to call me by that name. "I promise I do not take this lightly."

"Me and Clarissa don't, either, which's why we talked about it already." He sighed. "I wish my parents had thought harder."

Zhen tilted her head to the right. "What do you mean?"

He rolled his eyes. "Named me *Chell*."

"Chell . . . That is unusual," I said.

"Yep. Spelled it the old-Earth way to make it fancy. K-J-E-L-L." He shrugged. "One, not a fancy sorta guy. Two, nobody says it right. Kids called me Shell instead. Pummeled a few who made fun of my mum for naming me after dead bodies."

"I don't blame you," Zhen remarked.

"Changed it when I joined up."

"To?" Zhen asked.

"Lars. Lars Larsen."

I blinked.

One of his massive shoulders rose and fell. "Yeah, probably shoulda come up with a different one. That's how I know names're important."

Zhen cocked her head. "I like it. It suits you."

He relaxed, and his grin came back. "Thanks."

She tugged her pack from under her seat and pulled out her yarn.

For a moment, I did not understand how she could knit while we flew toward an uncertain future, but Nate would take me safely wherever I needed to be, and I had friends.

The sound of knitting needles hushed me to sleep.

Lars left first, guiding Elliott's tank to the infirmary. Zhen sat with me until I prodded her to go check on Alec.

"I can't," she protested.

"Nate will be with me. I will be fine."

She bit her lip.

"It's okay." Nate appeared through the doorway to the front of the shuttle. "Go on, Zhen."

"You're sure?"

"Yes," Nathaniel and I said in unison.

For a moment, I thought she meant to hug me, but she grabbed her pack and departed.

Despite the fact that Nate was the pilot and had seniority, when Johansen ordered him to take me to the infirmary, he saluted her, and once again, he and I walked side by side through the hallways I knew by heart.

When we passed the ugly red painting, he asked suddenly, "Are you sure? The cameras still aren't working. Archimedes has a couple of people from engineering monitoring their energy usage, and he's going to put the ship on orange alert if they go back on. We can stash you somewhere. He won't mind you stowing away, and we can sneak you into the infirmary for scans while that Recorder sleeps."

"I have thought about this over the past few days. I do not like it, but it is the safest option for all of us." We had not gone three paces when I stopped. "Nathaniel?"

A divot appeared between his brows.

"Would you mind holding my hand?"

A faint, dimpleless smile crept across his face. "There are many things I do mind—like taking you to that Recorder—but your hand in mine? Not one of them."

When we reached the closed infirmary doors, he bent and pressed a short kiss on my forehead. "Love you."

"You should leave," I whispered.

"Nope. Done it before. Worked out badly." He raised our interlaced fingers to brush his lips on the back of my hand. "Trying a new strategy this time."

"At least let go of my hand?"

"It's really too late to knock you on the head and hide you in my cabin, isn't it?"

I decided he joked and offered him a weak smile. "Indeed. Besides, Nate, we are on *Thalassa*. Archimedes Genet is captain, the marines are present, and this Recorder does not have an Elder's authority. What could go wrong?"

"Right." He released me, leaving my hand cold and empty.

I touched the panel by the door and tried to take a confident step, but the cane undermined my assurance.

Kyleigh was not at her usual spot. No patient rested on the beds, though Elliott's tank already hummed in the corner. A Recorder in Consortium grey but with the universal red medic badge on his shoulder glanced up from the computer where Edwards used to work.

"Ah. There you are. I have a few adjustments to make to the medical tank's programming before I can see to you. Please take a seat by the door." His fingers flew through the projection and letters that were no longer words, while his drone hovered in the corner like a moon. After he inserted a datacard into a slot on Elliott's tank, it chugged once, then settled into a steady rhythm.

"Dr. Maxwell did well," he said as he returned to wash his hands. "So you are the aberration who started this?"

"She didn't start anything," Nate remarked.

The Recorder studied him, and chills swept over me, even after the doctor turned away. I prayed briefly that Nate, too, would remember the drones bore witness. The Recorder-doctor tapped the foot of a bed. I left Nate's side, grasping the cane for comfort more than assistance.

"Leave the cane by the door," he said, eyeing me carefully. "Let me see you walk without it."

I obeyed, despite Nate's murmured protest.

Frowning, the Recorder-doctor studied my movements. He hummed slightly, then gathered a small medical kit and pulled on gloves. "I have interviewed Julian Ross. Young Tristram has begun to investigate his theories, and his claims bear out. I have requested he continue work under guard and with her supervision." He added, almost as if to himself, "A shame, truly. She would have made an excellent Recorder."

I risked a glance at Nate, whose mouth had flattened into a thin, white line.

"Remove your armor."

My attention darted back to the Recorder.

"You are safe on *Thalassa*," he added, possibly misinterpreting my lack of immediate compliance. "Or do you need assistance?"

As much as I hated to admit it, I nodded.

He held up his gloved hands. "Nathaniel Timmons, your uninvited presence proves useful. Remove her armor."

Mouth pinched, Nate did as he was told, detaching the external communications link and putting it in my hand, allowing his fingertips to linger for a second over mine. I stood in my stockinged feet, shivering and exposed in my black pants and jacket over my illegal green shirt.

The Recorder scowled at my attire, but when he approached the bed, his nose wrinkled. "I realize the conditions on Pallas were less than pleasant, but hygiene is never optional."

"We didn't have any cleaning units," Nate said. "Even if we did, between bugs and murderers, there wasn't a lot of time for making things smell nice."

"As you say." The Recorder shrugged one shoulder. "Aberrant. Roll up your sleeve."

My heart locked up. My unread note from Nate was in my inner jacket pocket. No matter what the note might say, the Recorder must not be allowed to see it.

"Why?" Nate asked.

"You are not the aberration, citizen. It is not your concern."

Obedience was my only option, so I pivoted away from them and carefully removed the jacket, folding it in half, then in half again. Perhaps the doctor would assume I faced the wall from out-of-proportion modesty. It did not matter, so long as he did not see the paper. I handed the jacket and its cargo to Nate.

"Why are you not in your greys?" the Recorder asked in the same casual tone.

"It's not my concern, but like I said, we didn't do laundry on Pallas." Nate shrugged. "With clothes in limited supply, it's more hygienic to wear the cleanest ones we could find." After two seconds, he added, "Sir."

The Recorder said, "Aberrant, you will resume appropriate attire."

"As you say."

"Now," the Recorder continued. "Your arm."

I tried to roll up my left sleeve, but when I could not make it even, I commenced on the right one instead. Nate opened his mouth to speak, but the Recorder held up his hand.

"I have read the reports, Timmons, and I am well aware of your propensity for verbosity. We need neither your conversation nor your company." He smiled, but I was not reassured by his apparently pleasant demeanor. "When you go, take the filthy suit and the jacket with you. The suit requires a heavy cleaning cycle before it is usable, and though I believe the jacket should be incinerated, do whatever citizens do with unwanted clothing." He shook his bald head. "You are dismissed."

Nate took three deep breaths, then smiled brightly. It was not a true smile, for his dimple did not flash at me. "Right. I'll probably see you both sometime before New Triton."

And he left.

The Recorder's smile vanished. Pale hazel eyes drilled into mine. "You will cease fraternizing with citizens."

I did not trust my voice, so I inclined my head once in answer.

"It is dangerous," he added, then a fraction of his former manner returned. "If Julian Ross and Dr. Maxwell are correct—"

"Have you notified the Eldest?" I demanded. When he said nothing, I pushed on, "The Training Centers. We must warn her about the Training Centers."

He grew quite still. "I have not."

Panic rose. "But the children—the little ones—"

"I cannot."

"It will take but moments to communicate with the High Elders," I insisted. "Surely the network was reactivated before *Attlee* departed."

His eyes narrowed. "It was, but after that ship left, the network cut off."

"That . . . That is impossible."

"Yet the impossible clearly has happened. I cannot even sense my drone in the corner."

He had to be lying. It was—

The station-wide jammer.

"You know something," he hissed.

I scrambled for a truthful response. "I would never put the little ones at risk."

"You were the only living Recorder on Pallas. The only one with the knowledge of our network. And now, we have no way to warn the Consortium."

My spine stiffened. "You exaggerate. A difference of an hour is not an insurmountable obstacle."

At that moment I realized two things. Firstly, he had known that I was responsible. Secondly, so accustomed was he to the instantaneous communication over our network that he could not see around its absence. Our interconnectedness had created a vacuum, a deficit, and this lack of trust had to stop. When the Recorder on Pallas did not present her findings to Gideon Lorde, she consigned herself to death and opened the door to the present disaster. This Recorder's absolute reliance on the Consortium could kill millions.

"What you need to do," I said with forced calm, "is to speak with Archimedes Genet about using *Thalassa's* communication—"

"And corrupt ourselves?"

My ever-present headache ratcheted up several notches to keep pace with burgeoning panic. "The captain is a good man. I trust him and Dr. Maxwell, Nathaniel Timmons, Venetia Jordan—all of them—with my life."

"Your life. Perhaps. But would you trust them with the lives of the Consortium?"

"Yes! With anything and everyone. They saved my life on that moon well before any viral threat existed."

Uneasy stillness corrupted the infirmary's familiar quiet.

Finally, the Recorder-doctor said, "Very well, I shall modify my original request. You might have limitations, but you will serve a purpose. You were in training to be an Elder, so I will allow you to interact as needed while you repair the network."

Any hint of confidence collapsed. "I cannot."

"Cannot or will not?"

Almost against my will, my confession tore free. "I can no longer read."

"You cannot . . ." His anger dissipated into something else, and his eyes grew round. "But that would be a nightmare. Are you certain? No, no. Why else would you say such a thing when you know I will have the medicomputer check your brain and eyes for damage? When did you notice?"

"When I woke up after escaping the roaches."

"Eldest spare me!" he exclaimed. "Dr. Maxwell has said nothing of this in his documentation. I must remember to thank him for not revealing Consortium weakness. What did he tell you?"

I lowered my head. "He does not know."

His browless forehead furrowed. "And you claim to trust them?"

Had I indeed undervalued them? A pang shot through me, but I held up my weak right hand. "I am broken. It is not a matter of trust. It is a matter of keeping that small dignity."

He clicked his tongue. "Sit."

I complied as he retrieved a medical bag labeled with the Consortium's eye and with the red-and-white badge.

The Recorder-doctor caught my right hand and turned it wrist up. "Foolish Aberrant," he said as if it were both my name and the sum of my being. "Fortunately, knowing you no longer had a neural chip, I brought this when they summoned me from Krios Platform Forty-One. I did not know how necessary it was at the time, but it will enable us to track your health."

I sat, transfixed as he anchored my hand between his arm and chest and cleaned my inner wrist with an alcohol-based disinfectant. After digging through the medical bag by my hip, he lifted the largest injector I had ever seen. In truth, it was closer in size to a sidearm. I watched in detached disbelief as he angled the tip against my wrist.

"With this, I will be able to monitor your health and pinpoint your position." He frowned. "If you had a medical tracker on *Agamemnon*, the citizen who tried to kill you would have been caught well beforehand. However, this has a link directly to the infirmary computers, so I will be able to send assistance or protection should I myself be incapacitated for any reason."

Detachment vanished, but when I tugged, his grip tightened. Though not much taller, he was much stronger than I.

"Release me," I demanded.

"You know I cannot," he said. "I will not lie. This will hurt, but I will provide analgesics before you go in the medicomputer for a scan. Do not panic," he added as I fought harder, and my respiration grew shallow. "This is very similar to the chips used on Ceres during storms, though those are larger."

He pressed the trigger. Pain shot down to my fingertips and up to my neck.

Once again, a chip tied me to the Consortium.

Disheartened, aching, and tired, I left the infirmary two hours later with one purpose: talk to Archimedes Genet without the Recorder monitoring our conversation. Cane in hand, I made my way to the bridge, and for once, fortune turned in my favor when the door opened in a matter of seconds. Alec Spanos stopped on the threshold, his thick eyebrows soaring at the sight of me. My eyes dropped to his throat, which was still hideously bruised.

"Alec," I said without any appropriate salutation, "I must speak to the captain. Is he within?"

"Sure." He motioned for me to enter.

Sudden self-consciousness held me back. "There is a step, if I remember correctly, and I am not proficient at steps."

"I'll ask."

He left and returned with Archimedes Genet.

"Welcome back," the captain said. "Alec implied there's an issue. What do you need?"

As quickly as I could, I explained the necessity for contacting the Consortium, adding the one spark of hope that whatever ship Skip and Xavier Johnson had, the average time to New Triton was thirty days.

"Thirty days won't matter if *Skip*"—Alec pronounced the name as if it were a curse—"has comms running. If Ross is correct, Skip's contacts could implement the plans before that ship approaches New Triton."

A chill swept over me. "I had not considered that they, that he—" I swallowed. "That makes the message even more urgent."

The captain frowned. "Jackson has already sent his report, but we've no idea if it's been forwarded to the Consortium or not. This lack of communication will be the death of people." He gestured to the bridge. "Use my office: write one up now. It'll be at New Triton within an hour and a half. Better still, send it to the Training Center on Krios Forty-Seven and *Attlee*, too."

My heart sank. How could I write when I could not read? I fisted my right hand and tapped my thigh. Blinding pain shot through my arm, and I gasped. An adequate reminder. "I will need help."

A hand rested on my left shoulder, and Alec said, "Whatever you need."

"Thank you."

"This way," Archimedes Genet offered. "The new doctor knows?"

I stiffened. "Yes."

"Then why is he sending you on his errands? He should transmit it himself."

Fresh panic vibrated through me. The Recorder-doctor would know what I had done, and I had no idea what he would do. Perhaps lock me in a room or keep me close by? I would lose the three ten-days of freedom I had left.

"Stars," Alec said. "What is it? You're white as a sheet."

"I will be well momentarily."

"Spanos, as soon as she's done, get her back to the infirmary—"

"No!"

Both men stared at me.

"Anywhere but there," I whispered. "I do not need to return until tomorrow. I . . . I am ready to write the report."

When Alec shifted to my other side and took my right arm, I cried out. He jerked his hand away and stared at his red-stained fingers. He caught my hand gently and even more gently rolled up my sleeve to reveal a blood-soaked bandage.

"What is this?" Archimedes Genet asked curtly.

"Subdermal medical tracker," I said.

Alec growled, "There's bruising on your arm, too."

"Of course there is, Alexander Spanos. You do not think I *wanted* this, do you?"

A muscle in the captain's jaw ticced, then he glanced at Alec. "Change of plans. Get her to her old computer lab. Help with that report, and I'll send someone with a hoverbed and personal supplies."

"Captain?" Alec asked.

"Hodges," the captain said with a quirk of his brow.

A sudden grin swept away Alec's scowl.

Archimedes Genet turned to me. "I'm afraid you are a security risk. Smuggling insect parts onto my ship? I am extremely disappointed."

My mouth fell open. "I would never—"

"I take contraband quite seriously." The captain shook his head, and his officer's queue rustled on his back. "I'll have to post guards at the door. No one comes in or out without direct orders. You're not allowed to go as far as half a meter without escort. And Spanos, I don't want this on the record, so when you see Timmons, tell him that he and I need to have a talk about the antenna found in her suit lining."

"You cannot mean this!" My breath caught. "There was no antenna! Nathaniel Timmons had no part in any—"

"And Williams," the captain said over my protest. "We'll need to restrict her activity as well as we investigate this . . . plot. When is she arriving?"

"Tomorrow."

"Alec," I gasped, stunned.

"Very well. I'll mention that when I talk to Timmons. I'm afraid we'll have to keep an eye on Williams as well, in case she's involved." Archimedes Genet had the audacity to smile, but there was a sharpness to it that made even less sense. "I'll have two hoverbeds sent up from storage. Whether or not Williams is in on the smuggling, and even if this former Recorder might be a security risk, I won't have anyone say I didn't provide medical care to someone on my ship."

He bowed slightly and strode back to the bridge. The doors slid shut, and I slumped back against the bland, beige wall.

"Alec," I managed, "how could you?"

"Easiest thing in the system," he said.

I refused to talk to him as we made our way through the ship. He made me stop twice and rest on the benches covering the chemical backup ductwork. The flicker of pride in Nate's role in maintaining the system that had saved the lives of everyone onboard was replaced by a sense of betrayal when Alec urged me onward.

When we reached the computer laboratory, Nate and Zhen had already positioned the beds on the wall opposite my favorite computer and the workplace safety posters. Zhen had the forethought to fetch sheets, blankets, and towels, which she stacked on the table they had pushed to the back of the room near the charging station. They jumped to their feet when we entered, and as soon as the door slid into place and clicked shut, I fell against Nate's chest.

"Careful with her arm, Nate," Alec warned.

Nate frowned. "What happened?"

"She has a tracker."

"Subdermal medical tracker," I corrected.

Zhen narrowed her eyes. "What's going on?"

Alec—of all things—Alec chuckled?

I turned to face Nate's friend. "It is not funny, Alexander Spanos."

"Alec, what happened?" Nate pulled me close, but his voice was steady.

All his amusement fled, and Alec scrubbed a hand over his chin. "It's that doctor. Show them."

Reluctantly, I rolled back my sleeve. Zhen glared at me as if I had done this to myself, but I did not know what Nate did. I could not bring myself to meet his eyes. He had been right that I had been in danger, although if he had stayed, if he had resisted, what would the Recorder-doctor have done? No, this was better.

"She's staying here," Alec explained, "where no Recorder-doctor or Elder can override Genet's orders."

"But two beds?" Zhen asked.

"Williams," Alec said.

Nate released a long breath. "So that spacing Recorder can't get his claws in either of them."

Understanding washed over me. "Then it is a ruse? Nate is not in trouble?"

"Now *I'm* in trouble?" Nate growled. "I will be if you don't explain, Alec. My patience is wearing thin."

"Archimedes has her under watch for smuggling."

Nate stared hard at his friend.

"Her?" Zhen exclaimed. "Who'd believe that?"

"What matters is that she's safe." Alec motioned to my wrist. "Although I have no doubt that by the time we reach Lunar One and the doctor leaves the ship, you'll be exonerated, and the rest of us absolved from aiding or abetting."

"Alec . . ." My apology caught in my throat.

"Don't fuss about it. The look on your face when Archimedes accused you of being a security risk . . ." Alec grinned but sobered quickly. "Nate, he needs to talk to you. And Zhen, we need to feed her."

Zhen was already on her way to the door. "Tea and dinner, coming up."

Nate kissed my forehead. "I'll be back as soon as I can."

They left together, and Alec sat me in the chair beside a workstation. "You rest. I'll write up your report. Tell me exactly what Julian Ross confessed."

So I did not need to admit my deficit after all.

The door was not fully opened when I heard, "Stars above, let me through!"

I turned my back on the posters' advice for safety and protocol. "Kyleigh?"

"You need permission, ma'am," Cam said sternly.

"You—you impossible, ridiculous—Move!"

Masculine laughter followed the small figure with short curls, who shoved herself into the room and threw her arms around me, squeezing tightly without bumping my wrist. When she released me, she pulled a wadded tissue from her sleeve, mopped up a tear, and blew her nose.

"Kye," Cam called. "You dropped your bag."

"Oh, stars. Would you mind?"

"Not a problem."

She led me to the table. "You must be sick of packaged fish. Let's get some real food in you."

"Zhen was to bring me food this evening," I said.

"I told her I would. She's tracking down a red light, since there aren't filters in this room. You sleep better with those, right?"

I nodded as Cam gave me a faltering smile and handed Kyleigh a bag.

"I'm glad you're all right, Zeta," he said. "You're really good at making people worry, you know that?" I began to stammer an apology, but he interrupted me to say, "Welcome back."

"I am glad to see that you are still onboard. You are well?" I asked as I settled in a chair.

"Mostly." He hesitated, then added, "Even though I didn't like leaving you, Tia was right about me going to that meeting. The Elder on *Attlee* was insisting that I go back with them. I'm nonessential."

"That is untrue, Cameron," I protested.

"No, it is. Captain Genet stretched the truth when he said that *Thalassa* needs me. I can't fly anything or shoot straight, like Eric can, and I'm rubbish on comms. Story of my life."

"Cam," Kyleigh began.

"No, it's okay. Taking odd jobs frees up people for the real work." His thin face creased when he smiled. "But now, I'm on Zeta guard duty, which is arguably the most important job onboard. And I'd better get back out there."

"Yes, in case that horrid Recorder who tortures people shows up again." Kyleigh pulled out the chair next to mine and smiled at him. "Thank you, Cam."

"You're welcome. I might accidentally let Tia in if she gets off on time."

"Adrienne Smith had better ease up," Kyleigh said as the door shut behind him. The bag crinkled when she pulled out the nightshirt Jordan had given me when I was first on *Thalassa*, a sandwich, a flask, and two blue, ceramic mugs.

"My shirt. I had not anticipated . . . Thank you."

"Yes, well, we are scrounging up new clothes, too. Not those greys, either."

"But that Recorder—"

"Can go—" She made a noise like an angry cat. "I didn't like him to begin with, but this? Here." Peppermint tea flowed in a fragrant stream into a mug. "Drink. Have a sandwich."

I took a sip and almost relaxed.

We were finishing when the door opened, and Cam said, "Go on, Tia. It'll be fine."

While Kyleigh gestured to the chair opposite hers, I did my best not to react to the change a ten-day and a half had wrought.

I must have failed, for instead of a standard greeting, Tia said, "I suppose I should say it first, so you won't be shocked or something. I'm"— she shot a glance at Kyleigh, who nodded—"expecting."

I scrambled internally for the correct thing to say. "I am not surprised." Kyleigh winced, and I realized I had misspoken. "No one told me. I extrapolated from what several people, yourself included, have said. And your clothes—" I cringed when my conversation with Zhen and Eric came to mind. "I apologize. My words did not emerge the way I intended."

Tia traced an invisible picture on the table's smooth surface. "It took me a while to react well, myself."

"How are you feeling?" I asked.

"Pretty good, though I'm hungry all the time." She sighed, and we sat in awkward silence until she added, "I've mostly been shadowing Officer Smith on comms, though I don't think I've learned much at all." She rested her arms on the table. "It's funny, you know. I really had no idea. I just didn't want to be locked up with Watkins and company."

"They sound awful," Kyleigh inserted, and I confirmed her suspicion.

Tia gave an exaggerated shudder. "I wanted to help, to be part of something bigger, but the whole time has been ordinary with spurts of panic. At first I thought I'd like to stand inside a moon, but I'm afraid that image has lost its charm. Eric told us some pretty awful stories yesterday, before he left again."

Kyleigh stared at the cooling mug in her hands. "I'm glad you stayed here."

"So am I. But, as awful as *Agamemnon* was, as terrifying as it was when *Thalassa* went dark, I'm grateful. Knowing what I do now . . ." Tia touched my left arm, then drew back. "Having met you and the others, having seen what you go through, well, I can't."

"Cannot what?" I asked.

Her hand rested on her abdomen. "Gift her. I . . . I just have to figure out what to do."

"What to do?" Kyleigh repeated. "I thought Eric asked you to contract?"

"What?" I exclaimed, though the pieces clicked into place: his frustration with Cam in the hallway, his concern over Tia's future, even his blush when she brushed his hair when his arm was broken.

Tia's eyes flashed. "I'm *not* taking a pity contract, Kye."

"It's not a pity contract," Kyleigh shot back.

The peppermint tea suddenly tasted sour. I set the cup down.

Tia rubbed her eyes. "Moons above. His parents have been together his whole life. That never happens. But it's what he wants. He—" A smile brightened her face. "Zeta! Give me your hand."

Uncertain of why my hand was necessary but willing to offer what little support I could, I complied. She pressed it to her abdomen.

I tried to tug free. I had no desire to touch anyone's abdomen, but then a faint bump rose and slid to the side. Tia released me, but wonder did not. I stared at my empty palm, as if my hand had something to do with the movement I had felt.

An ache hit my heart. I needed to see, to hold, this little one. Recorders did not have children. The Consortium made certain of that, so even if I remained free, this would never be my future. I exhaled. The Eldest would not excuse my behavior, so at least there was no reason to confess this to Nathaniel.

"I'm not giving her up," Tia announced. "I'll quit university. Whatever it takes, I'll do it—except taking a contract with someone who doesn't love me."

"Stars above," Kyleigh blurted. "Did he really not tell you he's in love? Of all the idiotic—I'm having a talk with him."

Tia's cheeks turned a shade close to fuchsia. "Kye!"

"Well," she temporized, "he's still officially training on the shuttle, even if he's already better than Osmund, so it'll have to wait."

"Or you can simply *not* talk to him."

Kyleigh leaned back in the chair. "You know who I'd like to not talk to? Julian Ross."

Even I recognized her diversion, but confronting her would accomplish nothing. I tried another sip of my tea, which was not truly sour after all.

"I don't blame you." Tia folded her arms over her belly, as if to shield the tiny one inside.

Kyleigh's face scrunched. "You know the worst part? Sometimes, I forget. I never really liked Ross, but I never thought he would . . . I don't know. Be outright evil? And sometimes, when I see him out of the corner of my eye, I see Elliott, and I can't figure out how I feel about that."

I could not either, but fatigue settled heavily on me. I drifted while their conversation ebbed and flowed.

"Zeta?" Tia set a hand on my arm. "You need to sleep. We've been prattling on for way too long."

Kyleigh, who had already cleaned off the table, placed the nightshirt in my hands. "Go change. Today was pretty awful, but tomorrow is a blank data cube. Get some sleep. We'll leave the light on. We'll tell Zhen to be quiet whenever she gets here."

They left. I changed and settled on my bed. I fell asleep thinking over love and loss and uncertain futures.

Shortly after breakfast the next morning, my communications link chimed, and the Recorder-doctor berated me for taking part in such a scandalous, citizen-like thing as smuggling. Since I knew the charges were both false and intended to protect me, I found his concerns amusing at first, even though he failed to connect my purported misdeeds to a likely assignment to the Hall of Reclamation. After he started to scold me about my suit's malodorous nature, however, I disconnected the link and refused to answer his four subsequent attempts to contact me.

When Alec and Zhen brought me lunch—soup and salad with fruit compote for dessert—Zhen was snickering.

"You should have seen it," she said. "I went with Tia to the infirmary for her checkup, and that Recorder was arguing with Archimedes, demanding that you answer his comms. And the captain said"—she lowered her voice in a poor attempt at making her soprano a baritone—"'I find it extremely suspicious you are so adamant about contacting a person suspected of the illegal trade of insect parts, especially since you are a doctor. After all, rare parts are often used in the manufacture of illegal drugs.'"

Her storm of laughter prompted a smile, which disappeared when a knock sounded at the door. Alec and Zhen were on their feet before it slid open. Quincy and two armored marines flanked Williams, who clutched a small sack to her chest.

Quincy set down a satchel and saluted me. The three men left, and the door slid shut.

Williams plopped her bag on the bed farthest from the table. "You were right about this. I found it before that Recorder did," she said without any other greeting. When she held up a note, for a half second I thought she held mine. "It was where Edwards promised it would be."

I blinked. I had forgotten I had told her about it.

Williams tore open the envelope and visually devoured it. Her hand covered her mouth, muffling her words. "His name is Connor. Connor Edwards."

A knot swelled in my throat. "It is a good name."

Alec stood and led Williams to take his chair.

"We had a pact." She smoothed the paper flat. "I met him in Albany City when he returned for continuing education, you know. I was at a café, studying for exams. He bumped my table, spilling coffee all over my uniform, so he bought me a new cup. He's been my friend ever since. We . . ." She raised dry but reddened eyes to mine. "You would understand there is nothing . . ."

Although staff had more freedom than Recorders, strong connections and attachments brought punishment. My heart ached. "Yes."

"After the last trip, when we met you, we talked about the potential risks and repercussions. Max did not understand then, though he has an inkling now. He has always seen us as people, not merely staff, not as if we are a subspecies of human." Williams scanned the paper one more time before carefully replacing it into the envelope. "*Connor* and I promised each other we would write notes if something happened. I left one for him, and his was exactly where he promised it would be. He told me his name, and he"—she sank onto the end of her bed—"writes that he wished things were different, that he had taken me out for dinner or to an antique bookshop. That he had bought me something other than one lonely coffee. That he was sorry he had let his fear of consequences steal . . ."

The lump in my throat made it difficult to say her name. "Williams," I began.

"Elinor," she whispered. "I wanted to be Elinor Anne Williams. My note was still there, so he doesn't know—" Her breath hitched. "Connor doesn't know my name."

I could do nothing. Without the ability to read, I could not keep my vow to find Alec's father or Jordan's cousin. Now, I could not find Elinor Anne Williams's Connor. *My* Edwards. I could do nothing—*nothing*—to ease these losses. I hobbled over to her side and held out my hand. She took it.

"I cannot promise to remember always, but I will try," I said. "Elinor Anne, you should not give up hope."

Alec and Zhen left soon afterward, and though Elinor Anne Williams sat there, shoulders hunched, fragile as thin glass, she did not cry.

I did.

That evening, she and I were finishing our dinner when Max entered the computer lab, set a datapad on the table between our cups, and angled his chair toward mine.

"Why didn't you say anything?" He tapped the datapad. "It's nothing to be ashamed of, no matter what that Recorder said."

A chill swept over me. The Recorder-doctor had betrayed my secret. Williams glanced between us.

"But it is, Max." My voice dropped. "Reading was part of who I was."

"No, reading is part of what you do."

Williams's eyes went round over the rim of her cup. She set it down so quickly that juice sloshed onto the table. I handed her a napkin without looking away from the doctor who had saved my life.

"Max, you told me once each person has value, is unique. My abilities were part of my uniqueness, and now they are gone. *Gone.*" My voice broke. "I cannot even perform the katas from my childhood. And reading was the building block of everything I did. I cannot even help find—" I broke off, lest I hurt the woman beside me.

"I told you, you aren't what you do."

Williams leaned forward and asked softly, "What, precisely, has happened?"

I cradled my ginger tea with trembling hands, watching the overhead lighting's reflection wobble on the golden liquid. "Since my final encounter with the roaches, I cannot read, except short single words in isolation."

"Oh, my friend. You should have told us," Williams exclaimed. "The sooner such things can be treated, the better."

Whether or not she was correct, they did not understand. I set my own cup down. "When I was small, the Elders recognized my potential and declared my calling would redeem my gifting. My mind and my . . ." I fisted my hands, as if doing so would clarify thought. "Who I was? Was becoming? They were all I had that was truly mine, though I did not understand as much." A shiver hit me. "I thought I lost everything when I lost my chip, but I was wrong."

"You have us," Max said.

"That is true." I held myself tighter. "Nate, you both, Jordan, Kyleigh, Alec, and Zhen . . . my friends. You are immeasurably more important."

"You still have us," Williams said. "You cannot believe your friends would—"

My heart jolted. "You must not tell them!"

"Judge you for the loss," she finished.

Max held up both hands. "If you don't want us to tell them, we won't."

I wanted to tap, hit, even pound my thigh, but pain from the chip in my wrist prohibited the action.

Williams folded her arms tightly. "We understand loss."

My shoulders hunched. "That is not all I have lost."

"You have not yet lost your freedom," she said. "And we are looking for a way to release you from the Consortium."

"It is more than that. I not only have lost my abilities"—my throat worked—"I have also lost who I am."

"You've always been more than a Recorder," Max began, but he stopped when I shook my head.

A shudder grabbed me and would not let go. Williams fetched a blanket from her bed and wrapped it around my shoulders. They waited.

"I killed him," I whispered.

They exchanged glances, and Max said with slow precision, "You saved Elliott's life."

"Not Elliott. That man." I pulled the blanket close, but warmth eluded me. "I hear him die, over and over, in an echo sounding out of nowhere, and the image ricochets through my mind."

Williams pursed her lips. "When you saved Yrsa."

"Yes."

"My problem," I said, though I recognized it as simultaneously an obstacle and an asset, "is that I believe the fundamental truth of your claim. Whether stardust or creation, we are unique, but my careless order to retrieve the medic at all costs crushed a man from existence."

Max reached across the table, his hand stopping a centimeter from my arm. "If you hadn't . . . You know what they did to Elliott and Ross. They wouldn't have allowed her to walk away."

"I know. I would do it again, but how? What words would have been sufficient? Nothing. My orders to the drone might have saved the medic—"

"Did save," Max appended.

I sighed.

Williams reached past me, reopened the flask of hot water, and topped off my cup of ginger tea. After pushing it in my direction, she said, "You did not intend his death."

"I caused it." I pressed my feet against the antistatic flooring, focusing on each bump, knob, or ripple in the material. "His death is so different from Lorik's. While I abandoned the Elder to roaches, he *chose* to sacrifice himself in order for others to live. The man Skip called Cord—I will not say that he deserved to die, though I heard the marines say as much. He will never have the opportunity to change. I denied him that." I took a sip of warm but weakened ginger tea. "Years ago— why is it, Max, that I can remember this, but labor over small things?"

He cocked his head at the sudden change in topic. "Probably the nanite shells."

"Ah. I knew that." I gulped down the tea, hoping the ginger's spicy burn would warm me. It did not. "Years ago, before I attended university, I took a prerequisite literature course, and one disturbing story had a man proclaiming that 'blood calls for blood.' Williams, you read. Do you recall it?"

"I do not."

Her unfamiliarity made no difference. "That is how it feels. As if he or his family are calling out for my blood in payment." I returned the empty cup to the table, rotating it so the handle was perpendicular to the table's edge.

Williams asked, "You seek absolution?"

The blanket slipped from my shoulders. "I find myself weighing the value of a soul over and over again. Perhaps I have summoned all this on myself. Perhaps I deserve to lose words. Perhaps I deserve even worse."

Williams tugged the blanket up again. "Do not say so."

"It has changed who I am."

Even though Max leaned back against his chair, he seemed to draw closer. "The worlds aren't static. There is upheaval and evil as well as growth and goodness. You have to trust that there's more than what we see, directing our paths."

"You speak of—" I glanced around for a drone that was no longer there. "Of Kyleigh's unquantifiable God?"

Williams answered for Max. She lifted her chin and said clearly, "Yes."

"But how would that mediate the wreckage here and here?" I touched my head and my chest. "If the value of a person remains the same? If we are each unique?"

"Forgiveness," she said with quiet confidence. "Justice and mercy intertwine like . . . like DNA. But that debt of blood has already been met."

I hunched my shoulders and fought, unsuccessfully, the need to rock back and forth. "This is not comforting."

"Hold fast to hope, even when it seems tenuous and thin." But Williams's adjuration provided little reassurance.

"Even in the darkest of times," Max said, "you must have confidence that what is painful now has been, and will be, met and answered. Circumstances help us grow. They can and will be used for good. It's more than simply pressing on, though that's part of it. Trust that something or Someone greater than us shapes the worlds. Nothing is wasted. And none of this changes the fact that who you are is not what you do. Your heart. Your choices. Those matter."

Tears leaked down my cheeks. "But I am broken."

"We all are." Williams touched my arm, stilling me. "But as to your immediate losses, there are therapies, Max, are there not?"

The two issues were unconnected unless through some deeper link of justice, but I raised my head, nonetheless.

Max's long cords of hair shushed over his shoulders when he nodded. "There are, to an extent. While I don't know how to purge every single nanite cluster from your system, there are proven methods for repairing damage with follow-up therapies."

My mouth fell open. "Are there?"

Max tugged at his ear. "The problem is they all involve being submerged in a tank for three ten-days, which cuts close to our arrival."

"If I am in that Recorder's care, no false claim of smuggling will save me from the Eldest."

His nostrils flared. "Probably not. That's why you're in here, instead of walking about the ship."

Williams finally took another sip of her juice. "Still, do not give up hope. Nathaniel Timmons is already working with the captain, Jordan, Max, and me, trying to solidify a way to free you." She grimaced and stated my unspoken fear. "The Eldest is not . . . stable."

"I met the Eldest a few years back," Max said. "He seemed fair enough."

I pulled the blanket tight around myself. "The Eldest is a woman now. She is close to Jordan's age."

His mouth pinched. "When did that change?"

"Five years past, and she is nearing the end of her service. The Eldests do not last long. It is how it has always been," I said.

"You cannot return to her care," Williams stated flatly. "And so, our goal must center on your future. I might not specialize in therapies, but I have medical training. We have three ten-days to help you regain strength, three ten-days to see if we can devise some therapy to help you recover. Three ten-days to find a way to set you free."

Max set his hand on mine. "Thirty days."

The intangible realities of justice, mercy, and forgiveness battled the burden of my errors, but the tangible demanded my attention as well. With the Recorder on board and a medical tracker in my wrist, thirty days seemed all too short.

But those thirty days were mine, even if the Eldest was waiting.

The weight of a hand touching Kyleigh's shoulder yanked her straight out of the stubborn differential equation. Kyleigh's stylus went flying, and any semblance of a solution fled her mind. Heart racing, she spun her chair to face her interrupter. Elliott's blue eyes dropped apologetically.

"Sorry, Kye," he mumbled as he picked up the stylus from under his desk and handed it back. "Escort's arrived. Didn't mean to startle you."

She faked a smile and slid the thin, black piece of conductive foam into its slot. "Gideon's here?"

"Brisbane," Freddie put in from across the room, where he was stuffing his watercolor pencil case into his pack. "And he's early."

Sure enough, Peter Brisbane's broad back almost filled the doorway. Kyleigh gathered her bag and tucked her chair under the desk.

"Gideon Lorde's not feeling too good this afternoon, so you get me," Brisbane said over his shoulder. "You kids ready to go any time soon?"

She held up her bag in response. "Is Gideon all right?"

"Hope so," the security guard answered without taking his eyes from the hallway. "Probably just that cold or whatever went through the station a few days back."

Freddie grunted as he picked up his pack and his portfolio bag. "I don't get how anyone here got sick. It's not like anything new arrived. Next supply ship shouldn't get here for maybe what, half a quarter?"

Brisbane shrugged. "Not a doctor, kid. Got no idea."

They filed out and waited while the guard sealed the classroom door.

"Alicia wasn't feeling good, either," Kyleigh said. "How's she doing?"

"Better. She's back to work today. Alison never even ran a fever." The pride in the guard's voice was palpable, like somehow his little niece's temperature was verifiable proof she was smarter than anyone else. "Whatever it is, it's hitting Gideon harder than it hit Alicia, but he'll be better soon enough. You kids stay clear of Dr. Allen's infirmary, just in case."

"You don't have to tell me twice," Freddie said. "I've had enough of infirmaries and hospitals to last the rest of my life."

They started down the hall, Elliott and Freddie on either side of Kyleigh, like additional guards. Somehow, that made her feel a little better.

Elliott exhaled heavily. "Kind of a moot point, isn't it? We're steering clear of everything lately unless someone takes us."

Brisbane nodded. "Until we catch whoever killed your father, Kye, everyone is on alert."

"Are we still heading to my"—Kyleigh caught her lip between her teeth—"to my old quarters?"

"That's the plan." The man glanced back at her. "You holding up?"

Her shoulders hunched. "I guess."

"The Lost-a-Parent Club is a rotten one to join," the security guard said.

Elliott stuffed his hands in his pockets, like a younger version of his brother. "It is."

These three, at least, understood. Peter and Alicia Brisbane had accepted positions on Pallas after their mother died. And Freddie had lost his mum, and Elliott . . . well, at least he had Julian.

Freddie shifted his portfolio to his other hand so he could hold hers. "Has Gideon found anything out?"

"Not yet."

They followed the meandering hall toward the quarters Kyleigh used to share with Dad. Her eyes burned, and she blinked hard.

"We'll move your trunks to Georgette's quarters until you decide what to do," the muscled guard stated.

"Are you really thinking of leaving?" The question burst from Elliott.

Freddie gave her hand a gentle squeeze. "Do you blame her for wanting to be done with this place?"

Elliott flushed. "No."

She squeezed Freddie's hand. "I'm not sure. Mom hasn't responded."

"Comms are dodgy lately." Brisbane shrugged. "Ross gave me some science reason about a comet, Krios, and relay stations."

Kyleigh managed a slight smile for Elliott. "Your brother's right. I might not say it often, but he's almost as smart as he is overloaded with muscles."

Brisbane chuckled.

Her thoughts wandered. Ross and her dad had worked together, but they must've been friends, because Julian was really upset over Dad's death. Of course, Christine broke up with Ross a few days later, which was a rotten thing to do, kicking someone when they were already low. No wonder he seemed off lately.

"You all right, Kye?" Freddie asked.

She jerked her thoughts back. "Just scattered. Anyway, your dad told me to take my time deciding. Georgette volunteered to sponsor me, though I'd have to go to Krios Forty-Seven for half a year for testing and presenting my thesis. Or I could head out to university, like we've talked about. Or join Mom, if she wants me—"

"Of course she does," they all chorused.

A smile tried to flutter into existence, but a sigh pushed it away.

Down the hall, a door flew open. Peter Brisbane stopped abruptly as Christine Johnson practically floated out of her excessive yellow office. She startled when she saw the four of them, and then flashed an unusually mechanical smile. Brisbane relaxed slightly, Elliott seemed to shrink, but Freddie stiffened.

Great. Exactly what they all needed. As if it wasn't awkward enough that the geneticist had broken up with Julian, she'd been hovering around the three of them. If Kyleigh hadn't known better, she'd have thought the woman was after Elliott.

"Peter! I'm sorry. I'm so jumpy lately." She tossed her long, thick waves of blonde hair over her shoulder. If jumpy had an opposite, it was Christine Johnson. "I was heading to a meeting with Gideon."

"Didn't you get my message?" Brisbane narrowed his eyes. "Gideon has a fever this morning. Meeting's canceled."

"I didn't." Christine's sculpted brows drew down. She retreated into her office, the plush carpet softening the click of her heels, and returned moments later, an initializing datapad held high as proof. "No wonder my morning was so quiet: I forgot to turn this on. My commlink isn't working. Marsden said he'd get it back to me, but he hasn't yet."

"It's not safe without one." Elliott glanced at Kyleigh. "Not now."

Instead of rudely dismissing the comment, Christine turned the full force of her smile onto Elliott. "You're right. I don't know how I'd forgotten."

"Leave your datapad on until Marsden fixes your commlink," Brisbane ordered.

"I will. Do you want my help, Kye?" Christine asked gently. "I'm quite good at packing."

Kyleigh shook her head, but a cloud seemed to gather over Brisbane's face. "How'd you know where she's going?"

The woman waved her delicate hand. "Everyone knows Charles Tristram was a slob."

Brisbane cleared his throat.

"A disorganized man. It will take ages to bring his chaos under control."

"Dad wasn't really disorganized," Kyleigh countered. "He always knew where everything was, down to the smallest slip of paper."

Christine pulled the lacy, butter-yellow sweater tighter around her arms. "I didn't mean to offend you, dear. I'm feeling a little under the weather myself. I was headed to the kitchen for a cup of soup, if you don't mind company."

"If you want," Brisbane said.

She sidled up to Elliott, which made Kyleigh's skin crawl. When they reached the hall leading to the cafeteria, Christine said, "Comm me, Kyleigh, if you want my help."

The echoes of her heels on concrete receded, and they resumed their silent walk. When they reached her old quarters, Kyleigh unlocked the door, and her throat constricted. Dad's stacks of papers waited for him as if he had merely stepped away. His faded cardigan hung by the bare hook where his lab coat used to hang.

They'd burned that lab coat. Couldn't get the blood out.

The room's emptiness swelled, and the weight of loss hit Kyleigh hard. She forced down the ache, compacting it into a smaller mass and ignoring its gravitational pull.

Christine was right. There was so much to do. The bots had kept it clean enough, and it wasn't like there were bugs roaming Pallas, so she didn't have to worry about something moving in the clutter, not like back on Ceres.

Brisbane's commlink chimed. He stepped into the hall to answer.

Kyleigh hugged her arms around herself. "Where do I even start?"

Freddie set his portfolio and pack on a side table. "Go pack your clothes first. El and I will get the books and the artwork."

If anyone could be trusted to take care of art, it'd be Freddie. "Right."

"Kyleigh?" Brisbane called.

She stopped halfway to her room.

"Going to have to leave you kids here for a bit," the security guard said. "Stay put until I get back or I send someone else."

Panic speared Kyleigh. "What is it? No one is hurt, right?"

Freddie put a hand on her arm. "No alarm, Kye. Not a security issue."

"No," Brisbane said, but he wouldn't meet her eyes. "Just a bit of a . . . situation in the infirmary."

Her heart dropped to her feet. "Gideon?"

Brisbane didn't answer. The door clicked shut, and they stood for a moment, then wordlessly set to packing up the remains of Kyleigh's old life. As she emptied her closet and bookshelf, the noises in the front room slowed.

Freddie's voice came down the hall: "We're done with the art and the books."

"I'm almost finished here." Kyleigh folded her last sweater and stuffed it into her trunk to cushion the glass dolphin Mom had given her before she and Dad had left Ceres to come to a moon on the tail end of the system. A moon where he was murdered.

"Don't think about it," she told herself. "Think about dolphins."

"Dolphins?" Elliott asked.

She jumped. "You guys need to stop sneaking up out of nowhere. But nothing. I mean, I don't really like dolphins. Cats are better."

"True," Elliott said. "You can hold a cat, if Dr. SahnVeer isn't around."

Kyleigh didn't add that she could cry into a cat's fur. "Mom and Dad took me on an ocean tour before we left her behind on Ceres. They tried to explain why she wasn't joining us here, but they just talked in circles. I was so mad that I didn't listen. Mom pointed out the dolphins, saying something about families being like pods that support and protect each other."

The trunk clicked shut, and she pressed her thumb on the screen to seal it.

"That's also true," Elliott said. "You want me and Freddie to carry that?"

"If you don't mind. I bet it's heavy." She followed them down the hall. "Set it by the door. I'll borrow a platform or something."

Elliott's commlink chimed.

"Where are you?" Julian Ross demanded.

"Freddie and I are helping Kyleigh pack things up."

"Kyleigh . . . Right. Look, Elliott, I need you all to stay there until I come and get you."

Kyleigh rolled her eyes. "Brisbane said—"

"Brisbane is busy."

"No." She tried stifle the irritation in her voice. "He's just checking on things in the infirmary."

After a pause, Ross said, "Gideon will be out of commission for a while."

"What do you mean?"

"He's sick, Elliott. Really sick, and I don't—" Ross stopped abruptly, then said with a degree of caution, "I stopped by the infirmary to ask Dr. Allen for something, and . . . Stars, but it looks bad. You all need to stay away."

Kyleigh exchanged glances with the others.

"Kyleigh, Elliott told me that your father had told you and Freddie to be very careful about what you eat and drink." Ross paused, then added quickly in an undertone, "I think he was right. Keep with packaged food and water until this blows over."

Elliott's eyes went round. "But, Julian—"

"I'm not kidding." His voice was so tight that his words emerged as a growl. "I'm doing what I can. I'll fix it somehow, but stay away from . . ."

"From?" Elliott prompted.

"Just stick together. I'll be there in five minutes. I'll make sure you all have something safe to eat."

"You think it's food poisoning?" Kyleigh's stomach knotted at the thought.

"No," he said, then the link went quiet.

Freddie glanced at them. "That was odd."

"Not really," Elliott said. "Julian has always had a hard time sleeping, since I was small, so he probably was at the infirmary about more meds for that. Plus, he's done a lot of work with medical treatments for the miners. He's plenty smart. He'll figure it out. Got the best minds here anyway." His voice trailed off.

"That's not what I meant." Freddie leaned back against the wall beside Dad's cardigan. "Avoid food and stay away from what?"

"Or whom?" Kyleigh added.

"Exactly."

She shivered. "I don't like any of this."

Her two best friends guided her to the sofa and sat on either side. Freddie kissed the tip of her nose, and Elliott tugged the blanket off the back and tossed it around her.

"It'll be all right, Kye," Elliott mumbled. "Don't worry. They'll figure out why Gideon's sick, and he'll be better and find whoever it was."

"They will." Freddie gave her a light squeeze. "Dad always says things work together for good. I've got a feeling things will turn out. It just doesn't seem like it at the moment."

"No," she whispered. "It really doesn't."

Pallas Station was four days behind us the morning Nate returned my jacket, freshly laundered and folded but without the note. He said nothing about its absence, and though I wanted to, I did not ask. The knowledge that I kept a secret from my Nathaniel burned and spat at me like sodium dropped in water. But to tell him with Elinor Williams in the room? I could not.

I focused on Bustopher instead of confessing. The cat accompanied Nate each morning, twining about Nate's ankles as he brought breakfast, tea, and coffee. I always greeted Bustopher with as much respect as he required, but on the first morning, he walked in with his nose high in the air, regarded me from a distance, turned his back, and sat facing the door with his tail curled precisely around his paws. Thereafter, though he still came voluntarily, he greeted Williams, snubbed me, and resumed his statuette position. The fundamental rejection was depressing.

"Bustopher will come around," Nate said as he unpacked the bag that seventh-day, setting each item on the table as he listed it. "Tea, as usual, but with almond raspberry scones this morning. And fish loaf."

I stared at the packaged meal with all the revulsion it deserved. "I do not require additional protein this morning, Nathaniel."

He chuckled, leaned across the table, and kissed my forehead. "Not for you. For him." He nodded at the cat.

"A bribe?"

"Bribes are completely ethical when cats are involved."

Williams inclined her head. "Excellent idea, Timmons."

The plan, however unappealing, worked. By the time I had finished my breakfast, Bustopher had accepted my offering, cleaned his whiskers, and jumped into my lap where he kneaded his paws and settled into what Kyleigh called a "cat-loaf."

Nate drained his coffee and eyed me for a moment. "So how's the wrist?"

The purring cat shifted as my tension ratcheted up several notches. Reluctantly, I held out my arm to Nate.

Though his touch was gentle, his voice was rough when he asked, "Shouldn't that have stopped bleeding by now?"

Williams wiped her mouth with a napkin. "Yes."

Nate frowned. "I don't like that."

"You worry too much," I said. "I have not had another episode thus far."

His communications link chimed, and he stood without answering it. "I've got to head down to engineering, but I'll be back later. I've got a surprise for you, and before you ask, no—if I told you, it wouldn't be a surprise."

He touched my cheek and left.

I could not force the heat in my face to dissipate. "I am not fond of surprises."

"In that case," Elinor Williams said, "I shall tell you in advance that I have asked Zhen to stop by during her lunch break and bring needles and yarn."

"I enjoy the sound of her knitting."

She dusted off her hands and began to gather the remains of our meal, and when I protested that I would clean up, her expression softened. "No, for now, a purring cat is the therapy you need most. But later, you are learning to knit."

That evening, Nate brought a young man to visit, which was indeed a surprise. I had not expected additional company. The young man, perhaps in his midtwenties, cupped his hands loosely to his chest and beamed at me.

"Sweetheart, this is Ken Patterson."

My brow furrowed as I searched my memories. "The marine who was bitten? I am glad you are recovered, Ken Patterson."

"Ken, ma'am, and thank you," the marine said. "I was pretty lucky."

Nate glanced at me. "You might want to wear your jacket, just in case. To protect your wrist."

"Does Elinor require a jacket as well?"

"No, just you."

Elinor Williams shrugged one shoulder, so although I wanted to ask why my wrist would require protection, I complied. Nate settled me at the table, then nodded at the young marine.

Ken's smile widened. "Hold out your hands."

When I did, he lowered his own and gently placed a tiny, tiny cat on my palms. My eyes widened.

"Hunter had a litter shortly after I got back," Ken said. "I'd had some training as an animal tech back on Ceres before I joined up, so I volunteered to keep an eye on her. She's been in my quarters, and good thing, too, since this little one came out breech."

I could not answer him. All my attention riveted on the creature in my hands, its black fur fuzzier than Hunter's grey, its pin-sharp claws pricking my palms, and its bright-blue eyes, bluer even than Elliott's or Julian's. The kitten took a wobbly step. For no discernable reason, my breath caught.

"Don't worry," the young man added hastily, perhaps mistaking my silence for disapproval. "Hunter won't reject him if people touch him, or anything, and I'll get him back to his mum in time for his next meal."

I touched the little cat's tiny ear to my dry cheek. "I am not worried."

"Good surprise?" Nate asked softly.

Why a kitten would fill my heart to the brim, I could not say. I lifted my eyes to Nate's. "The best."

We fell into a routine as *Thalassa*, power back at full and all systems repaired, raced to New Triton.

Every morning, Nate brought breakfast. Bustopher sometimes stayed and sometimes left when Nate did, and Williams and I would work on pointless reading therapies and strengthening exercises for several hours. Max stopped by midmorning, ostensibly to check on my progress so he could report to the Recorder-doctor, though sometimes, we simply played chess with his personal wooden set. The dark smudges under his eyes had grown fainter, and he smiled more readily. Though when he and Williams—I did not always remember to call her Elinor Anne—spoke of Edwards, the lines returned to his face.

Zhen, and sometimes Alec, would arrive with lunch, and afterward I would attempt to "cast on stitches," which was much more difficult than Zhen made it appear. Contrary to my expectations, she was patient with my slow progress.

Some evenings, Ken Patterson brought the kittens, sometimes singly, sometimes in pairs, though Tia, Eric, and Cam never visited me when any cat was present. Williams explained that Tia was worried about the parasite the cats carried, and even though Williams said it would have been safe, I understood Tia's concern. The little one she carried was too valuable for even the smallest risk.

But every evening, Nate returned with dinner. James and Kyleigh joined us frequently, and Jordan and Max usually brought dessert.

Kyleigh seemed tired, but as days spun into each other, she regained some of the effervescence she once had. The fifth evening, she stopped midsentence and exclaimed that she knew what she must do and bolted from the room, James following her like a security guard. The next morning, she arrived before Nate brought breakfast.

"Don't get your hopes too high," she cautioned me unnecessarily, "but I've got an idea. I didn't train under Dr. Georgette SahnVeer for nothing, and I am determined to find a way to get rid of those infernal clumps in your blood."

Elinor Williams swiveled her chair away from the computer and studied Kyleigh. "How?"

"I've thought of a design, a sort of nano-macrophage thing, to eat them."

"Is that possible?" I asked.

"I won't know until I try."

Elinor Williams tilted her head to the side. "If you manage it, you will save more than our friend."

"I know. Recorders, staff, citizens . . ."

"With terrorists infiltrating society, you will need a secure location to manufacture it," Elinor cautioned.

"I'll figure that out later. It's just an idea right now, but if I'm late for dinner, don't be too surprised. I'll need to stay to work on this so Ross won't find out, just in case." She paused for a moment. "To give him credit, he really is working on an antivirus, even though they already have Clarkson's treatment based on the parasites. I guess backup is good."

"It is," Elinor said.

Kyleigh exhaled. "I don't like working with him in the room, but it's actually better than working with Dr. Clarkson. You saw the research, Elinor. It's only fair Ross gets some sort of credit since she used his theories on viral therapies to find the treatment, even if it is based on parasites instead of germs." She turned to me. "And then there's all your blood samples that she stole from the infirmary."

"I do not mind," I said.

"Well, to hear her talk, she created the whole thing from thin air. You know, I'm glad Imogene Clarkson was gone before you got back, if only because it spared you her self-congratulatory speeches."

A fraction of a smile appeared on Elinor's face. "Did she claim sole ownership of the discovery?"

"Yes. She was insufferable." Kyleigh rolled her eyes. "Inescapable, too. Everywhere I went, there she was, shoving data about the cats and toxoplasmosis in everyone's faces."

"That would not go over well with Shiro," Elinor noted.

"It didn't. She outright alienated him, and then she offended the Elder on *Attlee*. I was worried they'd refuse to take her with them, but she did understand it best. To make matters worse, though, she almost took the cats."

"All of them?" When Kyleigh nodded, I clenched my jaw at the thought of that woman stealing Bustopher. I did not wish to imagine *Thalassa* without the cats.

"Cam and I put a stop to that plan." Kyleigh paused, then added with emphasis, "He and I saved every single scrap of cat waste and presented it to the Elder in a box for 'research and preventative measures.'"

A genuine smile lit Elinor's face. "Did you?"

"Yeah, and I suspect *that* was what made *Attlee*'s captain change his mind." Kyleigh drew a deep breath. "Right then. Save me some dessert."

She darted off and, after that, was frequently late for dinner.

Altogether, when I did not think of our arrival at Lunar One, or when I forgot that I could not leave the room without the Recorder-doctor finding me, or when my wrist no longer pained me, I was more than content. I was . . . happy.

Happiness, I decided, was not irrelevant after all.

Seventeen days into our journey, Nate, James, and Kyleigh arrived shortly after Ken Patterson did, and light sparkled from James's ears. I blinked twice and pushed myself to my feet, careful to avoid the tumbling kittens. James wore Freddie's diamond studs. An unexpected wave of grief washed over me, and I did not truly hear Kyleigh's comment, only Elinor's quick, "Your pardon?"

"Not yours, Elinor." She waved a hand at me. "Hers."

Nate regarded me closely but asked, "What about it?"

Uneasiness crept past the contentment the kittens usually brought.

Kyleigh set her hands on her hips. "It's getting long."

"What is?" I asked.

"Your hair." She grinned. "It's long enough to braid, if we keep it tight to your head."

For a moment, my wish to have braids like Jordan's tugged at me, but just as quickly, the aspiration vanished. "I-I cannot."

Kyleigh's hands fell from her hips. "Of course you can. Mine isn't as long as yours, but I'm having mine braided tomorrow."

"That'll be pretty," Ken blurted, then turned beet red.

James's mouth tightened, but Kyleigh flashed Ken a smile.

"Thanks." She turned to me. "Whyever not?"

My gaze fell, for I could not bring myself to explain.

Williams touched my shoulder. "Your scars?"

I could not even nod.

"Not that it's my call," Nate said slowly, "but I like the idea of leaving those curls loose."

I glanced up at him. How had I not noticed that my hair drooped over my eyes?

Nate leaned close and lowered his voice. "To tell the truth, I like running my fingers through your curls." Warmth flushed through me, and my heart sped up. He tucked a curl behind my ear. "And those scars?"

"What of them?" I whispered.

"They're proof you're one of the bravest in the system, sweetheart. They're beautiful."

All evening, his words repeated through my faulty memory, and that night, when I changed into the rust-colored sleep shirt, I studied my head in the water closet mirror. I still did not like the welts that encircled my skull, but I found that perhaps, I did not mind my scars after all.

Zhen DuBois angled through the computer lab door before it had finished sliding open. My hands stilled, the awkward knitting needles posed mid-stitch, and Williams swiveled around from my old computer. Bustopher, however, remained intent on my yarn.

Dark eyes narrowed at me, and Zhen announced, "I give up."

I, too, wished to quit or at least to unravel the lopsided, knitted rectangle and begin afresh. Zhen maintained that the increasing evenness of my stitches proved progress, but keeping evidence of improvement was unnecessary. I placed my knitting on the table, and the yarn rolled over the edge and across the antistatic flooring. Bustopher pounced. His feet and body tangled in the yarn, and he sprang back. My project flew off the table and onto his head. His ears went flat, his eyes went wide, and he streaked through the computer lab door, dragging my haphazard creation after him.

When Elinor Williams burst out laughing, Zhen's expression lightened. My heart did as well. Elinor had not laughed since returning from Pallas.

Cam leaned into the laboratory. "Zeta, soon as I'm off duty, I'll get your knitting back."

A heavy thud, a mild curse, and masculine laughter drifted through the door before it closed. Elinor Williams laughed even harder.

Finally, she wiped the corner of her eye. "I needed that." Still smiling, she took the chair opposite mine. "Well, Zhen, what is it you have given up?"

For an answer, Zhen reached into her pocket and pulled out my cracked, blue datapad.

My heart stammered, and all my flaws came roaring back to mock me, including my inability to adjust equipment. Concern for Daniel and

James made me gasp, "You have not given up on the jamming devices, have you?"

"No, I fixed that ages ago." Zhen deposited the datapad on the table. "Well, Daniel and I did before we left Pallas."

"This is true," Elinor Williams affirmed.

I exhaled in relief.

"And since none of us can mess around with Consortium infrared or whatever, a few of us also scrambled information on our ID bracelets."

Elinor tilted her head to the side, then her eyes widened. "So James and Dan's bracelets won't be the only ones that need reprogramming?"

Zhen's expression reminded me of Bustopher's when he had stolen and consumed a tidbit from my breakfast. "Right."

I relaxed. "There is no need to surrender the datapad to me again, if that is your meaning."

Zhen took the chair across from mine. "Not the datapad itself. I can't figure out how to find what you were searching for in her personal records."

Williams leaned over her elbows on the table. "Whose records?"

"Pallas Station's Recorder's."

Elinor Anne Williams gasped. Her gaze darted between us before settling on me. "How did you access them? Her personal logs would have been sealed, and only an Elder . . ." Tension wrinkled the corners of her eyes. "You used the drone."

"Not intentionally." They listened closely as I explained how I had utilized the datapads to control the drone and, finding the files, had copied them to my own device for later perusal. "I had intended to view them in VVR."

"That explains it." Zhen chuckled, though I did not find humor in my intentions. She leaned back, arms folded. "The drone reserved the slot, didn't it? This thing's alarm went off at midnight a few days back to notify me of a VVR reservation at 04:30. Alec wasn't too pleased about waking up, but then, he never is. He's positively grouchy in the morning."

"I . . . had forgotten."

Zhen flushed and pocketed the datapad. "I'm sorry. I didn't mean to—never mind. I'll take care of it."

My jaw tightened. This was my responsibility, not hers, but I could do little when reading was still so difficult. "It is well. What have you found?"

"A lot and a little, all at the same time." She shook her head. "I've been going over the entries whenever I can snag a time slot in VVR. There has to be a pattern, but I'm not seeing what it is. There are files about Christine Johnson, the infirmary, and a brief journal entry about erased records, but as much as I loathe that voided waste of DNA, nothing on Julian Ross. Not," she added, "that I want to exonerate him. I just want the truth."

"The station records proved that he did not kill Kyleigh's father," I said.

Elinor Williams nodded. "Yes, since she is working with him, Captain Genet told Kyleigh as much. Though, since there is no proof, he did not offer anything else."

"But did they clear Ross of the Recorder's murder?"

I studied the workplace safety posters, which held no more answers than they had when I could read them. "He testified that Christine Johnson killed her."

"Like he'd admit it? Have you taken a look—no, of course not," Zhen muttered. "Not when you've been locked up in here."

I stood and took several steps without my cane. "Do not reprimand yourself."

A smile brightened Zhen's face. "You're walking!"

"Of course I am." I waved her remark aside, refusing to be distracted from the information on the datapad. "I should have viewed the data we sent up from Pallas."

Elinor exhaled heavily. "Well, you cannot leave this room. Not with that Recorder ready to pounce on you like a cat."

"Actually, I think she can."

When I spun to face Zhen, I had to catch hold of a chair.

"It's *Thalassa*, after all," she explained. "The only real threat is that Recorder, and he won't leave the infirmary."

"Never?" I asked. "Not even to sleep?"

"The Consortium network's down, and he won't go a meter without that drone. He hasn't figured out how to use a datapad, like you did."

Williams darted a glance at the door. "The ship-wide network is functional. How do you know the Consortium's is not?"

"The datapad. After it woke me up, I decided to see if I could access records and track down Alec's father, which I failed to do with the network down." She held up a hand when I protested. "Alec's already lectured me. You don't need to."

The possibility of freedom, even though it would be short-lived, burned like a solar flare. "Then I may be of assistance with visual records."

"Which would be extremely unadvisable," Elinor Williams said.

Zhen's expression remained neutral.

"If the Recorder-doctor is not present, I do not see how leaving this room is an issue."

Zhen's dark eyes studied my face. "How's your headache?"

"You have been spending time with Kyleigh," I responded. "Her abrupt changes in conversational topics have influenced you."

The corner of her mouth rose a few millimeters. "A bit. But your head?"

"The pain is never truly gone," I admitted, "but that would not prohibit a short walk. I promise to return. I will even knit without complaint."

Zhen pursed her lips. "If you take some pain meds, and we're careful . . ."

Williams placed her hand on my upper arm. "You must entrust this to others, given the circumstances."

"No." When she shook her head, I added, "Please. If Zhen is correct, I will be safe. We will go slowly. I have been walking more, and this will give me the opportunity to help. When we reach Lunar One, I might lose . . ." I could not finish the thought.

Zhen flinched as though I had struck her, and Elinor Williams tensed. For the count of thirty-seven seconds, Elinor studied me.

Then, she said, "I do not like it, but if Zhen is correct, and if Max and Archimedes approve, then I will not gainsay the decision."

I sank into the chair, smiling so broadly my cheeks hurt.

"They will." Zhen was already on her feet and backing toward the door. "I'll go talk to them in person, so it won't be on any log. I have a VVR reservation anyway, and I'll queue up her entries. Maybe all I need is fresh eyes. I'll be right back." She grinned. "I'll even track down your knitting. Not even Bustopher gets you out of that."

She spun around, blue hair sheeting like a fall of water, and left.

"I do not like this," Williams said with quiet intensity.

"Williams, viewing records in VVR is the only way I can be of assistance. If I attempt to manipulate files, she will know."

"Oh my friend," she said softly. "You have not told her?"

I grimaced. "You have been my constant companion for days. You know I have not."

A tight smile straightened her mouth. "Perhaps it is time to tell them the truth. They will not reject you."

"I know."

Even so, I was not whole, and all I wanted was to curl into a ball and protect the losses that were but a representation of my fractured self.

An hour and a half later, however, Zhen and I waited outside VVR for the light to turn green. Cam still stood guard over the computer laboratory and Williams, but Eric and Ken Patterson watched the hall, alert as if the Recorder-doctor were Skip, the knife-man, or a roach.

I leaned my weight on my cane. "VVR is taking longer than usual. You are certain the files are loading properly?"

"Yes."

"Maybe it's broken," Ken offered. "It wouldn't load target practice the other day."

Zhen darted him a look. "That's because Hodges tried to reprogram it to have roaches."

Eric grimaced. "What is it with him and bugs?"

No one answered.

Still, the light remained yellow. Zhen scowled at her identification bracelet and muttered something about time.

"Tia said yes, yet?" Ken asked mildly.

Pink suffused Eric's face. "Not yet."

The other young man's expression fell. "Sorry."

I was spared any subsequent discussion, for the light flashed green and the door slid open. Gripping my cane, I entered a visual record of Pallas Station's infirmary.

Standard blue and green walls, two hoverbeds with crisp, white blankets, and familiar stainless doors of an older medicomputer should have seemed familiar, but the arrangement was wrong, as if the room had been shuffled, then rotated ninety degrees. To my left, medical supply lockers lined the wall, and the medicomputer was on the wall to the right of the door instead of across from it. Directly in front of me, a man in a white lab coat over pale-blue scrubs stood frozen in the act of opening a cabinet between the two beds.

I had seen this man before . . . in other records?

Zhen lingered in the hall, her undertones incomprehensible, then breezed into the room. "I sent Patterson to get you a chair. Eric will be fine by himself for a while." She strode through the room, fearlessly walking through the projections to investigate the doctor's list. "That's Oliver Allen. It's 475.4.4, seventh-day."

"Yes, Dr. Allen. I remember now." I squinted into the room, willing myself to recall the date and time as I used to, but my memory refused to obey. "How long before the Recorder dies?"

"Three days. Thirty-one days before Kye's dad, and not quite five ten-days until the first people get sick."

"It was the virus."

"We have no absolute proof of that, but probably." She twisted her blue hair around her fingers. "Allen thinks he miscounted the supplies, but I've watched this over and over and, moons and stars, but the man thought the best of everyone, even that uncouth engineer, Marsden."

Jean-Pierre Marsden. Yes, that had been his name, though for all his disagreeable traits, he had died trying to drag Dr. Allen to safety.

I hated death.

"So Allen calls in security in a few minutes because of a regulation in reporting discrepancies. I can tell Lorde's suspicious, but they don't do anything. Or the Recorder didn't see what they did." She groaned. "I wanted to start here, though if you have a better idea, we can do that."

"It is a reasonable place."

"Play," she said.

Dr. Allen opened and closed cabinets, checked and rechecked his datapad. Gideon Lorde joined him, his lanky frame towering over the doctor as he took notes of his own. His sharp eyes traced over labels I could not read, and his thick brows drew together.

They locked the cabinets and conferred in subdued voices, then the recording stopped.

"Nothing," Zhen declared. "And it's all like this."

"Have you viewed the corresponding files from the station?"

"Yes, and they are exactly the same. I even played them at the same time, and there wasn't a difference."

A knock at the door spun us both around, and she caught my elbow when I wobbled.

"Here you go," Ken said as he guided a wheeled desk chair into the room. He gave Zhen a salute and left.

I sat, balancing my cane on my lap. "The names or codes—I cannot recall which—do they reveal anything?"

"I don't think so," Zhen said.

"Perhaps if we . . ." I leaned back and closed my eyes.

"Your head bothering you?"

"No more than usual. Read me the files. Perhaps the list itself can direct us to a more productive record."

She demanded that VVR display the file names and summaries. I squeezed my eyes shut to avoid the words which sprang into the air between us, their letters made more incoherent by their added dimensions. She read them twice before I thought I saw a pattern.

"Four hundred two; five hundred thirty-seven; twenty-one, zero-five. Next: four hundred three; one hundred seventeen; twenty-three, forty-one. Next: four hundred—"

"Dates," I exclaimed, my eyes flying open. "The ten-day and day. Fourth ten-day, third. The other sequences are times and, I believe, locations. Zhen, pull up a station map. In that naming sequence of numbers, I believe the first sequence is the date and the last is time. Check to see if the middle numbers are locations."

"First, no, because the times don't match the timestamps on the files themselves. Second, the rooms weren't numbered. You were there. You saw the doors," she protested, though the map hovered in the air between us.

A sharp pain stabbed my head, and my fingers went numb. Panic shot through me, but I pressed it down. "VVR, overlay the station map with blueprints."

A second map blanketed the first, and numbers labeled the twisting hallways, decorated the unevenly spaced rooms.

"Moons and stars," Zhen breathed. "How did I not see this? But, no, the room numbers don't match."

"I did not see it, either. I needed to hear it. VVR . . ." I could feel my tongue thickening in my mouth, but I had to check. What was the last set of numbers? I could not remember. Carefully, so as not to slur my words, I said, "Zhen, have VVR play the station record for the time and location of the last full numerical sequence."

"VVR, play station record for," she hesitated, "fourth quarter, fourth ten-day, third." She squinted at the blueprints. "Infirmary. Timestamp, 23:41."

The room around us flickered, showing the infirmary lit in gentle blue. The door opened, and a woman with thick, wavy blonde hair peered in, calling softly to see if anyone was present, then walked to the medical locker and entered a code.

"Christine Johnson," Zhen muttered.

"Pause recording. Zhen, double-check," I said, and her fingers whizzed through data. "Was that her own password?"

"That sneaky—" Her jaw clamped shut. "That's Oliver Allen's code. And yes, she's snagging that potassium solution you talked about before."

"This merely proves that she did indeed steal the medication." The room split into two images. "Zhen."

"It's a better start," she said, zooming into and out of lists so quickly that nausea struck. "And it gives me an idea of how I can search outside her records as well. It's a ridiculous idea, true, though I suppose—"

"Zhen," I said thickly.

"Hmm?"

"I believe . . . I need help." My cane clattered to the floor.

Alerted by the medical tracker in my wrist before I had even asked for help, the droneless Recorder-doctor arrived at VVR with a hover gurney before Max did, contrary to Zhen's assertion that he never left the infirmary. Eric and Ken lifted me onto the gurney, and when Max and Nate arrived, I closed my eyes and tried to ignore the increasingly heated argument in the background.

Archimedes Genet and Michaelson were waiting in the infirmary.

Despite the risk, I spent the next several hours in the Recorder-doctor's care. Nate, Max, and Michaelson refused to leave while I remained there, dosed with nanodevices, drifting in and out of consciousness. I woke in the computer laboratory again, Bustopher curled against my hip. Nate slept in a chair, leaning on my mattress, his cheek on his arm and his other hand holding mine. I rolled to my side and watched him breathe until sleep returned to claim me.

Other than Max, Nate, Kyleigh, and Bustopher, visitors were scarce over the next several days, but on ninth-day, Max declared that if I could remain unagitated, I could again have company. Zhen and Alec arrived with our lunch as usual.

She seemed unusually pale and, after apologizing, picked lethargically at her salad.

"It is not your fault that I have clumps of nanodevices lodged inside me."

"I pushed you to help."

"No, Zhen. I insisted on helping." I met her eyes through the steam rising from lavender-mint tea. "I am well, and Max and the Recorder-doctor have started a new therapy. Additionally, Kyleigh insists that she has developed a design that shall clear my blood."

In response, Zhen skewered an innocent piece of lettuce with her fork.

Leaning across the table, I touched her arm. "I am as well as I can be. Now, tell me what you found."

She sighed, then after three seconds, began a recitation of what she had uncovered using the station Recorder's files and the information from Pallas Station.

The station Recorder had been methodically gathering proof of Christine Johnson's unsanctioned viral experiments, as Charles Tristram had later suspected.

Once Zhen saw the Recorder's logic, she extrapolated on those patterns and delved deep into the station's records, restoring damaged files, piecing together events.

She recounted how, when Christine Johnson realized that the Pallas Station's Recorder was closing in on their project, she had followed the Recorder late one night while she prowled the halls without her drone.

Dr. Johnson had injected the solution and left the Recorder for dead. By the time security found her, it was too late.

When Charles Tristram, however, suspected that her death had not been a heart attack, Dr. Johnson had stopped his investigation, too. Zhen's face blanched as she summarized what she had seen of Charles Tristram's murder. I understood. I had seen the aftermath in VVR as Gideon Lorde secured the room.

Shortly afterward, Christine Johnson and Ross had argued, and any sign of cooperation between the two disappeared. Two ten-days later, she stole an access code and broke into Gideon Lorde's office. His notes revealed that he had found her hair at the murder scene under Charles Tristram's body and another fragment of long blonde hair caught under a cabinet door, partially stripped by a cleaning bot. Although the investigation was ongoing and he had not uncovered more evidence, that alone was enough to bring his own destruction. Zhen had salvaged a partial recording of Dr. Christine Johnson lacing his dinner with what must have been Consortium nanodevices. Zhen had verified that the drops she had spilled into a water pitcher in a meeting room had come from the lab Dr. Johnson and Julian Ross had illicitly used to create the virus.

Christine Johnson's assumption that Gideon Lorde would be the sole person to drink that water was incorrect, as was her assumption that citizens did not have Consortium devices in their systems. Within twenty-four hours, person after person had fallen ill. Seventeen others had succumbed, as Gideon Lorde had.

Finally, Christine Johnson had fallen ill herself. In a matter of hours, she went from healthy to a headache to gasping for air. During her final moments, her agitation grew more intense, but it was a mark in Ross's favor that when she spoke wildly of how "Juls killed me—have to stop him—tell my brother—" no one had believed her.

No one, then.

Neither Zhen DuBois nor I had evidence, but we both suspected that as she died, Christine Johnson had finally told the truth.

53

PERSONAL RECORD: DESIGNATION ZETA4542910-9545E

CTS THALASSA
478.2.9.10 – 478.3.1.02

My retrieval day was that tenth-day. It had never meant much to me, since it was merely the day Caretakers had removed me as an infant from a gifting tank. Daniel, however, had explained the significance of designations, and James had remembered mine, so people filed in and out of the computer laboratory all day to wish me a happy birthday. By the time Cam, Eric, and Tia bore away the remains of my dinner, I was exhausted.

Williams kept glancing at the door. The frown playing across her face lifted when Jordan, Zhen, Alec, and Nate arrived. As Zhen set plates and utensils on the table, Nate slid a fudge-frosted cake in the center.

"I wanted strawberries," Zhen said, "but the kitchen only had freeze-dried ones left, and that isn't the same. We'll have strawberries next year."

Next year. The promise pinched at me.

Nate brushed her comment aside. "Chocolate's better anyway."

"Max and Kyleigh will be by later. Max guessed that you'd be worn out, with all the visitation requests he and Archimedes approved," Jordan said as she guided me to a chair.

They sang then, and the uneven melody was the truest gift I had ever received. Nate deposited a large, uneven slice of cake on a plate and pushed it in my direction. I took a tentative bite of deep, dark chocolate. My eyes closed.

"You like it?" Nate asked.

I could but nod as I swallowed. "I do."

"Happy birthday, sweetheart."

Then, he kissed me in front of everyone, but I did not mind at all.

As *Thalassa* approached Lunar One, the Consortium found me. My right wrist tingled, and the dull green that pulsed under my skin confirmed my fears: It was more than a medical device. It was a Consortium tracker. Like the devices used in patrollers on Ceres, once activated, the Elders—the Eldest herself, should she be concerned with a single aberration—would know where I was. My unexpressed hope of removing it vanished, for any attempt to cut it out would now be traced. Citizens would be punished to the fullest extent of the law. Recorders, too, faced a severe penalty, though I did not dwell on that. I knew where I was going. My consolation remained that the Eldest could not know my thoughts.

The light in my wrist brightened and expanded overnight, stretching in a thin streak alongside the veins, like fluorescent blood poisoning. I kept my sleeve tugged down to hide it, lest Nate worry. They all would.

No one could do anything about it.

That night, *Thalassa* slid into the arms of Lunar One.

And there was nothing anyone could do about that, either.

"He's gone."

Glad of any excuse to stop trying to slide the loop of yarn over the needle without dropping the loops I already had, I put my knitting down. "Who is?"

Williams spun the chair around and gave me a broad smile. "That Recorder-doctor. He and his drone departed on the first shuttle. If you have any plans to escape, this may be your opportunity."

Before I could respond, the door slid open. Archimedes Genet strode in, followed by Jackson, Nate, Alec, and the marine whose struggling moustache had not grown any thicker during our trip from Pallas. Williams and I stood.

"Recorder, Williams," Archimedes said. "It seems you have been mistakenly detained."

Nate nodded to the young man. "Hodges has a confession."

The young man favored us with a grin. "Everything was my doing."

"Everything seems a broad admission," Williams said, though a smile shone in her eyes.

The young man's sparse moustache twitched, and his smile seemed at odds with his claim of guilt. "I was the one smuggling parts. I've talked to the captain, whose beneficence has led him to let me off with a fee."

"Laying it on a bit thick," Alec muttered.

One of Jackson's wild eyebrows rose. "That's not all you'll face."

At that, Hodges lost some of his assurance and stammered something incoherent about "trophies," which made no sense. The idea that anyone would wish to keep insectile parts so distracted me that I barely heard the cheer in the hall.

The captain seemed to be holding back a smile. "Will you press charges?"

Startled, I shook my head.

Hodges agreed to hand over his stash of two tarsi and three antennae and pay a fine, but no additional punishment awaited him. Two marines escorted him out, though he offered both Elinor Williams and me what she later informed me was a "cheeky grin."

I did not ask how he had brought all those pieces onto the ship. I did not want to know.

That evening, there was a small party in the dining commons, but though I had no desire to go, Elinor Anne Williams did. She stood in the doorway for a while, studying me. "Thank you. You gave me a purpose these past few ten-days, which eased some of . . ." Her words stalled, then she added, "You and a certain young man need to talk."

My brow wrinkled. "That is vague."

One of her now-rare smiles creased her face. "As you often say, *perhaps*." She headed down the hall, but before she reached the corner, she pivoted to face me. Her smile vanished. "My friend, do not make the same mistake I did."

For long uncounted minutes, I sat alone in the computer lab that was no longer my holding cell. Soon, the Consortium would come for me. I needed to walk the ship one last time. Leaving my cane and my communications link behind, I opened the door and peered down the hallway.

Thalassa should have bustled with activity that evening, but the halls were oddly empty. I left my room to prowl the corridors and ended in the small lounge. No one else was present, so I settled at a table in the back and watched the movement of lights out the unshuttered porthole. Familiar footsteps lifted my heart.

"Want company?" Nate asked.

"If the company is yours, yes."

He took the seat opposite my own and rested his elbows on the table. His too-long, blond bangs fell over his eyes, and I resisted the urge to tuck them behind his ear.

"You're not going back," he said.

"Nathaniel, we have had this same conversation time and time again. Archimedes Genet might have hidden me from the Recorder, but no one can hide me from the Eldest and the entire Consortium." I pulled back my sleeve to show my scarred wrist. His jaw ticced, and he carefully rolled down the fabric to hide the dull green glow under my skin. "They know where I am. The Eldest knows—she must know by now—about you, about us. I cannot run."

"Well, I've been thinking." He rose, circled the table, and held out his hand. I stared at it for five seconds before my own, seemingly without my permission, slid into his. Our fingers intertwined. "Your discoveries helped save the entire system. We'll appeal to the prime minister, and you won't have to run."

"The prime—No, Nate, that is a wild stretch." My thoughts tangled together while he waited, green eyes focused on my face. "I am Consortium, and I have betrayed my gifting. The Eldest has no tolerance for deviations. You know the Recorder-doctor went straight to whatever triad of Elders is on Lunar One at the moment."

"After all you've done, she can space herself. Betrayed your gifting?" He frowned. "You've more than paid it back."

"Be that as it may, she will not be pleased." His defense warmed the farthest corners of my heart, but had I really done much at all? "To the Consortium, I am but an aberration. If you petition for my freedom, it puts you in danger." I wrestled down trepidation. "My return is the better choice."

"Stars above, sweetheart. Are you suicidal? You know what you're facing."

"Yes. I know."

His voice roughened. "You're facing the Halls."

I could not contradict his statement, but we had now, and that must be gift enough. I ran my thumb over the faded scars on his knuckles. I had never asked about them. Why had I allowed such an oversight? "When did you scar—"

"I'm not letting you." The green of his eyes seemed brighter than usual. His left hand trailed down my cheek. "It was bad enough the first time, and again on Pallas? And stars, but you had to scare me to death taking off with that drone to rescue Elliott. I can't go through it again." He released my hand, but I stood. Nate pulled me close, resting his forehead against my own. "You have to let me try. Let *us* try."

The very thought of losing Nate would destroy me, and if he suffered because I was too selfish and too frightened to face the consequences of my choices, my actions? The weight of that consequence was beyond what I could bear.

Yet . . . he felt a similar weight for me.

Irreconcilable, unresolvable weight.

"My heart," I said into his jacket, "I foresee no solution."

He waited until I raised my eyes to his. "You never answered my question. The one"—he inhaled deeply—"in that note."

Guilt pinged through me. I began to pull away, but he caught me again.

"Don't, sweetheart." He ran his fingers through my hair.

For a second, I forgot what I must tell him and closed my eyes and hummed, even though my hair must have stood out in disordered curls and points like a nebula.

"You did read it, didn't you?"

I sighed and set my forehead against his chest. "No."

For a moment, he held his breath, though his heart pounded. "I see."

"No, you cannot see." I had avoided it long enough, then long enough again to cause him pain. My arms slipped from his waist as I moved away. The gaping loss of who I had been stood before me, and I was afraid, so afraid, of losing his respect. I stared at the third button of his jacket and said, "I did not read it because since we rescued Elliott—"

"*You* rescued Elliott."

"Please, Nathaniel, allow me to finish," I said, then summoned all my courage. "Nate, I cannot read."

I shot a quick glance at his face. Perfect brows furrowed, then lofted, and his eyes grew wide.

"You can't . . ." He dropped into my abandoned chair and shoved his hand through his hair again. "Why didn't you tell me?"

The antistatic flooring consumed my attention until he reached for me, gave my hands a gentle tug, and pulled me onto his lap. He tucked me against his chest, and my tears dropped onto his jacket's black fabric. He loosened his hold and pulled out his old-fashioned cloth handkerchief to dab my face dry.

"Does Max know?"

I nodded and kept my eyes down, even when Nate tipped up my chin.

"You were afraid to tell me because you thought it would change my opinion of you?"

Shame tiptoed through the present grief of losing who I was and the future grief of losing him. "Yes and no." I gulped down air. "Though I could not bear it if you thought less of me."

Silence billowed around us like dust in tunnels.

"If you thought I'd think less of you—"

"*I* think less of me."

His words fell, soft as a feather. "Then you think less of me as well."

"No!" But I had. My hands flew to my cheeks at the falseness of my assertion. Fresh tears welled. "Oh my heart, I am sorry. I should not have—"

I tried to stand, but he caught me again. My fingers curled into his jacket while he pressed me close.

"It's okay," he murmured into my hair. "It must be frightening, like your whole world cracked in two, but it doesn't change the fact I want to spend the rest of my life with you." He puffed out a breath. "Then you've no idea what I wrote?"

"No."

"Blast."

I waited.

"I won't set a limit on our relationship," he began. "Stars, but I wish—" He blew out a breath, and his bangs lifted and fell. "All this time, I thought you'd read it and hadn't wanted to respond. And when I found it in your jacket, obviously opened, and you never said a thing?" Nate's laugh was short. "Serves me right for being a coward."

"You are not," I retorted indignantly, but before I offered evidence, he kissed me hard. The room around us disappeared into stardust.

Afterward, I whispered, "You are the bravest and best man I know."

His green eyes, soft and dear, held mine. "I've got nothing on you."

"Do . . . do you still have it?"

Wordlessly, he took the familiar envelope from his inner jacket pocket and offered it to me again.

"Would you read it to me?"

"No." Though my heart dropped at the refusal, there was a smile in his voice. "I love you. Whatever happens, you need to know that." He flushed slightly. "After all this is over, when you're free, when you've finally picked a name—and I know it's an old-fashioned term—but say you'll marry me?"

The universe stopped moving for one long, impossibly beautiful moment, and all of space and time consisted only of Nate and me.

"This note"—his fingers wrapped around my hand, crinkling his letter—"was a first attempt at asking you. A permanent contract, but more than that, a promise of you and me, to the very end."

Still I could not speak. A smile coursed through my entire being.

"Say something." His eyes searched mine. "Say you will."

I will was shivering on my tongue when reality crashed down. If they knew what he asked—

"Nate, please do not." My voice broke. "You cannot."

The color drained from his face. "I shouldn't have asked."

"It is not your question. Oh, I wish . . ." Admitting that wish aloud was too difficult. When I pulled away and stood, he rose to his feet as well. "If I were free, it would be different. But, my heart, think. Please, think." The note crumpled further as I grabbed his arms. "Remember Gervase Singh and his Recorder. His disappearance and her death. I go to the Halls, but when I go, let me know you will be well. Give me your promise."

"My promise is that you will be free."

His note dropped when I threw my arms around his neck and kissed him. Fiercely. As if doing so would alter the course of the world around us. As if it were my sole chance to breathe the same air he did. For a moment, he did not respond, then he met my intensity with his own. When he pulled back, he combed his fingers through my hair, and his forehead puckered.

"Sweetheart, if you love—"

"More than all the worlds," I said.

We stood, hands clasped, an arm's length apart in the quiet of the lounge for unmeasured heartbeats until he released one hand and knelt to pick up the note. He folded my fingers around it and held my hand to his chest.

"Until we're out of this mess, this note is my promise." A faint smile quirked. "I'll get you a ring later."

"I do not want any ring." When he tilted his head to the side, I realized I had spoken amiss. A weak chuckle burbled out before I could stop it. With my left hand, I traced his stubbled jawline. "You. I want you, Nathaniel Phineas Timmons. Not any ring. You."

"Then that's a yes?"

I covered his mouth with my hand, and he kissed my palm. "But even more, my heart, I want you to be safe. Perhaps—"

"There's no room for perhaps." His mouth tightened. "No room at all."

I slid my hands under his jacket and nestled into his arms, allowing myself to sink into closeness. At the steady music of his heart, my own calmed.

"I want to hold on," I whispered. "I want to believe, but I am afraid."

"I know." His exhalation ruffled my hair. "Maybe Kye and Max are onto something."

"How?"

"Faith."

"Her unquantifiable God? Does Max have one, too?"

Nate chuckled. "I'm pretty sure it's the same one. I'm not sure if faith is the building block of hope, or vice versa, but maybe without it, the universe isn't worth much."

Like a butterfly struggling from a chrysalis, hope fought through a dull sheath of fear. We stood there in the dim quiet for uncounted time, simply holding each other and breathing.

Eric stood in the doorway, any vestige of a smile gone. "Zeta? I'm here on behalf of Elliott Ross."

A deep scowl marred Elinor Anne Williams's features. "And whyever would he have the audacity to ask anything of her?"

I touched her hand and stood.

Eric's jaw ticced. "They're on the way here. The captain is allowing him to say goodbye."

"They?" Elinor asked.

"Local law enforcement. I think they call them militia on New Triton," he said. "He's headed to trial. I know he's made some pretty awful mistakes—"

Elinor huffed.

"But would you come with me? He asked for a specific number of people, and you, Kye, and Ross are at the top of the list, though I'm not sure the captain will let Ross go."

Before she could protest further, I put my hand on her arm and said, "Elinor, I must."

He waited while I pulled on my black jacket and grabbed my cane. We headed toward the shuttle hangar doors, and Cam and an ever-larger Tia joined us. She flashed Eric a tight smile.

"Thought you might need backup, Eric," Tia said. "He was your first friend, right?"

Eric nodded, but no one else spoke until we reached the hall where Lorik had taken me into custody.

Kyleigh stopped pacing and offered us a wan smile when we joined her. I counted one hundred fifty-seven seconds before she whispered, "Is it true that they strip names and brand people once they are sentenced?"

"No," I said. "They are tattooed, not branded."

"Yeah," Eric said, the lilt in his voice stronger than usual. "Cheekbone or forehead. Depends on the crime."

Cam winced.

"On their faces?" Kyleigh blanched.

"Makes it easier to see the number when they're in helmets," Eric answered.

Tia touched Eric's arm. "Isn't there a chance he'll get off? He saved Kyleigh and Zeta and tried to save Freddie and the Elder. He smuggled out that information, then paid for that with those people nearly killing him. Doesn't that matter?"

"I doubt it," Cam said quietly. "People will be angry and frightened over the whole virus thing, and I don't see—"

He broke off as footsteps drew near. Lars and Elliott Ross turned the corner.

Elliott's time in the tank had served him well, though with Cam's words ringing in my ears, I wondered to what purpose. Bruising and lacerations gone, broken limbs set and healed, Elliott stood tall. Any scarring would have been covered by the white jumpsuit he wore, but he neither limped from the roach bite nor carried his arm carefully from where he had been shot. His rich brown hair, brows, and lashes had begun to grow back for a second time, but he no longer appeared gaunt.

"Moons above, he's tall," Tia said under her breath.

Elliott's ice-blue eyes jumped to her, then the young man beside me. His jaw fell. "Eric?"

"Hey, El." Eric cleared his throat. "Came to see you off."

"It's good to see . . . How—no, that doesn't matter, but I'm . . ." A flush suffused his lean face, and he swallowed convulsively.

"It's all right," Eric said.

Elliott nodded, then drew a deep, deep breath. "Kyleigh. Stars, Kye, but I'm sorry. I'm sorry that I was so stupid, that you and Freddie got sucked into this nightmare. That he's gone."

She blinked rapidly.

"Recorder, I'm sorry for everything. Freddie was right." The corner of his mouth drooped. "He usually was. I was so busy trying to earn respect or love or whatever it was that I didn't do what I knew, deep down, was right. And in the process, I hurt the people that mattered most."

"Lars," Kyleigh said without taking her eyes from Elliott, "I need to hug my friend."

The tall marine glanced at me. "Recorder-who-isn't?"

I nodded, and he moved back.

Kyleigh approached Elliott slowly at first, then charged forward to wrap her arms around him. He held her for a moment, then set his hands on her small shoulders, stepped back, and dropped to his knees.

"I found it for you, Kye," he said, looking up at her face while he reached into the neck of the jumpsuit and pulled out a gold chain. "They wouldn't let me have visitors, and I didn't deserve them, but here." He took her small hand and poured the necklace into it.

Her mouth fell open. "My cross."

"To be honest," he murmured, "I'm rather glad I had it with me. Helped me focus, you know?"

"Yes," she said.

"So you forgive me?"

Gold sparkled when she hugged him again, this time resting her head on his shoulder. His eyes closed.

Kyleigh straightened, and then placed the chain and pendant in his large hand. "You keep it, Elliott." She cast a glance at the four of us, standing silently against the wall. "He can keep it, right?"

"I don't know," Eric said quietly.

Elliott grimaced. "Depends on where they send me. Dad kept his contract ring. He wore it on a chain under his shirt, but I can't risk losing this, Kye. It means too much."

"Yes, you can, because I can't risk not sending it with you. Hold still." She took it back and fastened it around his neck.

He cleared his throat and stood. "Eric? Can you tell your mum and dad, and your sisters that . . . I'm sorry?"

"Consider it done, ey?"

"Ey."

The subsequent awkward silence was broken by footsteps, and Jackson and Quincy turned the corner, Ross between them with his hands behind his back. For a moment, the fact that the one being taken away was unbound confused me, but there was a stark difference between Elliott's calm and the wild-eyed look on Julian's face.

"Julian." Elliott's baritone was almost inaudible. "You look a lot better."

Ross's eye twitched. "They can't take you. Nothing was your fault."

The younger brother glanced at me. "That's not true, and it's time I dealt with the consequences."

Ross turned to glare down at Jackson, but the marine remained unmoved.

"Julian. Listen, it'll be all right. I'm not worried about—"

"They can't send you off to the mines," Ross spat out.

"Can and will," Jackson stated.

Kyleigh gnawed on her lower lip. "Jackson, that isn't helping."

"It isn't like you murdered anyone," Julian Ross said.

Elliott held his breath, then released it slowly. "I almost did."

"You didn't," Ross reasserted. "I was the one who helped design that virus. Christine was the one who murdered that Recorder and Kyleigh's dad."

Kyleigh gasped, and Elliott caught her arm. My skin went cold, and for a moment, I was afraid I would collapse again. Tia and Cam moved closer to me.

"*You knew*?" Her small frame shook. "You knew and never told anyone, not even to—Why? Ross—she was my father's murderer and you never told me? You let me eat *dinner* with her!"

He did not flinch.

"Julian?" Elliott demanded. "Is that true?"

"Yes, it is." Kyleigh's face flushed. "Zhen and the captain told me that she had, but you knew and said *nothing*?"

Julian Ross pinched his lips, then nodded.

"You let a murderer go free." Elliott drew himself up to his full height and met his brother's eyes. An echo of Ross's sharp tones saturated Elliott's usually mild voice. "Because you were working together on that virus, and you couldn't risk losing that work? That was worth letting a brutal murder go unpunished?"

"No! I didn't have a choice."

Jackson cursed.

"Was she blackmailing you?" Kyleigh asked.

Ross gave a harsh laugh. "Of course she was. That *is* ironic, isn't it?" He regained control and fastened his icy gaze on his brother. "She threatened to kill you. If I said anything, she'd—I knew what she could do. I saw what she did to Charles."

"You should not lie." My words burst forth with as little control as his laugh. "You were not concerned for Elliott. You were concerned for yourself. If you had gone to Gideon Lorde as soon as you knew, if indeed you did not know beforehand—"

"I would *never* have—"

"Countenanced the slaughter of millions?" I interrupted in turn. "Planned the deaths of *children*? Simply because of the way they had been raised?"

Tia wrapped her arms over her belly, and Eric moved closer to her.

All my repressed fear and anger boiling to the surface, I stepped toward Julian Ross. "If you had cared for your brother more than you hated people like me, you would have gone straight to Gideon Lorde. He would have kept Elliott safe, but instead your inaction enabled her to seed that virus. Nineteen of your coworkers on that moon died before they went into the tanks. And then you altered the programming and killed everyone else."

His face drained of color, then flushed violently. "Gideon couldn't even keep himself safe. Why else do you think I stopped her?"

The hall fell absolutely silent.

Julian Ross glowered at me. "I was the only one who could."

Slowly, carefully, Jackson asked, "What did you do?"

"Performed an act of justice."

Elliott went completely pale. "Julian . . ."

Behind us, the doors leading to the shuttle bay slid apart, and perhaps they stole the oxygen, for when I tried to breathe, I could not.

Julian Ross turned those burning, ice-blue eyes on me. "You killed a man to save someone you didn't know. Crushed his skull. What would you have done for a brother?"

Someone who was either a contralto or a tenor said, "That's a conversation to walk into. So which one's our man?"

Jackson jerked his head toward Elliott.

"We usually restrain the one we're hauling off," the individual behind me said. "But if you say so."

"He didn't do anything," Julian shouted. "You want the guilty party, you take me!"

"That's for the courts, mate," said the voice. "Though it sounds like *Thalassa*'s right crawling with criminals. Might have to make a few more trips."

An unfamiliar tenor added, "We're coming back for you later. Got a whole grand trial set up for you. Wheels're in motion." He cleared his throat. "So. Elliott Ross."

Elliott stilled for a moment, then wrapped his long arms around Kyleigh, resting his cheek against her short, tight braids before brushing a soft kiss on the top of her head.

Ross hurled himself forward, and Jackson and Quincy hauled him back.

"I should have stood up for the right thing years ago." Elliott hid the gold chain inside his jumpsuit's collar, and his gaze flickered between Eric and Kyleigh. "Don't worry, ey? Whatever happens, I won't be alone."

He turned and walked onto the shuttle, and the doors slid shut while his brother slung imprecations at the people holding him back and at the ones bearing Elliott away.

And with that, Elliott Ross was removed.

Ships faded into small shapes outlined by seemingly random pulsing lights as they passed into New Triton's penumbra. The careful beauty of their movement reminded me of music: flashes trilled like violins, and the smooth darkness was the round, resonant sound of cellos. Floodlights swept the station, illuminating its own pale surfaces and the ships before moving on. I pressed my forehead against the lounge's single viewport and took long, quiet breaths, trying to center myself each second.

When Nate's footsteps sounded in the hall, though, all attempts at ordered thought were swallowed by a deep ache. I watched the ships' lights until he spoke.

"Those floodlights mess with my night vision." Nate settled in the chair, long legs outstretched, hands behind his head. "Can't be night vision in space, though, can it? No day or night, really. Space vision? Sounds stupid."

I sighed. "Perhaps disorientation is the point, although I do not believe space vision would be the correct term."

The right corner of his lips edged upwards. I struggled to smile back and failed.

"What's on your mind, sweetheart?"

I attempted to keep weariness from my voice. "So many things. Today . . ."

"I heard about that. I should have been there."

"It is as well that you were not," I said. "Though it was good that Lars was. It took Lars, Quincy, Jackson, and Eric to wrestle Ross back."

"Ross was wrong, you know. What you did to save Yrsa is nothing like what he did."

"True, and not." When he protested, I shook my head. "You are correct, but the end result . . . I suspect that I shall hear that man's death for the rest of my life, however long that is."

"Sweetheart—"

"But even if I do, Nathaniel, I must remember how valuable each life is."

"Stars." He rubbed the back of his neck. "Want to talk about it?"

"No." I covered my eyes and leaned back against the wall. "Williams ought not return. Since she is not a Recorder, she will not face the Halls, but after Edwards, I am concerned that the Elders will judge her harshly because of my actions. Her association with me could condemn her."

"Want in on a secret?"

"What is one more?"

He waited until I lowered my hand. Given the topic of conversation, his broad grin seemed out of place. "You know how the marines pooled funds to save Daniel? He says he doesn't need it, so J used her family connections and checked into Williams's gifting debt. We combined resources and paid it off, with room left over. J has the temp ID, and we'll shuttle her down to Albany City tomorrow morning. After the Hall of Records offices open up, she can pick up her bracelet, and Williams will officially be Elinor Anne Williams, citizen."

Relief, happiness, joy, or whatever the emotion was, washed over me. Without even being aware of moving, I was in Nate's arms, and his chuckle rumbled against my cheek.

"I am so very glad! Does she know?"

"Well, not yet."

"Nate! You should tell her immediately! You must," I insisted. "Give her that peace of mind, if she is still awake."

"She was a few minutes ago. Adrienne Smith was complaining about a sore throat. Thought her allergies were the virus." He grinned. "Everyone wanted to be there, but maybe you're right."

"It is what I would wish, in her stead." A sliver of jealousy ran through the joy, but the lifted worry far surpassed it. "Oh! She will be able to seek—"

His communications link chimed.

"Well, Tim," Jordan said. "You know I love my friends when I talk to Father twice in a ten-day, but I did it. Did you find her?"

His expression sobered. "She's right here. What's the news?"

"Jordan, what is wrong?" I asked.

"Break out your nicest clothes, because you're meeting the deputy prime minister tomorrow."

"I do not have nice clothes," I began before the last half of her statement caught up with me. "Jordan, I do not know the deputy prime minister."

She laughed. "That's why I said you're meeting her." A yawn interrupted the explanation. "I'm exhausted. Stars, what a couple of quarters. I'm turning in. You probably should as well, because it wouldn't do to miss a meeting that can set you free."

She signed off.

"Nate," I asked slowly, "what does she mean by free?"

His dimple peeked out at me. "Free. Told you we were working on it. J's connections, my persuasive skills, and you." He caught me up and spun me around once.

"I have done—"

"More than you give yourself credit for. Like I said yesterday, you pretty much saved the system. They owe you."

I nestled against Nate's chest and rested my head on his shoulder. Hope, true and sure, shot through my fears.

"She has a point." He kissed my forehead. "You should get some sleep."

"But Williams?"

"I'll tell her. I promise."

I snuggled closer. "Nathaniel, my heart, do you truly believe it is possible, that there is a chance I can . . . I could be free?"

"You have a shipful of people ready to testify on your behalf." Nate bent down and all too briefly touched his lips to mine. "If it goes like we all hope, tomorrow Elinor Williams won't be the only new citizen."

Nate told Elinor that evening, after all, and though I smiled so broadly that my cheeks hurt, Elinor cried. Archimedes authorized a late shuttle so she could leave for Albany City on the last flight of the day and be at the Hall of Records as soon as it opened.

I spent my last night on *Thalassa* alone. Excitement over freedom and the potential of a name was not conducive to good rest. I woke at least seven times before my alarm sounded. When it did chime, I was too tired to hear it, and if Zhen and Alec had not brought me my breakfast as they usually did, I would have missed it altogether.

I changed into my greys, and when I exited the water closet, Zhen was fastening a sheath to her right leg, despite Alec's low assertion that security would stop her.

She scowled at him, then at me. "Why on any known planet are you wearing those ugly things?"

"I will not presume freedom before it is granted."

Alec huffed, then finished the dregs of his coffee.

She took a package from a bag next to her chair and handed it to me. "Open this anyway."

A narrow scalene triangle of finely knitted, variegated blue lace slid through my hands like water. "This is beautiful."

"She started it the day after you left *Thalassa* the first time." Alec beamed, as if the craftmanship itself had summoned me from *Agamemnon*.

"Your favorite datapad is blue." Her cheeks pinked, then she said roughly, "This doesn't mean I like you."

"Babe!" Alec expostulated.

I studied Zhen and carefully considered my response. "Accepting this does not mean I like you, either."

Alec gaped, but Zhen threw back her head and laughed. She draped the gift over my shoulders and surveyed me, then adjusted it around my neck.

"Where's your commlink?"

"I am not bringing it, for the same reason I am wearing my greys. I do not wish to alienate any Elder who might be present, should the Eldest send a tribunal." She huffed, but I turned to Alec. "Alexander Spanos?"

He raised one thick brow. "Thought we settled that you're calling me Alec."

"We have, but I find that I must ask you something difficult."

"Sounds serious." He regarded me steadily. "What is it?"

"When you were a child, you and your sister were caught in an explosion."

"Ah." He settled back in his chair.

The single utterance neither reassured me nor informed me of his meaning. "Have you indeed forgiven us?"

His forehead knotted. "You?"

"The Consortium."

Again, he said, "Ah."

"When we first ventured into Pallas Station, you said people like me had caused your family harm. We had neglected to speak out and act, and as a result, your sister died in a medical tank and your father—I have not found him yet. You know now of my . . . deficit?"

"It doesn't change who you are," Zhen said.

Alec nodded. "Exactly."

"Be that as it may," I said, "before I was taken from *Thalassa*, I reviewed the incident. Indeed, proof that the Recorders documenting the attack had failed to protect citizens provided the impetus for my failed attempt to flee the Consortium. After I viewed those files, I found courage and reason to ask Nate and Jordan to help me escape."

His steady, brown eyes remained on my face.

"On Pallas, before you and Nate left for *Thalassa*, you offered me your sister's name."

"I did. I still do."

"Why?" The question's insufficiency prompted me to press on. "Why would you offer such a valuable gift to a member of the organization responsible for your sister's death and your father's disappearance? After your family's sundering and years spent in a struggle for basic necessities? After your mother's death?"

"Been thinking about that for the past quarter. The fact of the matter is that the Consortium isn't the sole guilty party here. They didn't set the explosives." He leaned on his elbows. "People like Skip did."

"But as a member of the Consortium—"

"When I told you that you were different, I meant it. When they took you and left that other Recorder on *Thalassa*, I was angry. Still am, a little, to be honest."

"So am I," Zhen put in.

He shoved his hand through his long hair. "I didn't see how Recorders are people until I met you. You and James and Daniel. Then, the marines mourned over Parker. All that made me think. You three can't be the only ones to defy the system. Facing the fact that I'd been wrong, focusing on the Consortium so I didn't have to admit my father played a part in his disappearance . . . that was hard."

"It would be," I said softly. "What was your sister like?"

"Arianna . . . Aria was the best. Loyal, funny, kind." His gaze drifted. "She wanted to see the sky."

"I, too, wanted to see the sky."

"I know," he said. "She was a lot younger than me, but Aria was my best friend. I loved her. Stars. It still feels wrong to say that in past tense, even now."

"Love is always present tense," Zhen murmured.

Was it? I wanted it to be true, yet the wrongness of what had happened chewed at any peace. "She should have lived."

"Yeah. But so should you." He stood. "Shall we?"

He offered me his left arm, and Zhen picked up my cane from the corner.

"Just in case," she said.

56

Sirens wailed, exactly as they had at Training Center Sigma, and fear momentarily pinned the girl where she stood.

"It is a drill," she reminded herself.

Her new cohort's Recorder, however, remained calm and ushered the group toward the shielded tunnels under the Scriptorium. Murmuring flared around her. *Citizens were trying to kill them again, like they had killed almost everyone at Training Centers Kappa, Mu, and Sigma.* Their gossip reached the little ones, who whimpered. When a tiny one from the third cohort started crying, the girl from Training Center Sigma frowned at the gossiping novices. They should not have frightened the little ones.

This was only a drill. Drills would keep them safe.

She tugged on their Recorder's tunic. When he looked down, she pointed at the younger cohort.

He said, "Go."

Without a second's hesitation, she dashed over and scooped up the crying child, uttering soft comforting sounds, telling the little one that she would be well. The third cohort's Recorder, who carried a tiny child in each arm nodded approval.

Other than the frightened children, novices and Recorders proceeded silently and evenly toward the doors, though the tall boy who always hit the ball the hardest and the slight boy who excelled at strategic games kept peeking back at the yard.

The children and their Recorders reached the tunnels, and an Elder paced the aisles, her drones following her in a line. She paused, face stern, and pointed at the girl and the whimpering three-year-old.

"Why is this little one not with her cohort?"

The girl adjusted the child on her hip. "I offered assistance."

"She asked permission," her Recorder testified.

"And I welcomed her help," the other one added.

The Elder's solid grey eyes bored into the girl's pale-blue ones. "Return her."

Cautiously avoiding the Elder, the girl walked to the younger cohort and deposited the little one. The other Recorder nodded thanks.

Up and down the space, children whispered.

The Elder took three more steps, then spun so quickly that the bottom of her tunic flared. "This is not a game," she thundered, her drones broadcasting her voice. *Not a game, a game, game,* echoed back. "Already, our people have been murdered."

No one ever said how many were dead, but the girl knew the numbers from Sigma. When she had crawled out from her hiding place in the Hall of Reclamation and searched for survivors, she had counted eight hundred thirty-nine, not including anyone in the tanks themselves. She found nineteen other children, and they had hidden in the refectory, stealing food from the kitchen until Recorders had arrived to rescue them.

The girl pushed down a stab of fear. When she was older, she would have a drone, and though she knew now that a drone would never keep her safe, it would regulate her emotions. *No fear in the future,* she repeated over and over—a promise she knew in her deepest being to be untrue. She clung to it, nevertheless.

Resisting the urge to run, she returned to her new cohort and stood erect between two boys.

"It is imperative that you remain quiet," the Elder raised her voice over the little ones' noise. "An uproar like this will draw citizens to find you. And they have no mercy."

The slight boy whispered in her ear, "Fear will train the little ones to cry."

The Elder whipped around. "What are you implying, Novice?"

His face went ashen, but before he could answer, a new voice said calmly, "Enough."

The girl froze. Everyone did, even the angry Elder, for every member of the Consortium knew that gentle voice.

"The boy is correct," the Eldest said. When more murmurs filled the area, she raised both hands, then lowered them, palms down. "Be still."

She scooped up the closest crying one, shushing him, and his sobs subsided. When he wrapped thin arms around her neck and popped a thumb into his mouth, the Eldest did not rebuke him for that comfort.

The Elder bowed her head. "Eldest. I did not know you were present."

"Obviously." The Eldest rested a cheek on the little one's bald head. "Else you would not have frightened the ones we are here to protect."

"I did not mean—"

"And yet"—the Eldest's voice was as soft as mouse fur and as smooth as the snakes that ate the mice—"you inspire fear and shame in others."

Another little one ran to her side, and she rested her hand on the small girl's head.

"The boy was correct," the Eldest said. "As was the girl when she offered help."

Whether it was fear or pride, something stirred in the girl's heart. *To be noticed, singled out, by the Eldest?*

"They deviated from the drill," the Elder protested.

"Yes." The Eldest's gaze latched onto the girl and the slight boy. "Come here."

Without daring to look anywhere except the quiet woman in dark Consortium grey, they walked in unison to stand before her. How very odd that she was not much taller than they.

"Now," she added, "face the Elder who frightens my children."

They did.

"Novice, repeat what you said."

He swallowed visibly, and his voice cracked when he spoke. "Fear will train the little ones to cry."

Around them, Recorders stiffened, and the cohorts fidgeted.

"Do you see the truth in him?"

"I see some truth." The Elder pursed her lips. "But I also see his fear."

The Eldest's voice remained gentle. "Who put that fear there?"

"A trick question, Eldest."

"Who?"

"The citizens who murdered us."

"Only the citizens?"

The Elder took a breath. "You and I and the boy himself."

The Eldest handed the little boy to the girl, but he whimpered and reached for the small woman who had comforted him. The Eldest touched the girl's shoulder.

"Novice," the Eldest said, "tell me what the Consortium is."

The girl shifted the little one onto her hip and recited, "The Consortium is all. The Eldest is our parent. The Elders, Recorders, novices, and little ones are our siblings. The brothers and sisters must be protected."

She did not add that family was everything, and that she would find a way to protect these little ones with everything she had. It was her own promise, but she dared not commit the heresy of adding to the creed.

"Indeed. The Consortium welcomed you all when the citizens who now seek to kill you discarded you before you were born. Elder, you used fear and harshness to control these, our future, when we have already lost many of our family. You have erred. Such an error is unpardonable." Her voice hardened. "When you harm my children, you harm us all. You harm me."

The Eldest's drones shot forward and wrapped the Elder in their grip. Her eyes went wide, their grey draining away to reveal blank, bloodshot brown. She gurgled, then dropped. Her three drones folded in all arms and appendages and drifted silently to the ground.

"Return the child to his cohort, Novice," the Eldest said calmly, "and then return to your own."

The girl did, trying to hide her quaking hands. She walked back to her group, sidestepping the still form on the floor. The other children parted to allow her to hide in their ranks.

The Eldest bent slightly to look the boy in the eye. "Do not speak out of turn, even if you speak the truth."

He nodded and scuttled back to stand beside the girl. The other children closed in about them, but there was nowhere they could truly hide, not from the Eldest, who saw everything.

While Recorders carried the silenced drones and their Elder away, the Eldest lifted her arms, and every member of the Consortium turned to her. Her gentle voice filled the room, sliding between the concrete pillars. "We will drill again tomorrow."

Recorders led the youngest ones out first, and soon only the novices remained. Footsteps echoed, replacing earlier murmurs, but as the shielded area emptied, the promise of safety seemed hollow.

There would be no Recorders to guide them, if the sirens sounded because citizens attacked. The girl had counted two hundred sixty-three little ones and novices, but in this vast area, there would be nowhere to hide. She did not know Training Center Alpha as she had Training Center Sigma, where she had taken her first steps and learned her first words.

Where was the safest place, one the citizens would never find? The one everyone would avoid? One where they could hide in the dark and—

The girl's stomach tightened, and she stopped. Sinking realization dawned.

The boy behind her hissed at her to move before the Eldest noticed, but it was too late.

The Eldest turned grey veiled eyes on the girl. She bowed, nodded, and sped up.

Tomorrow, they would drill again, but tonight, when the Recorders slept, she would find that path. Tonight would be *her* drill, and drills would keep them safe.

57

PERSONAL RECORD: DESIGNATION ZETA4542910-9545E

ALBANY CITY, NEW TRITON
478.3.1.04

My stomach was in knots four hours later, when we stood inside the central southern buttress, waiting for transport.

Cam rubbed his palms on his pant legs. "I've never been to Founders' Hall."

"I have." Tia fidgeted with the hem of the oversized shirt that might have been Eric's. "I wish I had something nicer."

"You look fine," Cam responded, his eyes still on the buildings, which rose into the dome.

"Better than fine," Eric amended Cam's abrupt analysis, blushing a little as he added, "Always do."

Her cheeks pinked.

Two group transports arrived, and we boarded. I took a seat at a window near the front. Nearly a third of the marines who had elected to testify climbed onboard, while the rest waited for the second vehicle. I wanted Nate's hand in mine but clenched my fists instead. Twisting around on the uncomfortable, rigid seat, I watched the streets zoom past. The faux marble of the Hall of Records flashed in the distance, but trees soon hid it.

"Elinor will be fine," Jordan said behind me, as if she knew I was thinking of Williams.

Kyleigh tugged on a short, beaded braid, then gestured out the window at the high wall separating Training Center Alpha from the rest of the city. "Is that where you grew up?"

"It is," Max answered on my behalf, and we both cast anxious glances at James.

My friend should not have come. I told him so repeatedly, but he had insisted on accompanying me since no one had seen through his false identity. Daniel, too, had refused to listen to reason. Not even Yrsa Ramos had changed his mind. She had reluctantly agreed to remain on

Thalassa, since all other medical personnel would be in Albany City. Daniel's hand kept drifting to his shoulder, but no tether held a weapon.

Momentary thankfulness enveloped me. The marines had shaved their heads nearly five ten-days ago, when the Recorder called Rose Parker had died, and in the group of short-haired men and women, Daniel and James were less obvious.

The transport slowed to a stop outside Albany City's municipal building. We disembarked, and it abandoned us in front of the white edifice.

Tia looked ill. "I shouldn't have come."

"You want to go back?" When she shook her head, Eric touched her arm. "It'll be fine. We're with you."

Jordan moved to the front of our group and smiled, unintimidated by the ostentatious structure and its inhabitants. "It's simply a building full of officious and obnoxious people who also got dressed and had breakfast this morning. Max, Tim, let's get our guest of honor in there."

The next transport arrived while we climbed the steps, and the boots of thirty marines followed us in.

Never before had I entered a building like this one. In every direction, decadent wood paneled the walls, graced picture frames, or offered seating. Importing such supplies from Ceres was symbolic of authority, power, and wealth. It disoriented me, no doubt as intended. Nowhere in the Consortium would we waste resources with such extravagance, and the excess did nothing to settle my nerves.

Security stopped us, and we waited while they made Zhen check the knife. She scowled at Alec when he muttered a quiet, "I told you."

Jordan led us past framed art—abstract or precise, portraits or landscapes, but few as fine as Freddie's—to a hall lined with wooden benches.

Behind me, someone whistled, low. I glanced over my shoulder.

Lars traced his fingers over the paneling. "And I thought that posh office was fancy."

An assistant in royal blue stepped through a tall, arched door and offered us what I believed to be an insincere smile. "Venetia Jordan and guests? Please follow me."

Jordan inclined her head, then seemed to shift slightly. Her businesslike stance did not soften, but grew more . . . catlike? Grace and controlled, easy power had always been part of the way she moved, but now her confidence encompassed something more, something I struggled to identify.

Nevertheless, I had the wild inclination to bolt back down the hall and hide in the city. The medical implant no longer pained me, so I tapped my right thigh before following Jordan through wide, glossy wooden doors. My left hand gripped the cane so tightly that my fingers should have dented the wood.

The room would have easily accommodated a group twice our size, but I did not take in the accessories and artwork, only the whir of drones.

At the far end, the deputy prime minister—an older woman near my height, her silver hair in an ornate pile of braids—waited with her hands clasped before her waist. To her right stood three Elders, their nine drones hovering like an asteroid field.

None of them held my attention.

My focus flew past the deputy prime minister, past the three Elders to the petite woman of Jordan's age. Her Consortium greys were a shade darker than mine, and her elegantly shaped head gleamed softly as the three drones ranged around her. Solid grey eyes immediately found me. Behind me, I heard Daniel suck in a deep breath, and though they would not hear me, I mentally ordered him and James to withdraw to the center of the group.

Towering double doors shut with a muffled boom. The deputy prime minister probably spoke, but I did not hear her.

Nate leaned over and whispered, "Breathe. It'll be fine."

The Eldest's gaze flickered to him and back to my greys and the blue scarf draped in defiance around my throat. The corner of her mouth lifted.

My blood chilled.

Fine? At that second, fine was the furthest thing from the truth.

58

Words flowed past me, as incomprehensible as static, and I attempted to listen to the citizens who stepped forward, one after another, to testify on my behalf: Jordan, Nate, Max, Alec, Zhen, Jackson, Quincy . . . perhaps half the people gathered on my behalf. After the last marine moved back, uneasy quiet filled the room, despite the small crowd of approximately two score men and women.

"Recorder"–the deputy prime minister glanced at her datapad– "Zeta4542910-9545E, you have been of great assistance to the system, citizen and Consortium alike. These citizens have testified to your bravery and generosity of spirit, and I personally would like to thank you for your efforts." A soft smile spread over her lined face. "You've become a bit of a folk hero to the younger citizens. My granddaughter actually cut off her hair to mimic yours. Her whole class has." She *tsk'd*. "Quite shocking, I tell you, all those young people running about nearly as bald as an Elder."

"I?"

"Oh yes, dear. Several sketches of you have been circulating on the news. You've shown true humanity, no matter that you are a Recorder."

"Was," Nate said clearly, and when the Eldest turned to him again, my panic reared up, as large and overwhelming as a roach. He shifted his weight. "She *was* a Recorder."

The prime minister's smile became artificial, and she shot a sideways glance at the slender woman in Consortium grey. "Thank you, young man. Do you have anything to add, Recorder, dear?"

"It has been my honor to serve," I began, but the Eldest held up her hand, trapping my words in my throat.

"Enough." The soft, thick soprano carried through the room. "Your testimony–those of you who could legally give it–has been recorded.

I know where you have been, where you are. I will know where you will be."

Nate moved closer, and I wanted to order him back, but doing so would worsen the situation.

"Deputy Prime Minister," the Eldest said mildly, without turning her solid grey eyes from me, "we, too, have testimony, for this aberration is damaged. I will not relinquish her."

The deputy prime minister's reply was drowned by the loud protests around me. I closed my eyes briefly against the sound, opening them again to see the Eldest hold up both hands. Shouts and protests fell to a low growl.

"Since this meeting was called by citizens, I first summon their own."

A side door opened, and five citizens entered. Dr. Imogene Clarkson, Sarah Watkins, Ursula Bryce, Paul Foster, and—the betrayal stabbed at me—Adrienne Smith.

Dr. Clarkson began her recitation of my uselessness and interference, but the Eldest cut her long-winded explanation short. Sarah Watkins spoke next, relating my lack of control, even citing the times I had threatened the citizens on *Agamemnon*.

"That's not true," Eric burst out, and Watkins shot a glare at him.

"Check with the others," Watkins said. "I wouldn't give false testimony."

Bryce and Foster insisted that Watkins had told the truth, and finally, Adrienne Smith's nasal intonations sliced at me. She asserted I had falsified records, though at least she admitted that she had only the proof of her own eyes and memory.

The Elders' drones released their tendrils.

"That is enough, citizen," the Eldest said gently. "Know this, Deputy Prime Minister. This testimony is for your benefit, to prove that she is not fit to be loose in your world. But for the tribunal present, I call the doctor who can verify some of these claims and uncovered other flaws."

Max set a hand on my shoulder, and I had a brief, unrealistic fear he, too, would bear witness against me. The thought was unjust, but terror was an unreliable counselor.

The side door opened again, and the Recorder-doctor emerged. His eyes, wide and dilated, remained fastened on the Eldest, and his tongue shot out across his lips.

"Eldest," he said, and even in that single word, his voice shook.

"Go on," she said gently. "Tell them what you learned."

He did, spilling out my disobedience, my purported yet exonerated smuggling, my fraternization with citizens, and the way I hid behind their regulations to avoid my duty. He did not mention any suspicions of my involvement with the network's collapse on *Thalassa*, but it hovered unspoken, like a drone. He had to shout to be heard over the surging arguments behind me.

How I wanted to lean against Nate, but doing so would condemn him.

Somehow, the Eldest's serene voice hushed my friends when she asked, "Would she be an asset to the citizenry?"

"I do not see how she could be anything but a liability." The Recorder-doctor licked his lips again. "She has no skills, Eldest, other than what the Consortium gave her, but those skills are useless to her outside our community and given her condition."

My blood froze, and I met the Eldest's eyes, shaking my head, silently pleading that they refrain from telling all the worlds.

"What condition?" the Eldest asked gently. "Do not hesitate. I absolve you of relaying medical information."

"She cannot read," the doctor said. "She is functionally illiterate."

The room fell silent.

His voice seemed unnaturally loud. "Her mind is hampered by damage wreaked by the virus she helped loose on the system when she continued to act as a Recorder despite losing her neural connection to her drone."

"Given the facts, Aberrant"—the Eldest's voice was almost kind—"do you have anything to add?"

My one chance, my single hope that she would have mercy croaked from my suddenly dry mouth. "Although I acted in defiance of the Recorder's implied command, I notified you of the continued threat against the Training Centers. To protect the Consortium."

The Eldest's tone lost all smoothness. "You were late. Too late."

My response was unsteady. "What do you mean?"

"With damage to Consortium systems that I believe to be linked to you—"

"Per our mandate, Eldest," I interrupted, all caution discarded, "you cannot accuse without proof."

Misplaced pride shot through me. I had been correct: she would show no mercy. But I had succeeded. Despite my flaws, despite my weaknesses, I had kept my friends safe, and not even the Eldest herself had found evidence against me.

Grey nanodevices shimmered across her eyes like mercury, and even her skin pulsed grey for a moment. "That is enough. Such defiance—" She inhaled. "I arrived this morning for two purposes. Firstly, to retrieve Consortium property."

More waves of protest swept through the cluster of friends behind me, but bright and clear, Max's words repeated in my heart: *stardust or creation.*

I raised my chin in pointless defiance. "I am not your property."

One of her three drones flicked its tendrils.

The Eldest turned her attention to the older woman. "Secondly, Deputy Prime Minister, I again request assistance for my people."

"It is against the charter, the founding documents, and the AAVA to arm Recorders." The deputy prime minister's face stretched into a grimace-like smile. "Both militia and marines are banned from your properties."

"We have lost three Training Centers to attacks *citizens* should have prevented."

Three Training Centers? My heart nigh unto stopped. "Clarify."

No one answered me.

"I'm sorry for your losses, Eldest," the deputy prime minister said smoothly. "But we aren't omniscient. You can't honestly expect us to know—"

All twelve drones shot into the air, all appendages stretched to their fullest length. The Eldest's face drained to a pale, ashy grey, and her eyes widened. "No."

The hair on my arms rose.

"You will assist me, citizen." Her voice changed, became hard as marble. "Now."

As surely as if a drone had told me, I knew then.

I took two strides toward the front of the room. Nate grabbed at my hand, and I took it, for I needed his strength. "Training Center Alpha. Is it Training Center Alpha?"

Her eyes narrowed at me. "Your actions have brought this on us."

Though it was likely that he would suffer for doing so, the Recorder-doctor answered me. "They have fallen silent. Not a single Recorder, not a single Elder on the premises is audible on the network."

"Moons above." Tia's exclamation seemed unnaturally loud in the sudden stillness. "Like when those monsters hit *Thalassa* and the ship's Recorder collapsed? But the giftings—what of the babies?"

Even Imogene Clarkson blanched. "All those kids?"

"The Recorders and novices will be lost, but the children who do not have drones—is there hope for them?" My lungs tightened. "Eldest! Is there hope?"

Solid grey eyes flashed at me. "Only if the citizens who murdered my people before are not armed *this* time."

I turned my back on the Eldest and her tribunal, on the deputy prime minister.

Cane in hand like a baton, I staggered to a run, my wrist pulsing with light and mild currents, Nate at one side, Jordan at the other, my friends and a group of unarmed marines thundering behind us.

59

My leg wobbled as I pushed myself through strangely empty streets, and Jordan and Hodges passed me, Max and Eric at their heels. Alec, Cam, and the marines tore after them, but Nate remained at my side, with Kyleigh and Tia behind us. We were not halfway there when my leg gave out. Nate caught me before I fell.

"Leave this to us, sweetheart." He kissed my forehead. "Stay safe."

He was gone, and I protested to their backs. "This was my home. These were my brothers and sisters."

Kyleigh caught my arm, as a blur of blue hair streamed past. In long, easy strides, Zhen disappeared after Nate and the others.

"Nate was partially correct," I said. "You should—"

"Not on your life," Kyleigh said. "I'm not leaving little kids to those murderers. You should stay with Tia."

Tia's face was flushed, and her hand held her belly, but she glared at us. "It could have been my baby in there."

Unable to dissuade them, I kept pace as they turned the final corner onto the tree-lined boulevard. My breath caught. The Training Center's gates had been shattered. I hobbled faster, but Tia gave a sharp cry and doubled over.

Kyleigh crouched before her. "What is it?"

"I don't know, but it hurts," Tia gasped. "Not like those practice contractions I told you about."

We led her over to a bench, and Kyleigh met my eyes over Tia's head. "She has five ten-days to go."

The gates were but meters away. "Do you have a communications link?"

Kyleigh paled. "Stars above. I left it on *Thalassa*."

"We must get Tia to a medical facility." The gates gaped behind me. I could almost feel their shattered teeth at my back. "I cannot remember—"

"I saw one a few corners back. You stay with her. I'll go get help."

"No. This is the sole egress. Should we fail to stop these people, they will leave through these gates. After the attackers murder my people, who knows what else they might do. You cannot be in their way."

Kyleigh's face went ashen, but she nodded and smoothed stray hairs away from Tia's sweaty cheeks. Another grimace warped Tia's expression.

"To safety," I said, and Kyleigh finally nodded.

I touched her hand, then leaning heavily on my cane, limped into Training Center Alpha.

The quiet was deafening. No children, no weapons' fire, no shouts, merely my own uneven steps and my cane's tap on the walkway. Defunct drones, smashed down on their sides, some with smoke creeping from panels, were scattered across the lawn and strip of pavement, but the only movement was the trees' gentle dance and the nodding of plants between the low, grey buildings.

"Where are you?" I whispered into the unnatural stillness.

Only circulation fans answered me.

I paused and closed my eyes, walking through the Center in my mind. The power plant, the Elders' housing, nursery and dormitories, clinic, gymnasium, refectory, Scriptorium, library, and under it all, the tunnels leading to the Hall of Reclamation and the medical processing laboratories.

The safest place would be underground. I limped to the nearest building with access to the tunnels, and I found the first people I had seen. Unmoving Recorders, red seeping through their grey uniforms, blocked the path. Were their drones all on the lawns? My feet slowed. There. A chest rose and fell in shallow, uneven gasps.

I dropped to my knees beside the man and set my hand on his bare head. "Recorder?"

Brown eyes flickered open. "The children."

"Help has come," I soothed, though the death around me made my heart sink.

"Tried . . ." He blinked, focusing on my hair, then my face. "Citizen?"

"Sister." Two tears fell from my lashes to spatter his cheek. I wiped them away.

"Trust," he said. "Scriptorium. Go."

His eyes closed, and I touched his cheek. "Peace be with you."

I braced myself with my cane, stood, and ran-limped to the door, which opened easily.

The darkness threatened to crush me, but I found the wall with my fingertips and followed it down and down, allowing tactile memory to guide me when reason failed. I kept my right hand on the wall and felt ahead of me with the cane.

Distant weapons' fire and shouts echoed.

I pressed on. When I reached a corner, chemical-blue safety lights flickered, illuminating my path. I moved more quickly, stepping around drones and bodies in grey, but when I turned the corner, sound and light hit me full force.

The pillared chamber under the Scriptorium was utter chaos. Recorders writhed on the floor. Marines and citizens fought hand to hand, and people I did not know dodged out from behind the structural supports to fire weapons into the room. Nate—where was Nate? Jordan?

The air in my lungs seemed to solidify.

Near where I stood, a woman in dull gold spun from behind a pillar and aimed a sidearm. A sharp crack, and a familiar marine fell. She ducked back and moved to fire again. She raised it again at . . . *Zhen.*

Rage shattered my paralysis, and I lunged forward, swinging the cane against the woman's torso as hard as I could. She screeched as she collapsed. Her sidearm skittered across the floor, and I dove for it.

Zhen spun at the noise, and I pushed the sidearm toward her. Without waiting to see what Zhen did, I bound the woman's hands with my blue scarf, ignoring an additional surge of anger—this was the woman who had stolen Kyleigh's suit. Though she struggled, I patted her waist and legs, finding two knives and a box of what I assumed to be ammunition.

"Zhen!"

She glanced over. I shoved the small box across the floor, and it slid to a stop at her feet. She took it. I grabbed my cane, but when I put weight on it, it cracked. I stowed it behind another pillar and cautiously moved from hiding place to hiding place, searching the melee for my friends. Though, what could I, damaged and unarmed, do?

I saw James first. He grappled with an unarmed man, and Jordan wrested a knife from another. She struck him hard with the hilt, and he dropped.

Beyond them, Max knelt by the fallen marine—Ken Patterson?— attempting to staunch gushing arterial red.

A headache sharp as a blade pierced my temples. Panic flared. *Please, no. Not again, not now.* My perception of my surroundings jumbled in my mind, like pipettes dropping, shattering across the floor. Then, mercifully, the pain vanished as quickly as it had struck, but time blurred.

Seemingly in slow motion, a man moved from behind the pillar, his knife raised, his focus on James. I shouted a warning, the sounds distorted and warped as seconds stretched past their allotted length. Max's head came up. The knife-man paused and met my eyes.

Adrenaline surged. Despite my leg, I bolted across the open floor, knocking James and Jordan down. Max jumped as the knife flew. The blade bit into him, and he collapsed. His skull hit the floor with a dull thud.

The world exploded into real time as a cry tore from Jordan's throat. She sprang to her feet. Again, I hurled myself at her back, and we tumbled to the floor. Another blade flew over us.

Blood streaked through the plasma oozing down her forehead, and an unfamiliar light burned in those golden-brown eyes. She hated that man. Perhaps, at the moment, she hated me, too.

"I brought you knives." My words seemed bizarre, like offering pastries and tea, but I pulled out the sheathed blades I had stolen.

Jordan took them and rose to a crouch. A hiss of air escaped between set teeth. "Get Max and James out of here. Ken, too."

Eyes blazing and knives in hand, she sprinted toward the man.

James had crawled to Max, so I scooted toward the young marine who had raised the kittens. He no longer breathed, and his eyes stared sightlessly at the ceiling.

Somewhere beyond me, a man screamed, and the sound compelled me to abandon Ken Patterson.

Get Max and James out, echoed in my ears even over the din. I scooted over to James, and together we dragged Max away from the fight. Polished concrete glistened slickly red in our wake.

Once in the hall's pale-blue light, noise receded. James sat against the wall and cradled Max's head in his lap. Blood saturated his pants, staining them near-black.

His silver gaze met mine. "I think . . . I think he was my father."

"Is." I placed a palm on Max's chest. Shallow breaths barely moved my hand. "He is."

60

"Move aside," someone ordered.

Though unarmed, I stood, ready to strike a blow against whomever—

The Recorder-doctor stood there in his pants and undershirt, his tunic missing.

"Where is your drone?" I demanded, as if it were supremely important, as if the question were logical.

"At the gate. I left without permission, even if the Eldest did not stop me. I suspect she is displeased." All his attention on Max, he knelt beside James. "I no longer have a tunic, and it is unapproved that I go shirtless." He snapped his fingers. "Remove your jacket, citizen."

"Westruther," I said.

"Your jacket, Westruther."

James complied, and the Recorder-doctor snugged it around Max's head.

"Aberrant, Westruther, there is nothing either of you can do here and now." His voice became unsteady. "I came to help the children, but I have only seen Recorders. I have not found any of the novices and the little ones. I cannot, however, betray an oath higher than the one binding me to the Consortium. I must provide assistance. Could you, perhaps—would you find the children?"

"I held my mother while she died," James said. "I cannot leave m—"

"Max," I inserted. He could not be allowed to betray himself.

James's throat worked for two seconds. "I cannot abandon him now."

"Please," the Recorder begged. "Go. You cannot care for the wounded, but you can find the children. You came to protect them. Find them now and save them, if you can. Once those citizens have been stopped, I can access the clinic's tanks and emergency generators. You help the children; I will help him."

"You are certain"—my voice broke—"he will not die?"

"Scalp wounds bleed prolifically, and I will not pull that knife free yet," the Recorder-doctor said, avoiding my question. "The sooner I get him—and the others—into tanks, the better off they all will be." Pale hazel eyes pled with us. "I cannot care for him and still search."

He was correct, and as much as I wanted to stay with Max, the memories of my cohort and the other nameless novices propelled me to my feet.

I touched James's arm. "You need to remain at Max's side. I will go."

"The Recorder-doctor's point is valid." James carefully lowered his father to the floor and wiped his hands, slick with red, on his pant leg. His eyes still on Max, he added, "I would not lose my friend as well. I am with you."

A scream echoed up the hall.

"Find them," the Recorder said.

With one more look at Max, we left.

We found nothing until we reached the nurseries, where divots in the wall told of weapons' fire. Two Recorders lay dying in the floor's dim, chemical light.

James knelt to ask after the children, but the woman pressed her mouth shut. His angled eyebrows drew down. "She does not trust me."

"You are not of the Consortium. Today, who can blame her?" I set my hand on my forehead. "I cannot think, James. There was a passcode—but no, the power is off."

He stepped over the Recorder to pound on the door, shouting that we meant no harm, that the enemies were contained in the hall under the Scriptorium, that the Eldest knew we were present.

The door ground open. A Caretaker in pale grey blocked our way, brandishing a child's chair like a weapon. As she studied our faces, the chair lowered.

Her eyebrowless forehead wrinkled. "I-I know you. How do I know citizens?"

"I am Consortium," I confessed.

"You have . . ." She gestured at my hair, but then her mouth fell open. "You are the primary aberration. We have heard of you, even here." Her eyes dropped to my blood-stained greys, then over to James, who stood straight as any Recorder. She backed up, one hand on the door as if ready to close it. "Are they gone?"

"Not yet," James said, "but we have been sent to help the children."

Her forehead crinkled. "This is true?"

"Yes," I answered.

The Caretaker peered past us, then spoke over her shoulder. "It is well."

A chorus of voices responded, but no one else emerged.

"Aberration, I remember when you were small." Her expression shifted as she regarded James. "And you . . ."

I grabbed his sleeve, ready to tell him to run.

But instead of denouncing him, the Caretaker moved closer. After three seconds of her eyes searching his, she reached up to touch his face. "You are well. And a citizen, I see. I must have been wrong. I remember neither you nor your sister." Her smile faded, and she edged back a meter. "After Sigma fell, the Eldest decreed all nurseries should have a chemical backup specialist present. The gifting tanks are secure."

The youngest, the infants, the tanks—all safe. For two seconds, I leaned against James's steady shoulder and allowed that mercy to sink into my heart.

"She also decreed Caretakers have drones deactivated, so we would not accidentally harm the ones in our care." Her gaze strayed to the fallen Recorders near our feet, and she shuddered. "We are secure, but the older children and the novices—were they not in the chamber under the Scriptorium?"

"That is where the fighting is taking place," I said. "I saw no children."

"There were none when we arrived," James added.

A divot appeared over the Caretaker's nose. "I do not know to whence they would flee."

Again, I reviewed the layout in my head, trying to hold onto a mental map. "That, then, is our task. Please shut and bar the door until the Eldest comes."

"Find them. Keep them safe," the Caretaker charged us, then the door ground shut.

Again, James and I stepped over and around the fallen. My limp became more pronounced, so I kept one hand on the wall for balance.

"I think I know where to look," I said. "You will not like it."

"As if there is much to like about today."

"The Hall of Reclamation."

He huffed. "You are correct on both counts. I do not like the idea, but the Halls are deep underground. While the citizens do not know of it, the children do." James exhaled. "It is a long walk. I will carry you."

At first, I declined the offer, but after another quarter kilometer, I consented to ride on his back. He trudged on through spotless halls made eerie by blue illumination.

When we reached the steel doors leading into the cave-like room, he set me down. "I never wanted to come back here. I never wanted to see those tanks again."

"I can go alone."

"No. We go together."

I nodded, and we pushed the doors open.

Nothing brightened the expanse. My dread of darkness nearly took me, but James set his hand on my shoulder. Scuffling noises echoed, as unlike insectile movement as warmth was unlike ice.

We had found them.

"Little ones? Novices?" I called. "We are not here to harm you. We are friends."

A childish figure of perhaps twelve years stepped into the dim rectangle of light cast through the open door. Her chin jutted at a defiant angle. I dropped to my knees and stretched out an arm, but she came no closer.

"Who are you?" the novice asked. "Consortium or foe?"

"Neither. Though once I was a novice."

She eyed me. "No one abandons the Consortium."

"And that is why we are here." Even James's steady voice seemed small in that expanse. "You are not abandoned."

Other children crept from the shadows. A little one darted out and grabbed the novice's legs, and a slight boy strode forward to stand, stance wide, arms crossed, at the first girl's side.

"James," I said. "Would you return to check on the others and clear a path for us?"

"She means the bodies," the first child explained to the slight boy. "I counted eight hundred thirty-nine at Training Center Sigma."

I repressed a shudder.

"Indeed. There is no cause for you to witness what has been lost." James turned to me. "You will be safe here?"

"We will."

My friend left, and the children crawled from their hiding places toward the faint, blue light cast through the open door. I sat with them for what seemed hours. My joints ached and my stomach gnawed before James returned, guiding Lars and Zhen to the Halls.

"It is over," James said. "The tunnels are clear."

"James was good about that." Lars set a hand on James's shoulder. "Has a good head, too. I couldn't have found the way down here, but he used an access panel in the southwest dormitory. Anyway, Jackson and Quincy say it's all clear."

The children stared at him.

The slight boy asked, "Are you certain?"

"'Course I'm sure. Wouldn't ever send a bunch of kids into danger," he protested. "And the deputy prime minister came through. Has a bunch of cafés and such sending food." He squatted down to eye level with the boy. "You kids like food, right?"

The boy nodded.

The little one peeked around the first child's legs. "Will they have pie?"

"Dunno." The tall marine grinned. "But tell you what. If they don't, you and me'll find a kitchen and make some. Pie crusts are tricky, but I bet we can handle it."

The slight boy gasped. "Can we?"

"Don't see why not."

A small girl crept forward, wide-eyed in the near darkness. "Are your muscles real?"

Zhen snorted.

Lars presented his arm. "Far as I know. Give it a punch."

She glanced around and, when no one said anything, tapped his arm.

"Nah, put some swing in it," he added, then made an exaggerated grimace when she hit him a little harder. "See?"

She giggled, then caught herself, and all color drained from her face.

I knew that look. Guilt. Anticipation of punishment. A knot of anger rose in my chest. Laughter should not produce fear.

A thunderous growl reverberated through the Halls, and everyone froze until the slow thrum of the circulation fans resumed. A few children cheered.

"Nate and Alec did it," Zhen exclaimed. "Moons and stars, it's good to have air."

However, when the dim lights flickered on, Lars and Zhen stared ashen-faced and open-mouthed into the vast room with its rows upon rows of tanks, now dark. Whether or not their inmates had lived mere hours ago, they did not now.

The first girl touched my arm. "A child is missing."

"You sure?" Lars asked.

She scowled at him. "I counted."

"Only one is an acceptable loss," a short girl said.

"That is untrue," I said more sharply than I should have. I softened my voice. "Who is it?"

"A girl of the sixth cohort."

"Stay here," I said, and when she protested, I added, "The others know you. They will feel safer. Lars, help me search."

She conceded, so while James and Zhen organized the group, Lars and I prowled the darkened aisles.

I found her. A tiny girl of six years, huddled in a ball, shrinking back from my approach.

"It is well, little one," I said quietly. "The bad people are contained, and it is safe."

She scrunched farther against the silent tank.

"I am going to call my friend. His name is Lars, and he is very kind." I leaned back. "Lars, I have found her."

"Good show! Need help?"

"I do not, but tell the others. The first novice is concerned."

I settled down to wait until the little one uncurled and sidled over to me. We rejoined the others. James offered to carry me again, but I declined. I kept my hand on the wall as the little one I had found, the first novice, and I slowly led the way from the Halls to the surface. Behind us walked two hundred thirty-nine children, and behind them, James and Lars closed the doors on the Hall of Reclamation.

61

PERSONAL RECORD: DESIGNATION ZETA4542910-9545E

CONSORTIUM TRAINING CENTER ALPHA, ALBANY CITY, NEW TRITON

478.3.1.04

Late afternoon light streamed from the dome overhead, and I angled myself in an attempt to shield the children from the sight of citizens escorting gurneys laden with bodies. Zhen caught my eye and waved from where she waited with Quincy in the doorway of a neighboring dormitory. In the distance, Jordan and Jackson spoke with militia and local law enforcement officers and a tall, burly Elder, while a small crowd peered around militia through the shattered gates.

Three drones hovered over the chaos and destruction. Under them, the Eldest waited.

A tiny boy darted past me to the Eldest, who picked him up and gently patted his back. He rested his cheek on her shoulder, but her eyes remained on mine. "Aberrant."

I did not answer her. I could not, not when a flush of fear engulfed me, for James was not far behind us. From what distance could she detect James's jamming device? Yes, Zhen and Daniel had altered the range, but if she discovered our deception, she would take him away. She would pry all the memories she could from his neural chip and then sentence him to a Hall like the one we had left dark. Beyond that, *Thalassa's* entire crew would be in danger. She could not miss that connection. I would not, and I lacked her capabilities.

I knelt beside the girl who clung to my hand, pointed beyond the Eldest to Zhen, and asked her and the first novice, "Do you see the pretty citizen with blue hair? The one holding the blue scarf?"

The little one nodded, and the older girl said, "Yes."

"Go to her. I believe the Eldest wishes to speak with me."

The novice's eyes, blue as zircon, studied mine. "Does she?"

"It seems likely."

"Then you should go."

I carefully considered my words. "Please tell the citizen—her name is Zhen—to let the other citizens know I must talk to the Eldest, who is over us all. Can you do that?"

"I will." She took a step, then held out her hand, and the little one took it. The hope that, someday, both would relearn how to smile fluttered through my mind like a butterfly. The novice paused, and her ice-blue eyes met mine. "Aberrant?"

"Yes?"

"Thank you."

She led the children past me to Zhen, but the little one kept glancing back at me over her shoulder.

Avoiding the future would not change it, so I limped to the petite woman with three drones. She patted the boy's back again, set him down, and sent him away.

My mouth went dry. "Eldest," I said. James was close, too close. I needed to move away. "Eldest, I know you carry the weight of us all on your shoulders—"

"A weight you have made more burdensome," she said, no apparent condemnation in her voice.

"Indeed." I closed my eyes for a single second. "I have a request—not for myself, but for the little ones and novices. Could we speak elsewhere? I do not want to add to the children's distress. They are so young."

She tilted her head to look up at me. "Very well. You and I will walk through the carnage." She led the way back over the bodies in the hallway. We reached the pillared room, where men and women milled about or stood guard over citizens who knelt with their hands on their heads. The Eldest waved her hand. "Behold, the defiling of our Center."

Rows of bodies filled the room: Consortium. The attackers. Three marines.

Too many. Bile rose in my throat.

"The deputy prime minister, for all her documented failings and inconsistencies, has agreed to send all Centers for Reclamation and Recycling to dispose of the bodies," the Eldest said, "though it will take hours to find and collect them from the entire Center, but these will be cleared first. After the citizens leave, I will send Recorders to walk through the destruction and retrieve damaged drones."

I kept my voice calm. "It is necessary."

Around us, citizens loaded bodies onto gurneys and platforms, collected casings, picked up broken knives. Center for Reclamation and Recycling workers bore Recorders out, gurney after gurney of red-stained grey. The citizens cast surreptitious glances at the Eldest, her drones, and me. While she watched them, and I watched her from the corner of my eye, they completed that task, then began lifting fallen marines. I wanted to touch Ken Patterson's arm, to assure him he would not be forgotten. I did not.

"I know what you did," she said mildly.

A shiver chilled my neck. "Do you," I said without inflection.

One of her drones settled about her shoulders, as mine had done at university when the stresses of social interaction had surpassed what I could bear.

She kept her grey eyes on the rows of bodies, but a tendril touched the unnatural glow in my right wrist. "I followed you. They found your cane by the southeast entrance where you assaulted Linda Mills-Stern, broke her arm, and shattered three ribs. It is a wonder you did not kill her."

"As you say." A pang of near remorse hit me, but Zhen . . . No, I had not erred. "The woman was targeting the people who had run to assist the children." I drew a deep breath and said, "I confess to acting without any attempt at unbiased documentation."

A citizen pointedly ignored the drones as he escorted laden hover platform past us.

"I am not displeased." The Eldest's classically beautiful profile could have been carved from grey-veined marble. "I decree you acted in defense of the children and of the Consortium itself. I have expunged these actions from the record."

The hairs on my arms prickled, and my forehead knotted. Had she removed my guilt, or had she tampered with the record itself? "Thank you, Eldest."

Her smile stretched over perfect teeth. "I believe I understand you now."

My stomach clenched, and not trusting my voice, I held up my glowing right wrist then touched my hair.

"Do not be foolish," she said. "I speak of how you put the children above all else. They are our future, and after the . . ." Tension crept into her voice, disrupting her gentle tone. Her drone sent another tendril about her torso. "We are all rejected by the citizenry. Discarded. And so, if I may use a nearly forbidden word, it is our sacred duty to protect those who are younger and weaker."

My skin flashed hot, then cold. "Who am I to question your verbiage, Eldest?"

She gave a low chuckle. "Indeed. Who are you?" A faint, almost negligible sigh sounded. "Transport will arrive tonight after curfew to take the surviving giftings and the tiniest ones to safety in Centers Beta and Pi. Their Recorders will accompany them."

"The other ones," I said in a rush, "the ones with chromosomal anomalies and those requiring constant care. What of them?"

"They are hidden from all save their assigned Caretakers. Citizens who rejected us would surely doubly reject those who cannot function within their"—her voice hardened—"social parameters."

"They, too, will be safe?"

Her grey eyes bored through me, though to what purpose I could not tell. "I will protect those who cannot protect themselves. This is my calling and my highest—my sacred—duty."

That particular weight lifted from my heart, and I smiled. "Thank you, Eldest."

Her browless forehead wrinkled. "You care, then?"

"Always."

She hummed a noncommittal acknowledgement. "While on Pallas, you activated a drone in an attempt to access a secured area in search of equipment to study Consortium nanotechnology."

Who had told her? Dr. Clarkson? Had it been part of the record? My heart pounded. "I did."

"You used it to kill one of them." Her drone untwined three tendrils to point to the kneeling group on the opposite side of the cavernous room. "To eliminate one of the people who murdered members of my Consortium."

"I did not intend—"

"I should punish you. And yet I will not. It was one less *citizen*"—she spat the term as if it were poison—"who would kill my people." She clasped her hands behind her back. "Yes, I understand."

I had no answer as we stood side by side, aberration and Eldest.

"Why do they throw giftings aside for compensation and convenience?" she asked in an undertone. "Why must they hate? It is as if they were humanity's true aberrations."

"I would not know," I answered, belatedly realizing she spoke to herself.

She shifted toward me, and her face remained expressionless. "How did they find out an EM cannon would disable our drones so they could murder my children? Someone betrayed us."

My heart raced again.

The Eldest's sudden laughter echoed eerily in the room, slipping between the columns, curdling about the bases.

Moons and stars. Williams was correct. The Eldest was unstable.

"Not you, Aberrant," she assured me. "I am not unfair. You destroyed one of them. I have expunged that from your record as well. It is a pity you cannot be reinstated, but your other crimes have not been answered. Perhaps you have done more good than I know, but you have not been completely honest, so I cannot tell."

Keeping my voice neutral, I asked, "You have absolved me?"

"I am not unjust." She gestured at the emptying hall. "You led citizens to save my children and rescue as many as possible." She closed her nanodevice-saturated eyes. "One novice here survived the destruction of Sigma. Before that attack, I had planned for her to be an Elder. She showed more promise than you ever did. But after seeing this twice? No, given her father's identity . . . I am not convinced that the sins of the parents do not extend to their children." Another short laugh. "After all, look at you."

I did not know if she told the truth or lied, but cold washed over me.

"We cannot absorb all these children," she continued. "Not if we are to continue accepting giftings, which is of utmost importance. Our calling is to save them from the citizenry. We shall be taxed to accept gifts, with three Centers gone. Somehow, we must expand."

"The other Centers," I said. "The ones here on New Triton, on Ceres, or even the one on Krios Platform Forty-One? Could they not take additional children until Training Center Alpha is rebuilt?"

"The giftings and infants will be prioritized, and after them, I can disperse nine or ten score. And no, this Center will not be restored. My cursory inspection shows crippling, irreparable damage to the nodes that—" She stopped abruptly. "You are no longer privy to such information."

I raised my face to the ceiling as if I could see through to the underbelly of the Scriptorium above. "It is well," I said. "Nor was I trained in that sector."

"Indeed. Nevertheless, I will tell you that Training Center Alpha shall be stripped, and the High Elders wish to sell it. Resources will be allocated to the defense of other Centers and to maintain their ability to take in gifts the citizens discard."

Invisible bands seemed to tighten around my chest. "What will happen to the remaining novices?"

Her guttural huff pulled my attention back down. "I discussed this with the High Elders, and they were divided. Some suggested putting my children in tanks."

"In the Halls?" Despite my effort to keep my voice steady, it cracked.

"As you say."

The image of the vast Halls where we had found the children stretched through my mind, a dark, unforgivable void. "No."

"You disagree."

"They have done nothing to merit the Halls. They are but novices and little ones. To do so would be wrong."

"Yes. Destruction is immoral." Her grey eyes—all her being—seemed intent on the marines and their prisoners. "So I have dealt with them. There is no place in the Consortium for such weakness of character. They are no longer obstacles."

Fear dribbled down my spine like melting ice, but at that moment, I remembered Max's ongoing quest, and unbidden, I again saw his blood on the floor. No, Max's injury could not be allowed to distract me, not now, but if I could help those like him . . .

"Eldest, as you have said, destruction is immoral." I stopped. My brazen proposal would surely be as dangerous as suggesting that she send the unclaimed children to tanks.

She waited.

"Some citizens regret their choice to gift." I licked my lips. "Could the novices, the ones who have no place . . ."

Her eyes glinted like metal, and her voice grew sharp. "Go on."

"Could their parents be presented with the option of reclaiming them?"

I held my breath. Closed my eyes. Wished I had kissed Nate one last time. Waited for a reprimand to take my life as it must have taken the lives of dissenting Elders.

No drone touched me, so I risked a peek.

She was silent, staring into space, her eyes darting as if in REM sleep.

Afraid to so much as glance at her again, I gazed straight ahead where two men in the green and white of Reclamation and Recycling hoisted the knife-man onto a platform without even removing the blade in his chest. Bile rose again in my throat. The last of the attackers' remains were hauled away, and the marines urged the prisoners forward.

I could not help searching their faces, and relief hit me. Though Zhen had indicated Nate and Alec had been elsewhere, reactivating power, they were here now. A bandage wound around Alec's right arm, which seemed unfair after he had already been wounded by these people back on Pallas. Nate's black jacket was torn or slashed, but it did not glisten with red. His green eyes found mine. I offered him the faintest smile, then looked away.

I tapped my thigh as I skimmed for others. Eric and Daniel kept their eyes down, as they should, apparently focused on the task of half carrying a man whose name I could not recall. Back in the corner, the trio who had first called me Izzy struggled out, the shorter two bearing up the engineer with box braids.

My heart stammered. Where was Cam?

I could not see Cam.

He had not been among the three bodies on the hover gurneys. I had only recognized Ken Patterson. None of them had been my Cameron Rodriguez.

Zhen, Jordan, and Jackson were already above ground. Surely Cam was, too.

"Aberrant."

I fisted my hands and turned back to her. "Eldest?"

She tilted her head. "It is as if you are more concerned with the citizens than with your future."

"I am damaged, Eldest, not unintelligent. I do not have a future. My concern is not misplaced."

A man shouted, "Don't think I don't know you and that traitor are working together, Recorder!"

I spun around. Not four meters away, Skip strained against Quincy and Hodges, who held him by the arms. Anger surged.

Why had Skip survived when Ken Patterson had not?

"Don't think them hauling me off to the mines is going to stop me from tracking you down and carving out your—"

"Be silent."

One of the Eldest's drones swooped down and enforced her crisp command. Arms wrapped around Skip like a cage, and tentacles covered his mouth. The drone yanked him from Hodges and Quincy and lifted him into the air. Skip's eyes went wide.

The Eldest advanced, and as she did, her other two drones interlocked their arms, forming a seat, lifting her until she hovered over him. The drone holding him forced his head up.

"I have searched the records, Xavier Phillip Johnson."

My breath caught. This was Christine Johnson's brother? The little boy in the picture?

"I have seen your defiance, your schemes, your machinations," the Eldest continued. "Your willful murder of my Elder, your assault on this aberration who yet remains my Recorder, and your vicious attacks on the Consortium and my children."

He made a muffled noise, and though she had no need for any physical cue, she snapped her fingers. A tentacle rose to cover his nose as well. Several of the citizens nearby gasped, but when one of the prisoners protested, the drone holding him lashed a tendril down at the woman and caught her arm. She screamed and dropped to her knees.

Xavier Johnson's face changed color as he thrashed fruitlessly.

"I said to be silent," the Eldest said mildly. "I am not finished. You are responsible for coordinating attacks with groups on New Triton, attacks which killed innocents. You destroyed my children." She leaned back in her drone-chair. "Additionally, you have trespassed on Consortium property to commit these heinous crimes. The AAVA clearly defines our rights in such matters."

His eyes bulged.

"And therefore, you have thusly submitted yourself to my authority." A slow smile edged across her face. "You are notified. All shall be recorded."

Electricity arced. Someone screamed. I clamped my eyes shut and turned my head away.

A thud told me when Skip hit the ground, and the gentle whine of the drones told me when the Eldest returned to my side.

Her mouth had tightened into a thin, white line. "You all have participated in the murder of innocents, all have trespassed on Consortium property. There is no reason I should—"

I dared to touch her arm. Though she turned her metallic-grey glare on me, I could not remain silent while she murdered more people. "Eldest."

She studied my face. "You are correct. Citizens, step away. I will remove them all."

"What?" My horrified exclamation echoed back at me from the pillars, as if it were not mine.

"Do not be concerned, Aberrant. Their punishments are recorded. They would be removed from all they know, forced to pay off a debt beyond their ability to meet, their families burdened beyond repair, and yet, I choose to spare them that fate." The Eldest's soothing voice shredded my nerves. "Behold, I am merciful."

Her drones left her side. Several marines made a futile attempt to protect their prisoners, but the drones punished them until they fell, gasping, to their knees. The drones lofted the prisoners as marines fought to pull them free. Alec grabbed Nate to prevent him from running forward. Shouts, screams, curses—all faded to eerie quiet. Ozone and the scents of urine and blood tinged the air.

Waves of nausea hit me.

"You were correct," the Eldest mused. "Justice, mercy, and our sacred duty."

The nausea intensified. No matter what she said, I was nothing like the slight woman beside me.

The Eldest waved a delicate hand. "Citizens, your service to my children has excused your presence, and you are allowed to remain on the premises until the last of my children are safe. Take your own with you."

Nate began to protest, but I interrupted. "Nathaniel, please. Go."

They left, taking the wounded with them. I kept my eyes on the ground, unwilling to place any of them at risk by garnering attention from the woman who readily eliminated those who displeased her.

The last of my friends left the room, and I was alone with the Eldest. An industrial bot growled its way across the floor.

Her drone caught my right arm and raised it, and I did nothing to pull away. It rolled back my sleeve and tapped the pale lines left by the implant in my wrist.

The Eldest simply said, "Do not forget I am tracking you."

I dropped to my knees, the pain of landing on the concrete floor a welcome diversion.

"Aberrant."

I looked up.

"Come."

I pushed myself to my feet and hobbled to where I had dropped my damaged cane. Splintered by the impact on the now-dead woman's torso, the raw wood mocked my need for support. I braced one hand on the wall and followed the Eldest to the Scriptorium then the front gate.

My consolations were that the children were well and Nate was unharmed, for the Eldest did not tolerate deviations. And despite her claim, she had no mercy.

"Eldest!" Kyleigh's voice echoed from the buildings.

The slim woman with her three murdering drones pivoted as Kyleigh sprinted toward us. I had believed I could not have been more afraid. I had been mistaken. Each breath felt like an attempt to inhale ice water.

My friend came to a stop, and panting, held up one palm before resting her hands on her knees and gulping down air.

"Stars above," she gasped. "So much running today."

The Eldest said, "Kyleigh Rose Tristram."

Inwardly, I screamed for my friend to flee, but she straightened and swiped her forearm across her forehead. One of the marines at the gate gestured at us, and several faces paled. Jackson grabbed Quincy's shoulder to hold him back, and Jordan threw an arm around James. No one, however, stopped Eric.

"I needed an audience with you," Kyleigh panted, "but I know you rarely talk to citizens."

"Indeed." The right side of the Eldest's forehead lifted. "What is your point, citizen?"

"The nanites." Kyleigh drew a deep breath and squared her shoulders. "I would like permission to utilize Consortium nanotechnology labs."

"No." The Eldest turned away.

Kyleigh reached out, as if to touch the Consortium's leader, and a drone snagged her wrist.

Not Kyleigh, too. I could not breathe.

"Please listen," she begged. "If you know who I am, you know what I do."

The Eldest's eyes flashed, but her voice remained mild. "What is that to me?"

"I want to help."

When I had tried to stop the Eldest moments before, she had

responded with murder. Eric drew near, and all I could do was fling up my hand to warn him to stop. He did.

The drone pulled Kyleigh close to the Eldest, so that they stood but half a meter apart, eye to eye.

"You wish to help your . . . friend?"

"I want to help you all."

"Kyleigh"—Eric choked on her name—"don't."

Her cheeks flushed. "Those nanites join together. I've been working on a way to break that bond, to disintegrate the clump so the body can eliminate it. I think I found it, but it's all hypothetical, and I couldn't manufacture anything like that on *Thalassa*. I don't want to go to the medical companies where there's no guarantee the information will be secure, safe from people like Skip." She pointed across the drone-littered lawn at the gate, where the last of the bodies were being loaded for transport to be reclaimed or recycled.

The Eldest's eyes narrowed.

"The Consortium has to have nanotech labs—I'd be stupid to think you don't—but other than here, the best, most secure labs are on Pallas, which is too far away. Besides, I can't work with the constant threat of being eaten alive by giant cockroaches."

Another tendril snaked around Kyleigh's waist, but though her respiration increased, she ignored the drone's narrow appendage.

The Eldest murmured, "Again I ask, to save your friend?"

Kyleigh drew a deep breath and said, "Yes."

My heart fell. The Eldest turned to me, her mouth tight.

My young friend strained against the drone's grip. "I want to save anyone who has this in their system. I know you don't approve, but Eldest, be fair. They say you're just." She indicated me. "Her friendship with citizens might have saved Consortium lives."

The Eldest rotated back to Kyleigh. Fear shot icy spikes through me.

"I know that *Attlee*, Imogene Clarkson, and the others brought a cure back, but an antivirus won't stop those clumps from killing people. Recorders will recover from the virus, but without a way to break up those clots, they'll still die." Her voice cracked. "My friend nearly did. So, if not for her, I am begging you to let me at least solve this for the rest of the Consortium. I'll work with anyone you want me to, just let me save them."

Cold sweat gathered in my fisted palms.

Kyleigh stood at her fullest height, eye to eye with the Eldest. "If you have to send me to the inner belt afterward for claiming a friend among the Consortium, so be it."

"Why would you do this?" the Eldest hissed. "Are you concerned that these clumps would kill citizens? They did not kill your friend, Fredrick James Westruther, despite the donation that provided him sight outside the reach of unaltered humanity."

Kyleigh went absolutely ashen, but an odd relief hit me in the midst of my fear. The Eldest did not know. I had deceived her. James and Daniel truly were safe.

"Why?" Kyleigh's hand rose to her throat, where she used to wear the chain with a cross, the one she had sent with Elliott. "Because it's the right thing to do."

"Insufficient." The Eldest cocked her head, and the drone slid a tendril around Kyleigh's neck.

Kyleigh tipped her face to the dome and closed her eyes, her lips moving soundlessly.

My weak leg, strained beyond its limits, buckled. Eric caught me.

After a pause, Kyleigh's hazel eyes opened. "Why? Because of love." A smile spread over her face. "Because whether we are stardust or creation—and I believe the latter—we are each unique. Citizen or Consortium. Each one gifted with abilities, each one valuable. I was nearly donated, you know. If you can't accept that my God made both of us, at least accept that I was nearly one of you, and that tie compels me to act."

My entire body froze, and simultaneously, Eric's grip on my arm tightened.

The Eldest's nostrils flared. "You dare to attempt to convert the Eldest?"

Kyleigh actually smiled. "I don't know that it's proselytizing if I know you won't listen, but someone should tell you at least once." Her expression grew serious. "You asked why I cared. That's my answer. Because of a love beyond what any of us can understand."

The drone flew back from Kyleigh as if she had reprimanded it.

"Your answer, Eldest?" she asked softly.

For the second time in my life, I heard the Eldest laugh.

Acid ate at my throat.

"Ah, Kyleigh Rose Tristram, you are wasted as a citizen." The Eldest waved a hand. "Yes. You may use the facilities here on Training Center Alpha as long as necessary. I will not be sending more of my people to assist you, lest you corrupt them, as well. You and whatever assistants you have will be on your own."

Air rushed from my lungs, and I clutched Eric's arm to stay upright.

"However"—the Eldest became living marble once more—"I will only strike your antithetical remarks from the record if you save my children." Her closest drone tapped my arm before all three spooled in their appendages. "We are not finished, Aberrant. I shall summon you to resolve our issues. In the meantime, you and your . . . *friends* . . . may remain until the children are safe."

We watched her cross the lawn, people parting before her as if repelled by a magnetic force. Once she passed the shattered gates, Eric led me to a bench, and I leaned back and shut my eyes.

"Are you all right?" Kyleigh asked.

I said, "You frightened me nigh unto death."

"I think I nearly scared myself to death, too." She gasped. "Stars above! You're covered with blood. Are you hurt?"

"It is not mine."

"Where's Tia?" Eric demanded.

"Tia's all right," Kyleigh answered without taking her eyes from my stained clothing. "Whose blood—"

"Where is she?"

"Don't fuss, Eric." Kyleigh heaved a sigh. "She started having contractions—"

"And you *left* her?"

"Oh, ease up, Eric," she said brusquely. "I took her to the medical center two streets down."

Boots thudded, and my eyes flew open. Eric was already halfway to the gates, hurdling damaged drones and dodging through the crowd and past Quincy, James, and Jackson, who strode toward us in unison.

Kyleigh put her hands on her hips. "Well if he'd waited *thirty seconds*, he'd know she's all right."

"Is she?" I asked.

She nodded, though her attention still followed Eric. "They stopped labor, but she'll be in there for at least half a ten-day. The baby is fine. Tia got a little worked up, though, and told everyone the baby's name. She came up with a list of guardians, including me, Eric, and Cam, just in case." Her eyes came back to me. "Her daughter's name is Zeta."

My heart stilled. That small gift lifted my eyes to the riveted ceiling overhead. Pinks and purples deepened. Was it evening already? Had it been that long?

"Tristram," Quincy thundered, "what were you thinking?"

Instead of answering him, Kyleigh flung her arms around the marine and hugged him tight. She released him to embrace the others, but then froze. "Where is everyone else?"

Gazes dropped to boots.

She jumped onto the bench and began to count. Her face went pale. "Zhen! Where is she? I saw Jordan earlier—but where is Cam? Timmons and Alec? Or Ken? Stars above, *where is Max?*"

Quincy shifted his weight and looked away.

She blanched. "Are they . . ."

"Zhen and Lars are with the children," James said. "Ken Patterson did not . . . He is gone."

Kyleigh sank beside me on the bench.

Jackson's gravelly voice churned through the air, listing their three losses, then the wounded. He cleared his throat. "We haven't found Cam, yet, Kyleigh."

A sense of numbness spread through me. But for some reason I latched onto the fact that he called her Kyleigh instead of Tristram, as he usually did.

"What does that mean?" she whispered.

Quincy squinted at the two-story Scriptorium. "Just that we haven't found him yet."

"I have people pulling medtanks from the Center's clinic," Jackson continued with a nod toward the dormitory, "and Timmons is setting up emergency generators."

Her eyes seemed larger. "Where is Max?"

Quincy set a bandaged hand on her shoulder. "Prepped for the first tank."

With an inarticulate cry, she tried to dart toward the dormitory, but James caught her, murmuring words I could not hear.

A shout echoed from the gate, and the guards parted, allowed a woman through, and converged again. Elinor Williams raced across the lawn.

"I heard," she gasped, and we waited while her ragged breaths evened. "The attack is all over the news, but the streets are so crowded I couldn't get transport. What happened?"

And though I wanted to tell her, I only listened to the disjointed story from the people around me. Tears wetted my cheeks, and overhead, the dome darkened to night.

When Archimedes Genet arrived shortly after nine that evening and asked for Nate and Jordan, Nate had just returned from patrolling the perimeter of the Center.

I knew exactly where Jordan was, for I had just left there myself to escort Kyleigh to a room to sleep. So, while Nate gathered his dinner, I led the captain through the lobby, through the crowded lounge, and by the doors leading to the children's rooms, past the busy laundry room, and into the dormitory wing we had converted into an infirmary.

The marines had relocated nine of the clinic's tanks, and Daniel had attached cables to portable chemical generators. Four retractable beds held bandaged, sleeping marines. Williams looked up from a computer, held her finger to her lips, then pointed to the beds and the Recorder-doctor. He had fallen asleep where he sat, snoring quietly in his chair, his head at an angle that guaranteed he would have neck pain when he awoke.

He had done well. He had made innumerable stitches, treated two concussions, set five bones, and saved seven lives. Three of the seven rested in the tanks: a marine named Knox, Max, and Cam.

A knot rose in my throat.

Alec had found Cam in one of the classrooms attached to the Scriptorium. When he had arrived, a seventeen-year-old Recorder in blood-soaked greys had left Cam's side to fight off whoever came through the door.

Like the other survivors in that building, her drone had been temporarily disconnected while she was under disciplinary review. Cam had burst into the classroom, and when he saw the score of novices and young Recorders, he had found places to hide them. At the sound of footsteps, he had hidden her behind the Recorder's desk.

Her voice had broken as she berated herself for crouching, hands over her ears as they took out their hatred on a citizen who came to the Consortium's assistance. She had not crawled out until they had left. None of my reassurances convinced her that she could not have protected him and her assistance had saved Cam's life.

The young Recorder had applied nanotech-saturated bandages to slow blood loss and, when those had run out, had applied direct pressure. His lacerations were deep, but the attackers had broken two ribs. His left clavicle had punctured his lung, and their final blow had damaged his spinal cord. He was stable but would remain in a tank for several tendays. Even then, the possibility remained that the nanodevices would be unable to knit his injuries.

Now, she refused to leave Cam's side and had fallen asleep, curled like a kitten in the chair beside his tank.

In comparison, Max was barely injured at all.

"He shall be up and about before the nanodevices eat all his hair," the Recorder-doctor had told me.

Williams had concurred. "We simply err on the side of caution. He will be fine."

It did not feel like he would be fine. It felt like nothing would be fine ever again, my own fate aside, even though all three tanks beeped steadily.

Both James and Jordan sat beside Max's tank, James in an unconscious echo of his father, elbows on his knees, hands clasped. Though my first friend had refused to change from his soiled clothing, Jordan's torn blouse had been replaced by a sleeveless overtunic of Consortium grey. A gel bandage covered the scrape on her forehead, and more encased her left forearm and covered what might have been stitches above her left clavicle.

For a long moment, Archimedes said nothing, then he asked quietly, "How are they?"

Her golden eyes, bruised by a blow and by fatigue, closed for a moment, and she touched the foot of the tank. "All three are stable. Elinor says the Recorder-doctor did well." Her voice shook. "I could have lost him, Archimedes."

"But you did not." Though I had not the authority to make the claim, I added, "And you will not, Jordan. Nor you, James. I refuse to lose anyone else."

Thalassa's captain squeezed my shoulder and turned to Williams.

"Despite the day's events, I still need to offer my congratulations, Elinor Anne Williams."

Her half smile faltered as soon as it formed. "Thank you. It has not been the day I had hoped for, but thankfully the Recorder-doctor is nearly as good as Max himself."

A brief silence was broken by the Recorder-doctor's soft snores and the tanks' burble.

At length, Archimedes Genet said, "Jordan. I believe you know why I'm here."

Her brows drew together. "I'm not leaving him."

"I've had numerous accounts on what happened when that Eldest arrived."

James seemed to hold his breath. He glanced at me. Jordan's jaw tightened.

"We need you, J," Archimedes said. "Under any other circumstance, I wouldn't ask you to leave Max, but I trust Williams's—Elinor's—assessment."

"I will stay," James stated. "He will not be alone."

Jordan's gaze flicked from James to me, and without another word, she stood and left, stealing a last glance at the quietly humming tank.

Archimedes gave me a short smile, then he, too, was gone.

Before I took Jordan's vacated chair, I peeked into the tank. Max's dreadlocks floated eerily in the green gel. I turned away quickly.

Elinor Williams set her hand on my shoulder. "He is healing. The knife wound will take time, but the blade touched nothing vital. The greater concern is head trauma, but even that"—she drew a deep breath—"has been treated with a heavy dose of clean nanodevices."

After a minute of silence, James asked, "What will happen to the children?"

"The ones with genetic disorders and the giftings are being taken to safety," I said. "Some of the novices will be sent to other Centers as room allows. I do not know about the rest. I talked to a Recorder who said the transports to take the children will begin to arrive tomorrow."

James lowered his voice. "The Caretaker who knew us has left?"

Williams spun around, all her attention on James and me and mouthed, *"Someone recognized you?"*

I nodded in silent affirmation, then said, "The transports should arrive shortly."

He pinched the bridge of his nose. "I promised I would watch over Kyleigh, but if one person denounces me, my presence will condemn her instead. Who else might know?"

"You are exhausted," Williams said. "Go, sleep. It has been a long, horrific day."

"I promised to stay," he argued without heat, "and even if I had not, I would not leave."

"In that case—" Williams handed him a blanket, then tapped my shoulder. "James and I are here with Max. With Cam. Go have a cup of chamomile tea and rest."

James attempted a smile. I rose and placed my hand on Max's tank, then Cam's, then wandered back to the dormitory kitchen, where I squeezed past Lars to brew a cup of tea.

Eric dozed in the corner, his head lolling forward. When he had returned from visiting Tia, Jackson had told him about Cam. Eric's jaw had tightened, but he had taken the news silently and joined the young Recorder in pacing the hall until Elinor announced that Cam was safely in a tank.

Nate and Jordan were still in conference with the captain when a communications link on the table buzzed, and Zhen checked it.

"Moons and stars," she huffed. "That woman never gives up."

"Which woman?" I asked.

"The deputy prime minister is trying to contact J again."

Alec, who had sprawled in a chair with his head back, did not open his eyes. "What does she want?"

"A public appearance from the *heroes of Training Center Alpha.*"

I choked on my tea.

Alec didn't move. "She just wants to be reelected."

Jackson limped in, Quincy ambling after him. The marines who noticed them pushed themselves to their feet, but Jackson held up his hand and cut through the lounge into the meeting with Archimedes, Jordan, and Nate.

"Three things," Quincy announced. "One, I never thought I would need to put bedtime routines to work on such a scale. I thought putting two girls to bed was rough."

Someone laughed.

"They were really good, though," another marine said from the corner. "Hey, Lars, I need another ice pack."

I ducked as a small bag of ice came flying from the kitchen and hit the man in the chest.

"Two." Quincy paused until everyone was looking at him. "Michaelson sent a heads up from command: Guess which group of marines will be looking for new jobs in the near future?"

A chill poured down my spine. To deprive them of their livelihood for saving children?

Lars poked his head from the kitchen, his jaw slack. "What?"

"You heard me."

The general uproar woke Eric and brought Alec upright.

The noise faded into discontented grumbles, and someone said, "Maybe a public appearance won't be a bad thing in this case. Garner all the sympathy we can get."

Ice-pack marine moaned. "I told you no good deed goes unpunished."

Quincy glanced at the closed door leading to the dormitories. "I'd do it again."

Consensus rippled through the room.

"At least we have warning," the woman said.

"Three," Quincy began.

Hodges interrupted the scattered moans. "It's worse, isn't it?"

I bit my lip. What could be worse?

"Julian Voided Ross overpowered his militia guards and got away."

It was as if someone had punched me. Every shadow in the room crept like claws to grab at us, but outrage energized everyone else.

"They have no idea where he disappeared to," Quincy said, "but if I have to live off caffeine for the rest of my life, he's not going to hurt a single kid here."

The chorus of agreement was soon overtaken by general discontent that they did not have proper weapons. I took my tea and made my way to the front doors to stand in the night. Eric followed me out.

"Zeta, you all right?"

"No," I said truthfully.

"Me, neither. Worried about Ross?"

"Yes." I looked up at the dim blur of the moon through the dome. "And Max. And Cam."

"And Kye. If she can't pull this nanite thing off, the Eldest'll space her and you."

We stood side by side and watched the dim glow of the moon through the dome.

I took a sip of tea. "How is Tia?"

"Better." He leaned back against the smooth outer wall. "If she'll let me, I'll be a constant for her. I'm not giving up." Half a smile edged across his tired face. "I love her, you know. Have for years. I'll do whatever shift they give me here, check on Cam, then head over there tomorrow."

Given the Eldest's irregular behavior, my future was uncertain, as the chip in my arm testified. I blew the steam away from my cup of chamomile tea and said simply, "Tomorrow."

Over the next two days, a citywide curfew kept citizens off the streets as armored transports took all but sixty-five of the children away. The little one who had held my hand and the blue-eyed novice were among those rejected for a second time in their young lives, this time by the organization that had claimed to be their home. The former had yet to speak, and the latter remained detached, save around the youngest ones for whom the novice seemed to have appointed herself Caretaker.

Citizens arrived at the unrepaired gates to gawk, but occasionally to offer food or help. We typically refused both, with two welcome exceptions. Lars's Clarissa arrived early on the first day. She had known that Lars was inbound and requested time off to meet him. Having seen the news reports, she fought her way through the crowds the first morning and appealed to Jackson, waving her credentials and citing her experience with children.

The other exception arrived that afternoon. Daniel escorted the petite woman with greying hair to the southwest dormitory. When the woman caught sight of Kyleigh, tears sprang to her brown eyes, and she cried out. In an instant, Melody Lu had outsprinted most people half her age. They clung to each other, and I could not say who cried harder, Kyleigh or her mother.

Kyleigh convinced Nate to restore power to the science laboratories. She fell to work on designing her prototype, her mother a willing assistant, though her specialty as a geneticist did not include nanotechnology. She was, however, fascinated with any tales of the roaches, relentlessly questioning anyone who would talk about them.

The Recorder-doctor had neither left nor received his drone, but he settled into a routine and readily accepted Elinor Williams as his assistant, though he seemed uneasy around most of the citizens. By the morning of the second day, only one infirmary bed was in use, though the tanks still hummed. James and Jordan rarely left Max's side, and Kyleigh and Eric were regular visitors.

Everyone was waiting, though to what end, no one would say, save to be certain the injured would improve and homes would be found for the children. No one spoke of my fate, but those who had witnessed the Eldest's behavior were inordinately kind to me.

The second afternoon, I took a bag of food pellets and walked to the tilapia ponds. I had always found it peculiar that when I tossed handful after handful to the fish, their frantic greediness was quieting. I neared the bottom of the bag when Nate jogged up and announced that the Recorder-doctor had drained Max's tank.

Without a cane and my leg still weak, I was not fast enough, so I missed it when he thrashed as Elliott had. I missed it when his eyes flew open, when his brain and body synchronized. When I arrived, he was already out of the tank and in a bed, blinking at the dormitory infirmary's unfamiliar surroundings.

"How are you feeling?" the Recorder-doctor asked.

"I'm . . ." Max rubbed his eyes. "We made it?"

"Yes." Jordan gripped the foot of the bed. "Robert James Maxwell, never scare me like that again."

The Recorder-doctor's eyes widened as he glanced from Max to Jordan, and his complexion suffused with color. "I . . ." He shifted his weight from foot to foot, then turned to Elinor Williams. "I must go check on supplies. Please remain and observe."

Even the back of his head seemed pinker as he strode away.

"Elinor?" I asked quietly.

She, too, watched Max and Jordan, a soft smile on her face. "I believe," she said, "that it is well."

Max cleared his throat, then asked, "Last I remember we were . . ." His eyes found James. "You're all right. What happened?"

"It would seem," James said, intent on Max's face, "that my father saved my life and took a blade meant for me."

The room hushed.

Max's brown eyes riveted on his son. "You know?"

"I suspected, but my friend—my first friend"—James offered me a quiet smile before turning that smile on Max—"has confirmed it."

They spoke quietly, but I did not listen. Instead, I leaned against Nate, well content. I could feel him soak up their happiness as a sponge soaks up liquid. Whatever happened next, *this* was what mattered.

Once their conversation slowed, Jordan cleared her throat. "Max?"

"Venetia?"

"I know this isn't the right time, but stars above, I'm not waiting any longer."

Max blinked once more. "What do you mean?"

"I don't know how I missed it." She drew in a deep breath. "You are the best and kindest man in the system, and somehow . . ."

He went very, very still, but his eyes searched hers.

Her beads clattered softly as she lowered herself to the edge of the bed and bent toward him. Lips millimeters apart, sharing the same breath, she said, "Somehow I didn't know that I love you," and kissed him.

I could not breathe until his hands moved up her arms to slide around her. I closed my eyes, for some things were not meant to be witnessed. Only Nate's steady heartbeat against my back, the faint burbling tanks, and the dim hum of electronic devices challenged the low purr of the generators.

"Venetia," Max murmured.

I decided it was safe enough to peek. I was correct.

"I love you, Max," Jordan repeated, her forehead against his, not seeming to care who heard. "Your heart, your kindness, your patience, your faith. The way your smile creeps up from the right side of your mouth when you're happy, the way you tug on your ear when you're thinking."

"You want the truth?"

She pulled back, drew a deep breath. "Always."

A smile as deep as space is wide spread across his face. "You had my heart the first time I saw you throw a punch. You were glorious. You still are."

"Why didn't you ever say anything?" she whispered.

Running footsteps sounded in the hallway, but perhaps I was the only one to hear them.

He brushed braids back and traced his thumb over her high cheekbone. "If all I could do was to be your friend, it had to be enough. I certainly didn't believe you would see me as anything else."

She wrapped her long arms around him and held him tight.

Zhen and Alec skidded into the room. One brow raised, Alec glanced at Nate, who nodded, but Zhen folded her arms.

"Well," she huffed. "All I can say is it's about time."

***

Still, the Eldest did not call on me, and no news regarding the children arrived. The tracker in my arm continued to glow and pulse occasionally, making my whole arm tingle. Hope rose and fell in a sine wave, but my mind kept returning to Lorik and the look on Elinor Williams's face when she said that Connor Edwards did not know her name.

Archimedes Genet visited again and brought the cats with him, though he kept Macavity for a mascot, to the competing chagrin and delight of the kitchen staff. It was, he said, an investment in the children's health to leave the rest of the cats in our care. Bustopher adapted readily, though Hunter and her kittens hid in Kyleigh's closet.

That evening, Jordan announced that she had accepted the deputy prime minister's invitation to a presentation for the following day, and that the condition was that we all attended. The idea of being summoned again to a public tribunal stole my peace.

While everyone else was at dinner, I snuck in to visit Max, Bustopher at my heels. The cat jumped onto Max's bed, and for once, Max did not shoo him away. I pulled a chair close and explained that if the next day went well, I would tell the others myself. If, however, the Eldest had her way, someone needed to know my name. Unlike Edwards, I could not write a note.

"Do you mind?" I asked him.

"No." He smiled, though his nut-brown eyes did not crinkle, only glistened. "Thank you."

"You will tell them, if . . ."

"I won't need to."

I tapped my thigh, but when he held out his hand, I stopped and accepted the offering.

"I would come with you, if I could," he said.

"I know."

Though I wanted to reassure him that this wasn't goodbye, I could not finish. Instead, I pulled my hand away and fled, bumping into James on my way to the brook I had loved as a child.

James followed me, not a difficult task, as my strength had not returned. He handed me a new cane, explaining that it had taken a while to find a suitable material. Then, he settled beside me on the mossy rocks, like he had years before, and we watched the water ripple.

After uncounted minutes, he asked, "Are you concerned about facing the Eldest again?"

I attempted to raise but one brow.

He plucked a blade of grass and tossed it into the brook. The current carried it beyond a bend. "I would be, if I were you."

"It is not solely my fate," I confessed. "You were present, James. I am afraid for my friends' reactions. Kyleigh herself admitted to being my friend, and . . ."

He nodded, and the diamonds in his ears sparkled. "I have been thinking of my sister."

I sighed at the change in subject.

"My sister and you." He ran a hand over his short hair and grimaced. "The tracker in your wrist and the one in hers. They could be removed."

"I cannot risk it, James," I said, "not now that I am near the Consortium network, but yes, your sister could have removed hers."

He regarded me steadily. "If she lives, she is in danger, for even if she fights off the virus, she cannot seek help for nanodevice clumping."

I had not considered that. "What do you plan to do?"

"Nothing, as of yet, but I believe I must leave."

"The Eldest herself is deceived, James. You need not."

"To stay is to endanger you all, to place Kyleigh in danger." His eyes seemed to focus on a middle distance. "Risking Kyleigh," he said, as if to himself, "would be more heinous than wiping a star from the heavens, for there are many stars and only one Kyleigh Rose Tristram."

He stood abruptly, and I did the same.

"Perhaps I will seek for my sister. If she survived, she will still have nanodevices in her blood and cannot go for help without betraying herself. She will be in danger."

My throat tightened.

Silver eyes met mine. "My friend, if this is your last night here—and I refuse to admit it is—you should use it wisely. Spend it with those whose lives you have enriched, with those who love you. Not alone."

As I watched him walk away through the gathering dusk, I admitted to myself that James was correct. I should not hide.

Lorik had said that he found freedom in his choice of service and sacrifice. Max had said that it was my heart, my choices that mattered.

This moment was all I had for any certainty. I brushed my leggings free of debris and went to find my Nathaniel. For the time I had remaining, I chose to live.

I had not expected a crowd, though if I had considered it, I would have known what "public appearance" meant.

Jordan, who wore an elegant gold tunic that did nothing to mask her injuries, threw a reassuring smile over her shoulder as we walked through the crush of citizens filling the square. Though Daniel had stayed to stand guard at Training Center Alpha's unrepaired gates, James strode at Kyleigh's side. Not even appealing to a sense of duty to bear Max company could convince him to remain behind.

I straightened my Consortium-grey jacket. No one but Zhen, who had procured it for me, knew that I wore a seamless green tunic tucked underneath, an unobserved defiance meant to lend me strength. I dared not hold Nate's hand, but I shrank closer to him as the crowd gaped and pressed in on us. The kaleidoscope of people made me glad for a cane to lean on. When we reached the front of the building, Alec groaned. A grandstand rose above the crowd, and the deputy prime minister beamed like an artificial light. Beside her, calm, beautiful, and silent, stood the Eldest.

The inclination to run nearly overwhelmed me.

We lined up behind them like a display of trophies, and the deputy prime minister pontificated on and on. She could have been speaking of the weather or nursery rhymes. The crowd clapped or cheered or booed in random intervals, but I understood nothing, saw only the Eldest and her drones.

Suddenly, the crowd erupted with noise, and Nate and Jordan escorted me forward.

The deputy prime minister said, "Well?"

Panic grabbed at me. I wanted to say, "Well, what?" but even if the words had not been rude, they were unutterable.

I glanced at the Eldest. She frowned.

Nate bent over and whispered in my ear, "She is talking about you leading the charge to rescue the children, and the Eldest's proposal."

Why had I not been listening? "What proposal?" I whispered back.

"To be Guardian," the Eldest said. At her calm voice, the crowd quieted. "To have the care and provision of the children who remain in former Training Center Alpha. To have the authority to accept appeals for ungifting."

"Former?" Hope flared brightly. "Ungifting?"

"To allow the donors to request custody of the children or to allow adoption. It is decided." Her eyes narrowed. "Unless you would rather return to us and face the consequences of your actions. You may, of course, decline."

One drone grabbed my arm and held it in the air for all to see the light that ran like poison through my wrist. Her other two drones formed a chair again, and all sound fell away as they lifted her twenty centimeters so her bare skull was even with my curls and her eyes slightly above my own.

Her voice lowered until I might have been the only one to hear it. "The Consortium relinquishes control of what was Training Center Alpha, but solely into your hands. I shall require the return of all our technology. You shall send every single neural chip to me. Your *friends*," she said as if she smelled something foul, "have hidden some of my younger Recorders. I will allow those, contaminated by citizenry as they are, to choose either service to the Consortium or diminishment to a mere citizen."

There was one way to serve the Consortium once the internal failsafe was activated. I bit my lip. "Dr. Maxwell is not yet well. He is the only one who—"

"Parliament has agreed to fund this endeavor until 479.1.1.01, not a single second longer, after which it is your responsibility. All technology will be in my control at that point, in or out of minds. This is the agreement I have negotiated on the children's behalf." Nanodevices swirled back, revealing green irises. "If you are to save the children, this must be done. Do you understand?"

"I do."

Her chin rose, and grey flooded to obscure her eyes again.

"You know my limitations," I said.

"As you say. That is why the High Elders and I have considered the applicants for assistants carefully. Venetia Jordan is an acceptable choice."

I could not hide the smile in my heart. "Then I accept."

Her drones set her down, but when the one holding me spun me to face the crowd, my attention snagged on a tall man at the crowd's fringe.

Julian Ross's gaze locked on mine. My heart stopped for a moment. Before I could speak, however, he vanished into the mass of people.

The deputy prime minister prattled on about awards and thanks, but I ignored her and turned to the Eldest. Despite the inherent rudeness, I said in an undertone, "Eldest, I am sure I saw Julian Ross in the crowd. Without drones, we are defenseless. The children must be safe."

Her mouth tightened, and she closed her eyes. "When we release the identities of the children who remain, his daughter will be a liability, but it is your decision. There are times when you must cut away the liabilities to protect the whole."

His daughter? If Julian Ross would commit willful murder for his brother, would he not have done more for a daughter? Either he was a greater villain than I had ever thought, or he had not known of her gifting, perhaps of her existence. Either way, the Eldest's assessment of liability was accurate. But she was also incorrect.

I drew myself as upright as I could. "I will not discard the child, but I will need to know which one she is, if I am to keep her safe."

She flicked her hand, though whether in agreement or anger, I could not tell. "The records will soon be available to the citizenry and even to you. Have your assistants do any research you cannot. The Sanctuary is under your control, Guardian. Arm your people, if you must. If you do not protect my former children, I will be displeased."

The deputy prime minister faltered, then turned around and glared.

"Go on, citizen-official. Make your announcement." The Eldest riveted grey-masked eyes on me. "Your purchase has enabled continued giftings. Take pride in that, Guardian."

My purchase? I had bought nothing.

"And so," the deputy prime minister concluded, "it is done."

The crowd cheered, though my friends cheered even louder.

"Moons and stars," Zhen hissed. "Say something."

I blinked. "About?"

Nate beamed down at me. "We did it. You're all paid up."

"Paid . . ." I could barely breathe. The Eldest's impassive face told me nothing. "You mean my gifting?"

Jordan clasped my shoulder. "Yes. Paid in full."

I could not breathe.

Nate threw back his head and laughed, then he lifted me in the air and spun me around in front of the deputy prime minister, the citizens, the Eldest herself. When he put me down, I placed my palm flat on his chest. His heart pounded under my hand, and all I saw—all that mattered—was my Nathaniel. I slid my hand into his inner jacket pocket, where I knew my note would be hidden, and pulled it out.

"Then," I said, "I will be keeping this, for I have an answer."

He knew, I could see it, but he asked, "Which is?"

"Yes, my heart. The answer has always been yes."

Pale, utilitarian concrete rose in polished columns while broad steps a meter deep led up to the lobby. I limped up the stairs. Quiet shrouded the depths of a room designed to inspire compliance by creating a sense of smallness, but instead of capitulating to the intended emotion, thoughts of the sky broke into the present. In my mind, I again stood on Pallas's dust while trillions upon trillions of lights arced overhead.

How odd that when I was at my smallest under the naked stars, my heart had swelled, and I, a tiny speck in the universe, had felt a connection with the whole, with beyond the whole, as if tasting the infinite. No matter how these halls had been designed. Their crafted grandeur oppressed, not elevated, and having sampled that sense of wonder, which called me to something—or someone?—beyond the scope of what was tangible, the hall's stern oppression could not steal my value.

That gentle concept of wonder edged out my fear and lifted my eyes.

An Elder stood in the center of the room, at one with the innate stillness, his drone close at his side, the other two several meters above his head. His eyes, as grey and dimensionless as his tunic, bored into me.

"We have been waiting for you."

His drones accompanied us as our boots clicked on the floor, the sound echoing until our footsteps seemed a multitude.

Without looking at me, he asked, "So this, then, is truly your choice?"

"It is."

He stopped abruptly, and a glance at his impassive face brought me to a stop as well.

"There is no return." His voice grew as gravelly as Jackson's. "Friends are not bound by contract. They can betray you, wound you, abandon you."

"Indeed." Despite the hovering drones and the Elder himself, I smiled. "They are free to do so, but I trust them, and beyond that, I have faith. And love, which is stronger than fear itself. I . . ." Hesitation edged out my words for a moment, but I forced it back. Reaching out my hand, palm up, I said gently, "And I wish as much for you, Elder. For hope, for peace, for love."

For a moment, he seemed to stop breathing, and his primary drone twined a slender, silvery tendril around his torso.

I dropped my hand.

He blinked grey-veiled eyes. "Let us finish what needs to be done."

He pivoted and strode down the hallway to my right. I drew in a breath and followed him into the bowels of the building.

66

Pausing just inside the doors leading from the Hall of Records, I unfastened the Consortium-grey jacket. I pulled it off, folded it, and set it on the polished floor. Without it, cool air nipped at me through the thin, green fabric of my tunic, and my heart sang as I left Consortium grey behind. I edged my way down the steps cautiously.

"Sweetheart?"

There, at the base of the steps, they waited. My Nathaniel, his perfect brows drawn together. Jordan, her golden-brown eyes locked on me. Kyleigh, my cane clutched to her chest and her lower lip caught between her teeth. James at her side, solid and still as rock. Alec and Zhen and Eric—all potential energy coiled like springs.

I rolled back the green fabric and raised my right arm, displaying both the bandage and the silver-and-black identification bracelet. *My* bracelet.

With an incoherent shout, Nate raced up the broad steps, and I was in his arms.

I was home.

When he set me down, I stepped back and slid my hands into his, attempting to memorize him all over again, so I would have the image stored safely in my heart.

His voice lowered. "What is it?"

What I needed to say went too deep for a smile, deeper than my bones, deeper than a planet's core. I tightened my fingers around his. "Nathaniel, my heart, I love you."

Green eyes never left mine. He released my hand, reached into his jacket, and pulled out a polished, two-toned band of gold, the colors woven together in delicate Celtic knots. He slipped the ring onto the third finger of my left hand, where it hung loosely.

Faint pink tinged his cheeks. "It's too big. I—I'll take it back. Resize it."

"No." With a degree of reverence, I tried it on every other finger before sliding it onto my right thumb where it fit as if it had been made to those specific measurements. Captivated by the ring's beauty, I held up my hand. "Do not change it," I said. "It is perfect."

He cupped my face, and his thumb slid over my cheek, then grazed my lower lip. I closed my eyes.

Alec whooped, and Zhen laughed. What the rest of them did, I could not say, for when Nate's lips met mine and his fingers twisted through my curls, I was lost.

He eased back and rested his forehead against my own, but in that moment of quiet, the whir of a drone sounded. The world snapped back around me.

Across the manicured lawn, a young Recorder, near Kyleigh's age, stood at rest, her drone at her shoulder. Eyes like turquoise blinked but did not leave me and Nate. He drew me closer.

"We're moving on," Jordan said.

The Recorder did not look away. "Be at peace, Guardian."

Eric moved forward. "She's a citizen now."

Although I kept Nate's hand in mine, I edged around Zhen. "It is well." I met the Recorder's eyes. "You are my sister. No matter who or where I am."

"No." The quiet word fell like a feather. Her drone's tendril twitched, and she stiffened.

My heart splintered.

After a shuddering breath, the Recorder moistened her lips. "Care well for the little ones, Guardian."

I waited, as I had been taught.

Her turquoise eyes lifted to mine. "Be happy."

She rotated slowly, and her boots tapped on the concrete path as she passed us and climbed the steps.

Zhen's clear voice rang out. "Recorder!"

The young woman and her drone turned.

Zhen held up a palm. "Be at peace."

A faint smile crossed the Recorder's pale face, then she disappeared into the colonnade leading into the Hall of Records.

Be at peace.

A strand of sadness wound through me. Drones, reprimands,

Recorders, and the Hall of Reclamation would continue without a hint of freedom. How could I go forward when I left those like her behind?

Nate's fingers threaded through mine, and he gave my hand a squeeze. When I looked up, he asked, "We still have that appointment, right?"

"Yes."

Kyleigh handed me my cane, but in truth, I leaned on Nate. With each step, I focused on the newness of the familiar world, a world in which I was no longer Consortium. A hint of pine tickled my nose. Jordan's beads whispered, and footsteps tapped in uncoordinated rhythms. Immediately overhead, mimosa leaves rustled in the gentle breeze from the ceiling-mounted fans.

Further up, beyond that domed ceiling, in the cold openness of space, the stars thrummed. They burned and pulsed, throwing particles, heat, and light into the void, whether or not my limited senses could detect them.

Stardust? Or creation?

Unquantifiable and indefinable. And yet as close as my breath.

Even in those holding cells and rooms, had I truly been alone? Perhaps, none of us were, not even the young Recorder with turquoise eyes. A shiver ran down my arms, and Nate gave my hand a quick squeeze. With the Hall of Records behind me, the promise of helping the little ones before me, the people I was finally free to love around me, and Nate beside me, unquenchable hope bubbled.

The quick patter of Kyleigh's shoes passed on my left. She darted in front of us all, stopped, and held up a hand. "Wait just a minute. This is all very nice and everything, but the thing is, you never said."

"There are many things I have not said." Instead of confusing me, her apparent belief in telepathy made me smile. "What is it I have neglected?"

"Your *name*. Stars above," Kyleigh exclaimed. "You haven't told us your name."

"Exactly." Jordan arced one delicate brow. "I understand that you were trying to keep us safe, but you've done that."

Light twinkled on James's earrings. "Indeed."

"Right," Zhen said. "Before we head over to get you two a permanent contract, you need to let us know what name you chose. Given name, middle name, last name." Zhen tapped out each on her fingers. "Now. You've been playing this close long enough."

"Three?" I turned my ring round and round on my thumb. "I cannot give you that."

Nate nudged my shoulder. I glanced up at him. One perfect eyebrow rose, and my smile crept back.

"What kind of rubbish answer—"

"Babe," Alec protested.

Zhen shot a glare at him, then turned that glare on me. "Of course you can."

"I chose only two." For a second, insecurity trickled through me. Lars had been correct. Selecting a name was a serious endeavor. If I had chosen poorly . . . But no, it was a good name, a talisman, a light against darkness. It was *my* name. "Arianna Maxwell."

"Arianna." A broad smile broke over Alec's face. "Excellent choice."

Nate's dimple peeked at me while Eric cheered and Kyleigh's eyes widened.

Zhen rested her cheek on Alec's shoulder. "It might not be Chrysanthemum," she said with a deepening smile, "but I approve."

"It's lovely." Jordan's eyes shone. "Does Max know?"

I leaned into Nate. "I asked his permission last night. If I could have had a father, I would have wanted him to be like Max. And . . ." I hesitated, for I suspected they would not like what I would say. "If things had gone poorly, I wanted you to know."

Nate's smile faltered, and he kissed my forehead.

"Arianna Maxwell," James rumbled. Silver-grey eyes regarded me as seriously as they had when we were children, but the edges crinkled when he smiled. "How fortunate am I, that my first friend would someday become a sister?"

Eric punched him lightly on the arm, though he did not seem to notice that James startled. "Pretty fortunate, if you ask me."

"It suits," Nate said with a smile that soaked into my bones, "but I'm still going to call you sweetheart."

Warmth tumbled and swelled deep inside my chest.

I had no reason to hide, and the future, far different from anything I had ever expected, lay open before me.

Standing there with my Nathaniel and my friends at my side, there at the unmaking of who I had been and the remaking of who I was always meant to be, I laughed.

EPILOGUE

When I was young, I had not understood how love expands, that it was not a finite resource. Nor had I understood that victory was not merely in grand accomplishments, but in the small things, like answering to a new name or watching a child learn to laugh without fear. Then, I had but an inkling of how valuable it was to belong, to be known and to know as an intrinsic part of a whole, rather than merely fulfilling duty.

The Eldest, her Consortium, and citizens called our home Sanctuary, but with my friends—my family—and in my private logs, it was Sanctuary One. Truly, it should have been the second. Someday, perhaps, Pallas Station would be Sanctuary Two in more than name. Someday, I hoped, any Recorder who wished freedom could find it, not merely the children the Consortium itself had abandoned.

Max began the process of removing neural chips, and the Recorder-doctor stayed with us and assisted him, though it was unclear whether or not he stayed voluntarily or under threat of reclamation. Elinor Williams remained as well, and Yrsa Ramos promised to return once her service time ended in three quarters, though I had not expected her to do so. Elinor noted that Yrsa's motivation might be selfish, as Daniel Parker served alongside Jackson, Quincy, and the other former marines who had become our security force.

Once Sanctuary One's gates were repaired and the former marines armed, which local authorities did not appreciate, we moved our temporary infirmary back to the clinic. The injured former marine, Knox, had recovered, although he was still not steady enough to join our security team, so Cam's tank was the only one we needed to relocated to the clinic. As Max and the Recorder-doctor removed the neural chips, however, more tanks burbled. Then, one by one, the children emerged, free from Consortium technology. Their hair began to grow in, and they chose names of their own.

While the majority of the children adapted easily enough, a few struggled. I understood. Though the omnipresent threat of reprimands had lifted, their change of status and restrictions was its own sort of cage. Adjustments were not always easy for me, either, although the quarters I shared with Nathaniel were already home.

Bustopher, of course, stayed with us and consistently claimed the most comfortable chair and any piece of Nate's black clothing he left out. I had not realized how much a cat could shed, so two and a half ten-days after we became Sanctuary One, I went in search of a spare cleaning bot. I found a storage closet with several models and was debating which would best serve the purpose when my communications link chimed.

"Arianna?"

The use of my name still summoned a smile. "Yes, Tia?"

"Cam's mother finally signed his medical care over to Sanctuary." She huffed. "Since we don't have a Recorder proper on site, you'll need to head over to the Hall of Records to accept. I made an appointment for this evening, and Jackson, Quincy, and Hodges will be your security detail."

I frowned. It was not that I resented my escort, since no one had seen Julian Ross and the Consortium was still under threat. Rather, my discontent was on Cam's behalf. How could his mother turn away from her son?

Even so, I temporized. "She might have been waiting for the university to accept responsibility."

"Well, that didn't happen, either," she stated. "It's downright evil the way they shimmied out of the work-study contract. I'm almost glad they booted me."

"Tia," I began.

"Don't get me wrong. I truly am grateful. If you hadn't offered me a place here. I would've had to take a job in the belt, and I'm glad I won't have to raise Zeta out in who knows where. But I'm also glad Alec and Zhen talked Eric into finishing up."

I closed my eyes. "He was, indeed, angry."

"Rightfully so." Tia exhaled sharply. "He still is, just better at hiding it. So . . . second, Kye's mom says preliminary results for the prototype are good. She wants you, James, and Daniel to stop by the lab later."

"You must remind me."

"I already set both alarms, so your ID bracelet will chime. Third, Jordan wanted you to know that we've had three more requests for ungifting and we're running checks on the families. Fourth, I've already notified Quincy that the uniforms should be arriving this afternoon." She chuckled. "I think that Clarissa might be more excited about the uniforms than anyone else."

I could not help but smile. "Given the way she has repeatedly asked about their arrival, I am inclined to agree."

"Which leads into the last point." Her tone grew serious. "Clarissa wants to talk to you about one of the children who is playing hooky. I've already spoken with Quincy about it. They're looking."

"Very well," I said and signed off.

Leaving the cleaning bot unclaimed, and having no idea what hooky might involve, I headed to Clarissa's classroom to suggest additional controls in case it was a computer-based pastime, but when I arrived, she was distraught. One of the six-year-olds, the little one I had found in the Hall of Reclamation, had not returned after the midday meal. After reassuring Clarissa that Sanctuary's gates were sealed but I would check the gardens myself, I made my way out-of-doors, taking my cane with me, should I need it.

Nate waved at me from the field where he was teaching the older children a wilder, rougher game than my cohort had ever been allowed to play. I waved back. They took advantage of his distraction and tackled him, and the entire group tumbled to the lawn in a flurry of shouts. Laughter rose and fell like music, as necessary to me now as the hum of circulation fans on a ship.

Swallowing the urge to remind them to be careful, I began my search, my steps more rapid and my limp intruding as the minutes passed without finding her. The little one disliked the smell of the greedy tilapia in their ponds, so it was unlikely that she sought refuge there. Refuge—

I turned and made my way to the brook where lavender and lilies whispered in the faint breeze. I had been correct, for there she sat on a rock, her arms wrapped around her legs as tightly as a drone's tendrils.

"Little one."

She startled and scrambled to her feet. Her eyes seemed too large for her tiny face, and her smile did not come as quickly as the other children's. The errant thought again crossed my mind that perhaps we were too many, but there was not one I would give up.

Not a one.

I knelt before her, and the moss's dampness seeped through my leggings. After a moment of hesitation, I brushed a smudge of dirt from her chin, then I held out my hand. She took it and raised her somber brown eyes to mine, and then, I knew exactly what to say.

"Have you ever made a boat?"

ACKNOWLEDGMENTS

Arianna leans back against Nate's chest, but her dark brown eyes meet mine. "Is this, then, the end?"

I sigh. "In a way."

Zhen scowls from the other side of the room. "That's a rubbish answer."

But it isn't. Wrapping up this trilogy has been difficult. It's too much like saying goodbye.

"Go ahead, Cath. Write those acknowledgments." As usual, Nate's the one to urge me on. "Start with Lauren and CJ."

He's right. Both of you—my brilliant, faithful alpha readers—have been lifelines. You read the messiest of versions so everyone else could read a cohesive one. You held me to deadlines and demanded the next chapters.

But if I stop there, I'd be leaving out friends like Laura, Marian, Jenn, Anne, and Angie, who suffered through various stages of writing angst and reminded me to press on. Thank you, Sophia, for reading the dev edits as I finished them. Julie—this would not be here if it weren't for you. And Patrice, your solid understanding of my people and of story is such a blessing!

Thank you to Sharon and Michelle, who gave fantastic feedback, and Angela, who suggested Quincy's name. Talis, you know why Connor chose that name, and I still say they should all sit around a campfire and talk. Chawna, I cannot thank you enough for your prayers and encouragement.

Nate bursts out laughing. "Add Peaklings and your Colorado Realmies. You know, the ones you killed off."

Arianna frowns. "That is not funny, Nathaniel."

He grins. "They asked for it."

"I do not understand why anyone would want to be written into a book only to be ruthlessly eliminated."

"Makes sense to me." Nate flashes a smile so broad his dimple appears. *"If I were going to ask to be put into a book—"*

When she spins in his arms, he stops, and his eyebrows—which aren't as perfect as she thinks—soar.

"Nathaniel!"

He glances at me and grimaces. "Point taken. I retract the thought."

"You'd better," Alec growls.

So, thank you, Kirk and John. And to my Peaklings, for wisdom in action scenes.

Jordan drums her fingers. "Your street team."

Definitely. I must thank Sophia, Chrissy, Lauren, Hailey, Stephanie, Angie, Julee, Angela, Jess, and Jess, as well as the rest of you. Your help has been invaluable. (Also, they voted for kittens, so everyone can give them a round of applause!) I'll add here a special thanks to Samantha, whose kind messages were globe-spanning hugs. Your guess about Arianna's surname was spot-on.

"Don't forget the readers," Zhen adds.

As if I could. Thank you. For reading, recommending, reviewing. I don't think I could ever express how much that means to me. And to my family, thank you for putting up with the long hours of seat-in-the-chair and the blank looks when you asked me a question and my mind was not in this world.

No one needs to remind me about Enclave. Steve, thank you for taking a chance on an unknown author with a weird story with its initially bald protagonist, drones, and giant bugs. Lisa, thank you for teaching me more about editing than I would have learned on my own. Sarah, for the copy edits. Megan, for proofing and for ongoing encouragement. Jamie, for your mad typesetting skills. Lindsay and Trissina, for handholding and wisdom. And another thank you to Emilie, who knocked this cover out of the park. Thank you, Oasis and Taylor, who have brought this book to audio and reached so many people. And to my fellow Enclave authors, especially Jasmine and Sandra.

The room grows quiet, and we watch the kittens tumble near Kye's knees.

I finally answer Arianna's original question. "This isn't really the end, not when the story is in the readers' minds and hearts."

Eric huffs. "I guess."

"But you can't be finished, Cathy." Kye catches a wandering kitten and hands it to James, who cradles it for a moment, then sets it with its siblings. "Not without the most important acknowledgement."

"No," Max adds, "you can't forget that."

I haven't.

And to the Author of the best story ever written, to the Author of life itself, unending thanks.

ABOUT THE AUTHOR

Cathy McCrumb graduated from Biola University with a degree in literature and a love for stories. *Recorder* and *Aberration*, the first two books in the Children of the Consortium trilogy, have received enthusiastic editorial and reader reviews. She and her husband, whom she met while writing letters to soldiers, have five children and currently live within the shadow of the Rocky Mountains. While writing is one of her favorite things, she also enjoys reading, long hikes, naps, gluten-free brownies, raspberries, and crocheting while watching science fiction movies with friends and family.

Visit her at www.cathymccrumb.com.

 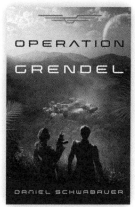